To Pam,

Enjoy

THE CHIP

By
Gary L. Dewey

Gary L. Dewey

Bookman LLC
Publishing & Marketing

www.bookmanmarketing.com

Also by Gary L. Dewey

THE PROJECT

Dedicated
In loving honor to my late mother
Lucille

All references to scriptural verses in The Chip were taken from the original King James version of the bible. Some are used in fictional dialog and not intended verbatim.

About the Book

Chicago based Electronic Solutions Inc. has brought an astonishing new product to the world: A Miniaturized, Implantable, Computer Chip, 'Signa-Chip'. With Signa-Chip comes the technology to assist physicians in monitoring critical medical conditions; the ability to communicate with the Global Positioning System satellites, aiding law enforcement agencies in the location of lost or kidnapped children, and a means of personal identification, taking man another step closer to a cashless society. But Adam Garrett knows something else the chip brings with it. A crucial bit of information that will cause society, as it is known, to forever cease. Knowledge that, if he tells, could cost him and his loved ones their lives.

'The Chip' takes you on a life and death struggle through real love, fear, tragedy and inner turmoil, racing you headlong to a time and place where a personal and critical choice must be made. A decision that, without knowing what Adam Garrett knows, may very well be your last.

1

Had he not been in the midst of a dream, where he was searching for his all to often misplaced cordless telephone, the incessant ringing of his actual bedside phone would have woken him. But it took a jab in his side from Carol, his twenty-eight year old fiancee sleeping next to him, on one of her rare sleep-over nights, to arouse him.

His first thoughts were to just lift the receiver enough to stop the '*insistent ringing*' and set it back down on its cradle. He ignored his initial intuition though, rolled over in his queen size bed and answered the 3:15 AM call with a groggy, "Hello?"

"Mister Garrett? Adam Garrett?"

Adam forced himself to stay conscious enough to respond, but not by much. "Yes?" He said, without opening his eyes.

A long day at work, a late Friday night dinner date with Carol, a couple of after dinner drinks at the restaurant's lounge, and he had no desire to be awake, let alone engaged in a conversation on the telephone.

No sooner though had the female's voice on the other end of the telephone say, "This is River Valley General Hospital," and Adam was fully awake.

Finding the switch for the lamp that stood next to the telephone on the night-stand, he turned it on. The dark bedroom was instantly illuminated by the lamp's bright, incandescent glow.

Forcing his eyes to stay open, despite the burning sensation the sudden, intense light caused them, Adam swung his feet to the floor. "Yes?" He said, prodding for more.

"There's no need for alarm," the voice responded. The nurse on the other end of the line, trying to calm the sudden, over amount of anxiety she heard in Adam's tone, spoke softly when she said, "Can you come in to the hospital?"

"Who is it?" Carol, aroused by the light and intensity of Adam's voice, stirred and sat up. With one hand she held the thin, semi-transparent sheet she was sleeping under to her chest, unconsciously covering herself.

Adam waved a backwards hand at her. Then turned and saw her, still half asleep, squinting against the light. Without a word he watched her brush her shoulder length, golden brown hair off of her face and slowly lay back down. By the time her head had touched the pillow, he knew she was asleep again.

Adam felt his heart pounding from the rush of being startled awake and in anticipation of the 'bad news' he knew what a call from a hospital at three o'clock in the morning meant.

With the apprehension still apparent in his voice, he asked, "What's wrong?"

The nurse tried again, in vain, to calm him. "There's no need to worry, Mister Garrett."

:

It had taken him only twenty minutes, from answering the call, to get dressed, out to his vehicle, and drive the three miles from his home to the I-94, 26 mile road intersection. The nurse's words; 'There's no need for alarm…no need to rush…,…no need to worry,' ran over and over in his mind as he turned his Black, two year old, Dodge Ram pickup onto the entrance ramp of the inter-state.

With the echoing words having the opposite effect on him than the caller intended, Adam felt an urgent need to hurry. *How ridiculous,* he thought, *three o'clock in the morning, I get a call that my mother has been taken in to the hospital and all they can say is, don't worry!*

At that hour on a Saturday morning, the traffic on I-94, the normally busy highway, coursing its way into and through Detroit, was all but non-existent. And where the entrance lane fully merged into the expressway, Adam pressed the accelerator pedal down hard against the floorboard. The 360 cubic inch engine of his pickup roared in response.

In his haste to get to the hospital, he had left Carol still asleep and reminded himself that he would have to call her later. Let her know what was going on. But, he'd have to find that out himself first. All he knew was what the caller had told him, which wasn't much, just that his mother had been brought in by an Emergency Medical Service vehicle and he should get there.

'There's no need to rush' flashed through his mind again as he looked down at the speedometer and watched the needle break the ninety mile per hour line. He eased his foot back just enough to hold his speed there.

River Valley General was on the opposite side of Detroit and thirty miles away from his suburban home. Half of the way there he felt a wave of sorrow course over him like a cold wind from nowhere. A lump formed deep in his throat.

"Hold on ma," he softly said, thinking the worst and fighting back a tear. "I'm on my way."

Too young...I'm too young to lose my mother and father. Twenty-nine is too young, he thought.

Adam reached for the button to turn on the radio and shut it back off again as soon as the music from it touched his ears.

In the silence, his imagination was getting the better of him. *It's bad enough I lost Dad to cancer three years ago,* he thought. *If I lose Mom now, it'd be almost too much to bare.*

Probably nothing real serious. Doctors today can work miracles, he tried consoling himself and wished he had woken Carol, so she could be with him. She had always been such a comfort to him through unsettling times during the four years that he had been with her and he could sure use hearing her soothing, reassuring voice now.

After a minute of anxious thoughts, the wave of anxiety abated enough for him to get a hold of himself again. To collect his thoughts. "Don't borrow trouble," he spoke aloud the advice his mother had always given him in troubling situations. "Wait until you know what's really going on," she would say, "before you get yourself all worked up."

Adam eased his foot off the accelerator. The Dodge slowed to eighty-five, then eighty.

I don't need to get pulled over by the police, he thought. *Even if I could talk myself out of the speeding ticket, the time I'd lose dealing with them would be more than I'd ever have gained.*

Trying to distract himself from dealing prematurely with the painful possibilities, Adam reached for the radio button again. This time letting it stay on.

:

The thirty mile trip from his house to the hospital should have taken him over an hour. He made it in just over half of that, pulling into the Emergency Entrance of River Valley General a few minutes after 4:00AM.

The five story, brick, multi-building structure, built ten years ago, along Michigan's shore on the Southern end of the

4

Detroit river, served the downriver communities of Wyandotte, Southgate, and Trenton. Trenton a small, quiet community, where Adam grew up and his mother still lived, was also home to the hospital And Adam knew it housed some of the most modern medical technology of the day.

At the front desk Adam found a small cluster of young people, dressed in knitted caps, pulled down over their ears, and jeans, whose crotch hung down around their knees. When Adam arrived the receptionist was barking out a disregarded command to clear the area in front of her desk and requesting them to wait in the available waiting room. From the tone of her voice, she sounded frustrated at having decreed the instructions repeatedly to no avail.

Adam wormed his way through the group of young adults, who Adam surmised were there to check the status of one of their friends. *Another of their gang members,* he thought, probably *brought into the hospital suffering from either a gun shot wound, or a drug overdose.*

Emitting sarcastic comments that Adam paid no attention to, the group of young adults parted in a wave to let him through. Like the water in a swimming pool does to a diver, they closed back around him instantly as he passed.

The receptionist had seen and heard enough disrespect from the group and threatened to call 'Security' if they didn't go to the waiting room and clear the front of her desk.

Amid a disgruntled outburst of vulgar expletives from the band of youths that didn't move back but a few feet, the receptionist looked up at Adam. "Can I help you?"

Adam saw her reaching under the lip of the desk and pressing the hidden button that would summons the security officer to the ER. "Adam Garrett," he answered, wondering if this was the same calm, collected woman who had called him earlier.

"I'll buzz you in," she said, nodding toward the locked, glass topped, double doors, restricting entrance into the actual Emergency Room area.

Adam moved over to the doors and stood looking through the safety glass at the flurry of activity on the other side of the wire reinforced widows. He stood there anxiously awaiting the sound of the electronically controlled lock to occur, signaling that he could enter.

The receptionist waited though for the security guard to appear and herd the group of milling young people toward the waiting room before she depressed the lock's button. Her delay prompted by the concern that the group would make a dash for the restricted area of the ER once the doors were opened.

"How come the 'honkey' can go in?" Adam heard one of the group ask, as he stepped through the doors.

Adam shot a quick glance over his shoulder and saw one of the larger male youths trying, unsuccessfully, to push his way around the unyielding security guard. He then continued walking up to one of the nurses standing behind the long counter in the ER room. Once there the pungent smell of antiseptic alcohol struck his nose, stinging his nostrils.

The thirtyish, over-weight, brown haired woman behind the counter glanced up at him from the patient chart she was reading. "Can I help you?" She looked back down at the chart as she spoke, obviously more concerned about what was on the chart than Adam's presence.

"I was told to come in here…My mother was brought in, about an hour ago."

"Name?"

"Adam Garrett."

She shot a sideways glance at him again that resembled a sneer. "Your mother's name," she said impatiently.

"Charlotte Garrett."

"Phyllis," the nurse called out to another woman who was just emerging from one of the many treatment rooms. "Mister Garrett is here."

Adam turned and watched the approaching nurse.

She was a pretty woman, with a tanned complexion. He guessed her age somewhere in her mid-to-late twenties. Her shoulder length blonde hair, pulled back into a ponytail, swung freely, seductively, behind her as she walked.

He saw her eyes darting up and down him and wished that he had spent a little more time making himself presentable before he rushed out of the house.

He let his head slowly drop and checked himself out in the process. He was a mess: The left side of his shirttail wasn't even tucked in, hanging crumpled, improperly buttoned, in a wad just above his gray un-ironed slacks. Hurriedly, Adam tried to tuck the shirttail into his slacks wadding it up even worse.

"Mister Garrett?"

Adam threw his head back in a jerk. The nurse was standing next to him. Her deep blue eyes, enhanced by the pale, blue uniform she wore, riveted to his.

It was too late to do anything about his shirt now without looking ostentatious. He ran a nervous hand through his rumpled, black hair and hoped that at least he had combed it, but couldn't remember for sure if he had. He had not. Parts of it stood out straight from his head.

She reached her hand in a gesture of greeting. "Phyllis," the nurse introduced herself.

Adam took her hand without answering. He felt a little flush and surprised by the strength of her grip. He had expected a gentler grasp. But hers was confident, sure.

"We have moved your mother up to the ICCU ward," she said without letting go.

"How is she? What's going on? What's happened?" Adam nervously fired out a barrage of questions, while mentally preparing himself for the bad news he was sure would follow.

:

Daylight was breaking across the parking lot, striking the reflective acronym; ESI. The large, translucent letters on the laboratory building for Electronic Solutions Incorporated, giving off a rainbow effect in the early morning sun. As the letters had been designed and positioned to do, they cast a multi-colored beam of light back toward the entrance gate. A prismatic greeting to those who entered in the early morning.

Un-noticing, indifferent to the panoramic array of colors, Ethan Blake pulled his Black, Cadillac Escalade up to the white brick pillar that stood just outside the locked steel gate. He slid his coded identification card into the provided slot next to the green, six inch monitor screen for the computer housed there. A soft, telltale buzzing occurred as the computer read the card's code.

"Good Morning, Mister Blake," a machine manufactured voice spoke out through the speaker. "Please look directly at the screen while I complete your identification."

Ethan turned his face toward the screen as instructed and stared at it for a moment while the computer performed a retinal scan of his eyes.

He always felt intimidated by the scanning process. Like the machine was peering, un-welcomed, deep into his inner-being. Ethan looked forward to the time, in the near future, when the antiquated ID card and scanner security system would be updated with the new personal identification chip system ESI was perfecting. And he would not have to endure the invasion ever again.

"Thank You Mister Blake," the machine said. "Have a nice day."

The steel gate just in front of him began to slowly retract, allowing him to drive through into the half filled parking lot.

With any luck, he thought, *by next week that new system would be installed and in place.*

At the set of smoked glass, front doors at ESI, the wide angle lens of a surveillance camera mounted inside the building, scanned the entrance. Ethan had to again wait until the on duty security guard, watching the scanned images, recognized him and 'buzzed' him in.

Such a waste, Ethan thought.

The daily routine of multiple security checks, to make sure unauthorized entry into the ESI laboratory was prevented, seemed a necessary nuisance to Ethan, just a few weeks ago, especially the manned one. However, now that the Design and Engineering Department had completed its work on the microchip that would do away with the hassles, the minor inconveniences of gaining entry seemed a bit more frustrating. He just couldn't see why the new system had not been implemented yet.

The electronically controlled door locks clicked open.

"Good Morning, Mister Blake," Joyce, the young, Receptionist/Telephone operator greeted him as he stepped through the doors.

"Morning," he responded as he, without looking at her, walked past the large, curved, black marble reception desk she sat behind.

As of late, he tried avoiding contact with Joyce as much as he could without offending her. For some reason, the thirty year old beauty, who had usually been reserved for the three years she worked the front desk, was 'coming on' to him. Ethan, though flattered by the extra attention, wanted no part of it.

Joyce's flirtations were really nothing outlandish; an occasional little extra show of cleavage; a sheepish, sideways smile; prolonged, deep eye contact; or just standing a little too close to him when they were together. Subtle little things, but nonetheless, to Ethan, her intentions were apparent.

And it was not that she was undesirable. Her salon kept, long, naturally blonde hair, deep set emerald eyes, and soft facial features had just the opposite effect. If anything, she was too pretty, too sexy. And Ethan also knew, that if he wasn't careful and kept his distance, he would find himself deep in an extra marital affair. Something he had no desire to engage in. Especially at this time in his life. Ten years ago though, when he was between marriages, it would have been a totally different story.

"Doctor Reece would like to meet with you this morning," Joyce said.

Ethan stopped, surprised to hear that the doctor, overseeing the medical aspects of the new chip, was in on Saturday, especially this early. He turned and glanced down at Joyce, while nervously fondling the bouquet of freshly picked flowers standing in a vase atop the marbled desk.

"Did he say what he wanted?"

Hoping that the mixed bouquet of flowers she had brought in impressed Ethan, Joyce answered, "No. Only that he wanted me to tell you that he needed to see you as soon as you arrived."

She held her gaze, her eyes glued to his, hoping she would see Ethan's drop toward the open neck line of her white satin blouse.

"Thank you," Ethan smiled. His eyes never left the mix of Daisies and Baby's Breath and headed for the elevator that would take him upstairs to the doctor's office.

From the tall, mid-wall to ceiling, black tinted widow in Doctor Reece's office, Ethan watched two more vehicles pull into the parking lot through the computer operated gate. He was nearly oblivious to the words of the doctor, who voiced his opposition over Ethan's choice, as Marketing Director; to make the new chip available to the medical community as of the coming Monday afternoon.

"Are you even listening to me?" Doctor Reece asked, turning his chair to face Ethan's back.

"I'm listening," Ethan responded and let a little more of his weight lean against the five foot tall, metal filing cabinet he had an elbow propped up on.

"You had no business okaying the sale of those chips until I was finished testing the reliability of those circuits. A bit premature don't you think?"

"How much more testing do they need Doctor Reece?" Ethan pulled his elbow down and turned toward the doctor. His voice carried the tone of impatience with it. "They have been run through every conceivable test we can give them...three times. And may I add they performed flawlessly."

"I'll agree to that. But..."

"But what doctor?" Ethan cut him off. "What part of this don't you agree with? The chip is working fine and will continue to do so. So what is it you don't go along with?"

Doctor Reece picked up a prototype of the narrow, half-inch long, cylindrical microchip that had been resting on his desk. He pinched it gently between his thumb and fore-finger and extended it out toward Ethan. "We have no idea how long this thing is going to last implanted, nor do we have any concept of the problems we're going to run into…once it gets out into the world."

"And?"

"And? I can't believe you asked that," Doctor Reece said, while he ran his other hand through his short, black, curly hair.

"Well, I did," Ethan said. He turned back to his view out of the window. He watched the early morning traffic, on the distant thoroughfare, rushing into downtown Chicago. *The doctor was right,* he realized. *The implantable chip did need more actual usage testing.* "But what better way to get that needed testing," he concluded out loud, "than by making it available to the public?"

"For starters…the costs and risks of implantation."

"Risks? What risks? The FDA has already approved of the hypo-allergenic coating on the chip." Ethan turned back around and walked over to the other side of the doctor's walnut desk. "Implantation is an out-patient procedure that doesn't take but a little cut, no bigger than a good sized sliver. Slip the chip in just under the skin and cover it with a Band-Aid. And costs," he said, placing his hands flat on the desktop and leaning in toward the doctor. "You talk about costs? Every day we delay making the chip available is costing this company three-quarters of a million dollars."

Doctor Reece leaned back in his black leather chair surrendering to Ethan's logic. The leather material made a soft scrunching noise, typical of the sound real leather makes when moved on.

"Besides," Ethan said, reading the doctor's body English and straightening up. "I think the benefits far outweigh any risks. The people need this thing and they needed it yesterday. If it helps save one life or locates one lost child, it'll be worth any imagined 'risks'"

"I still think it needs more actual testing before we can backup any claims about it," the doctor said, placing the prototype back down on his desk.

"I agree," Ethan responded and reached for the knob on the closed office door. "And what better way is there, that you can think of, to get that 'actual' testing than put Signa-Chip out there?"

Gary L. Dewey

2

Adam didn't know how long he had been sitting bedside, gently holding onto his comatose, sixty-two year old mother's hand, his eyes fixed on the heart monitor attached to her. The machine displayed her heart's 'beats per minute' rate and fluctuated between one-hundred-eighty and two-hundred.

Despite the oxygen tube, with the C shaped ring attaching it to her nostrils, she looked peaceful. Almost too peaceful and it scared him to look directly at her ashen and pallid face. Adam watched the heart monitor instead. Hoping that if he looked long enough and hard enough at it, he could will her heart to slow down, rest more between contractions and keep beating.

Every fifteen minutes; the sound of the automatic blood pressure cuff on her left arm, inflating, distracted his attention. He would turn from the heart monitor screen and watch the cuff expanding tightly around his mother's arm and slowly deflate itself, sending its reading to, he knew not where. Then realizing that he had neglected his assumed responsibility of watching the heart monitor, he would turn back quickly, hoping that the numbers, any numbers, were still being displayed.

The dim, quiet, stillness of the room, the rhythmic bleeping of the heart monitor, coupled with his lack of sleep the night before, caused his mind to wander. The effects of the initial surge of adrenaline he got was wearing off and he felt tired. Adam laid his head on the bed next to his mother's feet and had nearly dozed off, when Carol popped into his mind.

He remembered his promise to call his fiancée and let her know what was going on.

Slowly he raised his head back up and looked at the monitor again. There had been no change, the rate was still one-eighty. The cuff began to automatically inflate again and reluctantly he slid his hand out from under his mother's.

During the hours that he was there in her room in the Intensive Cardiac Care Unit, his mother never moved or opened an eye and fearing the minute he was not there, would be the minute she woke up, it took a few moments before he mustered up enough confidence to leave her. Adam stood, stepping out into the hallway outside her room, intending to keep his promise to Carol...If he could find a telephone. At the nurse's station, he asked if he could use the telephone there.

"Sure," one of the on duty nurses said, placing the plain, black telephone on top of the long, chest high desk.

"Do you know what time it is?" Adam asked, as his eye caught the bank of computer monitor screens behind her.

"Ten-thirty-five."

Adam's eyes and attention were on the two rows of monitors and the technician sitting in front of them and never heard the answer. Mesmerized, he watched the EKG reading scrolling across the screens in real time. Seeing the blood pressure readings super-imposed in large white numbers on the lower right hand corners of the five active monitors, he realized where the automatic cuff was sending its readings.

"Excuse me," he apologized. "What time did you say it was?"

"Ten-thirty-five," the nurse smiled. Reading Adam's gaze and answering his question before he could ask it, she added. "Yes, top row, on the far end is your mother's. We keep a constant eye on our patients."

Somehow, Adam thought, *that was supposed to make me feel better?* But, the knowledge did little to ease his anxiety.

He started to dial his home phone number but couldn't remember what it was. So rare was it that he called his own home phone that the not often used digits escaped his memory. He stood there staring off into space trying to recall the numbers.

The hospital's staff cardiologist, came through the doors at the end of the hall.

"Good morning Doctor Ching," the nurse at the desk called out in greeting.

Again distracted, Adam watched the oriental doctor, dressed in green surgeon scrubs and a white, cloth cap, walk past everyone without a word, and go directly up to the computer monitors behind the nurse's station.

A nurse appeared from one of the offices behind the bank of computer screens and held out a white, long sleeved lab coat to the middle aged doctor.

"Thank you," he finally spoke, removing the cap and exchanging it for the lab coat, that he promptly slipped into.

The doctor glanced back at the screens while he pulled a stethoscope from one of the coat's side pockets. As he turned away from the computers, he was handed a clip board with Charlotte Garrett's chart on it.

"Room seven," the nurse behind the desk added.

Adam, the call postponed for another time, was one step behind Doctor Ching and the nurse that accompanied the doctor.

They stepped into his mother's room before the doctor spoke again. "Who is this?" The doctor asked when he noticed Adam.

"I'm the son," Adam announced.

"Doctor Ching," the doctor introduced himself extending a hand.

Adam grasp the hand. "Adam...Adam Garrett," he said, holding the hand without squeezing or shaking it. The doctor's hand felt cool to the touch, the skin soft, almost effeminate. He could feel the skill in the surgeon's delicate muscles and Adam wondered how many lives that very hand had saved. And hoped that his mother's would be added to that list.

"Your mother has had a sever myocardial infarction. Complicated by her diabetes and being over-weight," Doctor Ching said, looking Adam right in the eyes. "She is very fortunate to be still with us."

Adam's eyes fell to the floor as the magnitude of what the doctor said impacted him. 'Sever Myocardial infraction' coming from the doctor sounded so much more grim than 'heart attack' did coming from Phyllis, the nurse who greeted him earlier in the ER. Her explanation of the condition seemed gentler, more compassionate. Suddenly, the cardiologist's hand didn't feel as reassuring to him as it did before. Adam let it go, pulling his back to his side.

"The next seventy-two hours are going to be crucial," Doctor Ching continued, stepping around him.

"We'll keep a very close eye on her, and the doctor will do everything that he can," the nurse said as comfortingly as she could.

Adam picked up his eyes and felt the salty sting of tears welling up in their corners. He watched, concerned, as Doctor Ching slid the stethoscope under the sheet, covering his mother, to listen to her heartbeat.

Anew, he felt hopeful and scared simultaneously. A thousand childhood memories of his mother raced through his mind as he watched Doctor Ching's facial expressions. Praying that in those expressions, he might find solace.

:

The Saturday morning sun climbed steadily higher into the clear blue sky over a sparely populated area in the suburban neighborhood of Sterling Heights, Michigan. The harmonic buzz of lawnmowers and leaf blowers filled the air as several residents of the upper middle class community tended to their typical weekend chores of outdoors maintenance.

As the summer's sun slowly climbed higher so did the temperature. By eleven o'clock, the mercury was already flirting with the eighties. The local weatherman threatening the temperatures would reach into the humid, mid-nineties before it peaked.

Thirty-four year old Gene Dawson, bent down and shut the push lawnmower, he was mowing with off. Glad that he was done with the lawn early enough to escape the real heat of the day, he straightened up and wiped the beads of sweat off his forehead, while wishing that he had gotten done even earlier.

Gene pushed the mower back into the garage, next to the family's new Dodge mini-van and his year old Ford SUV. He promised himself that he would come back out to clean the machine off and put it away, when he cooled down. And headed straight for the kitchen inside his home and something cold to drink.

Erica, his wife of ten years, loading the last of the breakfast dishes into the dishwasher, greeted him. "Done?" she asked.

"We need to get the air going before it gets too hot," he answered, heading for the refrigerator and a cold beer.

Typically they waited until later in the day, when it was really hot, enduring the summer's heat as long as they could, before turning on the three, large, air conditioning units it took to cool their two-story Colonial. The added cost of running the three 30,000 Btu units all day, their main reason for delay and the topic of many conversations about having a Central Air Conditioning Unit installed. "After sunset it naturally cools down enough anyway," Gene would argue against the expense of the Central Air, "and we really don't need it.

The weatherman's prognosis though was for even the night time to remain hot and Gene thought it less expensive, for today, to keep the house cool all day, instead of waiting until the heat built-up, before trying to cool it off.

"I thought that we'd take the kids and go out to the lake today," Erica suggested as an alternative the running the air. "I could pack a lunch, and we could make a day of it?"

Racing up to their mother, nine year old Bryant and his four year old sister Ashley, enthusiastically asked in unison, "Can we go out and play now?"

"For a while," Erica smiled down at the exuberant children. *Where do they get their energy?* She wondered, watching them dash out the same door their father had just sluggishly entered.

"The lake idea sounds good to me," Gene answered, keeping his face in the cool air inside the refrigerator. "I'll need to shower again, before I go anywhere."

"Should I make some sandwiches?"

"Might as well," Gene said, extracting his head and a bottle of 'lite' beer from the refrigerator.

He walked over to his wife, still dressed in her house coat, and kissed her on the cheek. "Let me drink this and get a shower," he said, "and I'll get the cooler out of the garage."

Returning the kiss, "No rush," she said. "I haven't even had my shower yet either."

"We could save some time and take one together," Gene winked at her and disappeared up the stairway toward the master bedroom and the adjacent shower.

What the hey, Erica thought. *The kids are outside playing and it's been a couple of days.* She followed him up the stairs.

:

"Hey, Bry!" Ten year old John Connors, pulled his bike up to the Dawson fence and hollered for his classmate and buddy Bryant.

Looking up from playing in the shaded sandbox with Ashley, Bryant answered a corresponding "Hey" and moved over to the double, chain-link gate that spanned the concrete driveway.

"Wanta come over to my place and shoot some hoops with us? Billy and Jake are there."

Bryant had been over to John's house many times and knew he would be allowed to travel to the next block over, where John lived and his other friends waited.

"Sure," Bryant opted for playing with his friends over his little sister, without a second's thought. "I need to tell my mom though."

"Play with me!" Ashley whined, coming up beside her brother.

Bryant never heard her, or just plain ignored her request and sprung for the house.

Inside the kitchen, he called for his mom with no reply. Moving over to the stairs he called again. Still without an answer. Listening for a response, he heard the water running

in the shower upstairs and a faint laughter. Figuring his
mother was busy with his dad, and that he would have her
permission anyway, he dashed back to the gate.

"Tell mom I'm over at John's," Bryant said to Ashley as
he lifted the U shaped latch that kept the swinging gates
closed and started to run down the driveway ahead of John.

"Wait for me," John pumped the pedals on his bicycle to
catch up.

In vain, Ashley cried out, "Play with me!" again. She
watched her brother turn onto the sidewalk and hurry away.

The U latch dropped on the wrong side of the gate. In his
haste to get away, young Bryant never made sure the gates
were locked. Slowly they swung open and Ashley ran out
trying to catch up to her brother. She reached the sidewalk,
in time to see the boys turn the corner three houses away.
Running as fast as she could, she followed. When her little
legs reached the corner, the boys were nowhere to be seen.

Just around the corner, already tired from running in the
warm air, her feet burning from the sandbox sand in her
shoes, her pink flowered sun dress soaked with sweat, Ashley
stopped her pursuit. Instantly her eyes widened, fear crept its
way into her mind. Why, she was afraid or of what she
feared, Ashley didn't know, but she felt scared. The very
first time she was ever this far away from home...alone, Ashley turned in all directions, looked for anything to help her
find her way. Nothing seemed familiar to her inexperienced
mind. And around just one corner and only a few houses
from home, young Ashley was lost.

Keep moving, Ashley's instincts told her and she obeyed.
Only her sense of direction was not developed enough to
know in what direction. Never before traveled afoot, all of
the terrain looked foreign and her movements kept taking her
farther and farther from home.

At the next corner she passed an undeveloped parcel of land in the suburban housing tract and was exhausted. She looked around again. All seemed frightening. It felt to her like she had been gone for hours, walked for miles, though her little legs had taken her only ten minutes and a block away from home.

The barking of a large, black Labrador Retriever across the street added to her terror. Scared, realizing she was lost, Ashley began to cry out loud.

Her instincts now told her to stay put, that her 'Mommy' or 'Daddy' would soon come for her, she again obeyed those instincts and sat on the curb of the street corner, sobbing. Her head hung low to her lap. The curls of her fine blonde hair touching her knees.

The sound of an automobile pulling up next to her caused her to lift her head. From the interior of the two-toned brown Buick, LaSabre, the reassuring voice of a man called out to her.

"Are you lost little girl?"

Ashley nodded, wiping the tears from her eyes.

"Well, come on," the dark haired man said, swinging the passenger door to the vehicle open. "I'll take you home."

:

Everything was blurred, when she first opened her eyes. The room spinning. Gradually, however, she regained her focus and the vertigo abated.

She was in a hospital, she surmised from the white walls of the room and the machines and tubes attached to her. Oddly, of all the things she could have felt, one of the first things she did feel was the cold, dryness of the air being pumped up into her nostrils.

From her mind, she got no adverse reaction to the realizations that she was hospitalized. Nor did she balk at the realization that the air being pumped into her nose was pure oxygen; the attached machines were monitoring her heart and blood pressure; the tubes were supplying her with live saving drugs, and that she was very ill, near death. The drugs she had been given as part of the medicinal 'cocktail' made sure her conscious mind, though seeing, was oblivious to all of it.

Nonetheless, despite the large doses of sedatives, her mind did respond when her eyes fell on the dark haired man sitting bedside, holding her hand. Her conscious mind, recognized her son, Adam.

She remembered nothing of how, or why she was there, or of her sudden collapse, or anything of the ambulance ride into the Emergency Room at River Valley General either. She did though recognize her only son and felt comforted that he was there with her.

Adam smiled at her and said, "Hi ma."

Charlotte wanted to answer, let him know that she heard him, tell him that she loved him, but felt too weak to form a verbal response. She lay there for a moment, fighting to stay conscious, until she mustered the strength to gently squeeze his hand. She closed her eyes again in sleep.

Almost on cue, a tall, brown haired technician, wearing a satiny, white nurse's uniform stepped into the room. The nurse's assistant was carrying a small basket of empty, glass vials. "I need to take some more blood," she announced.

Adam felt the technician crowding in close to him. He struggled to keep his composure with her closeness. He stood, quickly turning his back to the woman, hiding the tears in his eyes and stepped out into the hallway.

He needed a break from the tension of watching his mother, not knowing if her next breath would be her last. He had to get away for a minute, collect his thoughts. The blood drawing technician provided that opportunity.

"Where's the cafeteria," Adam asked one of the nurses standing within earshot. "I could really use some coffee."

The middle aged woman glanced, away from the chart she was reading toward him. Adam looked haggard, exhausted, and it took no professional to see it.

"It looks like what you really need is some rest, Mister Garrett," the nurse answered him. "Why don't you go home? You have been here for nine hours straight."

Adam's mind balked at the suggestion.

"She could stay like this for a couple of days," the nurse added. "We'll call you and let you know if anything changes with your mother. You should really go home for a while."

The suggestion seemed more viable the second time he heard it, though he was still hesitant.

Okay...okay, he eventually surrendered to the inner-voice that told him to obey the logic of the nurse. *You could use a shower, a change of clothes, something to eat, and a couple of hours sleep,* the voice urged him. *And you could be back by dinner time, fresh, rested, and better able to cope with this.*

The heat of the early afternoon in the city was close. The air thick and heavy with humidity. Adam stepped out off the main entrance of the air conditioned hospital into the asphalt parking lot and the suffocating heat. The black surface of the lot, shinny, almost sticky beneath his shoes, reflected back the heat of the sun. In the open, exposed parking lot it felt even hotter.

There was nothing much I could do anyway and she'll probably sleep while I'm gone, Adam again justified his decision to go along with the nurses observation and go home for a few hours.

He stood baking in the hazy, ninety-five degree heat, visually searching the parking lot for his pickup truck. His body and mind, near thermal shock from the abrupt twenty-five degree difference, between the temperature of the out-side air and that in the hospital.

To his dismay, his truck was no where to be seen. Des-perately, he reached into his pockets, searching for the keys that weren't there. In his haste to get into the hospital earlier, Adam concluded, *I must have left them in the truck's ignition.*

He turned, in a near panic back toward the main entrance to the hospital. When the cool air of the interior struck him, so did the memory that he had parked the truck on the other end of the sprawling medical complex, near the Emergency Room Entrance.

Relieved and again reassured that he was in bad need of sleep and making the right decision to go home for awhile, he walked through the hospital and exited out of the ER doors. The Dodge Ram, keys still in the ignition, sat waiting for him.

:

The call came into the Missing Persons Bureau division of the 3rd Precinct shortly after lunch. The initial conversa-tion; a familiar scenario of unintelligible prattle and one De-tective Floyd Keller had dealt with many times over his twenty-five year career of dealing with the hysterical loved ones of lost people. Still, despite the many times he had dealt with overwrought callers, being a parent himself of two chil-dren, and the son of an aging father suffering from Alz-heimer's Disease, he found it hard to stay totally objective: the initial calls always evoked compassion for the emotional victims with a lost child, or loved one.

"The first thing you have to do," Detective Keller told the sobbing, Erica Dawson as indifferently as he could, "take some deep breaths and try to calm down enough that I can understand what you are trying to tell me. I can't help you unless I know what is wrong."

There was a long pause. On the other end of the line, Detective Keller heard several snifflings and labored gasps for air as Erica tried to collect herself.

From experience Detective Edward Keller knew to just wait without speaking. Also from experience, he knew, even if the female caller did calm down, if he didn't wait long enough, before he spoke, that calm would be short-lived: the emotions would re-flair, as soon as she began to relate the information again.

Patiently Keller waited a few more seconds, "Who am I speaking with?"

"Erica…Erica Dawson."

"And where are you?"

"Eleven-three-seventy-five…Bridge road."

The detective quickly tried to get the basic information, knowing, as with most cases, there wouldn't be much else. He jotted down the address on the top sheet of the large, yellow, legal pad on his desk, followed by: Ms. Dawson. Under that he scribbled: Send Black and White.

"My baby is gone!" Erica choked out as he wrote.

"Gone?"

"She," was followed by more words the detective couldn't decipher, before he could make out the word "yard," as Erica tried to answer. "Yard", was then followed by even more words he could not understand then the word "gone" came through again.

It was obvious to the detective that he had not 'waited' long enough: The woman was crying again and unable to talk intelligibly.

Detective Keller turned to the windowed half wall that separated his office from the occupied, open area of the precinct's third floor. He knocked on the glass, trying to get the attention of one of the many other officers working in the area. Eventually a short, heavyset, uniformed woman looked up from the pile of paper work on her desk and glanced his way.

With his free hand, Keller pushed the top page of the yellow legal pad against the glass.

The woman squinted, trying to read the note ten feet away, leaned forward and nodded. She picked up the telephone on her cluttered desk and dialed the dispatcher's number.

3

The production process for the new implantable, miniature, Signa-Chip was on schedule and progressing steadily at the ESI manufacturing facility in Portland, Oregon. The five member team of engineering experts assigned to the task, promising to have the first completed batch of the multifunctional computerized chips available by Monday morning.

Ethan leaned back in the black, high-backed, leather chair behind his desk and smiled as the memo from the engineers at the Portland subsidiary scrolled across his computer screen. Ethan pleased that everything, unbelievably, was occurring as planned. Even the complex computer software that would interpret the infrared signals from the Signa-Chips, he was told, was ready for installation.

The computer card, making any computer capable of handling infrared signals and the final piece of the new identification system, Ethan knew was already on the market, had been for years, and was readily available. In fact, Ethan also was aware that even the Global Positioning System the Signa-Chip would use, had been in place for quite some time. And that, that GPS satellite system presently was employed by several companies and utilized in many differing aspects. All the way from personal GPS units, to vehicle recovery systems used by financial institutions to identify, locate, and repossess vehicles whose owners were in default on their loans.

Thinking back to the days of the 'chip's' conception, Ethan's ego boasted of his insight and the insight of the design engineers at ESI to foresee an implantable microchip for humans as the next logical, big step up in the evolution of the computer/information age. For the most part though, both the need and the technology were already in place and the only obstacles ESI faced were to get a computer chip small enough that it was implantable and get it encased in a FDA approved material that would not be rejected after implantation.

Both were accomplished easily: The finial chip, not much bigger than a grain of rice and encased in a pliable, hypoallergenic silicon plastic was, despite Doctor Reece's contradiction, ready to market.

Ethan's egotistical smile broadened, as he envisioned the trillions of dollars in sales the Signa-Chip, with its multiple applications would generate world wide for ESI. Especially, since Doctor Reece had discovered that through medical technology, the chip could be used to monitor a person's heart; blood pressure; brain wave activity, body temperature and a myriad of other medical conditions. The doctor had also discovered that when used in conjunction with the other implantable devices already in use, Signa-Chip could administer emergency treatments from afar. It could do this by providing the medium through which electrical nerve stimulation could be carried out. As in the case of those whose heart needs emergency defibrillation, or in the treatment of other cardiac arrhythmias.

And all of this on top of the Signa-Chip being used to assist law enforcement agencies in the location of; lost or missing persons, runaways and crime suspects. He knew it could also be used to track and monitor the activities and whereabouts of those criminals under house arrest; and completely eliminate the lost, or stolen, counterfeit credit card problems. Ethan's mind spun as he tried to imagine all of the applications where the new personal identification microchip could be used.

Despite this inability to foresee all, what Ethan could anticipate, was the potential for every human being on the earth to be implanted with ESI's Signa-Chip. And even many non-human applications.

His gloating over the envisioned success of the microchip was interrupted by an expected telephone call. The call, from the head of the Public Relations Manager at ESI, Carl Torre. Carl confirming that the conference room at the downtown Chicago, Hyatt Regency hotel was reserved for Monday evening.

"Are the PR people ready?" Ethan asked.

"Everything is all set," Carl answered. Confident that his team was ready for the presentation, Carl reassured Ethan that he had seen a preview of the program that would introduce Signa-Chip to the medical community and that it was adequate.

Knowing that this was the biggest endeavor the three member, Public Relations staff at ESI, Chicago, had undertaken, Ethan asked, "They are aware that over five-hundred doctors, hospital department heads, and even a few political people are going to be there, not counting the press?"

"Don't worry Ethan. I have everything under control. Everybody has their part and they know what they're supposed to do. It's just a simple, hour long, narrative, slide presentation, with a couple of computer generated charts and graphs thrown in for effect and everyone here has their roles well rehearsed."

"Simple?" Ethan leaned forward in his chair, his grip unconsciously tightened on the telephone handset as he firmly pushed it against his ear.

"Yes, simple," Carl responded with confidence. "The complexity of the product does not have to make its unveiling anymore elaborate than any other demonstration. We know what we are doing. I just hope that you will have your part down pat."

"I'm ready." Ethan relaxed his grip and leaned back into his chair again. As a Marketing Manager, he had participated in many product presentations over the years and was confident he could handle this one.

Carl said, "The statistical data itself will sell the Signa-Chip. All we have to do is let the world know that it's available."

Ethan had to agree: If, the thousands of lost or kidnapped children alone in this country every year, that are never found, or found too late, would have had the Signa-Chip implanted in them, ninety-nine percent of them could have been located within minutes and many of them rescued. That statistic alone, he knew, was enough to sell the chip to the general public.

:

The ringing of the telephone next to his head startled Adam awake from a sound sleep, where he had 'passed out', fully dressed, on his couch hours earlier. Exhausted both physically and emotionally, he had collapsed on the living room sofa as soon as he had gotten home from the hospital and had not moved since. The slept on side of his face was damp with sweat and creased from being firmly pressed against the course material of the couch for hours. The hair on that side was also matted and in total disarray. A feeling of panic already had a grip on him as he reached for the phone: Pessimistic intuition, telling him it was the hospital calling him back with dreaded news.

Half afraid to answer the call, half afraid not too, Adam picked up the handset. Still groggy from sleep, or the lack of it, Adam tentatively said, in a froggy voice, "Hello?"

"Adam?"

"Carol?" Relived and surprised simultaneously, Adam instantly recognized her voice. Instinctively, he checked his wrist for his watch. Not finding it on his arm, he quickly scanned the wood end table next to him for the time piece. "What time is it?" He asked, when his visual search came up empty.

"Six-thirty," Carol answered.

Adam shook his head trying to shake off the sleepiness. A bright daylight still came in through the living room widows, so he assumed correctly that it was PM, not AM.

"You all right honey?"

"Yeah. I'm just still half asleep."

"When did you get back home?"

Adam thought for a moment before he answered. "I really can't remember. Sometime after noon."

"When are you going back?"

"As soon as I can shower and get cleaned up a bit." Adam said, rubbing the quarter of an inch of stubble growing on his face.

"Should I cancel our reservation at the Black Angus tonight?"

Adam had to think again for a moment before he remembered the eight o'clock dinner date they had planned together at the popular restaurant.

"Why don't you try to make it for ten," he said. "If nothing has changed with my mother, I should be back by then. I just need to stop in and see her for a little bit and check up on her."

"That's kinda late for Lindsey to be up," Carol reminded him that her six year old daughter was included in that 'dinner date'.

Adam felt bad as he remembered that detail and the excitement the little blonde haired Lindsey displayed when she learned that she was invited along: Dancing in place, her blue eyes sparkling in anticipation of the event.

It would be the first time he would disappoint her, since he came into her life when she was just a baby, and it made him feel as guilty as if he was committing some unforgivable crime. Trying to justify himself, Adam said, "I have to do this."

"I know," Carol answered. "In fact, I'd be very disappointed in you if you didn't go see about your mother."

"But, I'd still...like...to see you tonight too."

Adam wanted to say, *I need to see you tonight,* but his mouth said the word 'like' instead. Afraid that Carol might misinterpret his use of 'need' as a weakness. A weakness his male psyche wasn't ready to show, especially during this time of distress. The truth of the matter though, was that he both really did want and need to see Carol: for her to comfort him, to supply him with moral support, to help him emotionally through another difficult time.

Adam wondered if Carol knew how much he had come to depend on her for such things. Hoping that if she did, she interpreted his need for her companionship as compassion and not as weakness.

She did. And from the way Adam stammered when he spoke, the way he hesitated between thoughts, she knew, the man she loved was mentally on guard. The way most men were when hurt and her mothering instincts were to help. "I could get a baby-sitter and go over to the hospital with you…if you want me too?" Carol offered, while allowing him the option.

Adam jumped at the opportunity of her company. "I'd really like that. Besides if mom wakes up, I know she'd be glad to see you too. It might just do her a lot of good."

On the other end of the telephone a slight smile crossed Carol's face. *Men*, she thought.

"You know it would be all right for you to tell me that you'd like to have me with you during this. That it would do you a lot of good too," Carol said.

"And it would," Adam admitted. "I just didn't want to impose…"

"Impose?"

"Well, you know."

"I love mom too," Carol responded, her feelings almost hurt by Adam's insensitive comment. She had thought that after four years, her relationship with Adam was such that she would be automatically included in his family matters.

In her mind, she was ready for marriage, if Adam would ask. But since both of them had just gotten out of bad marriages when they met, and they had promised each other that they would wait for at least five years before they ever thought of making that commitment again, he hadn't yet. Nevertheless, she felt that since she and Lindsey had met and spent enough time with Adam's mother to form their own relationship with her; it was insensitive for Adam to think that he was 'imposing' on her if she accompanied him to Misses Garrett's bedside. And she told him so.

"I'm sorry," Adam responded, feeling a bit ashamed of himself. "And yes I would love for you to go with me. It would be such a comfort to have you by my side through this."

"That's better," Carol said. "Now go get cleaned up while I get a 'sitter' and I'll see you in an hour or so."

:

There was not much else he could do but take down basic information, get a recent photograph of the little girl and gather any other pertinent information about four year old Ashley Dawson that the photograph didn't reveal. Such as the birthmark on her left shoulder and the small scar the girl had on her right calf. The scar; the three suture result of an encounter Ashley had last summer with a shard of busted glass while on an outing at a local park. The jagged piece of glass; the remnant of a beer bottle maliciously smashed by some inconsiderate teenager who thought it 'cool' to create the hazard.

"All I can promise you, Misses Dawson," Detective Keller said to the child's still weeping mother, "is that we will do everything we can to find your daughter. Maybe someone saw something…something that might give us a clue as to what might have happened to her and where we might start looking for her."

Both of the Dawson's shifted uncomfortably on the dark colored vinyl sofa that adorned the living room and matched the arm chair in which Detective Keller sat. Neither one confident that the detective's words were gospel.

Keller noticed the nervous discomfort and interpreted it as peculiar; worthy of further investigation.

Armed with the knowledge that of the children under the age of six reported to the National Incident-Based Reporting System as missing, nearly half were taken by a family member, Keller paid special attention to their reactions. He asked them personal questions related to their private relationship, watching their every expression. He felt, from the NIBRS data, that if his best suspect wasn't sitting right in front of him, they were somehow related.

"We have been married for over ten years," Gene barked back. He was offended by the detective's implication that somehow he or his wife were responsible for Ashley's disappearance. "And we get along just fine."

"I'm sorry," Detective Keller said, indifferent to both of the Dawson's stark reactions. "But, I do have to ask," he added. "The statistics show that most kidnappers are related in some way to the victim and I had to eliminate that possibility."

"I don't care what you've got to ask," Misses Dawson, whimpered. She wiped the tears from her eyes. "As long as it helps you find my daughter before something happens to her."

"I can assure you detective," Gene interjected. "Neither I, nor my wife had anything to do whatsoever with our daughters disappearance, or for that matter anyone we know."

"There's no way you can make that statement Mister Dawson. You have no idea what your neighbor three houses down, or just around the corner, is capable of. Yesterday he may have borrowed your lawnmower and today abducted your child." The detective waited for the impact of his statement to hit before continuing. "Nothing is as common as hearing; 'he was such a nice guy, quiet, kept to himself, always friendly, who'd ever believed he would do such a thing. I hear it all the time," Detective Keller reiterated, when he saw the sobering look appear on the couples face, "Now again, is their anybody that you can think of, relative or otherwise, who might be capable of kidnapping Ashley? Anybody who may have taken an abnormal interest in your daughter, man or woman? Showed her any kind of special attention?"

The detective waited while they thought, realizing another one of the NIBRS statistics that showed one of the seven, abducted, female children under the age of six were sexually assaulted while abducted. That fact, he would try to keep to himself, if he could. But would reveal it in an instant, if he thought it might inspire the parents to think and help identify a possible perpetrator.

The parents looked at each other questioningly for a moment.

"No one that either of us can think of," Gene eventually answered for both of them.

Anxious that the time being spent with the questioning could be better spent searching for Ashley, Erica Dawson stood. "I need to go," she said, heading toward the solid wood front door. "I have to find Ashley."

"We'll find her, Detective Keller stood also. "I have a team already out there looking."

The detective's words were of little consolation to the obviously distraught parents. They were even less so for himself: The detective knew the statistics. He knew the odds. And that the chances of finding the abducted child, unharmed, were very slim at best. And that the longer Ashley was missing, the slimmer even those chances became. Still, he had to try and encourage the aggrieved parents the best he could without betraying his doubts.

The one thing he did realize, after questioning them, was they were not involved in their daughter's kidnapping and it became clearer to him that the abduction was perpetrated by a stranger.

:

A canvas of the neighborhood revealed nothing. Not even a description of the vehicle. No one in the vicinity saw or heard anything unusual, nothing that could be construed as a clue. Ashley was gone, disappearing without a trace into the magnitude of the city.

Detective Keller sent the last of the uniformed officers, he used to assist him in the preliminary door-to-door inquiry, back to the precinct.

He sat alone in his car outside the Dawson house for another fifteen minutes, looking at the innocent child in the five by ten photograph, hoping that there was a small piece of good news he could give the child's parents. A tiny ray of hope. But, at present, there was nothing he had to give.

:

There was no change in his mother; she lay perfectly still in the hospital bed, her eyes closed, the machines still connected to her, the clear plastic tubes, attached to her nostrils, still supplying her with the life giving oxygen. No change was good though, they were told. It meant that she was holding her own. 'Stabilized' as Doctor Ching had called it specifically.

"We might as well go," Adam said to Carol, "and let her rest."

Carol, who sat bedside, next to his mother, holding her hand, looked over to Adam pacing around the small private room. And knew the waiting, the unknowing, the tension of being there this long was too much for him to bare. She gently slid her hand out from beneath Charlotte's and went over to Adam and put her arms around him.

He laid his head in the pocket where her neck met her shoulder and smelled the faint scent of her perfume. Somehow through this distressing time, he felt his love for Carol growing stronger and wished that they hadn't promised each other to wait for five years before marrying. He wrapped his arms around her in response to her hug and vowed to himself that after this was over, five years or not, he was going to propose.

More immediate though was the fact that he hadn't eaten for over twenty-four hours and felt the effects of neglecting his own body's needs.

"Let's go get something to eat," Adam said, easing his grip on her. "I'm starving and there's nothing much we can do here. The doctor said she should sleep through the night."

Carol pulled her arms back and looked at her watch.

"You're probably getting hungry too eh? "Adam asked.

"We've got about an hour before our reservation," she said, sliding the padded chair away from the side of the bed; pushing it back into its place along the back wall.

"That's okay," Adam said. "I have to stop at the bank before we get there anyway. I need to get a few bucks."

Holding hands, they both turned back and silently stared at his still sleeping mother, watching her breathe.

"Let's go," Adam tugged on Carol's hand and headed toward the door. "I want to stop at the desk and make sure they have my cell phone number…just in case."

An affirmative nod from Carol in response, signaled her agreement.

:

The ATM machine at the First National Bank drive-through was broken down; the jagged edge of a mutilated debit card improperly inserted into the narrow slot, the culprit for the malfunction. A sensor in the computerized machine interpreting the errant card as an attempt to defraud it, shut down.

Adam tried several times, unsuccessfully, to extract the jammed card from the machine, hoping he could free it and open the slot back up so his card could be used. Frustrated at his inability to remove the obstacle, Adam half shouted, "The only other ATM I know of is half the way across town. By the time I get there and back to the restaurant we'll be late for our reservation."

"That's okay." Carol placed her hand on his arm. "I can use my bank card to pay for dinner and you can pay me back tomorrow."

Reluctantly, Adam pulled away from the defunct machine. It had been a long time since he had felt that angry. And his ability to cope with even the slightest problem seemed non-existent. Hungry, overly tired, and stressed beyond imagination from spending the evening, watching his mother fighting for her life; now the ATM machine? It was all too much.

In failure, over his inability to control the circumstances of the last twenty-four hours, he stomped the accelerator of the powerful pickup to the floor. The rear tires of the Dodge Ram screamed in protest as the truck leaped forward. The dynamics of the vehicle's instant acceleration, pressing both of its occupants forcefully back into the seat.

"What was that all about," Carol shot a surprised, irritated glance his way when Adam eased off the pedal a few seconds later and let the truck slow down.

"Sorry," Adam answered. "Venting I guess…I needed that."

She chided him with, "Feel any better?"

"No! But, it did feel good for a moment."

Aggravated, not understanding the mentality that inspired Adam to do what he did, Carol reached down and turned on the radio without responding. She was surprised to hear the excited ranting of a 'fire and brimstone' preacher speaking about how the world was morally falling apart and that the predicted 'end times' neared.

"Find something else will you," Adam commented. The preacher's, blaring tone of voice grated on his last nerve. "Of all the things I don't need to hear right now, that is one of them."

Carol smirked at him as she reached for the radio's selector buttons. "It's probably just what you need to hear." She hesitated to push another of the control buttons teasingly.

"Come on," he pleaded. "You know I don't buy into all that hogwash. They've been saying the world was ending tomorrow for the last hundred years."

"No I didn't know that," she frowned when she realized that there were some things about Adam she still didn't know.

A practicing atheist, preferring to believe in some other, any other, explanation for the world's existence than creation by an unknown God, Adam reached over himself and tried to change the station.

Playfully, Carol gently slapped him on the back of his hand. "Okay, Okay," she said and chose one of the easy listening stations. The soft music filling the cab of the pickup with the soothing sounds of a popular vocalist.

Despite the relaxing melody, the sounds of the evangelist's voice echoed in Adam's head and reminded him of his mother's constant preaching at him when he was a teenager. About how the world was coming to an end twenty years ago and how he needed to be 'Saved'.

"Saved from what?" He remembered always responding to her with his prepubescent attitude. "The only thing I need saving from is all this preaching."

"You don't believe in all that God stuff do you?" Adam took the opportunity to present the question to Carol.

It was a topic they had never really addressed before. He didn't know how she felt about the issue and thought it important to ask before he proposed marriage to her.

"I don't believe. I don't, not believe." Carol answered. "There are just too many unanswered questions to accept it all. Too many things that suggest the existence of a supreme being to deny wholeheartedly. And there's just not enough proof, as far as I'm concerned, to believe either way."

"One of them middle of the roader's," Adam laughed. He was satisfied her answer was a 'safe' one. And relieved to realized, that in the long run, an agnostic was a lot more compatible with him than a 'believer', he dropped the subject.

Gary L. Dewey

4

The last bite of prime rib went down much slower than the first mouthful of the succulent steak did. Eating now more for pleasure than to satisfy his hunger, Adam tilted his head backwards and held the piece of meat between his teeth, savoring the taste for a moment longer before even starting to chew.

Across the white, tablecloth covered table, Carol sat watching him. The light from the trio of flickering candles on the table in front of her, dancing through her hair, giving it an extra golden glow. He closed his eyes and slowly bit down on the warm, medium rare piece of beef, letting the tangy, flavorful juices flow down the back of his throat.

He sure loves his steaks, Carol smiled. Watching Adam enjoy his Porterhouse steak, brought as much pleasure to her as the actual eating it did to him. She reached for her near empty wineglass, taking the last swallow of sparkling Chardonea just as Adam's head came forward.

Adam opened his eyes as he swallowed. In the dim lit Black Angus restaurant, the flickering candlelight, accentuating Carol's features, he found himself staring at her beauty.

"What?" Carol asked, noticing his prolonged look.

"I was just marveling at how stunning a woman you are."

Caught off guard. Slightly embarrassed by the sudden, unexpected compliment, Carol countered. "Then it is true what they say?"

"What is that?"

"Love is blind." She let the word 'is' drag out slowly.

"No I mean it. You are one beautiful woman."

As he spoke the words, a thought flashed through Adam's mind. The opportunity to expound was there. He waited for a moment as the part of him that said 'go for it' wrestled with the part that said 'not now'. The 'go for it' part won.

"The love part is right," he said. "But you're way off with the blind thing. I do love you very much and I think that you are the most beautiful woman in the world."

"Come on," Carol blushed. "I've already said I'd pay for the dinner tonight."

Feeling the blood rushing to her face, she was glad for the dim lighting inside the restaurant, that would hide her reddening checks. It was not that she didn't like the compliments, she loved them. She also loved the sincerity in Adam's voice. But, ever since she was a child, it always had made her feel self-conscious when she became the center of attention.

A serious look crossed over Adam's face. "No! I really mean it. If I had a ring with me…if we hadn't promised each other we'd wait the five years, I'd ask you to marry me right here and now."

Stunned, Carol sat speechless, but for only a second. "You'd better watch yourself Mister Garrett," she said seriously, staring deeply into his dark brown eyes. The flushed feeling long forgotten. "If you had a ring? If you ask me right here, right now?" She leaned slightly towards him and placed her hand atop his. "I just might say yes."

The tall uniformed waiter came up to their table and asked, "Can I get you folks anything else?"

Startled by the young man's sudden, inopportune appearance, both Adam and Carol sat back in their chairs. They felt like they were a couple of eight year olds who just got caught with their hands in the proverbial cookie jar.

"No," they both answered sheepishly in unison.

Picking up the empty dinner plates the waiter said, "Let me get some of this stuff out of your way." He placed a rectangular, black leather case containing the bill for the meal in front of Adam. "I'll be back in a second and take that up front for you...if you like."

After the waiter turned away to take the soiled plates to the Dishwasher's window near the back kitchen, Adam slid the leather case over toward Carol.

"Do you want to stop back at my place for a bit?" She asked, reaching for the debit card inside her purse. "After I take the baby-sitter home, we'll have the place virtually to ourselves."

The waiter was back, taking the bank card, bill, and leather case up to the cashier before Adam answered.

"Sounds like a plan," Adam eventually got to respond.

No sooner though had the words left his lips, when his cell phone started ringing.

"Mister Garrett?" A woman's voice asked, after he had answered it with the usual, "Hello?"

"This is River Valley General. They asked me to call you and tell you that you should come in."

"Let's go!" Adam said to Carol standing and hanging up the telephone at the same time. "That was the hospital."

Carol stood quickly and they rushed out of the entrance.

The waiter, his back toward them and on the other side of the crowded restaurant, never saw them leave. When he returned to their empty table with the leather case containing Carol's Credit/Debit card and a receipt, he assumed they must have both went to the restroom and would be returning momentarily. He placed the case on the table and finished clearing the remaining soiled dishes.

Immediately after the waiter had left the unoccupied table, a dark haired man in an adjacent booth, who had been watching the whole series of events at the nearby table, inconspicuously reached over, quickly pulling the leather case to his lap.

Back in his semi-dark booth, he pulled the credit card and receipt from the case and after checking again to make sure no one was watching, he reached out again, replacing the now empty leather case back on the table. He slid the ill-gotten bank card into his pants pocket as he stood, dropped a twenty dollar bill on his table to pay for his meal and nonchalantly headed out into the parking lot.

:

Two doctors and a team of nurses were exiting her room, everything that they could physically do for the critical patient at this time, done. The only thing left undone: the waiting. Only time could answer the question of whether she would survive or not. The echoing sounds of grieving, wafted out of the double swinging doors of the surgery recovery room as the doors swung open to let the doctors and nurses pass through.

Tears cascading down his own cheeks, as he looked at the swollen, battered face of his young daughter, laying motionless, near death, on the gurney, Gene Dawson reached out, placing a comforting hand on Erica's shoulder.

The weight of his hand, slightly a touch, was more than his wife could bare. Erica collapsed. Her brain, losing the fight to stay conscious. Her emotions, unable to bare the intense pain of seeing Ashley struggling to live, sought refuge in momentary unconsciousness.

Gene's reaction was lightning fast. Catching her as she stumbled, he held her limp body as he hollered for help.

Immediately, the team of nurses and doctors rushed back into the room, placing Erica on an empty gurney in the 'Recovery Position'.

The blackout wasn't of long duration, Erica regained cognizance within the next two minutes. Her skin clammy from perspiration, she tried to aright herself.

"Why don't you just stay laying down Misses Dawson...rest for a while," the older of the two doctors strongly suggested. "I'm going to order a Valium injection for you that should help you relax."

The doctor wanted to tell Erica that Ashley was going to be all right. That the sexually assaulted, severely beaten four year old, was going to be okay. He wanted to tell her something that might help ease the mental anguish, he knew caused her collapse...but couldn't. He himself didn't even know if the hemorrhaging in the child's brain would stop. If the cerebral swelling would subside before it killed her, or how much mental function the child would retain if it did.

"Just try to calm down," the younger doctor said and placed one of his hands on Erica's back between her shoulders. He made a gentle circling motion. "We're all going to do everything we can."

It wasn't long after the Valium injection, that Erica felt the effect of the drug and was able to relax enough that she could get back up. The grief over Ashley's condition was still there, present and foremost in her mind. The worry, the anguish still there. But the edge was taken off the agony by the drug, making it bearable.

:

She was awake when they got there, her eyes wide, but glazed.

"Hi Ma," Adam said, as he and Carol walked into her room.

She followed their entrance with her eyes without speaking. Not because she didn't want to say something to her son, she couldn't muster enough energy to move her mouth.

Carol smiled at Misses Garrett and placed her hand on top of Charlotte's.

The cardiac defibrillator, a new addition among the other machines in the room, caught Adam's attention. He shuddered as his imagination envisioned them applying the paddles of the device to his mother's chest and shocking her heart back to life.

"Mister Garrett?" A tall middle aged nurse with red hair, dressed in the typical white uniform, stuck her head into the room and signaled for him to step out into the hallway. "We would like to keep the visitors down to one at a time and only the immediate family," she said when Adam obliged. "And Doctor Ching left explicit instructions with me that we need to limit even those visitations to ten minutes at most."

"She's...", Adam started to defend Carol's presence.

"Doctor's orders," she cut him off. "Your mother gave us quite a scare not that long ago and we're fortunate that she's still with us. What she needs right now is rest and I'm sure you and your friend wouldn't want to do anything depriving her of that."

Adam's head dropped. "What happened?" He asked, looking down at the white and black flecked, tile floor covering and wondering why he was called into the hospital if he couldn't see her.

"Why don't you get your friend and go have a seat in the waiting room." She pointed toward the little room at the end of the intensive care unit. There's a couch, a couple of soft chairs, magazines, and a television in there, if you're so inclined. The doctor should be back shortly and he will come in and talk with you."

Questions left unanswered, not what Adam wanted to hear, but it was all he was going to get from the nurse. She turned back toward her desk, expecting that her instructions were to be unequivocally obeyed.

He watched her walk away before he stepped back through the doorway to his mother's room. Without a word, Adam, by waving his hand, gestured for Carol to come to him. Once out into the area outside the room, he timidly took her hand, leading her down to the waiting room.

They sat together on the pale green, vinyl couch. "They want her to rest," Adam said, "and only one of us can be in there with her at a time."

In the silence that ensued, the 'canned' laughter accompanying the sit-com playing on the suspended television set in the room, though low in volume, was under the circumstances, grating.

"That thing is getting on my last nerve," Adam said. His eyes searching for the remote control to silence the irritation, he said,. "Do you see the remote?"

Carol glanced around the room. "No."

Adam got up to manually shut the television off, but there were no exterior controls. Frustrated, he stepped out to the main nurses station and asked if the TV could be turned off.

The on-duty nurse floundered for a moment on her side of the long, chest-high counter/desk and handed him the remote. "Sorry," she smiled.

"I was wondering why the hospital called me in if I can't be in the room with my mother," Adam asked fumbling with the remote.

"Standard procedure," she said softly. "For a while, we thought we were losing her. And under those circumstances

51

Gary L. Dewey

it is hospital policy to call the family. But, the doctor was able to regain control and stabilize…" She trailed off.

The sound of the double electronic doors, at the far end of the unit, opening caught both of their attention. Doctor Ching appeared through the doors and walked up to the desk. He shot a quick glance Adam's way before he asked the nurse for the "Garrett chart."

"This is her son," she said while handing him a clipboard with several sheets of paper on it.

"I know," the staff cardiologist responded giving another glance. This time adding a nod of recognition.

"What's going on with my mother?" Adam asked, unable to contain the question any longer.

The doctor continued leafing though the papers on the clipboard. "I'll be right with you," he said without looking up. "I'll come down to the waiting room and talk with you in a few minutes."

No! You'll talk to me now, Adam held back from saying. *That's my mother in there and I want to know what's going on with her and I want to know now.* Logic got the better of him though. *The last thing he needed to do, was to start a commotion in the Cardiac section of the Intensive Care Unit and with, of all people, his mother's doctor.* He turned and walked away.

Another burst of irritating laughter emanated from the television set when he stepped back into the waiting room. At the tall, narrow window in the back wall of the room, Carol stood. The heavy, dark drapes that hung over the double safety glass window panes, held apart by her hand. She looked down through the nighttime to the flowing water of the Detroit River below.

Walking up to her, Adam pushed the off button on the remote, tossed it down on one of the chairs and put an arm over her shoulder in one move. "I love you," he said.

Without verbal response, she gently laid her face on his neck.

They stood there for a moment, locked together, watching the river meander its way through the city.

"Mister Garrett," Doctor Ching interrupted the moment of peace.

They turned simultaneously.

"Have a seat," the doctor motioned toward the couch. He himself pulled one of the chairs around so that it faced them and sat too. "Your mother is not doing very good," he spoke solemnly, but matter-of-factly. "She is stable now, but I don't know for how long."

"What's..." Adam started to ask.

The doctor continued speaking as if he never heard him. Preferring, to say everything he had planned on saying before answering any specific questions. "As it sometimes occurs, following a Cardiac infarction, the heart goes into a danger-ous ventricular fibrillation, in which case, it really doesn't function. Just sort of quivers," he explained, gesticulating with his hand, mimicking the motion. "The heart doesn't pump any blood and the condition, if not corrected immedi-ately, is fatal. Fortunately, in your mother's case, she re-sponded to the defibrillator and we were able to bring her heart back to a normal rhythm."

What he didn't tell Adam, was that his mother's heart had stopped functioning completely and that is what had ended the episode of ventricular fibrillation. Then jolted, by the electrical shock from the paddles of the defibrillator machine, her heart began beating again on its own, minus the quiver-ing.

"How long will it continue to beat normally? I don't know. Will it go into V Fib again? I don't know. What I do know is we have a couple of options available to us. One, we can try to control the tachyarrhythmia's with drugs, or two, I can implant a pacemaker. Which at this point in time, I think would be very risky to attempt."

Carol glanced over at Adam's face. It had lost its color. The depth of its paleness, assurance that the magnitude of the doctor's words were comprehended.

"Does your mother live with you?" Doctor Ching asked.

"No," Adam answered. He knew the doctor asked, not for information and wondered what the real meaning of the question was.

"They do have portable defibrillator machines," the doctor said, standing up. "And I suggest you get one and you should both learn CPR."

Shocked by the realization of what the doctor implied, Adam's face lost even more of its color. He felt sick in his stomach and wished he hadn't eaten so much at the Black Angus.

"If your mother does make it out of here," the doctor continued. "She is going to need to be watched and monitored for a while."

Doctor Ching stood, turned toward the waiting room door. He stopped, before stepping completely out. "We might have another option available to us soon," he said. "I have to attend a seminar tomorrow night. There's a new implantable device coming out on the market that promises, among other things, to alleviate some of the need for pacemakers. Don't ask me any questions." He put up his hand to stop any inquiries before they were even formulated. "I haven't seen it. I know none of the details about it. All I know, is what I've told you. Once I hear more, if it is applicable. You'll be the first to hear."

The doctor disappeared as suddenly as he had showed up and left them sitting, contemplating his words.

This time it was Carol who reached out a comforting arm, placing it around Adam's shoulder. She pulled him closer to her. "I love you," she whispered.

:

Ethan Blake stood in front of the full length mirror on the back of his bedroom door. He was rehearsing his speech and watching his facial expressions until he had it down pat. Satisfied that he had the correct verbal emphasis synchronized with the proper grimace, he smiled at his reflection and took a bow.

Narrative skill, an art he had learned long ago, was Ethan's earmark to success. It was an intrinsic ability he had, a skill that had sold many a product, even when the product was not all that he claimed it to be. As a youngster, he displayed his inborn ability to sell, many times. Purchasing items from local 'yard sales' with his weekly allowance and later reselling those items to friends and neighbors for a profit. Most times nearly tripling his original allowance.

One such incident, in which the young Ethan had purchased a rusty bicycle for a dollar and a can of black spray paint for a dime, that he promptly applied to the rusty bike, stood out in his memory most. Ethan resold that bike shinning like new, two days later for fifteen dollars. It was the first of many times his father, a career salesman himself, would tell him, he 'could sell the stink off a dead goat'. Ethan smiled every time he relived that day and thought of the old saying.

Confident his part of the presentation for the Signa-Chip was perfect, he turned away from the mirror. *Can't get much better than that,* he thought egotistically. Feeling this time, with this product, he really didn't need much of a 'sales pitch'. It was the sensation it was.

"Bravo!" Nicole, his wife and mother of their two children smiled at Ethan.

She, using all of her strength to hold back a guffaw, had been laying awake in their bed unbeknown to him, watching his fervid practicing.

Ethan had thought Nicole had fallen asleep long before he started his routine. If he had thought, for a moment, that she hadn't and was still awake, listening, he would have never cavorted in front of her and the mirror the way he had. Feeling a slight amount of compunction; half embarrassed; half proud of his performance; Ethan bowed again. "What no applause?"

Nicole complied, slapping her hands together while making a hissing sound with her mouth. The two actions together, resembling the sound a large audience would make when responding to a major event.

Ethan felt flushed. "Applaud this," he said, sidling over to the bed and lowering himself next to her.

5

"And there you have it, Ladies and Gentlemen." Ethan stepped to the side, away from the center stage podium, when he finished the presentation. An 'exploded' view of the chip appeared beneath the ESI logo on the suspended, eight-by-eight movie screen behind him. "The Signa-Chip by Electronics Solutions Incorporated."

A round of enthusiastic applause ensued. Intermixed with the applause, the flashbulbs of several newspaper reporter's cameras erupted.

"At the back of the room," Ethan continued, oblivious to the luminous distractions, "We have tables set up with informative brochures. You're welcome to help yourself."

Ethan paused, taking in a view of the congregation of people spread out beneath the small, portable stage. Never, in his previous presentations had he had such an audience with so many distinguished persons in attendance. *But, then again,* he thought. *I never had such a product to display either.*

As the applause subsided and the crowd began to disperse, Carl Torre came up beside him. "Good job," he said, patting Ethan on the shoulder. "See I told you there was nothing to worry about."

A quick sideways smile said Ethan was also pleased with the coordinated smoothness of the presentation. He looked at his watch. 9:30PM. *Perfect,* he thought. *Right on time.*

Carl added, "It'll only get easier from here,"

Together they stepped down from the stage. They were heading, as planned, to the back of the conference room, making themselves available to answer any questions that may have been left unanswered by the two hour long presentation. The two executives, confident the visuals and their narratives had explained sufficiently every conceivable aspect of the chip, were hoping there weren't many issues left uncovered, if any at all.   Nonetheless, if there were, they would fine tune and incorporate any that arose into the next major demonstration. That 'next' scheduled presentation was for New York city, the following Friday.

"Amazing technology," one of the reporters from a local newspaper commented to them as they walked passed.

"Not really," Ethan answered. They stopped walking and turned to face the reporter. "It's the same wireless technology that the cell phone in your pocket and the Global Positioning System works on," Ethan said. "The only thing ESI did was to make the chip small enough for implantation."

Abashed by his lack of expertise, the reporter tried to save face. "Well, the medical aspects are what I'm talking about."

"That too is old technology," Carl interjected. "Already in use in heart monitors, pacemakers, electronic thermometers et-cetera. All that we did was bring it together in a programmable chip and write the software that could interpret the electronic signals from the chip."

"Hence forth the name, Signa-Chip", Ethan smirked, enjoying toying with the naïve reporter.

"I see…Mind if I take a picture of you two together?"

Carl glanced over at Ethan for his approval.

"Suit yourself," Ethan said.

"Excuse me," a middle aged oriental man with straight black hair, wearing a navy blue suit, moved in beside the camera yielding reporter an instant after the flashbulb ignited.

"Yes?" Ethan turned.

The man extended his hand while introducing himself. "Doctor Ching, Department of Cardiology at River Valley General Hospital in Detroit."

"Doctor," Ethan said, grasping the hand in greeting. "Ethan Blake, Marketing Manager at ESI and this is Carl Torre, Public Relations."

"Doctor," Carl said, nodding.

"I was wondering about a particular aspect of the chip that wasn't addressed during the presentation," Doctor Ching started.

"Yes?" Ethan responded first.

"Does the Signa-Chip have two way capabilities?"

The information the doctor asked about, Ethan was not ready to make public. And not too sure of how the media would handled it when it was made public, Ethan looked beyond the doctor at the still present reporter and said, "Could you excuse us."

"Sure," the reporter said, backing away while pretending to fumble with his camera.

Doctor Ching, confused by the reluctance to answer his simple question said, "I can come back another time."

"No! No," Carl said, gently grabbing the doctor's arm and leading him a few steps away. "For some obvious reasons, ESI at this time, doesn't want that information out to the public. And at the very least not via the 'press'. We're not too sure how they are going to interpret it."

Still confused, Doctor Ching furrowed his eyebrows in question.

"Some might construe two way communications with the chip as an undesirable trait. A possible method of control," Carl explained. "A 'Big Brother' is watching you thing."

"Especially, if it is sensationalized as such by the media," Ethan added with a sideways glance toward the departing reporter, making sure the reporter had retreated far enough into the crowd gathering around the nearest brochure filled tables, to not over hear them.

"And we all know how they like to embellish things," Carl said. "We just want to have a little more command over what they get and what they do with that knowledge when they get it."

Nodding, Doctor Ching showed his agreement. He was not virgin to 'run ins' with the press and the tendency of the media to exploit simple details. Nor to the practice of the newspapers to make the proverbial mountain from a molehill for the purpose of selling subscriptions.

Doctor Ching recalled the last such 'run in' over an innocent bacterial infection that had occurred after minor surgery in three separate patients at River Valley hospital six months ago. By the time the media was done with the incident, the three occurrences were a major, infectious outbreak and the sterility of the operating rooms at River Valley were in question. The result: The whole hospital fell under the scrutiny of the Public Health Department until it was proven, unequivocally, that the hospital's procedures and sterility were well above established guidelines.

"So what you are saying to me is that the Signa-Chip does have two way communication capabilities?" Doctor Ching re-asked.

"Yes!" Ethan and Carl answered in unison.

"We anticipated a need for that characteristic," Ethan took over the rationalization. "Putting in a chip, both broadcast and receive capable."

"The reason I ask," Doctor Ching said, thinking of Charlotte Garrett. "I have a patient..." He abruptly cut himself off. He did so to eliminate becoming too personal with his inquiry. "What I guess I'm really asking," he began again.

"Is the Signa-Chip capable of acting as an implantable defibrillator?"

"That of course is dependent on the location of implantation. But you would know that," Ethan answered. A pretentious smile crossed his face as he reiterated, verbatim, Doctor Reece's words, when Doctor Reece was asked that same question. "It worked extremely well in that capacity when positioned near a branch of the sympathetic or parasympathetic nervous systems. In fact, we were able to invoke the potentially fatal arrhythmia in several different test animals and reverse it within seconds by utilizing the two way communication capacity of the chip."

"Excuse me," the newspaper reporter who had inched his way, unbeknown to the trio, back to within earshot of their conversation, interrupted. His pencil poised on a small pad of writing paper, "Did I hear you right? That the Signa-Chip can be used to both broadcast and receive electronic signals?"

"No, you didn't hear us right," Ethan sarcastically responded. "We were discussing the potential benefits, with the doctor here, what such a capability might have for certain heart patients."

"Isn't uninvited eavesdropping illegal in this state?" Carl asked Ethan rhetorically.

Ethan turned, and smiled an evil smile. "Yeah! I just watched a television program about that very thing. They likened it to an illegal telephone tap or voyeurism."

"Punishable by up to five years in prison." Carl said, turning his look from Ethan to the reporter.

"That's what I heard," Ethan sneered. "Now, what was it that you asked?" His ostensible glare refocusing on the backpedaling reporter.

"Nothing," the reporter said, walking away quickly.

"I didn't think so," Ethan called after him.

Carl reached out and touched the sleeve of Ethan's suit coat. "I wouldn't be so blatant," he said. "We need to stay on the good side of the press."

"I know, I just didn't like the sneakiness and I wanted him to know it."

"That's the impression I would have gotten," Doctor Ching smiled. Joining in on the chance to vent some of his animosity toward reporters.

"I think it's inherent in them. Almost a prerequisite for employment," Carl joked and all three of them chuckled aloud.

"In any event," Ethan redirected the conversation back to the Signa-Chip. "There is more clinical testing needed before we can make any substantial claims about the chip being used in the capacity of a two way communication device. Our doctor, a Doctor Devon Reece is working on setting up those additional tests as we speak."

"Since that is a secondary aspect of the Signa-Chip though, we are making the chip available now," Carl said.

"Fully capable of course?" Doctor Ching asked.

"Fully."

"Not to digress…but to get back to location," the doctor, ruminating questioned. "During your presentation, you pur-posed a left-hand implantation site?"

"That is correct," Ethan stated. "We wanted…needed… to choose a site that would best utilize existing conditions. Taking in of course all the foreseeable uses of the chip, con-venience, functionality, and to setup a universally standard site. So that someone who gets Signa-Chip implanted in Montreal can show up in Miami and everyone knows exactly where to find it."

The doctor understood the medical reasoning behind the Left-hand implantation site because of the direct connection the left arm has with the cardio-vascular system. However, he was not so aware of the other implications.

"Part of the impetus for choosing the Left-hand, besides the medical reasoning," Carl clarified, "is the left-handed location of the steering wheel in American made vehicles."

Ethan turned and surveyed the emptying conference room while his cohort explained the logic behind ESI's decision. Ethan made several gestures with his hands, supervising from a distance the maintenance crew dismantling the stage and gathering the various paraphernalia they had used during the presentation.

"It makes it so much more convenient for people," Carl continued, "to just reach out of their car window with the left arm and run the hand over the Laser Read Screen Signa-Chip uses. That screen by the way can easily be installed in existing ATM machines. Another incentive was the position of existing checkout counters and UPC code readers at all of the stores being on the left-side. This facilitates the use of the Signa-Chip as a personal identification device and capable of initiating electronic transfer of funds transactions, without much modification. These issues and more, made the left-hand site the logical choice."

"What do you have in mind for an alternative site? In the event of those unfortunates who have no left hand or for that matter even a left arm."

Ethan turned back to the doctor, pointing to the left temple area of his own head, just inside the hair line.

"Interesting," the doctor said, his eye focusing on the optional location.

"Ethan? Ethan Blake?" A woman's voice carried above the background drone of hammering sounds.

Ethan turned to see who owned the familiar voice.

An 'old' colleague, from GyroTech where Ethan had worked as a Product Representative six years ago, emerged from the thinning crowd.

"Beverly?" Ethan squinted. The voice and basic facial features of the woman were familiar, but the shape of the body didn't at all fit the memory.

"One and the same," the thirty-two year old red head smiled.

Torn between greeting the much slimmer, sexier, vivacious Beverly and continuing his conversation with Doctor Ching, Ethan turned back to the doctor and Carl. He wanted to confirm the most important aspect of their discussion before he was distracted. "You'll be sure to present the Signa-Chip to the Administrative board at River Valley?"

"Most assuredly," Doctor Ching said.

A hand touched Ethan's and he turned to look into the pretty, soft featured face and Hazel green eyes of Beverly.

She wrapped her arms around him, hugging him.

Ethan felt her firmness pressing against him as he returned the greeting.

"Excuse us for a minute?" He asked the two men, stepping away with her.

He gently pushed Beverly out to arms length. "Wow! You sure are looking good," he said. "You've lost some weight too."

"A lot of weight," Beverly boasted. "Forty-five pounds to be exact."

"How are you doing? Are you still at GyroTech?"

"One, I'm doing fine. Two, yes I am still there and I've been promoted to the Product Design Department."

"Wonderful!. I always thought that they were never using you to your full potential in sales."

"Well, thank you." A confident glow crossed Beverly's face. "And after the presentation I've just seen, apparently they were not utilizing you to your fullest extent there either."

Ethan just smiled and caught his eyes centering on the three inches of cleavage, Beverly's turquoise, low-cut dress left exposed. Quickly, after his mind realized what he was staring at, he lifted his eyes back to her face, wondering if she had caught his stare.

"When you are done here, want to go get a drink...reminisce?" Apparently, she had noticed.

"Umm," Ethan stammered, hesitating. He felt the gold band on his left ring finger. Eventually, ignoring his conscience, he answered. "Sure."

:

Despite the air conditioning in the crowded department store, it was extremely warm. Especially, crouched down in the narrow aisles, with rack after rack of clothing surrounding her and blocking any flow of air.

Carol held two brightly colored, flowered sun dresses up against Lindsey. "Which one of these do you like best?"

The six year old, indifferent to the stuffiness, contemplated her choices for a moment. She pointed toward a plain, pale orange dress still up on the clothes rack. "I like that one."

Carol had to admit that the white, embossed puppy, outlined in black on it's hem, was cute, but the basic color of the dress, she thought would do nothing for Lindsey.

"No. One of these," Carol insisted. "The blue one matches your eyes and makes them stand-out."

Instinctively, a little frightened, Lindsey reached immediately to her face. She felt for her eyes, expecting to feel them protruding out from their sockets, as she had seen happen to many cartoon characters. "They're not popping out!"

Her daughter's literal interpretation of the phrase 'stand-out' was too comical, Carol started to laugh out loud. "No, sweetheart," she explained. "Stand-out means that the color of the dress makes them look even prettier."

Lindsey felt her eyes again. Just to make sure.

"I like that one though," Lindsey said, again pointing to the embossed puppy.

The dress reminded Carol of the 'poodle skirts' of the 1950's. A look she never did care for. She hesitated. The proud, ear to ear smile though on her daughter's face, when she did take the dress down off the rack and held it against Lindsey was enough to seal the deal.

"Okay," Carol agreed when she saw the enhancing effect the pale orange dress had on Lindsey's blonde hair and ivory complexion. Nonetheless, she held onto the blue, flowered sun dress too. Deciding to purchase both.

"Yeahhh," Lindsey jumped in place expressing her delight over her mother's decision.

"Okay, settle down," Carol said, taking her daughter's hand and heading toward a checkout lane. Both now anxious to leave the store. Though for different reasons: Carol to get out into the coolness of the evening air and reconnect with Adam for a few hours before the weekend was over; Lindsey to get home and wear her new 'puppy' dress.

The line of people at the checkout lane was long. It took nearly fifteen minutes before Carol was able to lay the two dresses up on the counter for the cashier to scan.

The young, teenaged woman cashier turned quickly, greeting them with an indifferent, "Hello," while waving the UPC tags over the register's scanning lens.

Shyly, Lindsey looked up at the little silver ring that dangled from the corner of the woman's upper lip – the result of a body piercing. She timidly pointed toward the ring, her little elbow tucked close to her waist. "Don't that hurt?"

"Lindsey!" Carol turned away from looking through her wallet for her ATM card, and silenced her daughter's inappropriate question. But wondered the same thing herself.

Ignoring both of them the cashier said, "Forty-two-eighty."

"I know that thing is in here," Carol said, rechecking her billfold for the ATM bank card.

Growing frustrated, Carol placed the brown leather case on the track of the conveyer section of the checkout and quickly pulled out all of the plastic cards in it.

The young man, next in line, standing behind her, was not embarrassed to let his impatience show. He tished audibly, inhaled deeply, letting a loud exhale out through his nose and turned his back to Carol.

Without looking the man's way, Carol responded with, "Sorry!"

Amid the Health Insurance; Library; Video Store; Driver's License; Business, and Credit Cards in her wallet the ATM bank card was no where to be found. Frustrated, Carol went against her vow to only use the MasterCard account for emergencies and handed the Credit Card toward the cashier.

"You do it," the cashier rejected the card and pointed to the extension of the cash register mounted on the customer side of the checkout.

Carol scooped up the scattered contents of her wallet and dropped it all into her handbag and ran the Magnetic strip on the card through the slot on the Authorization device. READ ERROR. PLEASE TRY AGAIN., flashed up on the small screen.

Tentatively, Carol slid it through again. The same error message reappeared. Movement behind her caught her eye and she felt humiliated as she watched the customers in line behind her moving to a different checkout lane.

"Come on lady." The man behind her turned back to see what the delay was. "I haven't got all night," he rudely said.

Lindsey, standing patiently through the minor hassle, with the harshness in the man's voice, tucked in closer to her mother's leg.

"Here, try this, the cashier said. She offered Carol a semi-transparent plastic shopping bag to cover the scratched magnetic strip of the MasterCard.

The little trick of wrapping the slightly damaged card with the plastic bag worked to everyone's relief. Within minutes, Carol was buckling Lindsey into her safety seat, still wondering what had happened to her ATM card.

Once Lindsey heard the engine of the car start and felt the vehicle backing out of the parking space, she felt secure enough to voice her opinion. "That man was mean," she said, referring to the man in line behind them.

"Yes, he was," Carol agreed. Her mind refocused on the misplaced ATM card after being momentarily sidetracked by the thoughts of the ill-mannered fellow. Suddenly she recalled the last time she used the bank card. "The Black Angus," she said aloud. She remembered the distracting telephone call they had got from the hospital last night and forgetting to get her card back from the waiter.

"What's that?" Lindsey jerked her head around. Surprised by the off-the-wall comment.

"Mommy just remembered something."

:

As soon as she got back to her ground floor apartment, Carol called Adam. "Did you get my ATM card from the Black Angus last night?"

"No I didn't. We got interrupted remember?"

"Can I put on my new dress?" Lindsey asked, anxious to see herself in the 'puppy dress'.

"In a minute," Carol said. She set the bag containing the dresses down on the floor next to the over-stuffed, couch in her living room. Sitting first on the arm of the sofa, she allowed herself to slide down the arm, eventually collapsing onto the brocade material cushion. "Can you call over there for me and see if they still have my card?" She was almost pleading. A wave of anxiety coursed over her. She asked Adam to call for her in anticipation of a negative response from the Black Angus Restaurant. A response, she knew, she couldn't deal with directly.

In the fading daylight of the creme colored living room, Carol reached over to turn on the lamp on the end table. She noticed her fingers trembling as she pinched the lamp's switch. Everything she had, financially, was accessible via that ATM card and the mere thought of losing it was devastating.

Hearing, feeling and aware of the concern Carol must be experiencing, and knowing how upset he would feel in the same situation, Adam offered to make a personal appearance at the restaurant. "Sure," he said. "I'll take a ride out there and see."

"Call first," Carol said, "and get back with me. I don't think I can take waiting for you to drive out there, then all the way over here before I know if they have it."

Unable to contain her urges any longer, Lindsey grabbed for the shopping bag, fumbling through its contents. "Can I try it on now?"

Carol held Lindsey's enthusiasm back with one hand, while she spoke into the phone. "Get back with me right away," she said again.

"I will. As soon as I know."

"Love you."

"Love you too," Adam said and hung up.

:

He listened to the telephone ringing, dreading what he would have to say when Carol answered it. Nonetheless, there was no way around it, he would have to tell her what the waiter had said: that he remembered placing the ATM card and receipt back on their table and when he returned from the kitchen five minutes later, to finish clearing the table, the card and the receipt were gone. "Naturally," the waiter said, "I assumed you had taken them and left."

"Just try to calm down," Adam tried to console the near panicked Carol after he relayed the 'bad' news to her.

"What am I going to do?" She repeated several times, despite his efforts.

Her question was directed inward and more of a statement to herself.

"There's not much you can do on a Sunday night," Adam said. "But, call the bank in the morning as soon as they're open and cancel that card. I'm sure they'll issue you a new one."

"Should I call the police?"

"Why? No crime has taken place that you know of yet."

Adam caught himself, realizing the implication of including the word 'yet' in his comment and how insensitive the exasperating word was. "I'm sorry," he apologized.

"Every penny I owned was in that account."

"Don't borrow trouble," Adam echoed his mother's philosophy. "Don't jump to conclusions."

She knew he was right. She didn't know if anything was amiss with her bank account. Still, regardless of Adam's logic, she felt, correctly, deep within her that it was all gone. That whoever had taken her ATM card from the Black Angus wasted no time in deciphering her four digit identification number and depleting her account of the four-thousand-some odd dollars she had saved.

"Are you coming over?"

"I'm on my cell phone and half of the way there now. You want me to stop and get you anything?"

"No. I just need to be with you right now."

"I'll be there in a few," Adam said, pressing a little harder on the accelerator.

As he drove toward Carol's apartment, he couldn't help remembering his father telling him that; 'Bad things always came in threes'. First, was his mother falling deathly ill, now this! *What's next,* he wondered, as he pulled into the parking lot of the multi-building apartment complex where Carol lived. Before going inside, Adam sat in his truck for a moment, trying to think of what he might say to comfort her.

Gary L. Dewey

6

Sometimes it is hard to tell between what is the best outcome, in any given scenario, and what is the absolute worst. Sometimes, depending on the point of view; the logic applied, the differences between the two relative extremes are obscured. The two seemingly contrasting conditions, are in fact, one and the same. It was at times like these when that abstract rationalization made perfect sense.

On the one hand, the unrestrained wailing; the sorrow and grief Erica felt was so overwhelming, it crushed the very core of her being. The finality of her daughter's death, ripped and tore so vehemently at the very fiber of her soul, there were no other words to her that characterized the outcome, that anyone dared speak, than with the words 'absolute worst'. On the other hand, there was peace, unfettered, pain free peace. Ashley would suffer no more. She would not spend the rest of her life crippled, mentally and physically. She would not have to endure the inevitable ridicule; or the hellish, recurring nightmares that were sure to torment her through her days, had she survived. To four year old Ashley Dawson, her face and body irreparably disfigured; her brain permanently damaged by the swelling that resulted from the repeated blows at the hands of her ruthless abductor, her death was 'best'. Though no one involved even dared think it so, let alone speak it.

:

A thick, foreboding, lead gray sky, hung low over Southeastern Michigan early Monday morning. Periodically the moisture laden clouds dumped torrents of much needed rain on the drought stricken cities. The dense, humid air around each storm cell felt stifling. Even the normal chirping of the songbirds was stilled by the heaviness pushing ahead of the approaching cold front.

Adam waited on the covered, concrete stoop by his front door, until the occurring downpour eased. When it let up a bit, he made a mad dash for the shelter of his truck sitting in the driveway ten yards away.

Once inside, he started the engine and sat there trying to decide where he should go first. He could either go to the hospital; check in on his mother, who, at his last inquiry, was 'holding her own' or drive over to Carol's, be with her, when she called the bank to report the lost ATM card and check on her account.

Torn between choices, he sat there, unconsciously rubbing his wet hands along the upper pant legs of his black jeans. Staring blankly out of the windshield, he eventually decided on the latter. He reached over and turned on the wipers, backed onto the residential street that ran past his two story, red brick, colonial style home and drove toward the freeway.

Commuter traffic on the I-94 interstate was typically heavy. A steady stream of never ending vehicles in both directions stretched out as far as he could see. Carol lived only a few miles away so Adam opted to forgo the freeway and the hassles associated with trying to drive amid the madness of people more willing to die or be seriously injured in an automobile accident than be two minutes late for work.

When he arrived at Carol's apartment, fifteen minutes later, Carol was engaged in the daily frenzy of getting herself ready for work.

Still clad in her pink flowered robe, Carol asked, "Will you drop Lindsey off at the Daycare Center for me this morning?"

"Sure, "Adam smiled.

The site of her, standing in front of the mirror, brushing her teeth with one hand, blow drying her hair, at the same time, with the other made him chuckle.

"What?" She asked, when she glanced his way and saw the wry smile.

"Nothing," Adam dropped his head while shaking it slowly side to side.

"I got a late start this morning, what can I say?" She said, then playfully turned the hair drier on him.

The mini typhoon caused his black, four inch long, combed hair to blow askew.

"Hey! Watch it," he joked.

Carol giggled, "You need a hair cut."

Adam asked, "You call the bank yet?" He was hoping she had and the bank had given Carol 'good news' and that was why she was so frisky. To his chagrin, she shook her head no. *Prolonging the inevitable,* jumped into his mind.

And she was. If she was going to hear 'bad news', Carol at least wanted to get her personal hygiene matters for the day over with beforehand.

"One of us needs to get the Internet," Adam suggested again for the umpteenth time since they had been dating. But knew, though they both owned state-of-the-art computers, neither one of them would. Each having their own personal reasons for not re-subscribing to the service they decided years ago to eliminate out of their lives. "We could of gone online last night and checked the status of your bank accounts."

"Yeah I know, but you know how I feel about that. I'm not going to pay monthly for something I would rarely use."

Adam nodded.

"I spend enough time behind a computer at work. I'm not coming home and sit in front of one here all night too! Besides, whenever I need the 'net', I can get to it through work and it doesn't cost me a thing."

Subconsciously, Adam felt the same way: the Internet, as a whole, was overrated, he thought. In fact, on his desk, at Kendell Industries, where he worked as an in-plant electrical service repairman, a brand new, networked Gateway sat idle most of the time. The only things he ever really used the $2,000 machine for was inner-office memos and keeping track of inventories and completed work orders. Except for those few issues, all the computer ever did was take up much needed desk space. For him to actually log-on and access the Internet was a rare occurrence.

"Yeah I suppose." Adam relinquished, remembering his past experiences with the Internet. "All it is, is a giant porno factory."

"What's porno?" Lindsey asked, coming up behind him in the hallway, rubbing the sleep from her eyes.

Carol shot a look at Adam. The corners of her mouth turned downward. "Nothing sweetie. Big people talk,"

Adam scooped the still half asleep child up into his arms. "Good morning Sunshine," he said, planting a kiss on her cheek.

"What are you doing here?" Was the remark the kiss elicited.

"Yeah! What are you doing here so early?" Carol supported the question. "Why aren't you at work?"

"I had some vacation time coming to me and since Mom got sick, I thought I'd take some of it so I could be with her."

"Is Gramma here?" Lindsay's eyes brightened.

"No Sweetie Grandma's not here," Adam set her back down. He thought it cute that, though he and Carol were not yet married, Carol had opted to introduce his mother to Lindsey as Grandma. "Gramma's not feeling good today, so she's resting."

A look of disappointment crossed Lindsey's face. "I have to use the bathroom," she announced stepping into the small room.

"Excuse us," Carol said, closing the door, leaving him alone in the short hallway between the bedrooms and the lavatory.

"Any coffee?" He shouted through the door.

"In the kitchen," Carol shouted back.

:

The feeling was indescribable. A subtle sort of eerie, uneasiness. The way the quarry of carnivores must feel when being stalked; moments before their status changed from prey to victim.

He never saw anyone, but somehow he knew they were there. He could feel their eyes upon him, watching, plotting his demise.

He began feeling the uneasiness right after his late night rendevou with Beverly. At first, Ethan ascribed his acute wariness as a feeling of guilt; his own conscience condemning him for permitting the chance meeting with Beverly to turn into an adulterous act of infidelity. Ethan's imagination going so far as to conjecture that his wife was having him watched while they were apart.

Ethan later had dismissed those though with the improbability of Nichole hiring a private detective to keep track of him. He had never given her any reason to doubt his loyalty to her before and it seemed ludicrous that she would distrust him now.

Ethan cussed at himself for being so stupid; for allowing the seductiveness of Beverly to beguile his confidence in himself.

He searched his memory trying to remember if he may have said something or acted in a peculiar manner around Nicole. If he did or said anything that may have betrayed him, giving his wife reason to distrust him. When he found nothing, he dismissed completely the feelings of a private detective watching him.

Nevertheless, despite his finding nothing to support his feelings, he could sense that there was someone out there lurking. Someone who had a sudden interest in his day to day endeavors. *But, who, or why,* he wasn't sure of either. *Perchance, it was paranoia,* he thought, pulling his Cadillac Escalade through the exit gate of ESI's parking lot and onto the street.

His overwhelming day at work over, all Ethan wanted to do was get home, get his shoes off, relax. Out in traffic, he loosened his necktie, unbuttoned the top button on his white and black, pinstriped shirt, and found a radio station playing soothing music. He let his weight collapse into the plush leather seat and settled in for the long ride home.

An inconspicuous, two-toned brown, Buick LaSabre with Michigan license plates pulled in behind Ethan's SUV. Staying at least three car lengths back into rush hour traffic, the dark haired driver followed him across town. When Ethan turned onto the road that led to his large suburban home, the Buick turned with him. When Ethan pulled up into his driveway, the Buick continued passed until the next cross street where it circled back and came in from the other direction.

Renee', Ethan's eight year old daughter, as she usually did when her 'Daddy' got home from work, ran out to greet him just as the Buick, unnoticed, drove slowly by. The driver content that he had found what he wanted. His interstate spree of kidnapping, which already encompassed Ohio and Michigan would include, if he had his way, the state of Illinois.

He didn't know why he chose the Detroit area after he raped and killed the eleven year old girl in Cleveland nor why he decided on Chicago after the Detroit girl, he just followed his nose and found himself cruising past the tri-level Sandstone home of Ethan Blake, eyeing his next intended victim.

:

It was quiet. Almost too quiet. The only sound was that of their breathing and the fan of the central air conditioning unit gently blowing a cool breeze out of the wall vent above them. He felt comfortable in the twenty degrees cooler air, sitting on the couch next to her, his left arm draped around her shoulders, comforting her. "Do you want to go over to the hospital with me this evening?" Adam asked her.

"Yes I do," Carol said, picking her head up slightly off of his shoulder. "We've got to go pick Lindsey up from daycare first though, before we can go."

Her mind still reeling from the news she got earlier in the day that her checking account at the bank had been depleted of every dollar she had saved by the debit card thief, Carol gathered what was left of her emotional strength. "There's no sense in sitting around here the rest of the night crying over something I can do nothing about." She let a drawn out sigh drag from her lips. "What's done is done, I guess."

"All we can do now," Adam agreed, "is pick up the pieces and start anew."

"Anew!" Carol lifted her head the rest of the way and smiled. "Where did you get that word from? You must've dug pretty deep into your vocabulary trash bin and dragged that one out from the bottom."

"You're smiling aren't you?" Adam said and stood up in front of her.

Carol nodded.

"Then…it worked didn't it?"

"You're such a sweetheart." She responded while reaching out for his hand.

He took it, tugged on her gently until she too was on her feet. "I love you," he said, taking her completely into his arms. "And one of the ways we can start 'anew'…you and Lindsey can move into my place and you can save all the money you'd pay in rent for this place."

Carol pulled away slightly, her eyes widened. "Is that a proposal?"

Adam leaned back into her and whispered in her ear, "It is if you want it to be."

"You wouldn't be trying to take advantage of a girl in trouble now would you?"

"I'm hurt." Adam pulled away from her this time. He forced himself to frown and act offended.

"Come here," Carol said, pulling him back into her embrace and felt a lump welling up in her throat. "If we can get out of the rest of my lease agreement here, Lindsey and I would love to come and stay with you. Forever if you liked."

Adam leaned back, looked into Carol's face. "There is nothing I would like more," he said, while wiping the tears from her eyes with his thumbs and feeling a lump of his own forming in his throat.

:

She was awake and had regained enough of her strength to muster a smile when she saw Adam walk into her room. He carried a bouquet of her favorite white daisies in his hand.

"Hi ma," Adam said, responding to the warmth in his mother's smile. He was encouraged and noticed that the color in his mother's face had almost returned to normal. "You're looking good this evening."

"Hello," she managed back as Adam set the vase of flowers down on the nightstand next to her bed. Her eyes following the heart-felt present, hoping to see them as long as she could before they disappeared out of her peripheral vision.

Adam did a quick count of the hours that had passed since his mother came into the hospital, near death, three days ago. He felt a bit of relief when he figured out and realized that the dreaded, 'seventy-two hour, wait and see, critical time period', the cardiologist treating her spoke of, was nearly over.

"You're looking much, much better, Adam said and bent down and kissed her on the cheek.

"Better than what?" She responded to his surprise.

"I see your sense of humor is coming back," Adam smiled and took her hand in his. "That's a good sign."

She closed her eyes for a moment, savoring the love she felt in the touch of her only child's hand. A feeling she thought, for a while, she would never feel again.

"Has the doctor been in to see you tonight?"

"He was in earlier…Said something about a pacemaker and some chip…I don't want no chip," she added as sternly as she could.

Even though Adam had no idea what 'chip' she was talking about, it was obvious to him that the subject was upsetting to her. He reassuringly told her, "Don't worry about that now. Nobody is going to do anything to you, you don't want. All you need to think about right now is getting as much rest as you can and getting better."

Adam knew his advice was appropriate, but also knew that his mother probably wouldn't heed it. He knew her well enough to know that once his mother got something on her mind, she would dwell on it until she had rehashed it over and over a hundred times. "I've got some good news," Adam said, anxious to tell her and at the same time trying to distract her.

She glanced over at him in anticipation as he sat on the chair next to the bed.

"Carol and I are going to get married."

Her eyes widened. A broad smile crossed her mouth as she squeezed his hand a little tighter.

"I'll take that as your approval," Adam answered the increase in pressure he felt.

His mother nodded slightly. "She here?"

"She's in the waiting room just down the hall with Lindsey. We figured we'd take turns watching Lindsey and visiting with you…You want to see her?"

She nodded again, wishing that she could see Lindsey too. But knew the young child would not be allowed into her room. Nevertheless, just the mention of the child's name, that she had come to love so dearly, filled her with joy.

As Carol was in the room with his mother and he was baby-sitting Lindsey in the waiting room, Adam caught a glimpse of Doctor Ching walking past the doorway.

"Doctor?" He called out abruptly, setting the magazine he and Lindsey were leafing through down on the coffee table in front of the couch. He stood up and said to Lindsey, "Stay here for a minute. I need to talk to the doctor." When he saw a look of fear come on the child's face, he added, "I'll be right outside the door."

Lindsey picked the magazine up and scooted herself back into the couch just as Doctor Ching poked his head in the doorway.

"Hello doctor," Adam said, extended his hand in greeting as he led the doctor out into the open area of the Intensive Care Unit and beyond earshot of Lindsey. When he was sure that whatever was said between them couldn't be overheard, Adam asked, "How is she doing?"

"The critical period is not over yet," the doctor looked him in the eyes and said. "But, I think it safe to assume that your mother is going to make it. It was 'touch and go' there for a while. She gave us quite the scare."

Adam nodded his acknowledgment.

"She's a very fortunate woman. The infarction occurred near the sinus node. Damaging the…"

"Excuse me doctor," Adam interrupted. "Could you please keep it simple. I'm not much on medical terms."

"Your mother suffered from what is commonly called a heart attack," Doctor Ching resumed using the more common terms, even though he thought them inadequate to describe the condition. "The embolism…blood clot…sorry…anyway the clot caused damage to the heart tissue that controls the natural rhythm. Consequently she is going to need a device called a pacemaker to help her heart maintain a steady beat."

"Without it?" Adam furrowed his brow as he remembered how upset his mother had gotten when she spoke of the apparatus.

"Without a pacemaker there is no way to control her heart rate and it can go into a fatal tachyarrhythmia at any given point in time."

"Tacky…ah…rith…what was that?"

"Sorry," Doctor Ching apologized again. "The ventricle…the part of the heart that pumps the blood starts beating very rapidly and out of control…kind of fluttering like. The condition is fatal if the irregularity isn't stopped in a matter of minutes. With the implanted pacemaker, we can bypass the heart's natural mechanism and control the rate."

Adam's head drooped toward the floor.

"The only problem with this is that your mother is so weak, I don't dare do the required surgery. I don't think her system could withstand the trauma of it."

Adam never lifted his head and spoke toward the floor. "How long do you think it will be before she can? And what do you suggest in the interim?"

"How long will it take for her to recover enough for surgery? There's no way I can answer that definitively. Days. Perhaps weeks. It's up to her body, the amount of damage, and her own healing rate." Doctor Ching waited for his words to sink in a bit before he continued. "What do I recommend? Well, there's a new device called the Signa-Chip that I have just attended a seminar about last night. And in cases like your mother's it sounds very promising. It requires very little intrusion to implant and would allow us to constantly monitor, among other things and regulate your mother's heart rate."

So that was the 'Chip' his mother was so much against. Adam thought of telling the doctor, but didn't. At the time

Adam felt confident that he could persuade her to accept the new technology. Convincing her that without the device, her chances of living were slim to non-existent.

"When could you do that?" Adam asked. This time lifting his head until his eyes met the doctor's.

"Theoretically," Doctor Ching answered, this time was his turn to drop his eyes. "I could do it right now. Like I said, the implantation is only slightly invasive. Requiring only a local anesthesia and a very small incision." He looked up for Adam's response.

Adam's eyes were fixed on him…eagerly awaiting more information.

"The problem is that since the Signa-Chip is so new, it hasn't yet passed board approval for use in this hospital."

"Are you suggesting that the operation be done somewhere else?" Adam's suspicions rose quickly. The term *'Guinea Pig'* jumped into his mind and there was no way he was going to agree to subject his mother to that.

"No!" Doctor Ching immediately responded. "Not at all. Though from what I understand about the 'chip' it could be. Very easily too. What I am suggesting…," he stopped and restated. "What I'm informing you about is the fact that it may be a while before the Signa-Chip is approved for…" The doctor purposely left the sentence unfinished with an intonation implying that he was going to say more. But he wanted Adam to prod him for it.

"And?" Adam bit.

"And if there was a patient need…someone who could benefit immensely from the chip…and we got that patient's approval…it just might expedite things."

"And you think my mother just might be that someone?"

Doctor Ching nodded affirmatively. "Especially if you were to voice an opinion in her behalf."

Gary L. Dewey

7

They both leaned back in the recliner sections, on the ends of the four-cushion, off white leather couch, at the same time. Despite the opulence of the over stuffed sofa, Ethan felt uncomfortable sitting next to his wife. His conscience bothering him so badly over his elicit affair with Beverly Olsen the night before, that Ethan found it difficult to even look at Nicole without feeling debased. The presence of their two children, stretched out on floor pillows, watching the 'Big Screen' television just a few feet away, did nothing to make him feel any better either.

"What's the matter?" Nicole asked. She had noticed that he wasn't his talkative self and was avoiding eye contact with her when he did speak and it bothered her.

"Nothing. I'm just tired I guess," Ethan lied. "It was a pure madhouse at work today. Everybody and their mother called in today wanting details about the Signa-Chip and I haven't stopped talking all day."

Ethan caught Renee' turning her head when he mentioned the Signa-Chip. He smiled at her, knowing his little daughter had no idea what the 'Chip' was or what it did. But, he thought it cute that whenever he was talking about it, she usually listened intently. Little did he know that Renee', over the past few weeks, had learned more about the 'Chip' than he realized.

"As soon as the chip gets hospital approval, I'll get the kids over there," Ethan added reaching for the Daily Newspaper folded neatly on the cherry wood coffee table. *Perhaps,* he thought, *he could inconspicuously hide behind the 'paper and conceal the self-conscious look of guilt,* he knew, *must be written all over his face.* And since Nicole was the one who had insisted that their children get the implant as soon as it was available, he didn't expect, nor get any argument. He hoped that somewhere between the newspaper and his patronizing remark the evening's topic would turn away from him.

Aaron, who had heard only the words, 'I'll get the kids', from his father but nothing else of the comment, rolled off the canvas material floor-pillow onto his back. "What are we getting?"

"Remember that thing your father and I were telling you about?" Nicole answered.

"What thing?"

"That chip thing, in case you get lost or something, we could find you real fast."

"I know my way around. I don't need some 'thing' to find my way home."

Ethan opened the newspaper, covering his face and smiling behind it. Proud that his son was grown up enough to voice his opinion and glad for the subject change.

Nicole started to say something demanding and argumentative in response to her son's disapproval, but noticed that Renee' was still focused on her and listening intently, so she refrained herself. "Well, your father and I still think you need it," she said instead. In the process toning down her reply and keeping intact the agreement her and Ethan had to spare Renee' from any undo alarm when it came to the subject of the Signa-Chip.

"Did you see this?" Ethan folded the newspaper in half and stuck it in front of Nicole.

"I haven't had chance to read the paper yet," she said.

Her eyes fell on the bold print above the second page article: **Four Year Old Kidnapping Victim Dies.**

Nicole had just read the first part of the first sentence of the insert which said: Four year old Ashley Dawson died today, when Ethan pulled the paper back.

"Hey," she protested amid a burst of 'canned' laughter coming from the television. She glanced down at the children, who had both lost interest in the adult's conversation and resumed their positions, watching the 'sitcom'.

"Here," Ethan responded, handing the newspaper back to her. "I'm going to the kitchen and making some tea. Do you want a cup?"

"You know...I think I do," she smiled at him. "I can make it if you're tired?"

"I'll do it," he answered, more interested in separating himself for a few minutes and easing his self-conscious guilt, than in drinking tea. What he really felt like he needed, instead of a cup of tea was a couple of shots of Bourbon.

After filling the tea kettle and placing it on the stove to heat, he went back to the double-bowled, stainless steel sink and stared blankly out through the window at the street. Waiting to see where his thoughts would take him, he stood there blocking extraneous images from his mind. He pulled back the white, lacy curtain and watched as a two-toned, brown Buick drove slowly past the window. It looked vaguely familiar to him, peculiarly so. But he didn't know why. He tired but couldn't remember ever seeing the vehicle before.

No sooner had the car disappeared down the road and that strange feeling that he was being watched, flooded his mind again. *Who would be watching me at home? Too much worrying*, he dismissed the paranoid thought again. *Too much concern over things that 'might' happen.*

He turned away from the window. The digital clock be-hind the teapot blinked 9:55 PM. Right then he vowed to quit 'browbeating' himself...at least for the rest of the night.

When he got back to the large sunken living room with the steaming cups of tea, Renee' was sitting on Nicole's lap, the newspaper laying haphazardly on the floor at their feet. The 'paper, carelessly dropped from preoccupied hands. They were hugging each other and it was hard for Ethan to tell which one was clinging to whom the tightest.

As he drew nearer, he could see that it was Nicole who held Renee' closest. After reading the harrowing article in the local newspaper, envisioning what the dead child's mother must feel like and vicariously experiencing her grief, his wife, in tears, was clinging to their daughter protectively.

"What's the matter?"

"Nothing really," Nicole glanced up at him.

"Mom's crying," Renee' said, sadly.

"Am not!"

"Are to."

Nicole reached down and tickled her on the stomach. "Am not," she said above Renee's laughter.

Aaron turned to see what the distracting ado was about. "I'm trying to watch TV," he said.

"Sorry," Nicole said with a condescending tone, while pulling Renee' back into her arms.

Ethan, now irate that his son thought himself 'grownup' enough to voice his opposition, set the cups of tea down on the coffee table and announced that he thought it was bedtime for both the children.

"Ah mom," they both protested in unison.

"You heard your father," Nicole supported the unwel-come command.

Alone in silence, after the children had retired to their up-stairs bedrooms, Ethan finished perusing the newspaper, while Nicole switched television channels to watch the International evening news broadcast.

On the front page of the 'Modern Living' section of the newspaper, Ethan was not surprised to see the whole of the page devoted to the Signa-Chip presentation he and Carl gave Sunday night. He glanced over the page quickly for errors and exaggerations.

"Honey," Nicole called and interrupted his critique of the article.

Ethan dropped the 'paper from in front of his face.

Nicole pointed toward the television. "You might want to watch this."

On the television screen a video camera panned the front of Electronic Solutions Incorporated's main building and settled on a black haired, mid-aged reporter, in a dark blue suit. The look of seriousness on the man's face foretold of the magnitude of what he was about to say. The reporter turned and shot a quick glance at the entrance doors to the ultra-modern structure behind him, the ESI logo glowing translucent in the background.

"In a seminar at the Holiday Inn in downtown Chicago last night," the reporter started, "ESI announced the development of an implantable, personal identification chip, and promised that the 'new' Signa-Chip would change the way, you, I, our children and our children's children would live our lives.

"I don't know where those people get this stuff," Ethan frowned at the exaggeration. "Change the way we live," he snickered, mocking the reporter's choice of words.

Though Ethan knew the Signa-Chip would affect many aspects of life in the 'free world', he doubted the 'chip' would have the impact the reporter proposed.

Nicole said, "Well, one thing you know for sure, after tonight the whole world knows about your 'new' chip."

Ethan smiled inwardly, egotistically. *Yeah,* he silently agreed, *Signa-Chip was now a worldwide product.* The concept of a personal identification system was not at all 'new', Ethan knew and had been the topic of many for many years. Ethan's pride came from ESI being the first to perfect, miniaturize and market the device that would facilitate the process. Surprising to him though was how abruptly things were happening. He had not expected the news of the Signa-Chip to travel so far so quickly. It was as if the world was on the proverbial edge of its seat just waiting for something like this. Someone to announce its availability, before they all rushed out to purchase it.

:

He pulled around the corner and stopped the Buick. Three times he had been around the block, casing the neighborhood, looking for an inconspicuous place where he might pull off the abduction. There was none. Only house after house of manicured lawns, fenced yards and well lighted streets. *I'll just have to watch for now. Wait for an opportune time. Play it by ear.*

Satisfied that he had seen all there was to see, he pulled away from the curb and started back toward the motel room, miles away, where he was staying. But before he did, he headed out for the nearest main road, intending to find a place to stay closer to his intended target. As he rounded the

THE CHIP

corner three blocks south of the Blake residence, a small inner-neighborhood playground appeared.

The playground complete with all the amenities a child could hope for: Swing sets, Monkey bars, Merry -go-round, and a wooden structure that twisted and turned in several directions. The fort-like structure sat in the middle of what looked like a huge sandbox and provided places for the children to climb, run through, or just plain hide.

"Bingo," he said aloud, knowing that sooner or later, if he was patient enough, the child he was becoming obsessed with would show up at the park. *A perfect place,* he thought. The child vulnerable enough, that he could 'take' her unnoticed.

He sat there in his car wondering just how he had happened to arrived at the ESI parking lot just as the fancy Cadillac SUV was exiting. Why he followed the driver of the vehicle home. Why the little girl had ran out to greet her father just as he happened by. Why when he saw her, was he so captivated by the child that he had singled her out as he next victim. He had no answers for his questions. He just didn't know and attributed it all to fate. Whether it was the child's fate or his, he didn't know that either. Didn't care. But he knew he found the place where it would all begin.

⋮

He couldn't fall asleep. He tossed and turned well into the night. His mind fighting sleep until it finally overcame the tumultuous thoughts running through it and succumb to its need for rest. Two hours later though he was awake again. His head pounding. A horrid night terror the cause for both the headache and his being awake. Ethan climbed from bed and headed for the bottle of Ibuprofen in the medicine cabinet in the bathroom, adjacent to the master bedroom. The vivid-

93

ness of the dream still troubling him, he opened the bottle of pain reliever and swallowed two without the aide of drink.

He leaned forward and placed his forehead on the cool rim of the washbasin. Reliving the nightmare he had of identifying the grossly mutilated, lifeless body of his son at the city morgue, he vowed to himself again that he would get his family over to the doctor's as soon as possible and get the chip implanted in them.

:

Sitting at the Oak dinning room table sipping his morning coffee, it seemed sweetly odd to Adam, as he watched Carol in the kitchen cooking breakfast, Lindsey at her side, that something that felt as good as having them there with him, could come from the events as bad as it took to get them there.

He felt content, relieved and apprehensive all at the same time. Content that he had found the woman he was to spend the rest of his life with; Relieved that the years of lonely mornings, the days and evenings he spent alone in his empty house, since the end of his childless marriage, were gone forever. But still apprehensive with the lingering, bitter memories surrounding his divorce. Though those times of painfulness were so long ago, at times they seemed like only yesterday to Adam.

"Ta dah," Carol announced, coming from the kitchen with a plate of scrambled eggs and sausage in her hand.

Lindsey, an ear to ear grin on her face, trailed a half step behind her mother, carrying a handful of napkins like the King's Crown was atop them.

"Thank you ladies, "Adam smiled at them.

Carol placed the plate of food in front of him and gave him a peck on the cheek. "Your toast will be right up."

"And I helped," Lindsey beamed, setting a napkin on his lap.

Adam patted Lindsey lovingly on the top of her head, "And you did such a fine job too."

Both disappeared back into the kitchen and returned carrying their own plates of food.

"This is just great," Adam proclaimed. "My first breakfast at home with my new family.

"The first of many I hope," Carol smiled.

"I plan on a life times worth."

"Does this mean I can call him Daddy now?" Lindsey's naïve question took both adults by surprise.

They looked at each other for a moment, too shocked to respond.

"Well, does it?" Adam finally asked.

A lump welling up in her throat, Carol said, "I see no reason why you can't sweetie."

Since her daughter's biological father had disappeared, after the divorce over four years ago and had never returned, Carol pitied Lindsey who so desperately needed a father-figure in her life. She was delighted that at last Lindsey had found that 'someone'. And overjoyed that, that someone was Adam.

"Daughter," Adam reached out his hand toward Lindsey as if to shake it in a binding contractual agreement.

"Daddy," Lindsey responded taking his fingertips into her tiny hand and shaking them.

Adam used the contact to gently draw the child in closer to him and hugged her.

Lindsey returned the embrace.

Carol's eyes could not behold the sight of their bonding and hold back the tears of joy too. She felt the lump in her throat grow to the size of a bowling ball. A tear silently trickled down her cheek. The ringing of the telephone in the living room disrupted the moment. "I'll get it," Carol said through the lump. Glad for the distraction, she didn't know how much more 'joy' she could take and still hold back the flood of tears, she knew was waiting behind her eyes for the chance to gush forth. "It's Doctor Ching's office," Carol returned with the cordless telephone a few moments later.

Adam looked up at her questioningly.

She shrugged her shoulders, handed him the phone and sat back down to her scrambled eggs.

Puzzled, Adam said, "Hello?"

"Mister Garrett?" A woman's voice answered.

Adam closed his eyes and let his head slowly tilt backwards. "Yes? This is he."

"Could you hold for a second?"

"Yes," Adam pulled his head back down as he stood. He glanced over at Lindsey who had just taken a big bite of her toast.

He turned for the living room and some privacy. He hadn't taken two steps toward the large open room before a man with an oriental accent spoke. Adam recognized Doctor Ching's voice the instant the doctor said, "Hello."

"Hello," Adam said again.

"Mister Garrett," Doctor Ching said. "The Board of Directors at River Valley Hospital have approved the Signa-Chip we were talking about yesterday and I would like to schedule your mother for implantation later this morning. With your approval of course."

"Hold on doctor," Adam almost shouted to his own surprise. "We aren't going to schedule anything until I've had a chance to talk to my mother about this. Which by the way," Adam calmed himself. "How is she doing this morning?"

"There was a little improvement when I checked on her about an hour ago. She is still very weak though. Mister Garrett, I'm sure you are aware of how much your mother will benefit from having this chip…"

Adam reached the charcoal colored sofa in the living room, sitting heavily on the center cushion. *How arrogant of this doctor,* he thought, as he scooted to the far end of the couch and propped an elbow up on the couch arm, *to assume that I know the benefits of this Signa-Chip.* When, in fact, Adam had never even heard of the 'chip' until the doctor had mentioned it.

"Regardless," Adam heard himself say. "As long as my mother is aware enough to know what she does or doesn't want, it's her decision, not mine."

"Well, that is exactly why I called you this morning. Your mother had adamantly refused to even consider the implant, ranting on about some 'Mark'. I don't think she realizes what the chip can do for her and I was hoping that perhaps you could make that decision for her in her delusional state?"

"I won't do that," Adam said. "But what I will do is talk to her when I see her later today and see if I can find out why she has decided so strongly against it."

"As long as you don't take too long convincing her. The procedure was just approved two hours ago and already I have twelve people scheduled for the minor surgery and I suspect that by lunch time, I'll be booked solid for the next three weeks straight by the onslaught. I hope that you can convince your mother to give this a try before something worse happens to her."

For a moment Adam felt like he was talking to a high-pressure salesman instead of a doctor. One of those type agents, who while trying to sell him a life insurance policy that he didn't want was giving him the 'what if' pitch as a 'last ditch' effort to make the sale.

Against his better judgment, Adam said, "I'll see what I can do," and hung up.

Carol had placed his breakfast in the microwave until his conversation with the doctor was done. "You ready to eat?" She asked when he returned from the living room.

Not really hungry anymore, but not wanting to offend either, Adam agreed to eat. "I guess," he said.

Carol stepped through the doorway to the kitchen, on her way to the microwave. "What was that all about?"

"They want to put some computer chip in my mother that's supposed to help them monitor her heart better. Mom doesn't want it and they want me to go over her head and approve of it anyway."

Carol poked her head around the doorway. "That wouldn't happen to be that Signa-Chip I heard so much about at work yesterday, would it?"

"One and the same."

"The girls at work said that chip was supposed to be some type of identification tracking thing and that as soon as it came out they were going to get it for their kids. I didn't know it had medical applications too."

Lindsey lifted her head from her food at the mention of the word 'kids' from her mother and with a look of curiosity on her face stared at her.

Carol returned the inquisitive stare with a smile.

"I don't know much about it," Adam said. "I haven't been reading the newspaper or watching much TV either lately. But, I'm sure I'll be hearing a lot more about it soon."

There was a muffled 'ding' from behind Carol and her head disappeared around the doorway for a moment as she removed Adam's eggs and sausage from the microwave.

"I need to get over to the hospital and talk with mom this morning," Adam said, when Carol reappeared and placed the food in front of him for the second time.

"Are you going to have time to take Lindsey over to daycare for me?"

His appetite returning with a vengeance after the aroma from the food entered his nose, Adam answered. "Sure."

"I was thinking about getting it for Lindsey...just in case," Carol said. "But only, of course, after talkin' with you first."

Lindsey's stare returned again. The words 'in case' grabbed her attention.

Adam reached over and gently patted her on the head.

"If you're done eating," Carol said to her. "Why don't you go play until Mommy is ready to go."

Adam waited for Lindsey to leave before he answered Carols statement. "Well, I think we should just wait and see a bit. Give me a chance to learn more about this thing before we make any kind of decision. This world has gotten along for thousands of years without this chip and I see no need to rush into anything now."

Carol smiled at him. Again she realized that Adam's tendency to move ahead with caution was one of the things she loved about him. A reign for her impetuousness and if he had decided to marry her and become Lindsey's father, she knew it was done with much thought and consideration.

:

By 10:00 AM it was already getting warm. The day promising it was going to be another hot and humid one in Chicago. He rolled up the window of the LaSabre and turned the car's air conditioning on. The cool air blowing on his unshaven face and through his uncombed hair felt good.

From almost a block away, he watched the familiar figure of the man he followed home yesterday as the man walked out to the big sports utility vehicle parked in the driveway of the Sandstone tri-level house and pull away. He wondered how much longer it would be before the children of the household would be out playing, before the warm summer sun got too hot. Of special interest, the blonde haired girl.

Just over an hour later, he caught a glimpse, in his rear-view mirror, of the black and white police car coming towards him from down the street. A panic enveloped him as the patrol car neared. His mind raced as he tried to decide whether to try to drive away, just sit there as indifferently as possible, or slouch down onto the seat. Hoping if he did, the officers wouldn't notice him. In error, he chose the latter.

The scout car pulled up beside his Buick and angled in toward the curb, blocking any attempt at his escape. The policeman riding in the passenger seat jumped out and approached him.

He rolled down the window. "Good morning officer."

"What are you doing here?" The officer said, leaning forward, glancing into the back seat of his vehicle.

His mind thought fast for an answer without betraying his nervousness. "Picking up my buddy for work." He nodded back toward the house he was parked in front of.

The officer straightened up, suspicious of the disheveled looking driver. He looked up and down the street. No other cars were parked on the road except this one. Everyone else using the driveways each home had. Reaching down to unbutton his holster, in case he needed quick access to his weapon, he leaned back down toward the driver.

"You got any ID," the officer said.

"Yep," he answered, reaching into his back pocket for his wallet.

The radio inside the Patrol car crackled to life.

He fumbled with his wallet, trying purposely to delay getting the driver's license out, hoping for something.

"Officers in need of assistance. All vehicles in the vicinity of Broadway and Lincoln please respond," came over the radio speaker.

The uniformed officer sitting behind the steering wheel hollered out, through the still open passenger door, "That's us."

"You better not be here when we come back," the officer standing next to him said and jumped back into the patrol car an instant before it raced away.

"Stupid!" he cussed at himself. He tucked his wallet back into his hip pocket, his intent in no way dissuaded by the incident, but angry that he let himself be noticed in the neighborhood. *And of all things, by the 'cops'.* He pulled away from the curb, turned east at the corner and never noticed the young boy and his sister coming out of the tri-level Sandstone, a few houses down, on their way to a day of fun at the inner-neighborhood playground.

Gary L. Dewey

8

Every light on Ethan's five line telephone was flashing when he sauntered over to his desk. He sat down in his brown leather, high-backed executive's chair ignoring them and logged in to the company network first. When he saw that his two megabyte mailbox was also full, he stood up, took off his blue, suit jacket and set it down on the corner of his desk. Ethan then called his secretary on the intercom. "Misses Tyler," he said into the small black box. "Could you bring me a coffee?" Without waiting for a response, he turned the intercom completely off.

He was into reading the fourth e-mail before Katlin Tyler wrapped softly on his office door and walked in. She placed the cup of coffee he ordered in front of him. "There you go," she said. And picked up his jacket from the desk. She neatly draped it over the back of the two cushion couch sitting in the center of the office.

"Thank you," Ethan said, without looking at her.

Accustomed to such from her boss, Katlin simply turned around to go. On her way out she stopped at the window in the wall next to the door and rotated the four foot tall tree growing there, checking it for water. Satisfied that it was still moist enough from the last time she watered it three days ago, she departed as she came; silently.

After the eighth redundant e-mail, Ethan, already bored with answering the same questions over and over again, decided to listen to his voice mail messages. He listened to a few of those, which were basically the same as his e-mails. A few were even sent by the same individuals who sent the emails.

Ethan, turned the intercom back on. "Misses Tyler, could you come in here please?"

Katlin knew what he wanted. The forty-two year old, secretary just thought it was a lot sooner than she had anticipated.

When she stepped into his office moments later, Ethan said, "Could you go though all of these messages for me and see if we can come up with a standardized reply?"

His request, Katlin knew was not really a question, but a command. After ten years as Ethan's personal secretary she easily recognized the difference.

Ethan felt bad delegating that much work to Katlin. But saw no point in spending the better part of his day sorting through and giving his personal response to the repetitive flood of requests. All basically asking for the same information on Signa-Chip. Especially, when Katlin was capable of handling them in his stead.

Smug that she had second-guessed the intent of Ethan's call, she smiled and said, "Sure."

"There's a million of them," he said standing, relinquishing his desk to her.

"Well, did you expect anything different?"

"To tell you the truth," Ethan said, as he readjusted his clothes. "I didn't expect this much response until the chip gained widespread acceptance."

A puzzled look came on Katlin's face. "You haven't heard?" She said, "The chip has been approved at six local hospitals and nine others out-of-state. One as far away as Montreal."

"Canada?"

"Yep."

"No I hadn't," Ethan pulled his necktie up snug against his throat. "When did this happen?"

"Haven't you read any of your messages this morning?"

"Not really."

"Well, if it has continued as the day started, more approvals are probably occurring as we speak."

"Great!" Ethan smiled.

"You probably haven't read your message that there is a management meeting at eleven-thirty in the main conference room upstairs either?"

"No I hadn't." Ethan checked his watch. "It's eleven-ten already," he said.

"I suggest that if you have anything you want to do before that meeting, you best get to it."

Ethan pulled his suit jacket over his arms and buttoned it, "You wouldn't happen to know what this meeting is supposed to be about would you?"

"I don't have the foggiest," Katlin said. "But if I had to, I'd guess it has something to do with the chip,"

"Brilliant," Ethan said, jokingly. "From now on I'm going to start calling you Sherlock Holmes,"

"Well, how do you expect me to know what you big shots around this company are up to?" Katlin teased back. "Half of the time, I don't even know what's happening in this office."

"I wonder if Carl knows what's going on?"

Katlin grinned. "You need to ask him that, not me!"

:

The more he drove around thinking about it, the angrier he got.

"Who in the hell do they think they are," he said into the empty air inside his car. "I have just as much right to park on the street as anybody else."

He checked his mirrors. Traffic was clear and he quickly made a U-turn. The tires on the Buick squealed from the strain the sudden change in direction put on them. He decided to circle the neighborhood looking for the cops, before he went back to his vantage point, where they chased him from. As he circled, he passed the inner-neighborhood playground and saw the object of his obsession running between the swing set and the monkey bars.

The playground full of laughing, screaming children, oblivious to everything except engaging in having fun. No one, not even the chaperons who had accompanied their kids to the playground, noticed when the two-tone brown Buick pulled up adjacent to the unfenced playground and stopped. He sat there, the cool air blowing out from the dashboard vents on his face, watching, anticipating.

:

Ethan checked his watch again as he walked out of Carl's office. His short conference with the P.R. Manager, about the content of the meeting over, he still had ten minutes. *Just enough time,* he figured, *to make a quick call.* He quickly walked to his office three doors down the hall.

"I need to use the phone," he announced to Katlin, entering his inner office.

In the middle of listening to voice mails and jotting down the callers names, Katlin offered her phone. "Why don't you use the one on my desk," she said. "I'm kind of in the middle of something."

He retreated to the outer office and stood next to her much smaller desk and dialed home.

"The chip has been approved for implantation," he told Nicole excitedly. "And I'm headed to a meeting where the company is going to announce that it will provide several doctors for employees and their families to get the chip implanted this afternoon. So if you want to get the kids and come in, we can get them done here…today. Who knows when we'll be able to get an appointment at our family doctor."

"They're going to do it right there?"

"Yes," Ethan said. "We are equipped for medical research here remember? And it's not like it's major surgery, it's a simple procedure." He paused for a moment thinking. "Work crews are down by the entrance gates installing the new scanners and we'll have security people down there to let family in. So you don't have to worry about that either. If you want, just gather the kids and come on."

"What about…," Nicole started to ask for more details, but he cut her off.

"I've got to go," he said. "Or I'm going to be late for the meeting."

Nicole heard the telephone click during the disconnect. She stood there for a moment, the phone still next to her ear, trying to decide what she was going to do. They hadn't even had lunch yet. Aaron and Renee' would need baths before they went, and it was already hotter outside than she liked. She tried to come up with enough reasons to talk herself out of the unexpected task.

Her plans for the heat of the day were to just hang around inside the house, doing as little outside as she could. At least, until it cooled down in the evening. Maybe a couple of loads of laundry and straighten up the kitchen, but that was it for her plans. Driving half of the way across town and spending the afternoon at ESI was not among them. *Perhaps though, now that the chip was 'off the ground and running', her thoughts wandered. Ethan would get the raise he was prom-*

ised and I could talk to him again about getting a swimming pool for the backyard.

:

Hand in hand, Adam walked Lindsey up to the gate in the five foot tall fence surrounding the Early Learning Daycare Center. He bent down, lightly kissed the child on the check.

Anxious to show off her new puppy dress, to her week-day playmates, Lindsey reached, in a futile attempt for the gate's latch, well beyond her reach.

The female attendant, watching the half dozen or so young children already playing inside the fenced in area, turned to greet them. "My aren't we looking pretty today," she said.

Adam straightened, squared his shoulders, and ran his hand through his hair. "Thank you," he said, teasing the dark haired, robust woman, he guessed to be in her mid twenties.

"Not you," Lindsey snapped at him. "Me."

"Oh…sorry," Adam forced a fake frown, before he and the attendant smiled at each other.

"Thank you," the woman said, coming over and from the inside opening the gate Lindsey found impossible to over-come.

"Have a nice day," Adam said to Lindsey, as she raced past the attendant to join the other children. "You too," he added to the attendant, who thanked him again.

During the drive to the hospital, Adam 'shifted gears' mentally, trying to focus on his mother. So much had hap-pened and was happening in his life, he found it hard to con-centrate on any of it. Between, his proposal to Carol, Carol's bank account being depleted, Carol and Lindsey moving in with him, and his mother's heart attack, he found it nearly impossible to maintain perspective. Even the fact that he had taken the two weeks off from his job, robbed him of another thing that was mentally stabilizing.

By the time he did arrive at the hospital, he had promised himself that he would focus his energies on his mother's problems first. Everything else, he decided, could wait without catastrophic consequences.

He parked the four wheel drive, 'Ram' pickup at the back of the nearly full parking lot and climbed out into stifling heat. The outside temperature felt like it had climbed another ten degrees since he dropped Lindsey off. Though it had not. The stark difference between the outside air and the cool temperature inside the Dodge made it seem a lot hotter outside than it actually was. Before he had walked across the hospital parking lot to the main entrance, the back of his tan, short sleeved, pull-over shirt was wet from sweating.

In the cool air inside River Valley Hospital the sweating stopped abruptly and left him feeling clammy. Adam couldn't decide which feeling he hated most: hot and sweaty, or cool and sticky. He settled it by acknowledging he liked neither one equally.

"Hi ma," he cheerfully greeted his mother, despite the uncomfortableness of his clinging pant legs.

She looked at him. Her eyes were much brighter, but her skin still looked pale, nearly ashen. "Hello," she answered him.

Encouraged by hearing the strength in her voice, Adam slid the chair, sitting along the back wall in her room, bedside and sat. He was also encouraged and a bit surprised to see that a couple of the machines, his mother had attached to her the last time he visited, had been removed. He took her hand in his. "You feeling better today?"

She nodded and squeezed his hand.

"What's this they tell me that you won't let them put that new chip in your hand? The doctor said that it will help them help you. Let's them monitor your heart and blood pressure better."

Her eyes widened. "I don't want no chip," she mumbled. "It's the devil's chip."

"Ma," Adam smiled. "It's not 'the devil's chip'. It's a tiny computer device that they can use to keep track of what's going on inside your body when you're not here in the hospital. And from the way you're improving, I don't think they're going to keep you here much longer."

"No chip...the devil's...Promise me you won't let them do it," she said and tried to sit up.

"You just relax," Adam gently placed a hand on her shoulder preventing her from raising. "Don't you worry. I'm not going to let them do anything you don't want. I just don't see why you think this device is the devil's. From what I understand, all it is, is a computer chip."

"Revelation 13:16," was all she said and allowed herself to lay back down.

Adam, watching the increase in his mother's heart rate on the monitor, said nothing for a moment.

"Promise me son, you won't get it," she said. "Don't let them put it in Lindsey either."

You know I don't believe in that stuff, he started to say but stopped himself. The one thing he didn't want to do was argue with her and if he said what he thought, he knew it would start an argument. "Have you seen your doctor today?" Adam, despite knowing that she had, asked anyway, trying to divert her attention from the upsetting issue of the chip.

"Promise me you'll at least look into it?"

His diversion didn't work. "Promise," he said to appease.

She closed her eyes and mouthed something unintelligible.

Adam watched her lips moving. Thought he heard her say, Thank you Jesus.

Religious right to the very end, he thought, admiring his mother's commitment to her beliefs.

"Will you, at least, let them put in a pacemaker?" Adam asked. He was sure he wasn't going to convince his mother to accept the chip no time soon and opted to try and persuade her to let the doctor, at least, put in the life-saving pacemaker device.

She shook her head no. "Don't trust them."

"Ma!" Adam pleaded. "Without it you could die." He paused again. "You're going to let them put in a pacemaker. It's the least you could do. I'll make absolutely sure that's all they do, or we'll sue them and we'll own this place."

Misses Garrett slowly opened her expressionless eyes. She said nothing. Her blank expression; neither agreeing, nor refusing.

"You should let your mother rest now," the uniformed nurse that had been watching Misses Garrett heart monitor out by the main desk, stuck her head into the doorway. She didn't like the irregularities that she was seeing on the screen and thought it best that the visit be cut short.

Adam looked up at the blonde nurse in her late thirties and frowned.

"You mother is still very ill," she returned his frown. She still needs lots of rest."

Reluctantly, Adam acknowledged her advice. "I'll be back later," he said turning back to his mother and standing up.

He bent over, kissing her on the cheek.

"I love you," she whispered in his ear. "You promised." She reminded him then closed her eyes and said, "Luke 9:24."

:

Well, I suppose if it's going to get done, now is the best time to do it, Nicole thought, setting the cordless telephone down in its' cradle.

Dressed in red shorts, tennis shoes, and a white cotton blouse, she started out the door of their central air conditioned house. She re-thought her motive: to walk over the playground and get Aaron and Renee', when the hot, humid air outside hit her in the face. She retreated back into the house, getting car keys and her purse.

She rounded the corner of Forest Avenue, a few moments later, just as a haggard looking man stepped into the street, in front of her. She had to brake her vehicle hard to avoid hitting him.

The man jumped back, surprised by the sudden appearance of the Black Mercury.

Nicole gave him a dirty look and continued past him, pulling in across from the two-toned, brown Buick parked on her left. She looked over into the playground and saw Aaron chasing another young boy, through the play fort. She tooted the horn, while visually searching the area for Renee'.

Aaron never responded to the sound of the horn and disappeared deeper inside the fort, emerging seconds later. This time, Aaron was the one being chased.

She tooted on the horn again letting it resound a little longer. Nonetheless, she still got no response from her son. But it did seem to Nicole that everyone else in the park was looking at her. Including the man she had almost run over.

The man, Nicole noticed, had moved over onto the playground and was sitting on one of the benches placed around its perimeter.

Realizing that she would probably have to get out and get the children herself, facing the dreaded heat and the man she could have killed, she tried the horn again. Again to no avail. She cussed aloud into the car.

Nicole climbed out and embarked on a path that would intercept Aaron, while still visually searching for Renee'. She spotted her in the sand box amid the group of kids playing there, just a few feet from the bench where the man sat. *Great,* she thought, *just my rotten luck.* If she was going to get Renee' she'd have to walk right past the man. "Renee'!" She hollered above the voices of the frolicking children.

Renee' looked up, surprised to hear her name being called. Instantly she jumped to her feet when she recognized her mother.

The man turned quickly too. Angry the girl he had gotten so close to, was escaping and he could do nothing about it.

"Go get your brother," Nicole commanded Renee' when her daughter came up to her.

"Aaron!" Renee' ran five steps toward him and yelled. Her young, screechy voice cutting through the air.

Aaron instantly stopped. So quickly in fact, that the boy chasing him crashed into him and they both tumbled to the grass. Melodramatically, Aaron got up and hobbled toward the car, embellishing the results of the impact.

"Come on," Nicole encouraged him, knowing he wasn't hurt and anxious to get back into the Mercury, where it was much cooler.

Children aboard, Nicole pulled away from the curb. Glancing up into her rearview mirror, she felt a chill run through her, as she saw the haggard man heading back across the street to his car.

:

Katlin was stunned, confused. She didn't know what to do, or how to respond to the voice mail message she had just listened to. The message from some lady named Beverly Olsen, offering to setup a rendezvous with Ethan for Friday night was alluring, almost seductive in tone. It had her doubting her boss's marital fidelity: Not that she thought it any of her business. She really didn't care one way or the other, what extra-marital activities Ethan engaged in, or what he did, or did not do in his private life. But what she did care about was her job, and this, she was sure, would have a negative effect on it.

Katlin was in a dilemma. She knew she couldn't just ignore the implicating message, Ethan would know she had heard it. And she had no idea what he might do, knowing that she had that hanging over him. Nor, neither could she just delete it, pretending the voice-mail was never there. Surely if she did, Beverly would call back when Ethan didn't respond and he would not only learn of the message and be constantly self-conscious around her, but he would also be irate with her for deleting it. And with just cause.

She decided, her best course of action was to delete all the voice-mail messages, when she was done copying the names and addresses of the business callers, vowing to deny any knowledge of any private calls altogether.

Katlin hurriedly finished up with the voice mails and as she erased them, she heard footsteps coming through her outer office and quickly turned to face the computer monitor. With the same look on her face, a child has when caught with their hand in the proverbial cookie jar, she glanced over to the wooden door separating Ethan's office from hers.

"Is my husband in?" Nicole asked, stepping through the door, a worried looking child on each hand.

:

Armed with the knowledge gleaned from his preview with Carl, the meeting held no startling issues that Ethan wasn't anticipating. The only thing that was anything akin to a surprise was the announcement by the CEO that ESI would suspend normal company operations, if needed, increasing them to meet the predictable, escalating demand for the Signa-Chip and the matching computer software. But that too Ethan had figured was an eventual inevitability.

"This thing is taking off a lot faster than we thought it would," Ethan said to Carl after the meeting concluded. "My message boards are overwhelmed."

Somberly the two men walked down the hallway towards their respective offices. Each trying to get a grip on the situations they now faced: Primarily announcing to their departments and implementing the changes in company procedures, the chip was bringing about.

"But one good thing," Ethan said, stopping outside Carl's office door.

"What's that?"

"The media is doing a lot of the leg work for us. I'll bet several of our out-of-state presentations won't be necessary."

Carl reached for the brass handle on his office door and nodded.

"Hey," Ethan asked as an afterthought. "Are you going to get the wife and kids done here."

"Either today or tomorrow," Carl answered. "The doctors are supposed to be here 'til Friday. You?"

"Hopefully they're on their way now."

Carl looked at his watch. "Doctors aren't supposed to be here until two," he said. "Still got over an hour."

"Well, if they're early, I'll just take them to lunch, or something."

Carl turned the door knob to his office. "Sounds like a plan." He pushed it open and stepped in.

Ethan slowly walked down the hallway to his office, contemplating his choices for lunch.

"Daddy," Renee' greeted him excitedly when Ethan stepped into his office. Both children, jumped up from the couch and rushed up to him.

"Hey," Ethan scooped his daughter up into his arms. He kissed her on the cheek and gently set her back down, hugging Aaron in the process.

Katlin, watching the greeting from behind the desk, felt a twinge in her stomach. *How could you do that to your children?* The provocative voice-mail message still on her mind. She looked at Ethan with the same anger in her heart as if he had betrayed her personally. She forced a smile. "How'd your meeting go?"

"Fine." Ethan silently questioned the awkward expression on her face. "The messages?"

"Mostly financial institutions, banks, and law enforcement people trying to confirm their own ideas of what the Signa-Chip can and cannot be used for." Katlin stood and began gathering her notes. "I've got some thoughts and I'll see if I can't get the Advertising Department to print something up." Katlin stepped out from behind the desk and added, "Something we can mail out to them and answer all of their questions at once."

"That's what we're looking for," Ethan said, as he circled around behind her, a stern tone to his voice. Matter-of-factly he added, "Thank you."

"Just doing my job," Katlin responded.

Nicole smiled smugly as Katlin walked past her, not anxious to engage in conversation with the woman.

It had been almost a year since she had seen her husband's secretary and that was just 'in passing' at the annual company get-together and the fewer the words that passed between them, then and now, the better Nicole liked it. However, she said, "It was nice seeing you again," though she really didn't mean it.

Katlin retreated toward her office. "Nice seeing you and your children again too," she smiled back, meaning her smile as little as Nicole did hers.

Neither woman was of the arrogant type, but neither had any desire to socialize with each other either. Nothing more beyond the niceties required in their occasional 'passing'. Each preferring to keep their private lives, private, and completely separate from the workplace.

Gary L. Dewey

9

Adam didn't understand why his mother would so vehemently reject something that was touted to help prolong her life. Perhaps, she didn't realize the seriousness of the damage to her heart. Perhaps, despite her opinion, he should go against her wishes and okay the implantation of the chip. Perhaps, she was unable mentally to make that decision and he should make it for her.

Alone in the dim lit, quiet solitude of the waiting room, just down the hall from her room in the ICU, he wrestled with the resolution. He stood up from sitting on the couch, paced, sat back down, stood up again and paced some more. He stopped at the window, brushed back the room darkening drape with his left arm letting in the full brightness of the day. He leaned awkwardly against the window frame, peering down at the bustle of life in the parking lot below. A long moment passed, devoid of thought, while his subconscious mind weighed the pros and cons of the dilemma he faced.

It's all that religious hogwash that stood in the way, he concluded. *How can people let something as abstract, as the un-provable existence of a God guide their decision making processes,* he wondered. *Especially, when it came to matters of life and death. Martyrdom,* he answered his own question. *My mother is a martyr, or wants to be.*

He turned away from the window, took two steps toward the waiting room door on his way out to the main desk. His mind made up to okay the implantation.

When he remembered his promise to his mother, Adam stopped. On the bottom shelf of the rack of magazines and books standing against the wall of the waiting room, his eyes fell on the black, imitation leather cover of a bible. He hesitated as he reached for the book he hadn't had in his hands for decades.

Himself, 'by nature', an honest, kind, peaceful, and law-abiding person, Adam didn't believe people needed instructions to live ethical lives. 'We all knew right from wrong at a very early age,' Adam's argument with anyone who approached the subject with him: 'And the way people conduct their lives are conscious choices they make on their own. Not because some 'preacher' somewhere told them what to, or what not to do. And surely not because of something someone wrote in a book 2,000 years ago."

He continued his reach for the bible despite his philosophies, choosing to honor his promise to his mother.

The book felt oddly strange in his hand. Cooler than he expected, heavier than it looked. He went and sat back down on the couch, staring blankly at the unopened bible on his lap. Giant Print, Reference Edition, King James Version, he read imprinted in gold letters on the book's cover. Adam took a deep breath and flipped open the first few pages. He lifted his eyes toward the blank television screen, trying to remember what verses his mother had directed him to. *Revelations something was one of them,* he recalled flipping through the bible looking for that book. *'Biblos', a collection of books,* he remembered the Greek meaning of the word bible, but couldn't remember that Revelations was the last one in that collection. Eventually he did stumble across the book of Revelations. And the numbers *13:16* jumped into his mind.

Arrogantly, he thumbed through the pages looking for chapter thirteen, verse sixteen: *'And he causeth all, both small and great, rich and poor, free and bond, to receive a mark in their right hand, or in their foreheads:'* the verse read.

Confused, unable to grasp what verse sixteen meant and why it would adversely effect his mother's decision about the chip, he read the verses before and after it, hoping for more clarity. *'And that no man might buy or sell, save he that had the mark, or the name of the beast, or the number of his name,'* Verse seventeen said. It did little to help enlighten him. However, when Adam read the last part in the proceeding verse, he began to comprehend. *'…, and cause that as many as would not worship the image of the beast should be killed.'*

She foolishly thinks this chip is the beast, whatever that might be, or some sort of mark, Adam reasoned.

"Ma," he spoke aloud and shook his head contemptuously, half out of scorn, half out of pity. Adam closed the bible and set it on the small, end-table next to the couch. If he could find out where the intended site of implantation for the chip was, and found out that it was not the right-hand or the forehead, he was sure he could convince his mother that it wasn't the beast, or the mark, or whatever else she, naively, thought it might be.

Adam went out into the ICU hallway.

"Doctor Ching is not in now," the nurse at the main desk told him.

Adam lifted his arm and looked at his watch.

"Between six and seven," the nurse answered his question before he had chance to ask it. "He should be in making his evening rounds about then."

With about three hours to wait and too long to spend sitting idly around the hospital, Adam decided to pursue the issue of this chip he was hearing about and find out as much as he could before confronting his mother again.

:

At 3:20 the intercom on Ethan's desk jumped to life, startling him and his family.

"Mister Blake?" Katlin's voice rang over the small, black box.

"Yes," Ethan responded.

"They are ready for you in the Infirmary room."

"Thank you!"

The box went dead again.

"Well, this is it," Ethan looked over at his wife and children. "We are one of the first. Let's go be part of history."

Flooded in the barrage of inquiries she had to answer concerning the chip, Katlin, the telephone held against her ear, glanced up at them, as one by one, they filed past her.

"You're going down too, aren't you?" Ethan asked his secretary.

Katlin nodded and put her hand over the mouth piece of the telephone.

"We're scheduled for first thing tomorrow morning," she said, referring to all the non-essential employees. "Today is just for the 'big wheels'."

"I'm a little scared," Renee' said.

"Nothing to be afraid of," Ethan turned his attention back to her. "Daddy will go first and you'll see."

The truth was, that even though Ethan knew the implantation procedure was a mere quarter-inch long incision at the base of the hand, he was a touch apprehensive too. Not for himself but for his children's sake.

In silence the Blake family walked the rest of the way down to the small, in-plant clinic that ESI had set up for its employees. A small congregation of the management group had assembled outside the doorway. Some already implanted with the Signa-Chip, some waiting for their turn.

"Let me see," Ethan heard Robert Jason, one of the Product Managers from the fourth floor, ask Carl to show him the incision.

Carl peeled back the edge of the small bandage and everyone around him, including Ethan leaned in for a better view. Some thought the cut a bit more than they expected, others a bit less. To Ethan it was what he had envisioned: a small spot the size of a good sized sliver.

Nervously, one of the many children that had come in to get the implant asked, "Does it hurt?"

Ethan recognized the child as Larry Kohl's, eight year old son.

"Naw," Carl smiled. "Don't even know they did it." He did know though, when the Novocain in the anti-biotic ointment they used to numb and disinfect the area wore off, there was some discomfort.

A RN nurse, appeared through the closed clinic door. "Ethan Blake?" She called.

Ethan glanced at the short, uniform clad woman in her late thirties. "That's me,' he said, sidestepping Carl.

"Is it just you?"

"No," he answered, turning to locate his family. "My wife and children are here too." He stretched out his arm to encompass them and gathered them in with a sweeping motion of his arm.

"Right this way," the short haired nurse beckoned.

Ethan went over toward her, stopping at the door, holding it open. "Come on guys," he said, pausing just long enough to let his family in ahead of him.

There were several people inside the usually empty Infirmary, used primarily as a first-aid station. Enough people to make the small, well-lit room feel crowded. Three additional tables had been brought in and placed in the center of the room in a neat row beside one another.

The six foot long, paper covered tables spaced equally apart with just enough room between them for a small square extension table near one end and a wheeled stool.

On the stool between the first and second tables Doctor Reece sat. He nodded a greeting when his eyes met Ethan's. Of the other stools, the one nearest them was empty, the other occupied by a young doctor, Ethan surmised had just graduated from medical school, or had, not very long ago.

"Any allergies, hypersensitivity's, or other medical problems we should know about?" The nurse asked, holding a clipboard in one hand, a poised ink pen in the other.

"None that we know of," Ethan answered. Then added with a sense of pride, "We're all healthy and in good shape."

"Are you going to want to sit with the children while the procedure is done on them?"

"Yes!" Nicole jumped in. She placed her hand on her daughter's shoulder for reassurance. "Especially with Renee'."

A third doctor emerged from the door at the other end of the room carrying a new box of surgical Latex gloves. He set the box on the end of the center table and removed a pair of the thin gloves from the box. Stretching his hands into them, he took his place on the empty stool.

"My boy and I can go on the other tables," Ethan said, guiding Aaron toward the front table and the older, more experienced looking doctor. Leaving Doctor Reece open for Renee' and his wife, he stepped around the tables and went for the intern.

"Up here," Doctor Reece patted the table when Renee' and her mother neared.

Nicole helped Renee' up on the table and laid her down on her back. Ethan and Aaron followed suit on their tables. Immediately, the nurse came by, outstretched their arm over the small extension table and swiped the base of each of their right palms with an orange colored antiseptic solution and a dab of gel.

Within seconds, Ethan felt a numbness in his hand spreading out from the gel. "Hey!" He said, loud enough to get everyone's attention, including his wife's. "This is the wrong hand."

"No it isn't," Doctor Reece said. "We had gotten word from upstairs," he referred to the upper management, "that the left-handed site wasn't compatible with world needs, so they have decided to go with the right hand instead."

"What kind of incompatibility?" Ethan sat up. "And why wasn't I told about this before this point?"

"Relax," Doctor Reece said firmly. "Not everybody in the world has a left sided system like we do and it was just a minor change. Management decided it would be better, to satisfy the majority, if we used the right side in place of the left, that's all."

What the doctor didn't tell him; there was an infection in the left-handed site on one of the test monkeys and that the infection had spread up the animal's left arm. With the direct connection between the left arm and the cardiac system, the bacterial infection threatened to affect the animal's heart. And if it had not been for early detection and the aggressive use of the correct antibiotics, a very serious condition could have arose, but was averted. He also didn't mention that the incident was also instrumental in 'upper management' deciding to switch locations to the right side.

Ethan, laid back down. "I just wish for once, I could be kept up to date around here. Anything else I should know about?"

"All done," Doctor Reece said to Renee'. He placed a brightly colored bandage over the tiny incision and let her sit up. "Mom's turn."

The doctor tried to keep his attention on what he was doing and keep himself from telling Ethan, in front of everyone, that against his wishes, Ethan was the one insisting on 'pushing' the chip before he thought it ready.

Ethan shot a quick, concerned glance toward his daughter.

Renee' hopped down from the table like nothing major had happened. The fingers on her left hand lightly rubbing the bandage, she stepped away from the table, making room for her mother.

With an intense interest, Ethan watched as the young doctor made the incision at the base of his palm, central in his hand, three-quarters of an inch above the wrist. It was a peculiar sensation for him to see the skin part beneath the blade of the scalpel and the tiny wound start to bleed slightly without feeling a thing.

"You're done too," the doctor at the first table said to Aaron.

Ethan shot a glance his son's way as the doctor helped the boy down from the table.

The tearing of paper nearby brought Ethan's attention back to his doctor's actions. The doctor, using a pair of tweezers, extracted the Signa-Chip from its, just opened, sterile packaging. Ethan watched the doctor place the 'cooked rice' sized chip over the cut and it disappear into the incision in the valley between his thumb muscle and the thick flesh that composed the outside of his hand.

"That's it?" Ethan asked, when the young doctor placed the flesh colored bandage over the cut.

"That's it. Just keep the area clean and dry until the incision heals over."

Amazingly simple, Ethan thought. Even more uncomplicated than he had originally envisioned.

"This left to right hand thing has been taken care of hasn't it?" Ethan asked Doctor Reece, as he stood and watching the doctor conclude his wife's procedure.

"The change has been made in all the brochures and a new instruction sheet is going out with the packaging," the doctor answered without looking at him. "There you go Misses Blake," he added, pressing down the adhesive bandage after positioning it. "Welcome to the new age of personal identification."

:

He pulled his car into the parking spot in front of room nine at the El Dorado Motel. He climbed from the Buick; angry from the belittling his own mind was bashing him with. He slammed the car's door closed and went inside his room, throwing the keys hard against the wall above the dressing table. They ricocheted off the wall, bounced on the table top and fell to the carpeted floor.

He pulled his wallet out of the back pocket in his jeans, tossed it on the bed and went straight for the shower. He kicked his tennis shoes off along the way and except for the shoes, he, fully dressed, took the coldest shower he could stand. The chilling water washed away the sweat that was making his black, crew-neck T-shirt cling to his back.

Still dripping wet, he stepped from the shower and paced around his room. Still cussing himself for not taking the girl when he had the chance, for walking right in front of the child's mother, and allowing himself to be seen by the police. Nonetheless, despite the obvious deterrents, he was not dissuaded. In fact, the more unlikely it became that he would pull the intended kidnapping off without being caught, the more challenging the task appeared and the more determined he became.

He took off the wet clothes and dropped onto the bed naked. Within minutes he was asleep, napping for just over two hours. When he awoke, late in the afternoon, he dressed in fresh clothes and drove past the playground again. It was during the hottest part of the day; no one was at the playground. Out of frustration, he slammed the palms of his hands hard against the top of the steering wheel.

He felt even more frustration when he drove past the residence of his would be victim and saw no vehicles in the driveway, or any activity in the darkened house.

Watching the house disappear in his rearview mirror, he said, "I'll get my chance again," and drove away. His resolve to return as many times as it took to get that 'chance', renewed.

:

Adam phoned Carol, a few minutes before she got out of work. "You want to go out for dinner tonight?" He asked.

"Sure," she answered, while stacking the day's unfinished paperwork in the basket labeled 'To Do'. "Where you going to take us?"

The word 'us' on the end of her question caught him off guard for a moment, causing him to pause as he remembered his life with Carol now included Lindsey and most everything they did would now be the three of them.

"But, we can't stay out too late, I need to get over to my apartment and start packing up some of our belongings," Carol filled in the silence. "I only have a week to get out of there, or I'll have to pay another month's rent."

Adam said, "And I have to get back to the hospital this evening too. I need to talk to Doctor Ching."

"Anything wrong?"

"Naw! Mom is just being stubborn, that's all. And I need to find some things out about this chip the doctor wants to implant in her, before I can try to convince her to accept it. If she doesn't, I may have to decide for her."

One of Carol's co-workers stuck his head around the partition that separated her office cubicle from the other ten cubicles on the floor, mocking her for delaying her departure. "You working overtime tonight?"

She stood up and sneered toward the Company Accountant. Not believing, that at one time, before Adam came into her life, she had actually thought about dating the obnoxious man, three years her junior.

He never saw the sneer though, his head retracted, his body three steps down the hallway before she had time to respond.

"Can we talk about this over dinner?" Carol spoke into the mouth piece of the headset she wore. Waiting for Adam's reply, she reached over to the keyboard on her small desk and logged off the company Internet,.

"I'll pick up Lindsey and meet you back at the house," Adam said somewhat offended.

He wanted to talk with her then. To get some of the frustration he was feeling off his chest and to ease the pressure he felt. But, he also knew what it felt like, wanting out of the workplace at quitting time. "Love you," he said, ending his part of the conversation. He reasoned, that it would be better, anyway, to talk with Carol face to face. He waited for her; 'I love you too' response. When it came, he hung up and headed for the Daycare Center and Lindsey.

The restaurant he chose for their dinner was no place special: a family owned and operated type diner on Twenty-two mile road, he had eaten at many times, called the Pelican Place. Decorated with several large, carved wood statues of the namesake, in different poses, placed strategically around the interior, the restaurant's evening menu offered the usual sandwiches and 'home cooked' dinner specials.

Adam liked the Pelican Place mostly for the service he got when he was there; always prompt and courteous. He also liked the relaxed atmosphere in the diner, especially when sitting in the section at the front of the restaurant. Its tinted-glass, walls and ceiling especially appealed to him. He always felt more relaxed, surrounded by the multitude of live plants in the little section, that was joined to the main part of the restaurant, yet separate from it,. And that was something he needed to do: relax.

He went straight for the 'plant room', as he called it, ignoring the, 'Please wait to be seated' sign near the entrance door and took the empty table in the back corner.

"Is this okay?" Adam asked Carol, though he knew it would be.

"Sure."

"Is it okay for you," Adam smiled at Lindsey, who had already climbed up into the booth.

Lindsey reached for the clear, plastic covered sheet that contained a list of the daily specials.

"I guess so," Adam answered for her, when she didn't respond.

Carol slid into the empty spot next to her.

"I want a hot dog?" Lindsey announced.

"Don't you want to eat something more nourishing?" Adam said. "So you can grow up big and strong like mom."

Lindsey thought for a moment. "Okay. I'll have French fries too."

Adam laughed aloud for the first time, in a long time.

Three other groups of people sat at the booths in the section and Adam thought it just crowded enough that they could talk openly without drawing attention to themselves, yet empty enough to allow for quick service.

From nowhere it seemed, the waitress was there standing next to their table. Menus, a box of crayons and a colorable place-mat in her hands. "What can I get you to drink," the young blonde haired girl, in tan shorts and maroon top asked. She laid the menus on the edge of the rectangular table and placed the coloring sheet in front of Lindsey, handing her the box of crayons too.

"Coffees," Carol answered, pointing her index finger and waving it back and forth between Adam and herself. She leaned over and asked Lindsey, what she wanted to drink.

Lindsey preoccupied with opening the box of crayons froze at the question, contemplating the choices, like her mother had just asked her what the meaning of life was.

"Can we get a small milkshake?" Carol turned to the waiting waitress. "Strawberry?"

"Sure."

"Strawberry milkshake okay?" Carol turned back to Lindsey.

She nodded her approval, extracting the red crayon.

When the waitress left to get their drinks, Adam picked up one of the menus and leaned back into the padded bench seat. "I don't know what to do about my mother," he said. "The doctor wants to put that chip in her. He says it's the newest thing and it will give him the ability to monitor her heart twenty-four-seven, along with her other medical problems." He returned to his normal sitting position, pursed his lips and frowned. "And she flat out rejects it. She thinks it's some 'beast', or its mark."

Carol furrowed her eyebrows and leaned into the table. "Beast?"

He leaned in to meet her. So Lindsey, absorbed with the crayons and colorable place mat couldn't hear him, he whispered, "Some religious thing. And I'm afraid she is going to have another heart attack and die without it."

Carol leaned back, this time the look of contemplating the 'meaning of life' on her face.

"I just don't know what to do." Adam also leaned back. "I promised her I wouldn't let them do anything to her she didn't want them to do. And now this. I just can't sit back and do nothing."

"What did she say?"

"Not a whole lot…only that she was very much against it. She gave me a couple of bible verses to look up and made me promise her that I'd look into them."

"Did you?" The look on Carol's face changed from contemplation to one of questioning.

The waitress interrupted when she returned with their drinks. "Are you ready to order?" she asked, after placing the beverages in front of them.

"I want a hot dog and French fries," Lindsey said, without looking up from the picture of the circus clown she was coloring.

"Can you give us a few more minutes?" Adam asked, finally opening the menu.

"I'll be right back then," the waitress said, turning away.

"I think I'll just have a chief's salad," Carol said.

"Sounds good," Adam agreed, closing the menu and setting it back on the table, without really looking at it.

"Well, it seems to me that no matter what you might, or might not believe," Carol resumed the conversation. "As long as your mother is mentally competent, you just can't ignore her wishes and make her take that chip."

It was not what Adam wanted to hear from her, even though he knew she was right. He wanted Carol to encourage him, to support the thoughts he was having to okay the implantation. But, he knew that wasn't going to happen. His shoulders drooped as he let his weight settle deeper into the booth.

"Did you read the verses like you promised?" Carol wondered.

Adam nodded. "I read one of them."

"And what did it say?"

"Not much. Something about some beast, some number, and not being able to buy or sell without it."

"Six, six, six," Lindsey looked up from her coloring.

Stunned, surprised by the comment, both Adam and Carol turned to her. "What?" they both said in unison.

"Where did you hear that," Carol asked.

"I heard the ladies at daycare talking," Lindsey answered the question. "She said the 'beast' was a number. Six, six, six." She returned to her picture taking a different colored crayon. "And we shouldn't have it."

A moment of subdued silence ensued.

"'Out of the mouth of babes'," Carol looked at Adam.

"Are you ready to order?" The waitress returned.

10

Dark, thick clouds covered the Chicago skyline, hovering above them like a battleship gray blanket, threatening to make their drive home a wet one. Ethan kept glancing skyward expecting a deluge at any second. The regular programming, on the radio inside his SUV, was interrupted for an announcement by the National Weather Service. The service issued a sever thunderstorm warning for the greater Chicago area. With the approaching storm, the meteorologist said, there was also the possibility of large hail and damaging winds. The news of inclement weather did nothing to ease Ethan's nervousness.

The Novocain used on the incision had worn off and the implant site on Ethan's right hand was quite tender. He was reminded of it, wincing every time he bumped his hand against the steering wheel.

He looked over at Aaron, buckled into the passenger seat; his right hand resting in his lap with the palm turned upward. The boy's eyes were fixed on the bandage, trying to stare through the Band-Aid and the wound below it. Envisioning, with pride, the computer chip buried just beneath his skin. Aaron saw himself in a new 'light', as some sort of infallible bionic man. Empowered by the computer chip, capable, as the fictitious character Superman was, of 'leaping tall buildings in a single bound'.

"Does it hurt?" Ethan asked his son, as the first drops of rain began to fall.

"Not really," Aaron lied. His pride and boyish ego not allowing him to admit to the discomfort.

"Mine hurts a little," Ethan said, reaching for the windshield wiper switch with his left hand. He glanced up at the foreboding sky again, then at his rearview mirror. He spotted his wife's car in the traffic behind him. He wondered how she and their daughter were doing. If they were experiencing the same level of minor pain as he and Aaron.

"What about if I fall on it or something? Aaron wondered aloud. "I might break it or something."

"The chip is pretty flexible and in a few days you body will surround it with a thick layer of very strong scar tissue," Ethan explained. "Unless you purposely hit yourself there, very hard with a hammer or something, you're not going to hurt it."

The storm clouds thickened and blocked enough daylight to cause the sensor in the Cadillac's front grille to activate and the automatic headlights on the Cadillac Escalade came on. The rain increased to a torrent. The gusts of wind driving the rain sideways in blinding sheets. Ethan checked the sky again, worried that the storm would suddenly dump hail, large enough to damage the custom paint job on the fifty-seven thousand dollar vehicle. He checked the mirrors again and saw Nicole's Mercury two cars behind him. He scanned the visible distance ahead and spotted a gasoline service station with a protective cover over the filling pumps. He pulled into the center one.

Nicole followed, pulling her car up next to his and lowered her side window. "What's the matter?"

"Nothing," Ethan said. "I just don't want it hailing all over my car."

She looked out at the driving rain. "Well, we just can't sit here, blocking the pumps like this until the storm is over."

"I'll just fill them up then while we're here. Check the oil. Maybe go inside and get some coffee."

"Well, I'm not waiting, we're almost home."

Ethan climbed out of the SUV. "How's Renee' doing?"

Nicole pointed into the back seat of her car. "She fell asleep…I don't know why you just don't go home and park the car in the garage?" She added turning back toward her husband. Her eyes never seeing the two-toned brown, Buick LaSabre that had been following her pull over to the curb and stop.

"It's the getting between here and there I'm worried about. The worst part of this storm will be over in a few minutes and I don't want to take the chance of any hail chipping the paint all up. I just got this thing."

"I'm going home."

"Suit yourself, but leave the garage door open for me. I'll be home right behind you." Ethan turned away and took the hose down from the pump next to his vehicle.

Nicole and Renee' circled the station and pulled back out into traffic.

The rain eased for a moment then came in a deluge again. Ethan went in and paid for the gas. He also purchased himself a coffee, Aaron a soda and a cinnamon donut. They went back out to the Cadillac, content with their drinks to wait out the storm.

:

As soon as she rounded the corner on Pine Groove Avenue, Nicole pushed the button of the automatic garage door opener. Still half a dozen houses away from their garage, responding to the infra-red signal, the door opened. By the time she swung her car into the driveway the door was completely open. She drove in and glanced into the back seat.

Renee' was still napping. And figuring that she would probably have to carry Renee', Nicole went to get the house open before she woke the sleeping child. She ran toward the front door through the pouring rain. One hand covering her hair the best it could, keys in the other, poised. As she unlocked and pushed the door open, she could hear the telephone inside ringing. She shot a quick glance back to the open garage and Renee' before dashing into the house to answer the telephone.

The call was from her mother, on the other side of town, concerned that, in light of the severity of the storm, she and the grand kids were all right.

"We're all fine, Mother," Nicole reassured her. "Just a lot of rain over here is all."

"Well, not here," her mother told her. "We had several trees blown down and we have lost our power."

"Is it still raining out your way?"

"Nope, sun is shinning again. But my air conditioning won't work and it's hot as blue blazes again...muggy."

"Well, I'm sure the power company will have your electricity back on in a little bit," Nicole said, as a loud blast of thunder rumbled through the house. The telephone crackled and went dead for an instant.

"You still there?"

"Yes Mother, I'm still here. But we should get off this thing. I've got to go get Renee' out of the car."

"Okay. I'll talk to you later."

"Okay," Nicole said, ending the conversation. "I'll call you after the storm passes."

:

It was still raining quite hard, when his cell phone rang, but no hail had fallen.

"Renee' is gone!" He heard Nicole, in a panic, screaming on the other end of the line.

"What?" Ethan asked again. He had heard her the first time, but couldn't believe what he had heard.

Nicole was in a full fledged hysteria. "I left her in the car for a couple of minutes, while I opened the house and when I went back for her she was gone!"

"Have you called the police?"

"I saw that same brown car going around the corner that I seen at the park this morning," Nicole cried. "I think he's got her."

"What brown car?"

Aaron, sensing something drastically wrong, looked up at him. "What's the matter Daddy?"

"Nothing," Ethan said, putting the vehicle into gear and pulling away quickly. Knowing he wasn't going to get much more from his hysterical wife, he said, "I'm on my way. But hang up so I can call 911."

"I already have," Nicole's voice was raspy.

By the time, Ethan turned onto his street the rain had eased to a shower. A black and white scout car was blocking the driveway. He pulled the Cadillac with the driver's side wheels against the curb and ran into the house. Aaron was just behind him.

Nicole was crying uncontrollably when he took her into his arms. Ethan couldn't think. His heart pounding wildly.

"Mister Blake?" The shorter of the two uniformed officers asked him.

"Yes," he choked and read the name Hodge on the officer's badge.

"A detective is on his way," the officer said.

"What's the matter," Aaron began to cry too, though he didn't know why.

Somebody has taken your sister," Ethan let a protective arm drop and scooped Aaron in against his leg.

"Taken her? Where?"

"We'll find her don't you worry," the tall, dark haired officer said. The statement lacked a reassuring tone.

"We can find her ourselves," Aaron said, as sternly as a young boy could. "She's got the chip."

Stunned for a moment, Ethan grasped what his son had said. He let go of both Nicole and Aaron and stepped back. "That's right," he said, heading for the desk phone in the dinning room.

The short officer fell in behind him. "What are you talking about?"

Ethan never broke stride, never answered. The phone to his ear, he dialed ESI's number. "Frank? He said sharply, demanding, when he recognized the man's voice who answered the call. "Your first test," he said without even waiting for a response. "I need you to tell me where my daughter Renee' is!"

Frank, the Computer Systems Administrator at ESI was sitting in front of the main File server computer at the company and had not as readily recognized Ethan's terror driven voice. "Ethan?" He asked.

"Yes. FIND HER! And I mean now, or your ass is mine!"

"I'm on it," Frank said. Then silence.

Ethan heard the tapping of a computer keyboard in the background. A pause that seemed like forever, though it was only about a minute. Then more tapping.

"Hello," Detective Jacobs announced, coming into the room.

Ethan spun around and saw that everybody in the house including, the two officers, Nicole, and Aaron where standing in the arched doorway to the Dinning room, staring at him. Nicole holding her breath. His eyes fell on the suited detective in his mid-forties, pushing his way through the small group.

Ethan turned back to the desk, ignoring the greeting. He grabbed an ink pen and a small scrap of paper from the clear plastic holder on the desk top.

"What's going on?" Detective Frank Jacobs asked. All he had gotten from the two officers he asked was a shoulder shrug.

"Yes," Ethan said into the phone. The room went silent, as Ethan jotted some numbers down on the piece of paper.

Out loud Frank read the latitude and longitude coordinance information, The Global Positioning System satellite had provided for chip number 100027387, assigned to Renee' Allison Blake, again.

"Got it," Ethan confirmed the numbers.

Frank asked, "You want to tell me what this is all about?"

"Where is that?" Ethan ignored the question.

Frank tapped a few more keys. "Hold on. The software is giving a street map overlay of the site."

Ethan held his breath. He glanced over his shoulder at the silent crowd in the doorway.

"That chip is east bound on Pennsylvania Avenue around Thirty-Ninth street," Frank said.

Ethan immediately, moved the telephone down from his ear and pressed it against his chest. "My daughter, is in a brown car, headed east on Pennsylvania Avenue near thirty-ninth."

"How do you know that?" Detective Jacobs, eyes widened.

"A two-toned brown car," Nicole almost shouted.

"Don't you think we need to get my daughter first. I can explain how later."

"Get on it," the detective turned to the officers. "Call it in and get all the units in that area to intercept any brown cars, on Pennsylvania Avenue.

"What if he turns off somewhere?" Officer Hodge asked.

"We can track him," Ethan said. "Wherever my daughter goes, the system will find her. Just keep an open communication with your dispatcher and I'll tell you where she is."

"Call it in!" Detective Jacobs commanded again.

"Any changes?" Ethan returned to the telephone as Officer Hodge disappeared out into his squad car.

"No," Frank reported. "Still eastbound on Pennsylvania. Now he's around thirty-fifth."

Stay with me Frank," Ethan said. "I need you to keep tracking her."

"He's headed toward that old industrial section downtown," Detective Jacobs said, when Ethan relayed the message.

"We've got three units converging on the location," Officer Hodge said, coming back into the house. "And the chopper's up."

"Is it still pouring out there?" The detective asked Officer Hodge.

"No it's starting to let up some."

"Good."

The stress of the situation was too much for Nicole to bare. Nor could she believe what she was hearing; her daughter was kidnapped, her child's life in the hands of a complete stranger and all the police could talk about was the weather. She turned away and kept any sarcastic remarks to herself. If she busied herself, Nicole thought, thinking about, or doing something else, she wouldn't have the time to worry so much. Especially since it was something she could not control. She withdrew towards the kitchen. She rubbed the dry streaks of mascara below her eyes, trying to gather as much of her composure as she could. "Would anybody want some coffee?"

Nobody did, but realizing that the act was really just an attempt by the woman to distract herself from the building tension, they all agreed to the offer.

"You want to help?" Nicole, extended her hand out toward Aaron.

Aaron wanted to stay. To feel a part of the excitement, a factor in what was going on. His young ego subconsciously needing, already, to be among the men, in times of trouble.

"Go help your mother," Ethan said, when he noticed Aaron's reluctance.

Unwillingly, Aaron took her hand, feeling embarrassed, as all watched the two of them disappear into the kitchen.

"You've got quite a boy there." Officer Hodge smiled.

Ethan heard Frank's voice come over the phone. "She's turned south on Twenty-Eighth Street," Ethan announced excitedly. Within seconds Frank relayed a new direction. "Now he's headed east again," Ethan passed the new information on.

⋮

Officers Jawoski and Lawden in unit number 492 were the first to spot a two-toned brown car eastbound on Pennsylvania Avenue. The vehicle made a sudden right turn onto 28th, a smaller side street in a little industrial section. The officers followed it around the corner.

When the driver of the car noticed the police car coming in behind him, he sped up and made another quick turn onto Indiana avenue, looking for a place to hide. The wet pavement, on the building lined street, caused the Buick's back end to slide sideways; The driver fighting the vehicle back straight.

Officer Lawden forcefully pressed the accelerator of the squad car to the floor, while Jawoski hit the switch for the siren and reached for the two-way radio. It was obvious to them the car was trying to evade them and the chase was on to find out why.

The Buick's stock engine was no match for the powerful 'magnum' in the police car; the skill level of the driver; no match for Officer Lawden's either. Quickly the distance between the two vehicles was reduced to a few feet. The wail of the siren echoing off the brick factory buildings that lined both sides of Indiana Avenue, piercing the night.

"Unit 492, Officers in pursuit, east on Indiana," Jawoski spoke into the hand-held microphone. "Requesting support." He leaned forward, straining to read the license plate number. "Plate, Michigan; EMA 561. Elizabeth...Michael...Adams; he gave a name for the letters on the plate, then repeated the numbers 561.

"Units 878 and 397 are in the vicinity," the dispatcher responded.

Officer Lawden allowed the scout car to overtake the Buick, clipping it in the left rear in the process. The Buick spun wildly out of control. Immediately, Lawden slammed down hard on the brake pedal.

The officers watched as the awkwardly impacted Buick spun in a complete circle before it stopped, pointing in the opposite direction, facing them. It leaped forward charging them and they braced for the impact. At the last instant the

Buick veered, jumped the curb and raced down the narrow sidewalk past them.

Lawden swore as he locked his one foot down on the brake pedal to hold the front wheels of the squad car from moving, and mashed the accelerator to the floor again with the other. Driven by the power of the engine and a lesser amount of traction on the road, due to the rain, the rear wheels broke loose from the payment. The Scout car spun around in place. Half of the way through the spin, Lawden released the brake pedal. The front tires free to turn, the police car leaped forward in pursuit.

"This guy is better than you thought he was," Jawoski, chided.

"Not as good as me," Lawden boasted, confident that he would reclaim the distance separating them from the Buick.

The chase would not go on much longer and ended as the Buick approached the intersection of Indiana and 28th street: Unit 397 and 878 were there just before, and stopped front to front, blockading the roadway.

There was no room to get around either vehicle without a collision and the tires on the Buick locked as it slid sideways down Indiana. With it's passenger side, the Buick impacted both police cars simultaneously, hard enough to stun the occupants but not injure.

Officers Lawden and Jawoski were out of the squad car and on the Buick in an instant.

"Out of the car." Lawden, out from behind the wheel, stuck his service revolver against the windshield and commanded.

"Hands where we can see them," Jawoski, stepped in and pulled the driver's door open. In another quick move, he had the scruff of the driver's neck in his grip, pulled him out of the vehicle and flung him to the street. Jerome Parrish landed face down on the wet road, Officer Jawoski's knee in his back. His days as a free man over: DNA evidence would prove that Jerome was the one the states of Michigan and Ohio wanted for kidnapping, sexual assault, and murder.

"It's all right now. It's over," Lawden said, reaching in to get the traumatized child from the back seat.

Renee' withdrew herself from his grasp.

"It's okay," he reassured her again and took her trembling arm. "We're not going to hurt you."

Officer Kerney from Unit 878, stuck a donated teddybear in over Lawden's shoulder. He enticingly shook the white, furry bear with a bright Red scarf tied around it's neck in front of Renee'. "Want this?"

Lawden felt her continued resistance and didn't force her. "I bet she wants to see her mother," he said, releasing his hold.

"I'll bet she does too," Kerney said, as he felt Renee' take the teddybear from his hand and clutch it close to her.

"Well, when she comes out we can take her home," Officer Lawden smiled at her and backed his way out of the Buick.

Two more squad cars pulled in behind Unit 492 as Jawoski threw Jerome, handcuffed, forcefully into the caged back seat of the car. He slammed the door before Jerome was all the way in, purposely pinning his leg.

Jerome screamed out in pain.

"Opps, sorry," Jawoski said and opened the door slightly. When Jerome's leg was free from the door Jawoski kicked him the rest of the way in, then slammed the door closed again.

"You got her," the officer from one of the units asked pulling up beside Jawoski.

Lawden, turned at the question. "Yeah we got her. But she won't come out. Still too scared."

"We can call the parents and have them come out."

"Let me ask her," Lawden answered. He stuck his head back into the Buick. "You want us to bring your mom and dad here, or you want to get out so we can take you home? It will be much faster if you let us take you home."

Renee' scooted toward the door. Officer Lawden took her by the hand and helped her out. "We'll take her home," he said, turning Renee's hand over to officer Kerney.

:

Standing in line at the drug store near his house at 23 Mile road and Van Dyke Avenue, Adam felt odd paying for the day-old news.

The young woman running the cash register looked up at him. "You know these are yesterday's papers?"

He felt self-conscious as he responded, "I know". All eyes within hearing distance were on him.

Adam heard some ridiculing from two customers behind him.

"Heck, I'd sold him my old ones for half the price," one of the hecklers said.

Adam wanted to respond but held his tongue. He took the papers and his pride and went home.

Though the small articles in the day old newspapers didn't provide much, they were the only source Adam knew of for the additional information he sought on the Signa-Chip. The articles however, did address some of the virtues and intended uses of the chip, singing its praises as a medical, financial, and personal identification, 'breakthrough'. The more he read about the financial and personal identification aspects of the chip though, the more he realized he couldn't use the data to convince his mother into accepting the implant. He folded the newspapers and tossed them on the floor in front of the over-stuffed recliner he was sitting in.

The frustrated looked on his face prompted Carol to ask, "Didn't find what you wanted?"

"No," Adam answered. "In fact, just the opposite."

Carol furrowed her eyebrows in question.

"They're talking about using this thing to replace Credit; Debit; ATM cards; personal ID's; and a whole bunch of other things," Adam answered.

"And?"

"And those are the very reasons why my mother doesn't want the chip in the first place."

"I don't see why that should stop her, just because the chip is good for other things?"

"Well," Adam admitted. "I agree with you. But, it doesn't take a big stretch of the imagination to see how that chip could be used to control buying and selling. Not that, there is anything wrong with that. Just look at all the illegal activities that would stop; Prostitution; Drugs; Theft; Embezzlement; the list could go on and on, but that only plays right into what those bible verses say and why mom is so opposed."

"There's always going to be those things," Carol contradicted.

"How? Prostitutes and drug dealers going to go around with specialized ATM machines? Besides, the chip will make everything easily traceable. Even the people."

Lindsey looked up from the floor, where she sat between them, playing quietly with her doll set. "What's a prosa...toot?"

"Big people stuff," Carol smiled at her.

Content with the answer, Lindsey went back to her toys.

"You trying to tell me you think your mother is right?" Carol returned to the conversation.

"I'm not telling you anything," Adam let his eyes fall toward the floor. "But, the bible verse did say that without this mark, whatever it is, people wouldn't be able to buy or sell anything…sure does make me wonder. Especially, since this was foretold a couple of thousand years ago."

"What is it that you're wondering?" Carol asked, really wanting to know what was going on inside Adam's mind.

"I'm wondering if there isn't a little more to this religious stuff than I'm willing to believe."

A silence ensued, except for the sounds of Lindsey rearranging the furniture in the small doll house that came as part of the play-set.

The subject of religion was something Carol was not opposed to discussing. "What does that mean?" She said, breaking the silence.

Adam thought for a minute before he answered. "I guess it means I'm going to look a little more closely at this thing, before I try to convince anybody of anything…The newspaper article says some company in Chicago…Electronics Solutions Incorporated, invented this Signa-Chip thing, so I suppose the best way to find out what I want to know, is give them a call and see what they have to say."

"I thought you were going to talk to your mother's doctor about it?"

"I am. But, he's only going to know the medical side," Adam said while twisting his wrist, looking at his watch. "Speaking of such, it's getting about that time," he added, standing up from his chair. "Are you going over there with me?"

"You bet," Carol answered. "I would like to hear what the doctor has to say too."

"Are we going somewhere?" Lindsey glanced up from her dolls.

"Just for a little while sweetie," Carol said. "We need to go over to the hospital and see Grandma for a few minutes and talk with her doctor."

"When is Grandma coming home?" Lindsey frowned.

"Mommy doesn't really know. But, soon I hope."

11

"In the National News today," the channel eleven late night Newscaster reported. "A high speed chase in southwest Chicago, ended early this evening in the capture of Jerome Parrish."

A small, grainy, photograph of the unshaven, un-groomed, Jerome was superimposed in the upper right hand corner of the television screen.

"The thirty-three year old, Michigan man, had kidnapped Renee' Blake the eight year old daughter of Ethan and Nicole Blake, just hours after the young girl was implanted with the new Signa-Chip." The photograph in the upper right hand corner changed to one of the innocent looking Renee'.

Adam sat up bolt straight from his prone position, resting his head on Carol's lap. Both he and Carol's eyes widened, giving their full attention to the newscast. The couple had been relaxing together on the couch in front of the television. Carol slowly, methodically, running her fingers though Adam's hair almost had him asleep, when the subject change on the 'news' occurred.

"For more on the story," the newscaster continued. "Here's Linda Palmera, in Chicago…Linda."

The whole scene on the TV changed to a blonde haired, female reporter, in her late twenties. She was standing in front of the ESI headquarters building in Chicago. A light rain was falling and she stood holding an umbrella in one hand a wireless microphone in the other.

"Dan," she said. "Thanks to the new computer chip, in-vented by Electronics Solutions Incorporated, the company you see just behind me, a kidnapped young girl is home safe in her mother's arms. Just minutes after being taken from the back seat of her mother's car, in the garage of their suburban Chicago home…Chicago police, with the help of the child's father, were able to locate and track the exact position of the child and make the arrest. Like I said, just minutes after the child was taken."

"I understand that the child's father works for ESI?" The scene went back to the station in Detroit, while Daniel Heron asked the question, then went to a split screen for Linda to answer.

"Yes he does," Linda said. "Mister Blake is the Marketing Manager for ESI and one of the persons responsible for making the chip available to the public."

"It is also my understanding that the child had received the chip just hours before she was abducted?"

"Again you are right Dan. In fact, they had just gotten home from having the procedure done here at ESI when the incident occurred. Also, of interest to our viewers," Linda said, as the television screen changed back to a full picture of her. "Jerome Parrish is a suspect in the kidnapping and death of Ashley Dawson in Detroit. As you know, Dan, Ashley was the kidnapped four year old who died yesterday after being found severely beaten and sexually assaulted. Chicago police are awaiting DNA test results to confirm that suspicion."

The TV screen flashed back to Daniel. "Thank you Linda," he somberly said. "We will keep an eye on this developing story. But, for now, thanks to the new Signa-Chip from ESI, this story has a happy ending. More on the news when we come back."

The news program gave way to commercials. Adam clicked the television's remote control mute button and looked over at Carol.

He had purposely avoided talking about his discouraging trip to the hospital. The conversation he had with Doctor Ching and his mother concerning her implantation with the Signa-Chip, did not go as well as he had planned and he really didn't want to talk about it. But, in light of the news broadcast they both had just watched, his feelings changed.

"You know," Adam said. "We need to think very seriously about having one of those chips put in Lindsey. With all these kidnappings, runaways, and lost children stuff going around, I think we would be smart to have it done."

Without taking her eyes off the television, her mind wanting to agree, but her heart cautioning her, Carol answered, "I'm not so sure."

"What?" Adam stood up. Shocked at what he heard.

"Just what I said," she slowly turned her head up at him. "I'm not so sure."

"And why not?" Adam stepped over, squatted down in front of her and placed his hands on her knees.

Carol hesitated for a moment with her answer. "Well, I've been thinking about what your mother said," she paused again. "An awful lot." Another pause. "What if what she says is true? What if there is a God and taking this chip is taking 'the mark'. Then what? Are we condemning Lindsey, before she has a chance to make up her own mind about things?"

"Not you too?" Adam stood, turned away. "It's not bad enough I have to fight with my mother on her death bed, now you?"

Carol's eyes followed him up. "I'm not 'fighting' with you. I just don't agree, or disagree with you."

"Well then, what are you saying?" Adam put emphasis on the word 'are'.

"I'm saying that before I agree to let them put this chip in our daughter, I think we need to find out more about it and why mom is so against it. Don't you think we owe at least that much to Lindsey?"

Adam turned back and squatted again. "Do you really think that if there is a God, that God would condemn someone for having a computer chip implanted in them that could possibly save their life. Look at this little girl in Chicago we heard about." Adam turned, nodding at the television. "That chip may have just saved her life. Do you think 'God' would condemn her for that?"

"No I don't," Carol said. "He wouldn't be much of a 'God' in my eyes if he did. But, we don't know all the facts yet either. The executioner who throws the switch on the electric chair, ridding the world of a killer, doesn't make him right either."

"I know," Adam spun around and sat next to her on the couch. "The end never does justify the means does it?"

"You wouldn't mind, would you, if I bought a bible and have it around the house so I could read more about this 'mark' thing?"

"No I wouldn't," Adam put his arm around her shoulders. "I was thinking about doing the same thing myself."

:

Sitting at the kitchen table across from his wife, taking the last swallow of morning coffee, Ethan, was 'torn' between taking the day off, staying home with his family or going into work. His devotions contrasting one another. On one hand, he felt a moral need to stay with his family after they had endured the trauma of the night before; on the other, realizing, because of the overwhelming surge in the request for the very chip that spared his daughter, he felt obligated to go into work. Ethan knowing ESI also needed him. Especially at this time in light of the chip's proliferation.

"Go to work," Nicole reassured him. "We're fine. It's over and as far as Renee' is concerned it was just a wild ride in some stranger's car."

Ethan still reluctant, nodded. "Thank God we got the chip in her when we did. It could have been a lot worse."

"Don't thank God," Nicole snarled her lips. "Thank you and ESI for all your hard work and getting the chip out when you did."

Ethan didn't respond and set his empty coffee cup down on the table.

"Now go out there and help get that chip into as many innocent little girls as you can before something happens to them. We'll be just fine."

The drive into ESI was uneventful, except for the several times Ethan contemplated turning around and going home. There was something about the thought of losing his daughter, so young in her life, that made him feel like he should spend as much time with her as he could.

The cold front that had pushed the thunderstorms, of the night before, ahead of it, brought cooler, less humid air with it. He lowered all of the windows in his vehicle and let the wind blow through it, invigorating him.

He turned up the approach to ESI's parking lot and out of habit reached into his suit jacket pocket for his ID card. Extending the now defunct card toward the slot, he noticed the new, flat panel screen that had been added to the security computer by the technicians the day before. Out of curiosity, he withdrew the card and placed his right-hand on the black, six inch by six inch, pivoting screen.

Instantly, a thin, red beam running from top to bottom on the screen slowly moved horizontally across the screen under his hand.

"Good morning Mister Blake," the computerized voice greeted him to his surprise. He was as equally surprised as the locked, heavy steel gate, blocking entrance into the secured parking lot swung open.

Now that's a little more like it, Ethan smiled.

His satisfaction with the speedy switch over of the security process at the front entrance gate was short lived; he still needed his coded ID card to get into the building and the visual recognition by the security guard. If he had his way, that part of the entrance process would soon be history too.

"Good Morning, Mister Blake." A different woman than Joyce glanced up at him then back to what she was doing.

"Morning," Ethan said, recognizing the woman who looked in her mid-forties, but didn't know her name.

He walked over to the chest high counter the woman sat behind. "What's wrong with Miss Holett this morning?" He glanced for the name tag, he hoped the woman wore.

"Joyce is no longer an employee of this company," the tag-less woman said.

Ethan was shocked. He stammered for a moment wondering what might have happened. Not that he would miss Joyce. He was actually somewhat pleased: He was getting tired of fighting off her unwanted advances. Although he had to admit to himself that Joyce was a lot more pleasing to look at.

"She refused to accept the Signa-Chip so they fired her. They had to."

Stunned again, Ethan put both of his hands on the top of the counter and leaned in on it. "I didn't know that it was mandatory to take the Chip."

"It's not. But how else are you going to get onto the property?"

"Did they transfer her to another position somewhere else?"

"Why? All of the ESI locations require the Signa-Chip for entry." Ethan glanced down at the woman's right hand and saw the bandage there. "Are you going to be her replacement Miss…?"

"Teresa Klouse," she answered. "No I'm just here on loan from Design and Engineering. Until they hire somebody to take over permanently."

He remembered where he had seen her. She was Jim Peter's secretary. "Well, welcome to Marketing," Ethan told her, pushing himself back straight.

"Thank You," Teresa said. "Oh, by the way, how is your daughter this morning?"

"A little upset but okay," Ethan said and walked away.

The outer office was empty and Ethan thought for a moment that his secretary might have been fired too, but the top of her desk was strewn with partially finished sales reports, so he knew Katlin wasn't far away.

He stepped through the door into his inner-office with the telephone ringing and answered it before he sat down.

"Thanks for returning my calls," Beverly Olsen, sternly said.

"Who is this?"

"Sleep with me and don't even remember my name? I see the kind of guy you are."

"Beverly?" Ethan's voice took on a more passive tone. He heard the door to the outer office open and Katlin step in. He quickly turned his back to her. "I'm sorry," he said into the phone. "I can't personally answer all the messages that come into my office. Especially since we have been swamped with requests for information on the Signa-Chip. But, if you'll leave me your number, I'll return your call as soon as I can. He glanced over his shoulder to see if Katlin was watching. She wasn't.

Katlin didn't have to. She already knew, that Ethan was talking to 'that' woman. Either from a 'woman's intuition', or from the 'deer in the headlights' look he had on his face when she caught him off-guard,.

Ethan jotted down the telephone number Beverly gave him on the corner of his paper desk pad and said, "Thank you for your interest in the Signa-Chip and either I or my secretary will get back to you as soon as we can."

Katlin smirked to herself. She then became nervous, knowing that her boss now knew, that she knew about his little extra-marital, Sunday night, activities. And she had no idea how he would respond. *Maybe it wasn't even her,* she thought trying to calm her growing anxiety. *If it was, he'll feel to self-conscious to talk to me, he'll just close his door.* She watched out of the corner of her eye as Ethan walked over and put his hand on the edge of his office door.

Ethan stood there for a moment, thought of saying, *Good Morning*, but slowly swung the door closed. He collapsed into his chair behind the desk and glanced over at the number he had just scribbled onto the pad. He wondered if Katlin had gotten the messages from Beverly intended for him.

"Carl Torre on three," Katlin's voice came over the intercom on his desk, startling him.

"Miss Tyler," Ethan leaned forward and pressed the return button on the intercom.

"Yes?"

"Did I get any messages from a Beverly Olsen...from Gyro Tech yesterday?" He had to know the answer; he couldn't have this hanging over him.

Katlin mustered her strength. "Not that I know of sir. Your wife came in before I had a chance to finish up and I didn't get all of them. Was it important?"

"Not really," Ethan relaxed back into his high-backed leather chair. "I was just expecting a call from her that's all."

Both breathed a sigh of relief, each confident that neither one knew anything for certain.

Ethan switched from intercom to telephone and punched line three. "Carl!" He said almost too cheerfully.

"I'm surprised to see you're in this morning. How is your daughter doing?"

"You already heard about that?" Ethan answered a question with one.

"Sure. Everybody has. It was all over the news last night."

"Well, Renee' is fine. Resting I hope."

"I bet that was hell?"

"That's the understatement of the year. But, we can chalk one up for Signa-Chip already."

"That was almost unbelievable," Carl said, slowly shaking his head. "It couldn't have happened any better if we had planned it."

"Tell me about it."

There was a pause in their conversation.

"How's your hand this morning?"

Ethan looked down at the redness surrounding the cut. "Still a little sore but nothing to worry about. Yours?"

"Probably about the same as yours. Doctor says it might take a couple of days before the soreness goes away."

Ethan knew both of them had piles of work to do, trying to catch up to the sudden demand and the conversation was beginning to sound like small talk. "To what do I owe your call this morning?" He asked, trying to get to the matter. "I know it's not to check up on the progress of my implant."

"Well, no it's not," Carl said, his eyes rolling toward the ceiling unbeknown to Ethan. "They want us to fly out to Detroit tonight and give a presentation there first thing tomorrow morning."

Ethan sighed, closed his eyes. This was shaping up to be one of those days. *I knew I should have stayed home,* he thought, but said, "Can't we fly out in the morning? It's only an hour flight."

"No! They want us there tonight so they can be sure that we are there for the eight o'clock presentation...The setup crew is already on its way."

Discussed with the news Ethan said, "My daughter just survived a kidnapping and they want me to leave my family the very next night."

"Come on now Ethan," Carl said. "If you think they give a rat's behind about anything but the Chip, you are sadly mistaken."

"What time are we leaving?"

"Our flight is scheduled out at ten o'clock on Northwest gate five."

"I'll be there," Ethan surrendered without more argument.

:

"That's the lady," Lindsey pointed toward Melissa Elsworth.

"Don't point, it's impolite," Adam told Lindsey as they approached the playground gate at the Early Learning Daycare Center.

On the other side of the chain-link gate Melissa looked up from the book she was thumbing through. The twenty-seven year old caregiver turned to face the pair. She stood up from the picnic table where she was sitting, perusing a children's activity book. "Good morning Lindsey," she said and shot a quick glance back to the small group of toddlers in the playground, she was supervising. Seeing that they were all safe, she walked up to the locked gate to let Lindsey in.

"Good Morning," Adam greeted Melissa and extended his hand toward her when the gate was opened.

"That's my new dad," Lindsey beamed proudly.

"Pleased to meet you," Melissa took his hand for a brief moment. "Congratulations."

"Well, congratulations aren't in order quite yet," Adam smiled. "Can we talk?"

Melissa glanced back at the children as Lindsey joined them in the sandbox.

"If you have a few minutes?"

"Sure," Melissa said and stepped back. In the process she swung the gate open wider for him. "What can I do for you?"

They made their way back to the picnic table and sat.

"Lindsey tells me that she overheard you talking with someone else about some 'Mark' thing in the bible."

Melissa's initial reaction was one of dread; fearing Adam was one of those Atheists who was about to chastise her for talking about God in front of his child. She tensed her spiritual muscles ready to engage in verbal battle with him. She understood Atheist had their rights, but she had hers too and if this man was going to try to stop her from expressing her beliefs, he was in for a heated discussion.

"I have to admit," Adam started passively. "I don't know much about this 'Mark' and can't say that I really believe in any of it at all. But, my mother is in the hospital, very ill and the doctor seems to think this new Signa-Chip will be very helpful in keeping her alive. She of course is refusing the Chip, claiming that it's this 'Mark'."

Melissa relaxed and smiled at him.

"And I'd like to know more about it." Adam let his head drop in an act of humility. "You see I don't have anybody I can go to...to help me understand and when Lindsey said that she overheard you talking about it. I thought I'd take the chance and ask."

"What is it you want to understand...mister..."

"Oh I'm sorry," Adam picked up his head. "Adam Garrett."

"What is it that you want to understand Mister Garrett? The Mark or the Chip? Because I can't tell you much about the Chip...What'd you call it?"

"Signa-Chip," Adam looked at her furrowing his eyebrows. "I can't believe you haven't heard about it yet. Its been all over the news."

"Well, my husband and I were in Church for most of last night and most other nights we're studying scripture and don't watch much television. Though I have to say, I have heard bits and pieces about it."

"So, you wouldn't have an opinion about having it implanted?"

"There's your first mistaken assumption," Melissa smiled. "I am totally against it and I applaud your mother for rejecting it."

Adam sat up straight. Frozen by the woman's power of conviction over something she confessed she knew so little about. *Must be one of them religious fanatics*, he thought. Anticipating a 'fire and brimstone' sermon, Adam thought of ending the conversation. For his mother's sake, he didn't.

"Don't get me wrong," Melissa said. "I don't think anything is wrong with the Chip itself. In fact, it sounds like something very useful. But, it's what the Chip signifies that I'm against."

"So you think it's the 'Mark' too?"

"There's not much doubt in my mind about it. And apparently not in your mother's mind either. Though I don't think the chip itself is the 'Mark…just the culmination of the system. It's the number that goes with it."

"Six-six-six?"

"Actually Mister Garrett," Melissa leaned back. "Six-six-six is just the prefix code to contact one of the two massive computers. One of which is in Rome, Italy, the other in Luxembourg, Germany. You see, one of the computers uses six-six-six, the other the inverted sixes, nine-nine-nine." She paused to let Adam digest the meaning of the sixes. When she saw that he didn't, she continued. "That's why they chose that digit because it was the only one that when inverted it becomes another number. That way they could use the same digit to prefix two different computers."

"What is that all supposed to mean?"

"Nothing in itself. Until you hear all of it."

"Well, please continue," Adam said, leaning in and placing his elbows on the table.

Melissa looked around at the children, rechecking on their safety. "The service code into those computers, for United States citizens, is four, seven, one. Followed by your social security number."

"So what you are telling me is that this new Signa-Chip has those numbers in it and 'Big Brother' can watch us?"

She shrugged. "I don't know for sure what numbers are in them now, but it is feasible that they are there. And I'm sure 'Big Brother', as you call him, wants to do more with it than just 'watch' us.

"This is starting to sound like a fairy tale," Adam smirked.

"Believe what you like Mister Garrett. But it was you who asked me to tell you about the Mark remember?"

"That I did," Adam felt defensive. "But, I haven't heard anything about the Mark yet."

"It's all about the Mark," Melissa leaned in to him, her face stopping inches from his, her eyes fixed on his. "All the way from the Trilateral Commission, the European Union, and right on down to this new Signa-Chip."

"Hold on a minute," Adam said, moving back away from her. "You're making this sound like some kind of conspiracy and I don't buy it."

"It's not any 'conspiracy'…it's a new, world wide, monetary system." Melissa paused and looked around like she was afraid somebody might be listening. "The chip is just the final piece of the puzzle and whether you 'buy into it' or not, doesn't make it go away."

Adam was intrigued. "How do you know all of this?"

"In the bible," Melissa told him. "God foretold of this 'new' monetary system, thousands of years ago, and warned his people not to become a part of it. That this system would lead to an evil one world government and church. And this new system, He also foretold, was to be mankind's ultimate decision to accept or reject him. And those who choose to align themselves with it, by accepting the mark, would seal their own fates and that they would become the objects of his final wrath."

Adam smiled and sighed through his nose. "More of this end of the world stuff."

"I'm not saying anything about the end of the world," Melissa leaned back straight. "The Lord said, 'when we see these things happening, know the end draws near'. So is it the 'end'? I don't know." She leaned back in. "But what I do know, just as sure as I look up in the sky and see, from the gathering of the clouds, that a storm is coming." Melissa stopped and pointed skyward toward the thickening, lead gray clouds, then said, "it is coming."

Adam listened without response, he felt like he was being reprimanded.

Melissa stood, signaling the end of the conversation. "I have to get back to the children now and get them inside before it starts to rain," she said. "But, I want you to answer this and tell me Mister Garrett...no answer for yourself; who but God could know and predict such things, with such accuracy, thousands of years before they ever happened? And if this God, you don't want to believe in, predicted it and said don't become involved in it...I, your Mother, and many other Christians, aren't...No matter what the cost."

Adam sat, his head hung low, he couldn't understand why, but he almost felt ashamed of himself.

Melissa started away, but turned back to him and said, "You wanted to know about the Mark? Well Mister Garrett, it comes down to this: 'Choose you this day whom you will serve, as for me and my house we will serve the Lord'." She walked away, stopping at the locked gate, waiting for him, so she could let him out.

Adam took a moment to gather himself. He had not anticipated the magnitude of her words. He had enough to know that there was no way he was going to convince his mother to take the chip; enough to make him doubt even if he wanted to try to convince her. But not enough to satisfy his desire to know more. He stopped at the gate next to Melissa.

"Thank you for your time," he said. "You have been very helpful."

"My pleasure, Mister Garrett," Melissa swung the gate open and Adam stepped out onto the sidewalk and stopped again as Melissa closed the gate and re-locked it.

"Would you mind," Adam turned back toward her, "after work one of these nights, if I asked you and your husband, you'd come by the house and we could talk more about this?"

A wide smile crossed Melissa's face. "We would be happy to, Mister Garrett. You just name the time and tell me where you live and we'll be there."

"How about tonight, around nine-thirty, after Lindsey goes to bed? I would love to hear more, as I'm sure Lindsey's mother would too."

"Well, why don't you talk to Miss Wendell and make sure...I'll call my husband and make sure it's okay with him too, though I'm sure it is, and when you come back this afternoon to get Lindsey let me know where you live."

"I will," Adam said, as the first droplets of rain began to fall.

12

With his fiancee' next to him, Adam stood next to his mother's hospital bed, mute, his body trembling uncontrollably. He felt Carol's hand touch his ever so gently. He knew he didn't dare acknowledge the tenderness in her fingers, or for sure his knees would buckle. He wanted to weep, burst into tears and cry like a child. But, he held back the flood of tears he knew would come if he let go. The more he held back, the larger the lump in his throat grew, the harder it was to fight against the urge to breakdown.

Something had to give; it was either turn around and leave for a moment, or collapse. He glanced up to Carol's face. Dark streaks of mascara were running down her checks.

His voice broken with emotion, crackling, "Can I be alone with her for a minute," he managed to ask.

Carol nodded and let his hand fall away from hers.

Alone in the room with his mother, Adam reached out and took the lifeless fingers of her right hand into his and let himself cry.

I love her, I have a right to cry without shame. His thoughts raced, before he crumbled beneath the weight of his loss and he openly wept. *She's gone, gone forever,* he wailed. *Never again would she smell the sweetness of the roses in her garden or sit on her porch and feel the coolness of the breeze on a warm summer's night. She would never hold her grandchildren, or spoil them as Grandmothers do.*

Adam wept holding onto his mother's hand for nearly half of an hour. Until his eyes were puffed and burned from the saltiness of his tears. When there were no more tears left within him to cry, he folded her hands over her heart and stepped out of the room.

Carol met him, wrapping her arms around him. They stood there, just outside her door, comforting each other.

"Mister Garrett," Doctor Ching came up to them. "Would you like to step into the waiting room for a moment?"

Adam and Carol followed like lost sheep as the doctor lead them into the room.

"Have a seat," Doctor Ching motioned toward the couch. Seating himself across from them in the over-stuffed chair. His tone emotionless when he spoke. "As part of hospital policy, when one of our patients passes on, and out of concern for the family, I'm here to answer any questions that you might have concerning your mother's death."

How considerate, Adam's first thoughts mocked. His mind wanting to lash out at anyone, or anything to help ease his suffering; someone to blame for the pain he felt. The last thing though Adam wanted to do was to put Doctor Ching, the one who could answer his questions on the defensive with derogatory, unbecoming words that he knew would accomplish nothing. He refrained his thoughts. He needed answers and expressing his grief might hinder getting them.

After a few moments of silence Adam realized Doctor Ching and the hospital had done every thing humanly possible to prevent his mother's death and that his pain did not give him license to be obnoxious. "Thank you," Adam said, and let his head droop low.

Doctor Ching said, "I know how you feel Mister Garrett. I too was devastated by the lost of my mother at a young age." He paused, hoping that the words would somehow lighten Adam's burden. When he saw they didn't, he added, "I can offer you a mild sedative if you like?"

Adam shook his head no.

"How about if I just tell you what I know? After that, if you have any additional questions…I'll be happy to answer them for you…if I can."

With a slight nod from Adam, Doctor Ching started to explain. "Well, you know your mother was brought in here last Saturday morning suffering from a major cardiac infarction…heart attack," he said. "And at best she had a thirty percent chance of surviving the damage to her heart muscle. She was overweight, had high blood pressure, her cholesterol levels were over three hundred and I would venture to believe, she probably lived a pretty sedentary life style…Many times in such cases an embolus…a clot forms somewhere in the body and eventually blocks the blood flow to the heart."

Adam nodded to show that he understood what a heart attack was. He lifted his head until his eyes met the doctor's.

"The part of the heart tissue that is deprived of blood flow dies," Doctor Ching continued, "and as was the case with your mother that section of tissue ruptures from the pressure within the heart itself, resulting in death."

A vision of his mother's heart exploding within her chest flashed through Adam's mind. He cringed, recoiled in his seat and felt ill as an intense wave of nausea coursed its way through him. He grabbed hold of the front edge of the couch cushion with both hands to steady himself, took a deep breath, and exhaled with a long, drawn out sigh.

"Are you all right Mister Garrett?" The doctor stood, readying himself to catch Adam.

Carol wrapped her arm around his sagging shoulders.

The vision and nausea passed as fast as it came. "I'm fine," Adam said.

"Can I get you anything? Water?" Doctor Ching offered.

"No I'm all right," Adam gathered himself. Oddly enough, he did feel better, stronger. His brain, reacting to the stress, was producing its own sedative in the form of endorphins.

"I just have one question doctor and I think I already know the answer," Adam managed to say.

"Ask."

"That chip you wanted me to okay for you to implant in my mother wouldn't have made a difference would it?"

"No," Doctor Ching shook his head. "It wouldn't have mattered a bit."

It's over. Adam pondered the finality of his mother's death. Now all he wanted to do was go home, wallow in self-pity until he couldn't stand it anymore, pick himself up, make his peace with it, and get on with his life.

Adam stood. Regaining more poise every second, he extended his hand. "Thank you doctor for all that you've done," he said somberly,.

Stunned by the sudden turnaround in Adam's demeanor, Doctor Ching shook hands with him. "Wish there was more I could have done," he said.

Adam reached down and helped Carol up. "Can we stop by mom's room one last time?" Adam asked both of them.

"Sure," Doctor Ching answered as Carol nodded her approval.

He really didn't go back into the room, but stood in the doorway looking in at her. Laying in the narrow hospital bed, his mother looked peaceful to him. Like she had almost welcomed her death. Adam thought that he saw what appeared a slight smile upon her face. And for a moment, she didn't look dead to him, but more like she was sleeping, like he had seen her do many times while he was growing up. But reality came crashing in on him again and he fought back the tears once more. "Bye mom," he said, leaned his head into the room and whispered. "I love you."

The late afternoon air outside of the River Valley Hospital was warm and humid. The rain showers they had earlier in the day did nothing to cool things off and the heat was oppressing.

"Feels like we might be in for some heavy weather this evening," Adam said, looking up into the thick sky.

"It'll fit the way I feel," Carol spoke for the first time since they had arrived at the hospital two hours ago.

"But, after every storm," Adam put his arm around her waist and headed for his truck, never finishing his sentence, never looking back. "I've got some people coming over later tonight," Adam said, when they reached the vehicle.

"Are you sure that's a good idea?"

"It's just the lady from Lindsey's daycare and her husband."

"Melissa Elsworth?"

"Yeah! I was talking to her when I dropped Lindsey off this morning. She was telling me about the Mark, but never got to finish, so I invited her and her husband over."

"Yeah, but that was before...," Carol stopped and climbed in the passenger side of Adam's truck.

"Well, I did promise Mom that I would check into this chip before she...," Adam couldn't form the word to finish his sentence and felt another lump welling in his throat. He swallowed hard and started the Dodge. "And I have every intention of fulfilling that promise."

Carol forced a weak smile. "Amiable. I just think it might be better for us to wait a couple of days. Give ourselves a chance to deal with our loss before we jump in to anything else."

"You're probably right," Adam pulled away.

"I even think it might be a good idea to let Lindsey spend the night at my parent's tonight," Carol said.

:

Both of them were accustomed to being in and around large groups of strangers, so the throngs of people at Detroit Metropolitan Airport bothered neither one of them. They moved steadily through the busy terminal concourse, without talking, single minded in their destination; the front exit. The masses paid no attention to the two, suited, businessmen either. To them, Ethan and Carl were just two more faces in the crowd.

Once they reached their goal, they stepped though the automatic doors out into the cool night air. Ethan raised his arm to flag down one of the many yellow taxis shooting in and out of the covered area just outside the terminal doors.

"That won't be necessary," a woman's voice, near them, called out.

Startled, they both turned to see who had called. To see if the words were intended for them. Immediately, Ethan's head dropped.

Beverly Olsen, dressed in a tight fitting, white, V-necked sweater and a pair of dark blue, creased, slacks strolled up to them. "My car's parked just over there," she pointed behind her. "We'll give you boys a lift."

A tall, lanky, curvaceous brunette, with munificent lips, sidled up beside Beverly.

"This is my friend Delia," Beverly introduced the thirty-two year old woman. "You remember Delia Brown from Accounting don't you Ethan?"

Distracted by Delia's beauty, Carl turned away from the cab, anxious to accept Beverly's offer.

Ethan gave a sideways glance. All he needed to see of the woman was her long, tanned, shapely legs, hanging down from her white, cutoffs and he knew who she was from his days at GyroTech.

Pushing out of the gathering crowd near the main exit doors, an impatient businessman in his fifties, grabbed the rear door handle of the cab that pulled up to answer Ethan's hail.

"Hey!" Ethan objected, "that's our cab."

The man ignored him and pulled open the door. Tossing his small, overnight bag in ahead of himself, he snarled back, "I haven't got the time to wait while you and your friend stand around gabbing half the night away."

Delia started to chuckle.

Ethan swung his carry-on bag at the cab as the door closed. The bag bounced harmlessly off the window with a dull thud. "Ignorant idiot," he shouted as the taxi pulled away.

By then Delia and Beverly were in a full laugh.

"Come on tiger," Beverly stopped giggling long enough to say. "I'll give you a ride before you get us into an all out brawl."

"We're just going over to the Holiday Inn." Ethan gathered his composure, but still reluctant.

"We know," Beverly passed an evil grin his way. "We are too."

"Come on," Carl urged, already starting to walk away with Delia.

"We don't bite...unless you want us to," Delia smiled back, parting her lips seductively. In the process, showing her snow white teeth and repeatedly champing them together with a slight, clicking sound.

Ethan hesitated for a moment and found himself looking at the backsides of the trio as they walked away. He let his shoulders droop and started after them.

The white, Lincoln Towncar with all the 'toys' they climbed into, to Ethan looked way beyond what he thought was the ability of Beverly's salary to afford.

"Nice car," Carl remarked, tossing his one piece of baggage into the spacious trunk.

"Not too shabby for a woman eh?" Beverly boasted.

"Not too shabby for anybody," Carl grinned back at her.

Ethan suspiciously asked, his baggage still in-hand, "You never did say what you ladies were doing in Detroit, at this time of night, and at the airport?"

"Aren't you going to put that back here?" Beverly avoided the question.

"I'll keep it with me…if you don't mind."

"Suit yourself," Beverly said, as she lower the trunk lid.

The soft whine of the electric motor pulling the deck lid tightly closed filled the silence.

Beverly pulled the new Lincoln out of the parking lot onto Merriman Avenue.

"You never did answer my question," Ethan said, without looking at her.

Beverly reached over and turned on the stereo. "What question was that?"

"What you ladies are doing here."

Beverly glanced up into the rearview mirror. "Waiting for you guys." Then added, "What kind of music do you like Carl?"

"Oldies is fine with me."

Beverly hit the radio's scan button until she heard an old Beetles song playing.

"How did you know we were here?" Ethan said.

"You're doing a presentation on the Signa-Chip tomorrow morning in the Conference Center at the Holiday Inn," Beverly smiled. "Our boss wanted us to be here for that conference and it was a piece of cake to find out you were coming here tonight and on what flight. The rest is history."

"How'd you find all of that out?" Ethan turned to look at her.

"Easy," Beverly eased the Towncar to a stop at the traffic light. "Your secretary. Katy…Cathy…," Beverly purposely stumbled, though she really did know the name.

"Katlin," Carl leaned forward and said.

"Yeah, Katlin," Beverly smiled that evil smile again. "She was actually very willing to help us out." She glanced back up into the rearview mirror.

Ethan closed his eyes, leaned heavily into the white leather seat and let his head fall back onto the head rest. *Oh God*, he thought, *Katlin knows.*

Almost shouting, Ethan sat forward. "What do you want Beverly?"

"I don't want anything," Beverly acted surprised. "What's got into you?"

"Stop the car. I want out," Ethan shouted, his voice forceful, demanding.

Stunned, Beverly ignored him.

"Stop the car," Ethan demanded again and reached for the ignition keys to turn the motor off.

"Stop it," Beverly said slapping at his hand. "You don't want to do that."

Carl reached up and pushed Ethan back to his side of the front seat.

"Then pull this junk over and let me out."

"You don't want to do that either," Beverly said. "This is not the best neighborhood for some suited businessman to be

wandering the streets. Especially at this hour of the night.
You wouldn't last five minutes out there."

"Still I'll take my chances 'out there'.""

"What's going on with you," Beverly said. "I just want
us all to be friends."

Carl put his head up into the front seat. "Yeah, why can't
we all just settle down and be friends?"

Ethan let out a sigh and closed his eyes until he felt the
Lincoln slow and make a left turn into the entrance of the
Holiday Inn. As soon as the car came to a complete stop, he
jumped out, bag in hand and headed for the entrance doors.

"If you change your mind later, I'll be down in the
lounge," Carl called out after him.

Ethan never answered and kept right on walking.

"Can I take that for you?" A dark haired bellhop met him
at the door.

"I got it...thanks," Ethan said and rushed past him, up to
the front desk.

"We're not going to let his lousy attitude ruin the whole
night for us are we ladies?" Carl said, reaching up and pulling
Ethan's door closed.

Beverly opened the glove compartment and pushed the
automatic trunk release button. The power deck lid opened
with a clank.

"As far as I'm concerned the night is over," Beverly said,
glancing up into the rearview mirror again.

"Ladies, the night is young," Carl whined. He looked at
Delia. Her frown told him she agreed with Beverly. Carl
paused. "You sure?"

Delia nodded.

"Well, thanks for the lift," Carl slid over and opened his
door. "Nice meeting you," he smiled at Delia. "Maybe next
time?"

"Maybe," Delia said back without expression.

Carl collected his bag and slammed the trunk lid down out of habit.

"Sorry, he waved as the Lincoln pulled away. Carl rushed into the hotel door, also ignoring the bellhop's request to carry his bag.

"Wait up," Carl called, just as Ethan stepped into the elevator on his way up to their room on the fifth floor of the hotel.

Ethan held the door for him and waited.

"What in the God's name is wrong with you?" Carl asked when they were in the elevator.

"I'm a married man," Ethan answered. "And I have no particular desire to be 'just friends' with either of those women."

"I'm married too," Carl defended himself. "But, I sure wouldn't have minded a roll between the sheets with that Delia chick."

:

Adam was still awake for the late night news announcement that Electronic Solutions Incorporated was planning a presentation of the Signa-Chip in the morning. He was on the telephone to the Holiday Inn, trying to secure himself a reservation for a seat at that presentation, before the announcement was completely over.

"I'm sorry sir," the telephone operator told him. "That conference isn't open to the public. Besides even if it was, I couldn't get you in, all the seats are accounted for."

Adam thanked her and hung up as Carol, wrapped in just a towel, stepped back into the living room, fresh from taking a shower. Adam looked at her sleek, flawless, frame and marveled at her beauty. *What a lucky man I am*, he thought.

And despite the tragedy of losing one woman in his life, he felt fortunate to have gained another. Though he knew Carol's love could never replace his mother's, she did bring her own love into his life and he appreciated it.

"Have I told you how beautiful you are lately," Adam said.

"Only every time you look at me and smile."

Adam let a wide grin cross his face as Carol walked over towards him.

"I thought we just might need something to get our minds off of our troubles," she said, undoing the knot in the bath towel. The Tangerine colored cotton towel fell to the floor at their feet.

:

The usually true observation that men fell asleep afterwards and it was the woman who stayed awake did not apply to Adam, at least not this night. He tossed and turned well into the early morning hours, while Carol, contented, dozed off right after their love making.

At around three o'clock in the morning, Adam got up again. He made a hot cup of tea and sat alone in the darkness of the kitchen, reliving events of his childhood days, when both of his parents were alive. He broke down and cried a few times from the joyous memories. When he finished his tea and reminiscing, an hour later, he felt much better, stronger, the sharpness of his pain ebbing into a dull ache, deep in his heart.

For the rest of his life, Adam realized in the peaceful, darkness of that morning, he would always miss his mother and have a place in his heart for her were she would live on.

He set his cup in the sink and went back to bed. Cuddled up next to Carol, feeling the warmth of her next to him, Adam dozed. At seven o'clock, he was awake again, thanks to his biological alarm clock, and got up to take a shower.

Carol, awaken by the noise of the shower, stuck her head into the steamy bathroom. "How come you're up so early and where you going?"

Adam slid the glass shower door partially opened. "They're having one of those presentations on the Signa-Chip this morning," he said. "I'd like to go by there and see if I can learn some more about this chip. Hear it right from the 'horse's mouth' sort-a-speak." He slid the door closed. "If I can sneak my way in."

Still half asleep, Carol said, "Well, if you don't mind, I'm going back to bed?"

Adam shut the shower water off and slid the door open again. "Don't you have to get up and ready for work?"

"If I was going to work...I'm going to take a couple of days off." Carol handed him his towel. "I need a few days." She stepped out of the bathroom and went back to bed.

By the time Adam dried himself and dressed, un-typically in a gray suit and tie, she was asleep again. He bent over her, kissing her lightly on the cheek. "Love you," he whispered and quietly left the house.

Armed with the announcement from the newscast, the night before, as to where the presentation was to take place and at what time, Adam had no trouble finding the Holiday Inn on Merriman road and the I-94 expressway. Even if he had not, the over-filled parking lot of the eight story tall, ul-tra-modern hotel, and the line of backed-up traffic, on

Merriman, still trying to get in, told him something major was happening at the hotel.

He pulled into the near empty Ramada Inn parking lot across the street and crossed the busy road afoot, dodging in and out of the moving traffic.

Adam glanced at his watch. *Still have half an hour before the presentation is supposed to start,* he thought, *plenty of time for some coffee.*

He made his way into and through the groups of people milling around the closed, heavy wooden, double doors to the entrance of the large conference room.

Dressed in his suit, he fit right in with the crowds, hoping, as he had planned, that because he did, he would be able to inconspicuously slip into the presentation amid one of the groups.

Adam noticed name tags that said, 'PRESS' pinned onto the suit pockets of several people. *I wonder,* he schemed, diverting from the restaurant, heading off to the gift shop just across the hall.

He purchased a clear plastic name tag holder, a black felt tipped pen, and a thick pad of Legal sized paper from the Gift Shop. Afterwards he stepped into one of the stalls in the men's room. Alone in the stall, he took a sheet of paper from the pad and folded it several times to size and on it, in bold letters, with the black felt pen, carefully printed the word 'PRESS'. He slid the paper into the holder and pinned the holder to his coat pocket. Adam backed up from the mirror and smiled at his craftiness.

When he stepped back out into the crowd waiting for the conference room doors to open, a dark haired man in his mid-thirties and dressed in a crumpled looking corduroy sports jacket asked him, "What paper are you with?"

Adam, caught off guard for a moment by the question, answered "Times Herald," a bit to loud. Several other people in the group looked his way and Adam thought he felt himself blush. He was glad, when an instant later, the conference room doors swung open and distracted everyone.

Adam stood on his toes and looked past the crowd of people into the room.

The main body of red, padded, metal folding chairs stood in the center of the expansive conference room and reached from just beyond the doors, all the way up to the portable stage one-hundred and fifty feet away. A ten foot square movie screen hung suspended above the stage and just behind a small podium. To one side of the main body of chairs, after a narrow aisle, was another bank of similar chairs, one third in number as the main body and arraigned in corresponding rows. The other side of the room was filled with manned, long folding tables. All covered with explanatory pamphlets and brochures about Signa-Chip.

"Press around to the left," one of the ushers pointed to the small rows of seats along the west side of the room.

Adam moved into the room with the group he was with and along the back wall, he found, mid-section, a seat.

"Hello, Ladies and Gentlemen. And members of the press," Ethan stepped up to the podium microphone.

Adam couldn't help but smile.

"I'm Ethan Blake, Marketing Manager for Electronics Solutions Incorporated."

I'm Adam Garrett, reporter for The Times Herald, Adam smiled.

A slide of an outside shot of ESI's headquarters building in Chicago appeared on the movie screen behind Ethan. "Along with the Public Relations Manager Carl Torre," Ethan paused long enough for Carl to step forward next to him and nod toward the audience. "We'd like to welcome you to this exposition on the virtues of the Signa-Chip."

An hour later, the presentation over, Ethan and Carl stepped down from the portable stage, allowing themselves to be interviewed. With the crowd of legitimate reporters who responded to the opportunity, Adam worked his way in closer, still engaged in his facade. He had several questions he wanted to ask, namely those that referred to the alleged relationship between Signa-Chip and the Mark. He eventually did get his chance to ask.

"Mister Blake," he started as reporter-like as he could. "Have you received any feedback from religious groups on the supposed relationship between your company's chip and the 'Mark of the Beast'?"

Ethan and Carl both turned and stared at him, their eyes furrowed, boring into him. Adam felt ashamed he had asked.

"What kind of question is that?" Ethan chided as a mocking chuckle erupted among the other reporters.

Adam felt his body retract slightly.

"First off," Carl jumped in. "What is this 'Mark of the Beast' thing?"

"Some deluded religious malarkey, I suppose" Ethan answered still staring at Adam. "And as such, we at ESI fail to see any co-relationship between what we are doing and the delusions of a few religious fanatics."

Adam sunk back into the group and found his way to the other side of the conference room, near the brochure covered tables.

13

Two hours after the Signa-Chip presentation was over, Adam sat at his kitchen table, across from Carol, mulling over the list of 'virtues' he had written on the purchased legal pad.

"Personal Identification, Security issues, Credit/Debit card replacement, Lost or Missing Persons location, Thief, Prostitution, Street Drugs, Illegal Monetary Transactions deterrent…"

Carol sat, sipping on her coffee, dispassionate, impatiently listening as Adam read off the list to her. Presuming that he was using the distraction of researching the Signa-Chip to occupy his mind and keep it from dealing with his mother's death, she tried to show some interest, because she was. But, she also felt there were more immediate concerns for the day that they needed to address.

"Heath Conditions Monitor, Medical Alerts," Adam looked up from the pad of paper. "You know they're even talking about digitally storing x-rays, drug allergies, and surgical histories on this thing. It almost sounds," he raised his hands and made the parenthetical motion with his fingers, "too good to be true."

"That's great," Carol said. She set her coffee cup down on the white Formica table top. "But, you do realize you're only getting one side of the story? And that, from the people who stand to profit most from it?"

"I know." Adam's eyes dropped back to the brightly colored brochure he had gotten while at the presentation, sitting next to his list.

"Of course, in their eyes, it's going to be the greatest thing to come along since sliced bread."

The kitchen went silent as Adam thought about what Carol said.

Carol, hesitating to say what she knew she had to, was searching her mind for a gentler way to redirect Adam's thoughts. But when she couldn't come up with one, she said, "I know you have been trying to avoid it, but you have to call a funeral home today and have them pick your mother's body up from the hospital."

Her statement brought the reality of the day crashing in on Adam.

Watching the look on his face as it turned from the excitement of discovery, to one of shock, she hated herself for her bluntness, for pushing him. "I know that sounds cold sweetheart," Carol paused, hoping to justify, to ease the blow. "But, it's something you have to do."

He thought for a moment, struggling to regain his composure, before responding. "I know," Adam admitted. "I have to call her life insurance company too and let them know she has passed."

Carol went around the table and placed her hand on his shoulder to comfort him.

"I know she has a burial plot next to Dad's at the Woodland Cemetery out on twenty-two mile road," Adam said. "And we have to think about what we're going to do with her things too."

"No immediate relatives?"

"None that I know of. She and I were the last."

"Well, I think we ought to just take it all, hers and mine, and put it in storage for now until things settle down a bit," Carol moved her hand away and put her cup in the sink.

"Then we can go through it a little at a time and figure out what to do with it."

"Sounds like a plan," Adam forced a smile at her. He knew that his mother had a house and a ten year old car that he had to consider what to do with. But, he figured, those larger items could wait.

"I'm going to go take my shower and get dressed," Carol said, walking past him. She bent down and kissed him on the forehead. "I want to pickup Lindsey before it gets too late."

Adam turned back to his list. He stared blankly at it until he heard the water running in the shower. He pulled out the telephone book and scanned it for numbers.

By the time Carol was done, he had called the Mutual Life Insurance company and three Funeral Parlors, before he found one close to the grave site that would pickup his mother's body.

"The funeral will be Friday at one," Adam told Carol matter-of-factly, when she returned to the kitchen, dressed in cutoffs and a blue, tank top. "At the Bruncowski Funeral home in Utica." He paused, swallowed the lump in his throat. "I need to get a death certificate from the hospital and get that off to the insurance company before they can do anything." He paused again. "Her policy they said, should be enough to take care of most of the costs."

"We'll get though this sweetheart," she walked up and hugged him.

He smelled the essence of her skin, cool against his face. Somehow, the fragrance empowered him. Just her scent was enough to make him feel stronger.

"As sad as it is," Carol pulled away and looked into his eyes. "As much as it hurts…life goes on."

The words, unintentionally, hurt. His mind reeled at the thoughts of life going on as if his mother was still alive, as if nothing had happened. Still, she was right and he knew it. Life did go on, no matter how cruel it seemed.

He wrapped his arms back around her, holding her close, loving her even more for her courage.

After a moment he released her, his mind made up to do just what she implied. And that was to do what he had to do; mourn, hurt, but get on with 'life'.

Adam regained control of his racing thoughts and asked if she wanted him to go with her and get Lindsey.

"I can handle that," she answered and said," Why don't you stay home and rest. I know you didn't get much sleep last night and we'll be home in a few minutes."

Adam agreed.

Carol pulled out of the driveway and made a left turn at the corner heading for the expressway and her parents house twelve miles away. As soon as she was out of sight, she pulled over and cried. She cried for Misses Garrett, she cried for Adam, and the cruelty of life. She also cried for herself.

:

Frustrated, Ethan removed his jacket and tie, tossing them both on the hotel bed on his side of the double occupancy room and started pacing.

Carl covered the mouth piece of the in-room phone, he was talking on, with the palm of his hand. "The best I can do commercially is five-thirty this evening," he said to Ethan.

Unbuttoning the collar button on his starched, white shirt with one hand, Ethan looked at his watch. The numbers 11:49 showed back. "And just what are we supposed to do for the next five and a half hours? We could drive back to Chicago by then."

"Do you want me to make the reservations or not?" Carl snarled at him.

"Well, I'm not flying one of those private paper cubs back."

"That's Piper Cub," Carl remarked.

Ethan didn't vocally respond. He just looked at Carl with piercing eyes.

"Do I make the reservation or not?"

"What choice do we have?" Ethan walked over to the window and pushed back the heavy, dark green drapes. The traffic five stories below went past in a steady stream in both directions.

"No! Eight, nine, five, three," Carl reread the last four digits off of the company credit card into the telephone. "That is correct...Two, Ethan Blake and Carl Torre." He said, "Yes," once more and hung up.

Ethan turned away from the window and let the drapes fall back into place. "Now what," he said, walking over and sitting on the edge of his bed.

"I know I'm hungry," Carl said. "For starters we can go downstairs and have some lunch."

Ethan stood up and headed for the door without speaking. Carl was one step behind him.

"I don't know why we couldn't fly back on the same flight as the setup crew," Ethan said, pushing the down arrow for the elevator.

"Because the setup crew is headed to New York."

Ethan turned quickly and looked at him. "We're not going to New York are we?"

"Tomorrow night. I thought you knew."

"Nobody tells me anything anymore."

The elevator doors opened and Ethan sighed.

"You knew this might get a little crazy," Carl reminded him of the potential for the chip to 'explode' onto the scene.

"Yeah, but my daughter wasn't supposed to be kidnapped on top of everything else." Ethan looked down at the almost healed surgical cut in the palm of his right hand for the hundredth time. *How could he be upset that the chip was keeping him away from home,* he pondered. *If not for the Signa-Chip he probably wouldn't have a daughter right now to worry about.* "Well, it sure would have been nice if somebody would have booked a return flight for us."

"Somebody did," Carl glanced down at his palm too. "They just didn't know when the presentation would be over, or how long we would be detained after it answering questions. So, they just left it open."

The elevator doors opened again one floor down and two more men boarded the conveyance. They got on and immediately turned their backs to Ethan and Carl. From the matching dark suits, hats and round nosed black leather shoes the men wore, Ethan guessed them either FBI or CIA agents. He nudged Carl and nodded towards the bulge he spotted under the left arm of one of them.

Carl squinted questioningly at him.

Ethan formed a child's replica of a revolver with his thumb and forefinger.

They rode the rest of the way down in silence, until the two men got off at the ground floor.

"Those guys were at the presentation," Carl said, when the men were far enough away not to overhear him. "I remember their faces. They were sitting up front, center...like in the second or third row of seats."

Ethan thought for a moment, envisioning the area Carl was referring to. "Yeah, I remember them too," he said.

Carl looked a little nervous. "Maybe we have the 'Feds' watching us?"

"So? Maybe our Uncle Sam has an interest in our little chip," Ethan smiled at him. "Could you imagine the size of the contract we could get if they wanted to replace those little metal dog tags the soldier boys wear with the chip? Millions!"

"How many?" The Hostess met them at the restaurant entrance.

"Two," Ethan said and lifted as many fingers in case the pretty, well dressed, young woman didn't hear him.

"Smoking or non?" She asked and pulled two menus from the box hanging on the side of the small podium she stood behind.

"Non," Carl answered.

The Hostess, walking away from them and smiling, glanced back over her shoulder to make sure they were following her. She swayed seductively as she lead them past the long, self-serve, salad bar in the center of the restaurant.

"Friendly little thing isn't she?" Carl commented under his breath.

Ethan smiled back, still lost in his thoughts about the government men they had seen on the elevator trip down, never heard Carl's comment.

"Your waitress will be with you in a moment," the young girl said, stopping at a booth along one of the windowed side walls. She placed the menus on the rectangular table. "Can I get you something to drink?"

"Coffee," they both answered in unison.

Watching her walk away, Carl undressed her with his eyes.

Ethan opened his menu and hadn't read the first item when he heard; "You boys eat here often?" He glanced up toward the familiar voice.

Two booths away, Delia waved an energetic hand at him.

Ethan cussed quietly, his mouth hidden behind the menu.

Carl turned to see what Ethan was cursing about.

Beverly Olsen, still not quite over being offended by Ethan's rudeness from the night before, beckoned with a reserved smile, "Why don't you guys come join us,"

Carl was sliding out from his side of the booth before Beverly had even finished inviting them. "Come on," he waved to the reluctant Ethan. "It will certainly kill some time."

Slowly, Ethan forced himself out.

The Hostess showed up with the coffees in time to see the relocation. She grabbed the menus, following them over to the new table.

"I like the casual thing you got going on there," Beverly pointed to Ethan's rolled up sleeves and open collared dress shirt. She padded the seat of the cushion next to her.

Already sliding in next to Delia, Carl had taken away his only other option. Ethan managed a tepid smile as he sat.

"We were just talking about you guys," Beverly scooted over to allow enough room for him, but barely.

"We were just talking about you ladies too," Carl lied, as he eyed Delia, clad in a sleeveless, white cotton top.

"What are you boys still doing in town? I thought by now you'd be on your way back to Chicago," Beverly scooted away another inch.

"Can't get a flight out 'till this evening," Carl answered much too quickly, giving too much information for Ethan's liking. "We've got the rest of the day to kill and don't know how."

There was nothing he could do to modify Carl's statement. Nothing he could say to make it escapable. Carl had set them up for what Ethan knew was coming next and come it did.

"How nice," Delia chimed in on cue, "We don't have to be back either. We can spend the day together." She turned sideways like she was looking behind herself and lightly brushed against Carl. When she felt the contact she leaned her weight in toward him, pressing firmly against his arm. "And I'm sure, together, we can figure out something to do."

"What can I get for you folks?" The waitress came up to the table and asked.

"I'd like French Toast and bacon," Carl chimed.

Ethan waited for the ladies to order.

"Nothing for us," Beverly said. "We've already eaten."

"Can I get a ham and cheese omelet?" Ethan said.

The waitress nodded, "What kind of toast?"

"Whole wheat."

"Thank you," the waitress said, scooping up the menus.

"So, if you ladies have already eaten, what are you doing hanging around here?" Ethan said, hoping the answer would give him something to excuse them.

"We're waiting for the pool to open up," said Beverly.

Delia said, "Hey, why don't you hang out by the swimming pool with us for a while that'll 'kill' a couple of hours?"

"We didn't bring any swimsuits, or towels," Carl frowned.

Ethan was getting angrier with Carl for his open-ended comments. He didn't want to spend the rest of the day defending himself against Beverly's advances. He didn't know how much more he could. They were being given opportunities to bow out gracefully, but instead of taking them, Carl was getting them in deeper. At that time, it never occurred to Ethan that Carl knew exactly what he was doing.

"That's not a problem. There's a K-Mart right down the street. Delia and I could go get you some of those one size fits all suits and be back before you even finish eating."

"That's all right, we…," Ethan started to say.

"Nonsense," Beverly pushed herself against Ethan, sliding out. "Come on Delia let's go shopping."

Both men stood, letting them out of the booth.

"Be right back," Delia smiled at Carl. "Don't go anywhere."

"What are you doing?" Ethan scolded, when the ladies were gone. "We've both got wives and kids at home."

Carl's face tightened. "Why don't you just relax a little? Two beautiful, vivacious, willing women." Carl waved his hand back and forth between them. "Two virile, successful, businessmen, three-hundred miles away from home…They'll probably even follow us to New York, or wherever else ESI wants to send us next. If we wanted them too." Carl leaned back in his seat with an egotistical audacity as the waitress placed their plates of food on the table in front of them.

"More coffee?" She asked.

"Sure," said Carl.

When the waitress was gone, Carl leaned back in. "And I see no problem with a little extra-curricular activity, when the opportunity affords itself. Breaks the dull drum and keeps the home fires burning bright."

"You don't understand…," Ethan said, unwilling to confide in Carl that he had already been with Beverly after the last presentation. That after a 'few' harmless drinks reminiscing, their innocent reunion turned 'heated' and ended up in a motel room.

"I understand a lot more than you think my friend." Carl took a small bite of his French toast. "I saw you leave the presentation in Chicago with Beverly…and it was probably good…too good!." He swallowed. "If you don't watch it, you could get caught up in a full blown affair, ruin your happy home, and that scares you." Carl took another bite of bacon. "Won't happen unless you let it…What you're feeling…natural reaction…You'll get used to it."

Stunned, Ethan's chin dropped. His eyes widened. His mouth hung slightly open. This wasn't the Carl, he thought he knew. This was someone else that just looked like Carl.

Carl swallowed. "Don't worry pal your little secret is safe with me and after today, I hope mine is safe with you!"

The look on Ethan's face didn't change. He sat there staring at Carl, wondering how many other women Carl had been with; How Carl knew about him and Beverly.

"Aren't you going to eat?" Carl returned his stare. "The girls should be back soon."

Ethan lifted a slice of toast to his mouth.

"It doesn't get any better Ethan, this is it," Carl smiled. "Why don't you just take it for what it is? A roll between the sheets with a beautiful woman."

:

Adam didn't want to stay around the house, waiting for Carol. He knew that once she got with her mother it could be hours before Carol got away. He wasn't adverse to her spending time with her parents, he really promoted it. But, he didn't want to wait for her either. He wrote her a short 'sticky' note explaining that he had just stepped out, that he would be back soon. Sticking the lime green, paper note on the cupboard door above the kitchen sink, where he was confident Carol would see it, Adam grabbed his cell phone and left.

The late morning air was already hot and humid but the weatherman had forecast a stormy afternoon with falling temperatures as a cold front moved across the state from west to east. Adam, hoped it was an accurate forecast. He'd had enough of the unseasonably hot weather. It was only the middle of June and Michigan had already experienced eight, ninety degree plus days. Three quarters of the number of days they usually endured for the whole summer.

He drove by the Early Learning Daycare Center, hoping to talk more with Melissa. She was too busy though to afford him but a few minutes of time. Much of which she filled with condolences on his loss.

"Can't you and your husband stop by later?" Adam sounded almost pleading, when Melissa told him that she didn't have the time to visit much with him. "I'd really like to talk more with you about this chip,"

"I'm really sorry," Melissa said. "We would really like to talk to you and Carol too. But my husband and I have commitments for tonight and tomorrow."

"When do you think you can?" Adam felt despondent from the news. He didn't know the reason why, or why he even cared, but he had a burning desire to learn religion's view of the Signa-Chip.

"We might be able to make it on Friday. But, I'll have to check with Jack to make sure."

"Good," Adam started encouraged. "No wait." His hopes fell again. "Friday's the day of the funeral. I'll won't be able to make it…Can we shoot for Saturday?"

Melissa thought for a moment. "I think Saturday is free. Though we do have to be at the church around five. The teens in my Sunday School class are rehearsing the program they're doing for Sunday service."

"You teach Sunday school?"

Nodding, Melissa said, "For six years now. My husband and I both teach. I teach the teens and my husband teaches the young adult class."

"I'm impressed, said Adam.

"Ah it's really nothing. The Lord does all the teaching. All we do is keep it organized and lead the way, help explain something if somebody gets confused."

It was either the way she said it, or the way it struck him, but Adam was intrigued by her words. He had never heard that approach to teaching before. He was, for the first time in his life, looking forward to discussing a 'religious' topic with somebody. "Well, if you and your husband are free," he said. "Saturday morning will be fine."

"Like I said, I'll have to make sure with Jack first." Melissa said, leading him toward the gate. "But if it's all right...How about we make it for around ten o'clock."

Adam stepped out of the gate onto the sidewalk inspired. "That would be great."

:

Ethan was not about to let Carl's eagerness draw him into something he wanted no part of. He loved Nicole and his children and would do nothing intentional to hurt either of them. He pushed away his half eaten lunch. "You go on ahead if you want to," he told Carl. "I'm going to rent a car and take in some sites."

"Suit yourself," Carl said. "I'm going to take in a few sights of my own." He let the word 'sights' drag out.

Ethan used his company charge card to pay his bill adding an exorbitant tip for the waitress out of anger at ESI for
the inconvenience of the unexpected lay-over. He then
stepped out into the covered entrance to the hotel and waved
in a cab. He took it back to the car rental at the airport.
Where he procured a dark blue, Ford Taurus, again using the
company credit card. He spent the rest of the morning and a
few hours of the afternoon just driving, going no where in
particular. A little after three o'clock he returned to the hotel,
went up into the room and called home.

"I should be home around seven o'clock," he told Nicole.
And explained the circumstances why he would be late.

"That's a bunch of crap," Nicole said. "ESI should have
made return reservations at a decent hour."

"I agree," Ethan responded. "But, there's not a whole lot
I can do about it now. All I can do is wait."

"Where's Carl?" Nicole surprised him.

Ethan stumbled. "Ah, I don't know. I think he's down in
the lobby."

"What's going on?" Nicole asked, suspicious by his answer.

"Nothing!" Ethan answered too quickly, to loudly.
"There's a lounge down there and he might be there."

"Come on, Ethan, I know you better than that. Something is going on. I can tell by the tone of your voice."

"I'll tell you about it later," was all he said.

14

Except for a muffled sob, the small, dim lit room, where his mother was laid out in the Bruncowski Funeral home, was near silent. Occasionally, someone in the small gathering would stand up from the rows of padded folding chairs behind him and walk up to the gleaming, open casket sitting at the head of the room.

From their seats, front and center, Adam and Carol watched the mourners come and peer in at the body. They would all whisper something softly to her before turning and offering their condolences. Adam forced a smile at each of them. Not knowing what else to say in response, he simply thanked them for coming.

During the times when no one was paying their last respects, Adam stared at the bright yellow, white and red blossoms of the Irises, Orchids and Gladiolas encircling the dark gray casket. The vivid flowers at times seemed appropriate to him, while at others the effulgent bouquets looked out of place. *Too much color, too much life,* Adam would think. *Too festive, for such a solemn time.*

Adam turned around and glanced over the group of mourners behind him. A few of the people present, he recognized from his Dad's funeral and knew them only as distant cousins of his mother. The kind of relatives you only see at weddings, funerals, and family reunions. Everyone else were strangers to him. Friends of his mother's he assumed. Friends and acquaintances from the church she attended. All coming to pay their last respects; say a final farewell to the woman they knew and loved.

"Charlotte Garrett," the pastor of her church spoke as he stood from his front row seat, next to Adam. He slowly walked up to the casket, peering in. With his back to the gathering, he started the eulogy. Slowly he turned to face them, his hands clasp together in front of him. "So near, so dear to those of us who had the privilege to know her while she walked God's earth," he said.

Adam glanced up at the gray haired man with thick glasses he had heard his mother quote many times over the years. Pastor Wyans looked pensive, his face drawn. The weight of serving as the minister of the non-denominational church, Adam's mother attended, for over thirty-five years showed. He was tired and looked it. The, 'too many', funerals of his congregation members and their families that he had presided over, along with the burdens of the day to day maintenance of his 'flock', taking it's toll.

Pastor Wyans said, "Of all the beautiful things I can say about the kindness and generosity of Charlotte," he paused. "Most importantly...she loved God. She lived with him in her heart. She died with him in her heart. And because she did...she'll live again."

Someone from the crowd said, "Amen!"

Adam's head sank slowly floor-ward. How he wished he could believe that. How he wanted to think, that somewhere in this great universe his mother was alive in another form. Happy again. Reunited with his Dad and all those that she had known who had passed on before her. And that someday too, he would join them. Try as he might, he couldn't. But, deep within his heart, neither did he think that this was all there was to life; that for his mother, this was the end. He struggled against the gnawing thoughts from within that told him there was more.

Although Pastor Wyans was only a few feet away and spoke clearly, the minister's words seemed muffled to Adam, aloof and distant, as though coming from afar. And though the pastor, while delivering the eulogy, spoke with enough volume to his voice that all within the room could hear and maybe a few beyond it, Adam, lost in thought, heard little of it, wrestling with the inner turmoil.

The sound of the group singing, as Pastor Wyans led them in a chorus of 'Amazing Grace', his mothers favorite Gospel song, brought Adam's mind back to the funeral. He didn't know the words but mouthed it the best he could, anticipating the obvious words and singing them loudly. To his surprise Carol, knew every one of the words to several verses and sang along with the congregation as if she had been doing it for years.

It was the first time he had ever heard her really sing and the sweetness of her voice as she sang the hymn with sincerity, made his heart feel good. It would be one of the moments he would remember for the rest of his life.

:

Just after lunch hour on Friday afternoons, one of the responsibilities Ethan, and every other manager at ESI, had to do, was hand out the paychecks to the employees in their respective departments. This Friday though would be the last time they would do that job. Starting the following week, the Payroll Department at ESI would implement a mandatory, 'Direct Deposit' policy.

The company, choose to mandate the electronic system of wage dispersal, because of the nearly one million dollars it would save annually in paperwork and extra costs to print out paychecks. That savings did not include: the big reduction in man-hours required by the Payroll Department to provide those paychecks, for the fifteen hundred ESI employees in two locations, nor did it include the valuable time spent by management distributing those checks to the employees.

The policy of paying wages electronically, company wide and making that policy mandatory was nothing 'new' either. Several other large, nationally known companies were already doing it, saving millions of dollars. Several more were in the process of making that conversion. ESI's name could now be counted among that growing list of companies utilizing the automated system.

The complaints were minimal. As with every change, a few could be expected. But Ethan was fortunate, none of those protests came from within the Sales Department and he didn't have to deal with any disagreements. Everyone of the thirty-five people he had working under him were anticipating the change and accepted it as 'the next logical step' at ESI. Especially so, since the emergence of the Signa-Chip and the implementation of the totally electronic security system.

Carl telephoned Ethan in his office at two o'clock. "Are you almost ready? We need to be at the airport by three-thirty,"

Ethan said, "Just about. My bags are packed and I'm ready to go. I've only have a few more of these paychecks to hand out and that's it."

"Did you run into any trouble with the consent forms for the mandatory direct deposit?"

"Not really. Just a couple of times I needed to explain how to fill them out. You?"

"A couple of people were a little hesitant about giving out there bank account numbers on the consent form. Until, I showed them their account numbers were on the bottom of every check they wrote."

Ethan chuckled. "I find it hard to believe there are still people out there who don't realize that."

"That's nothing Ethan," Carl chuckled back. "I have one guy who doesn't even have a bank account. Still does everything with cash, or money orders."

"You're kidding?"

"No I'm not. In fact, he took the rest of the afternoon off to open one, so he could get paid next week."

Exhaling through his nose, Ethan shook his head. "Well, let me go hand these things out," he said, picking up the stuffed 'pay envelopes' off his desk and leaning back in his chair. "So, I can get this over with."

"Ethan," Carl said before he hung up. "I'd like to apologize for Detroit. I was a bit out of line."

Ethan held the phone to his ear without responding. They hadn't talked about Beverly and Delia since the restaurant in Detroit, In fact, they hadn't talked much at all afterwards and Ethan wanted Carl to know he wasn't happy with the whole incident.

"You could say something can't you?" Carl felt the pressure of Ethan's prolonged silence.

"What would you like me to say Carl? That it was okay? Because I won't. I was in a very awkward position there and at home and I didn't appreciate it."

At that point, Carl could have easily allowed their conversation to escalated into an argument, Ethan's denial of his role in the situation, opening that door wide. "Like I said," Carl digressed instead, "I'm sorry for that and hope we can put this behind us."

"I don't see why we can't, if you don't involve me in anymore your little escapades." It was Ethan's turn to feel the pressure of Carl's ensuing silence. "I know some of this is my fault," he said. "I should have never allowed myself to be taken in by Beverly in the first place. But what can I say? I had a moment of stupidity…a moment I now sorely regret. But it's over now and I want no part of anything else, Miss Beverly Olsen, or her friend Delia have to offer."

"That's fine," Carl said, feeling better that Ethan had, at least, acknowledged his part in the affair.

"Well, let me go finish handing out these paychecks so we can catch our flight," Ethan said and hung up.

:

Only four of the eight and a half hours he laid in bed that night were spent sleeping. The other four and a half, Adam tossed and turned fitfully. Even the four hours of sleep he did get were not consecutive. Twice he had been awakened by night terrors. Dreams of being lost and confused. Wandering aimlessly through the dark, endless maze of an abandoned, windowless, factory building. Searching for his only way out, every doorway he passed through in the similar dreams took him deeper into the maze…to a darker, more desolate place.

In one of the nightmares, his last and most frightful, he was pursued.

Something unseen, unknown, shapeless, raced him for the only exit in the cold, empty building. Something he knew he had to beat there. And no matter how fast or hard he ran, the 'thing' stayed always one step behind him. Taunting him. In the dream, Adam realized that if he didn't beat this 'thing' to the exit, the door would be forever sealed. He would be caught, forever imprisoned in the icy desolation.

He ran blindly through the building, his footsteps echoing behind, in front, and beside him. The deep throated laugh of the pursuing force cut through the emptiness. Mocking. Finally he reached the exit: A thick steel, electronically operated door without handles, he was unable to open. A steady stream of projected, roman numerals scrolled past the door in a beam of iridescent green light. He turned to face the source of the laughter as the taunting increased in pitch. Only the image of the Signa-Chip, he saw on the slide screen at the presentation was there, floating, suspended in the stagnant air. He reached out to grasp it, somehow knowing the chip was the key to opening the exit door.

His fingers had nearly touched the chip when a voice from nowhere, everywhere, said, "But Adam...what is beyond the door you seek to past through?" Adam jerked awake.

He laid there in the stillness of the morning, beads of sweat on his forehead, listening to Carol breathing softly next to him. He turned, "Six-thirty," he mumbled, looking at the clock, setting on the dresser across the bedroom. Disappointed that it wasn't later, he rolled to his back staring toward the ceiling, half hoping for, half apprehensive of more sleep. Sleep didn't come. At seven-fifteen, Adam climbed from the queen size bed and took a long, cold shower.

Wrapped in his black and white speckled bathrobe, his hair still wet from the shower, Adam sat at the kitchen table, lost in thought: *Why,* all of a sudden, had he become so interested in religious things? *Why,* was he so obsessed with learning about this Mark thing?

I've done what I promised, he tried to convince himself that he needn't pursue this issue anymore. *All I really vowed to do; was read the biblical verses and I have done that already. What else do I expect to learn?*

Invigorated by the shower, but still sleepy, he got up from the table to make a pot of coffee. As he waited for the coffee, he wondered if it was too early to call Melissa and cancel their ten o'clock, Saturday morning meeting?

The hands on the octagon shaped clock over the refrigerator pointed to eight-forty. He could make the call if he wanted. He hesitated, pouring a cup of the coffee instead.

Adam set the steaming cup on the table and went into the living room. He retrieved the yet to be opened bible Carol had purchased two days before. Going back into the kitchen, he laid the black leather-like book next to his coffee. He sat staring at it for a moment before he leafed through it, looking for the thirteenth chapter of Revelation. Rereading the verses in chapter thirteen he had promised his mother to read, Adam had less comprehension of the words, than when he had read them the first time. Feeling desperate to understand, he tried reading the whole of the chapter. That though only caused more questions. Frustrated, more confused, he wondered how anybody ever learned anything from the maze of dragons; lambs, beasts, crowns, and horns, talked about in the chapter.

Walking into the kitchen and seeing him, Carol asked, "What ya reading?"

Adam jumped, spooked by her sudden appearance.

She apologized, walking over and kissing him lightly on the cheek.

Adam said, "I wish somebody would tell me," and flipped the book closed.

"Well, I thought that was why Melissa and her husband are coming over?" Carol said, heading for her own cup of coffee.

"I don't know," Adam frowned. "I was thinking about canceling."

"Why?" Carol turned quickly.

"I don't even know...really," Adam said. His resolve to learn the religious aspects of the Signa-Chip waning. "It just seems kinda useless to me at this point."

"I wouldn't jump to any conclusions just yet," Carol went back to her coffee. "Let's talk to them. What could it hurt?"

Adam shrugged. "I guess," was all he said.

Carol said, "I need to get Lindsey up and get my shower." She sat across the table from Adam. "I want in on this too."

"Of course," Adam looked confused, surprised. "I always thought that."

"Then why were you going to cancel without even telling me?"

"I didn't did I?"

"Are you guys fighting?" Lindsey appeared in the doorway, rubbing the sleep from her eyes.

"No sweetie," Carol calmly said. She extended her hands and made a beckoning motion with her fingers. "We were just talking about Miss Elsworth coming over today."

Lindsey climbed up onto her lap. "The lady from daycare?"

"Yes," Adam smiled at her. "We have some things to talk about."

Lindsey looked concerned. "I wasn't a bad girl was I?"

"No sweetie," Carol said, hugging her.

"I'm hungry," Lindsey pulled back.

"I'll feed her," Adam said, standing up first.

"Then I'm going to go get my shower," Carol announced and set Lindsey into her vacated chair.

Adam had gotten dressed in black jeans and tee shirt and was drying Lindsey's just washed orange juice glass and cereal bowl when Carol, showered and dressed reappeared.

"Where's Lindsey?" She asked.

Adam placed the bowl in the cupboard next to the sink. "Should be in the front room watching TV."

"Let's not fight okay?" Carol moved up behind him, wrapping her arms around his waist.

"I wasn't fighting," Adam turned around and looked her in the eyes. He playfully laid the dish towel over her shoulder, kissing her on the lips in the process.

She melted into his embrace. "I love you," she said, laying her head on Adam's chest.

The door bell rang interrupting the moment.

"Good morning!" Carol said, opening the wood, entrance door.

Jack and Melissa Elsworth smiled back. Both toting two black bibles under their arms.

"Are we too early?" Melissa said.

"Not at all," Adam stepped in behind Carol. "Come on in."

Carol swung the door wide and Adam led them into the kitchen.

"Coffee?" Carol offered, as Adam motioned for them to sit at the table.

"Sure, Jack nodded.

Melissa sat. "Not me, she said. "Thank you anyway. But I think I've had enough for the day."

"This is a nice home you have here," Jack glanced around while making small talk.

"Thanks," Adam responded and set the cup down in front of his guest. "Are you sure I can't get anything for you?" He redirected to Melissa.

"I'm fine...Well, hello there," she said, noticing Lindsey peeking through the doorway."

"Hi Miss Elsworth," Lindsey said, looking overly concerned.

"Why don't you go watch television sweetie," Carol smiled at her. "We're just going to talk about some big people stuff."

Lindsey disappeared around the corner as quickly as she had showed up.

"Such a sweet child," said Melissa.

"Well, now Mister Garrett," Jack said. "My wife tells me that you are interested in learning about 'the mark'?"

Adam pulled out his chair and sat. "I was hoping that perhaps you could enlighten me as to why my mother was so against this new Signa-Chip, referring to it as this 'mark'? She was so opposed, even to the point, that if it could have saved her life, she was prepared to refuse it."

"Your mother never told you about the mark?"

"She tried," Adam let his head hang low. "Several times, but I would never listen to her."

"And now you think you are ready?"

"I think so."

"How about you Miss Wendell?" Jack turned toward Carol while sipping on his coffee.

"I want to know what all this is about too," Carol answered quickly. "I have a young daughter, as you know, and in light of the story about that little girl in Chicago who was kidnapped… Adam and I were thinking about having the chip implanted in her, for safety's sake." Carol paused and thought for a moment. "And before we go ahead and have it done, I'd like to know where people like…," she caught herself before she said, 'you' and said, "What the bible says about it."

"That's what really has us puzzled," Melissa said. "From what I understand you really don't believe in God, so why would you care what he has to say?"

"You're puzzled?" Adam grunted. "Well, let me clarify how this all got started."

As indifferently as he could, Adam told them the story of his mother; how the hospital wanted him to usurp his mother's refusal of the chip and how she had made him promise to find out about the chip. Giving him, as a reference, the sixteenth verse of the thirteenth chapter of Revelation, just before she died. "Obviously my curiosity was pricked by the verse and now I want to know more," Adam said and leaned back in his chair.

"And before we made such an important decision about Lindsey we wanted to know what 'God' had to say about it," Carol finished for him.

"We may not be 'believers' as you call us," Adam smirked a little on the defensive. "But we don't want to deny Lindsey the chance to make up her own mind, when she is ready either."

"Well, that is exactly what you would be doing," Jack said authoritatively.

"As you might believe," Adam said.

The room went into a strained silence. Carol frowned at Adam.

"We didn't come here to argue with you Mister Garrett," Jack said, feeling a bit attacked, ready to leave. "And it really doesn't matter what we, do or do not believe. The prophecy says what it says." He stood to leave

"I am really sorry," Adam apologized. "Please don't go. I just feel so much pressure with my mother's death, this chip thing, and I didn't get much sleep last night either. I guess I'm a bit temperamental. Sorry!"

Jack sat back down. "I understand completely," he said. "Been there a few times myself. But, we're here to help you...that is if we can."

"And we appreciate that," Carol said. "We are so happy that you have come."

There was another, much less tense silence.

Melissa broke the silence jokingly. "Well, now that we have gotten the pleasantries out of the way, why don't we get started?"

Jack leaned forward, took another swallow of coffee. "How about if I just give you a sort of biblical overview of the mark? Any particular questions you have after that, Melissa and I will try to answer if we can?"

"Sounds good to me," Adam said. He leaned into the table, looked across it to Carol.

Carol nodded her approval.

"God predicted," Jack began. "Let me restart that. God foretold that just before the last days of life as we know it. Ten nations would get together and form a pact. The final, original ten nations in that pact...a conglomeration of the countries belonging to the old Roman Empire. We have seen that part of the prophecy fulfilled with the formation of the European Common Market." Jack looked around the table for response. "Later known as the European Union," he said when he didn't see any. "You have both heard of that haven't you?"

Adam and Carol both nodded. But, neither really knew what it was, what it meant or that it was predicted to happen.

"It's the old Roman Empire?" Asked Carol.

"Greece was the tenth nation to join," Melissa said. "Completing the confederacy."

Jack said, "It's one of the 'beast' referred to in Revelation,"

"The ten heads with ten horns and ten crowns?" Adam, excitedly stated.

Realizing the meaning of the verse, he proudly proclaimed his knowledge.

"The heads; individual entities. The horns; armies. The crowns; kings. "Ten countries, ten armies, ten rulers combined into one?" Carol gasped.

"The European Union," Jack nodded. "But the real strength is economical. You control the money…you control the world."

"This is too much," Adam stood up. "You trying to tell me this was all predicted…foretold in the bible?"

"Thousands of years ago," Jack nodded. "But that is only the proverbial 'tip of the iceberg'. We haven't even began to touch on the mark."

"I don't think we have too. I think I know the end of this story already," Adam paced to the kitchen. "How's your coffee?"

"I'm good," Jack said.

"I want to hear," Carol said. "And I could use a refill." She held her empty cup up.

"Well, the mark is a number. And the beast, I'm not sure if it's the Common Market itself, or someone that rises up out of it, or both, really it doesn't make much difference which, but the beast will cause everybody to have the mark on them."

"How can that be?" Adam poured the coffee. He headed back to the counter in the kitchen to replace the pot on its base. "They couldn't force anybody that doesn't want it."

"Who said anything about 'force'. There's a big difference between 'cause' and 'force'. If you don't have the mark, you can't access your money."

"Which you won't have," Melissa said. "Because without the Mark you won't be able to earn any."

Adam sat, shaking his head, smirking again. "And how are they supposed to do that?"

"Already doing it," Jack smiled at him. "Ever hear of Mandatory Automatic Deposit? Several of the larger retail chains in America have it. No bank account…no work…no mark…no access to your account. Simple and most importantly, it's history."

"And I suppose God is totally against this mark?" Adam leaned in almost whispering.

Most assuredly," Melissa said. "Let's open our bibles to Revelation chapter fourteen.

The flipping of pages could be heard as Jack and Melissa waited patiently for Carol and Adam to find it.

"Read verses nine and ten," Melissa said, when the page turning had stopped.

Mouths fell agape as they read the verses depicting God's anger with all those who received the mark of the beast, or the number of his name. Adam realized why his mother, if she thought it was the mark, was so against the Signa-Chip.

Adam felt angry again. "If it's just some personal identification thing why would this God who is supposed to love everybody condemn them for just trying to survive? There's a lot worse things he could come down on us for."

"For one thing it's a lot more than 'just' a personal ID thing," Jack explained. "It's the final straw. God has let mankind get away with all kinds of atrocities against him, themselves, and each other. This is it. There will be no more middle of the road, no more gray area. You'll either choose to be with Him, or you'll choose to be against Him. And let me tell you which ever way people choose…it will be their final choice."

"You're talking end of the world stuff," Adam stood again. "The fanatics have been hollering that on the street corners for centuries. But here we still are."

"Just calm down," Carol said to him.

"Well, I don't believe all this crap." Adam paced around the kitchen.

"The prophecy says what it says," Jack turned toward Melissa. He knew that Adam wasn't really angry, but afraid. Afraid of the truth. Afraid of what it meant. Jack had seen the same reaction many times in the last few weeks. Even from some of the people that attended the very church he did.

"How does all of this fit in with the Signa-Chip?" Carol turned back to Jack.

"That I don't know for sure. Is the Signa-Chip the means by which the one world government is going to control currency? I can't answer that, I don't think anyone can yet. But it doesn't take a real stretch of the imagination to see it as viable. And I don't think it will take much longer to find out."

An eerie silence fell in the room. Adam stopped pacing, leaned against the sink countertop.

"Can I go out and play," Lindsey poked her head around the corner of the wall again.

"No sweetie," Carol said. "We're almost done talking in here and Mommy will take you out."

"Sounds more like you're fighting," Lindsey frowned.

"No," Carol smiled at her. "Daddy just got a little excited."

"I think we should get going," Jack announced to Melissa when Lindsey went back to the Saturday morning cartoons she had been watching. "Let these people think about what was said."

This time Adam didn't stop them, though Carol wished he would. She had more unanswered questions and this was her best chance to ask them.

"Like I said," Jack turned toward Adam. "It really doesn't matter what you, or I believe, or don't believe, the prophecy says what it says. Your only real choice now in the matter is to heed, or ignore the warning...But, as you're thinking about it, you may want to ask yourselves, who but God could know these things eons before they happened?"

"And your newspaper confirms them," Melissa added to Carol. "You are watching them happen right before your very eyes."

"Church Service starts at eleven o'clock tomorrow," Jack picked up his bible. "We would sure be glad to see you there."

Gary L. Dewey

15

No sooner had Ethan and Carl stepped out of the elevator door, mid-Saturday morning, into the lobby of the hotel in New York, where the late running seminar had taken place the night before and the reporter's cameras started flashing. Caught off guard by the sudden, unexpected volley of glaring lights, Ethan squinted, turning his head away from the blinding lights.

"Looks like we're becoming celebrities," Carl nudged him.

The questions came so fast and furious as the group of television and newspaper reporters pressed in on them, that neither was able to hear any of them. Only bits and pieces.

Confused by the unforeseen attention, Ethan pushed his way toward the exit door. "Excuse us," he repeated several times.

The group gave way but followed.

As they neared the exit, Ethan did distinguish a question coming from the group. He stopped and spun around. Narrowing his eyes, he scanned the small band. "What was that?" He asked for a reiteration. Not because he hadn't heard it the first time, but he couldn't believe what it was he had heard.

"Is it true that ESI was sold this morning to the German conglomerate World Technologies?" A short, stocky man with dark rimmed glasses asked.

"Did World Technologies purchase a block of controlling shares in ESI?" The second question came from another reporter.

Ethan focused on the tall, brown haired man in his late twenties who asked it. "Where did you hear that?"

The reporter hesitated.

Ethan turned to Carl. "Have you heard anything about any take over?"

Carl shook his head. "News to me."

"I'm sorry," Ethan said, turning back to the reporters. "We know nothing of this. So if you will excuse us, we need to catch a flight back to Chicago."

A new barrage of unintelligible questions came again.

Carl pushed open the glass entrance doors and stepped out under the covered approach to the hotel. A yellow cab pulled up and stopped.

Amid a new onslaught of flashing cameras, Ethan and Carl climbed in.

"To the airport James," Carl called out to the Asian driver.

The cab sped away as an American version of the paparazzi hurried after it.

Stunned by the news of a possible take over by a larger, European company, Ethan and Carl rode speechless until they neared the airport.

"This is starting to get too much to keep track of," Carl shook his head. "No doubt a restructuring is in the making."

"No doubt," Ethan agreed, worried about how secure his job was.

Something he never even had the slightest concern over for years. ESI was a profitable corporation and Signa-Chip promised to make it even more so. *Why*, he wondered, *would ESI want to sell out?*

Carl put Ethan's thoughts into words. "Promotions are more of a probability, I would think, over the possibility of dismissal."

"I'm not going to worry about it," Ethan said as the cab pulled up to the main airport terminal and they climbed out. "And I don't think you have anything to worry about either.

Carl tossed a twenty dollar bill at the cabby for the fifteen dollar fare as Ethan walked away. "I'm not," he said, catching up to him. "But, I know one thing for sure…if it's true ESI won't be the same place."

Ethan stopped and turned toward him. "And that might not be all that bad."

:

Adam lay down for a nap just after lunch. His head pounding from the lack of sleep and the turmoil within. Some of his questions about the mark had been answered by the little meeting with the Elsworths earlier, but he still had many more and it seemed to him the whole issue was a Pandora's box; the more answers he got, the more questions he had.

Carol came into the bedroom and pulled the drapes closed making the room a little darker. She sat on the bed next to him and ran her fingertips through his hair.

"I've got a headache that would kill the average man," Adam frowned.

She moved her fingers from his hair to his temples, rubbing them gently in a circular motion.

Regretting his unbecoming reactions to the biblical prophecies, Adam apologized for his earlier outburst.

"You don't need to apologize to me," Carol leaned over and kissed him on his forehead. "You did nothing to me. But I think you should say something to Jack and Melissa…After all you invited them over and were kinda rude to them."

"I know." Adam's mind wandered, totally enjoying the feel of Carol fingers.

"Well, Lindsey and I are going back over to my old apartment to get some more of our things," Carol told him. "And I need to stop by the bank before it closes and cash my paycheck."

"You want me to go with?"

"I don't think it's necessary. You should try to get some rest anyway." Carol sat back straight. "We're not going to do anything heavy. But, if you don't mind I'd like to use the truck?"

He reached into his pocket and handed her the keys.

Carol took them and stood. "We shouldn't be too long."

Adam turned onto his side toward her. "I just need an hour or so," he said, closing his eyes.

She kissed him again.

"Be careful," he said, without looking at her.

He was asleep, before Carol was out of the door. A deep, dream filled sleep. Forty-five minutes later, he awoke sweating. The dream containing the haunting images of his mother's funeral, cut his nap short. Adam rolled over and climbed off the bed to his feet.

He got up to an empty house with his head still aching. But the pain was no where near as sever as before. Nonetheless, he appreciated the relative silence in the house.

As he made a fresh pot of coffee, the thought of returning to work the day after tomorrow went through his head and made him mentally cringe. He'd like to...he needed to take another week off if he could get it. But knew, the way things had been going for him lately, he wouldn't. Though he knew he had the vacation time coming, that he could use, the company would surely want him in. Things would be an electrical mess in the machine shop. It was every time he was off for more than a day or two. He would have to straighten things out, before Kendell Industries would even think about allowing him anymore time away from the job.

Job security, Adam let himself smile. He could always count on the machinist to 'jury-rig' the components of the machines, to keep them running in his absence and a full time job getting the machines back in order, when he returned. He took his coffee, went toward the living room, still smiling at some of the ingenious, makeshift things the machinist had come up with over the years to bypass the elaborate circuitry on the computerized, metal cutting machines.

As Adam walked past the dinning room table, the bibles still in the same places as they were when Jack and Melissa left, he noticed a pamphlet one of them must have left behind. He picked it up on his way into the living room, reading the title, printed in big bold letters; **Revelations Revealed**.

He sat on the couch, set the pamphlet on the end table next to him and turned on the television. Changing the channel from the cartoon station Lindsey had been watching, he settled for the twenty-four hour news station.

Typical stuff, he thought, listening half-hearted to the detailed report of the suicide, terrorist attack in Israel that killed eight people.

"Just ahead," the newscaster announced after the terrorist story was over, "The expanding forest fire in Colorado, a four point two, earthquake in Japan, and the unannounced takeover of the maker of the new Signa-Chip, Electronic Solutions Incorporated by the Germany based World Technologies."

Adam sat up straight, abruptly, nearly spilling hot coffee on his lap.

Gary L. Dewey

Awaiting the 'takeover' story, wondering if World Technologies was a European Union governed company, he picked the 'Revealed' pamphlet back up and opened it.

There are many places in the Scriptures, the author of the two page pamphlet wrote, were God speaks to us of the final days of mankind's' allotted time on the earth. Among them: Jesus spoke in the twenty-fourth chapter of Matthew, of wars and rumors of wars, kingdoms against kingdoms, pestilence's, and earthquakes in various places. But, no where are we given such a detailed account as we are in the book of Revelation.

The news broadcast came back on after the commercials and Adam set the pamphlet down again, vowing to read more of it later.

As anticipated the 'takeover' story was the last of the three the newsman talked about. With compassion for the plight of the people involved, Adam listened to the reports about the Colorado fire that had already destroyed over five-thousand acres of forest and the earthquake that rocked Japan's coastal region killing three-hundred and twenty-seven people.

"In a four-hundred million dollar move," the newscaster started the buyout report. "World Technologies purchased a controlling block of ESI stock at the close of the New York Stock Exchange last night. The surprise, last minute move, by the third biggest European based electronics company would give it control over the manufacturing and sales of the new Signa-Chip that is taking this country by storm. The announcement was made this morning by CEO of World Technologies via satellite and caught even the upper management at ESI unawares. For a report here is our New York corespondent Elisa Holmes."

220

Adam leaned in toward the television for a closer look as the scene changed to a split screen of the station's news desk and the lobby of a large hotel.

"Good morning Elisa," the newscaster said.

"Good morning Matt," the blonde haired, reporter responded.

"Elisa, we're being told here that even the management at ESI had no idea that the company was being sold."

"That is correct," Elisa said, as the screen changed to a full view of her in the busy lobby. "In an attempted interview earlier today…"

The view changed to the film of Ethan surrounded by a group of reporters in the hotel lobby.

Elisa's voice could be heard behind the film. "We asked Ethan Blake, Sales Manager at Electronic Solutions if he knew of the purchase," she said. "Ethan and Carl Torre, the Public Relations Manager at ESI, were in New York after giving a presentation of the Signa-Chip to an audience of about five-hundred people last night."

"Is it true that ESI was sold this morning to the German conglomerate World Technologies?" The question was heard as the taped interview ran.

The look of surprise on Ethan's face was obvious as he spun around to face the reporters. His eyes narrow.

"Did World Technologies purchase a block of controlling shares in ESI?" The reporter asked again.

There was a slight jump in the tape as Ethan turned to Carl. "Have you heard anything about any take over?"

Carl shook his head. "News to me."

"I'm sorry," Ethan said, turning back to the reporters. "We know nothing of this. So if you will excuse us, we need to catch a flight back to Chicago."

There was another jump in the tape. It resumed, showing Ethan climbing into the back seat of a yellow taxicab with Carl and the taxi pulling away.

The TV screen went back to Elisa in the lobby. "So, as you could see from that tape Matt, all indications are that even the managers at ESI had no idea about any takeover of the company."

"Thank you for that report," Matt said, as the view changed back to him at his news desk.

"Coming up after the break...more on the continuing search for members of the terrorist group responsible for the deadly bombing Wednesday of the British Embassy in south-east Africa."

Adam, lost in thought, leaned back on the couch and closed his eyes. The opening of the front door jerked his mind back to the present. Carol and Lindsey came in. Each carried a box proportionate to their size.

"Is there more?" Adam stood up to help.

"Lots and lots," Lindsey rushed into her bedroom with the box of toys she carried.

"Most of it can stay in the garage, or go in the basement," Carol said. "It's just a bunch of odds-n-ends."

Thirty minutes later, all three of them flopped down on the couch, Lindsey between them. The pickup truck load of boxes full of bric-a-brac, toys, and kitchen utensils, stacked neatly along one of the walls in the semi-finished basement.

"That was a lot of work," Adam patted Lindsey on the head. "Why didn't you wait until I could help?" He directed his question to Carol.

"You did," Lindsey looked up at him and answered for her. "How else did all them boxes get downstairs?"

"I meant over at the apartment," Adam smiled at her.

Carol asked, "How's your headache?"

He nodded that it felt better.

"You get any sleep?"

He kept nodding. "'Bout an hour," he said.

"Feel good enough to go to the bank for me?"

"Sure."

"Can I go?" Lindsey chimed in.

"Didn't have time to make it?" Adam eyed her disheveled hair.

She caught his look and brushed the strands of hair hanging in her face back over her head. "No," she said. "I did go to my bank but they wouldn't cash my check. Said since I didn't have an account there anymore they couldn't do it. Can you believe that?" Carol was hurt, angry, almost shouting, remembering the incident. She brushed her loose hair back again "I've been dealing with that bank for twelve years. They've even financed two cars for me. And now because that creep depleted my account they won't even cash my paychecks."

"Well, why didn't you just use your check to open a new account? We have enough money to make it for the few days it'd take for your check to clear the bank."

Lindsey's head slowly swung back and forth, looking intensely at whoever was speaking.

"That's just it," Carol stood up, walking toward the kitchen. Signaling Adam that she didn't want Lindsey to hear the rest.

Adam delayed following her, rolled over onto Lindsey, tickling her armpit.

Lindsey burst out in laughter as she struggled to get free. Adam wouldn't let her go. Tickled her again. When she was done laughing, he sat up, switched the television back to the 'Kids Cartoon Network'. He joined Carol in the kitchen, leaving Lindsey behind in a trance, mesmerized by the cartoon show.

Adam walked up next to Carol and put his hand on her shoulder. She was trembling. Mascara tracks under her eyes said that she had been crying.

"What's wrong babes?"

"Nothing," she said turning to the paper towel dispenser hanging under the cupboard. "It's just that bank," she said, pulling off a sheet of paper towel and dabbing the corners of her eyes with it.

"What's with the bank?" Adam stepped beside her.

"I tried to open a new account, but I couldn't, they wouldn't let me."

"What's up with that?" Adam felt himself getting angry too. "I've never heard of such a thing."

"Welcome to the new age," Carol went and sat at the table. "My bank has a new policy...Are you ready for this?"

Adam sat across from her and nodded.

"All new accounts are totally electronic. No ATM cards, no checks, no walk-ins or drive through, only direct deposits."

"Sounds like a dream come true. You'd never have to worry about someone stealing your ATM card ever again"

She glared at him. "Except you have to have the chip to access and use the funds."

The room grew quiet except for the sounds emanating from the television in the living room.

"This is getting a little too freaky for me," Adam said. "I don't like it at all."

"What if your mother and Jack and Melissa are right about this chip? That this thing is one of the 'end of times' signs?"

"You know what you are saying," Adam stood up, his headache starting to return with a vengeance. He paced around the table.

"I know exactly what I'm saying. I'm admitting the validity of the prophecy and consequently the existence of a God, we have both denied all of our lives."

"I'm not ready to admit to that," Adam circled the table again. "Just listen to all the crap out there. Everybody has got it right in their own minds and everybody else is wrong. I don't buy into that and neither do you."

"No I don't," Carol's eyes followed him around the table. "That though doesn't mean there isn't a truth 'out there' somewhere among all the 'crap'. And just because there are many false religions doesn't negate the legitimacy of a God."

The more Adam listened to Carol's reasoning, the more agitated he felt. The part of his mind that, in light of the prophecy; could no longer deny the existence of a God, was mocked by the other part that rejected the logic. Agitated, not that he didn't give credibility to the prophecy, it was becoming to obvious to ignore, but he simply couldn't deal with the guilt he felt. Adam realized the possibility that he had woefully denied God and his mother all of his life.

"Why don't you sit down honey?" Carol said. "I'm getting a headache following you around the table."

"I'm getting one too," Adam stopped behind his chair, put the thumb of his right hand on his right temple and stretched his finger across to his left temple massaging his forehead.

"Maybe we should talk about this at some other time?" Carol offered.

"No I want to get this over with now." Adam sat, still rubbing his temples.

"Well, as far as I'm concerned," Carol said. "It is over already."

Adam let his hand drop to the table and looked across at her. His eyebrows slightly raised.

Firmly, Carol said, "There's just too much symmetry between the mark and this Signa-Chip for it all to be just coincidence. And that along with all the other details of this Revelation stuff, which I'm sure we only know a small part of, there's just too much similarity to take the chance. Especially as far as Lindsey is concerned."

Adam nodded his agreement.

"Jack's words keep coming back to me," Carol reached out and took his hand in hers. "'Who but God could have known these things, thousands of years before they happened?'"

The part of Adam that didn't want to accept the connection between the bible prophecy and the chip tried to justify its use. "The chip does have its good points!. Look at that girl in Chicago." Adam spoke more trying to convince himself. "And I'm sure that scenario has been repeated several times in the last few days. The more popular the chip gets the more lives it will save."

"I'm not contesting that at all. I'm sure with all the things they can use it for, some of them are going to be great. But, you know as well as I do, this Signa-Chip is going to come to no good. And if it's part of this 'mark' thing. I want no part of it! For me, my daughter, or anybody else I care about, including you."

"I hate this," Adam stood up again, but didn't pace. "I feel like I'm being backed into a corner with no way out."

"Isn't that exactly what Jack and Melissa said? It's time to choose. No more gray areas. No more middle of the road.

It's either take the chip, deny God forever, and reap the rewards of that decision or make a stand."

"You know you might make a great preacher someday," Adam squeezed her hand and smiled. "Sound just like one."

"This is serious honey," Carol squeezed back. "This just may very well be the most important decision of our lives."

Adam's smile disappeared. "If this chip and the mark are one and the same," he said. "There is no doubt in my mind it will be. But it's a decision that's being forced on us and I don't like that…not one bit."

:

Ethan spotted the two, dark suited men leaning against the back wall, as soon as he stepped out of the collapsible tunnel that connected their airplane with the terminal. They were the same two men he had seen in the elevator at the hotel in Detroit. He elbowed Carl and nodded in their direction.

"Looks like we got company," Carl said, recognizing them also.

Ethan looked ahead at the line of passengers dispersing into the terminal. "I wonder what those government guys want with us? They're starting to get on my nerves."

"Getting a little paranoid in our old age are we," Carl mocked him. "I'm sure of two things," he added getting serious with him. "One, its got something to do with Signa-Chip. Second, we're about to find out."

Ethan turned to look for them but they were gone. He scanned the crowd of passengers and those who showed up to greet them.

"Ethan Blake?" A deep, stern voice from behind startled him.

Gary L. Dewey

He turned quickly to face the indifferent, eyes of the taller of the two men, staring directly into his eyes. The man towered over Ethan's five-foot-eleven frame by a good three inches and outweighed him by fifty pounds.

"Douglas Kolar, World Technologies," the man flashed his ID. "My partner, Jake Miller."

Jake, about an inch shorter than Douglas, twenty-five pounds lighter, weighing in at about two-thirty, never flinched, never smiled, or changed his countenance with his introduction.

Uneasy with the thug-like appearance and demeanor of the men, Ethan reached behind him and pulled Carl beside him. "Carl Torre," Ethan introduced his counterpart too. He pulled Carl around, figuring that if these guys wanted to 'get rough', he wanted them to know there were two of them also. Though he knew if they did, he and Carl were no match for the much bigger, stronger men.

"We know who he is," Douglas said.

"What can we do for you gentlemen?" Carl responded, putting as much depth to his voice as he could.

Ethan scanned the area for a security guard but couldn't see one.

"Mister Randolph would like to speak with you. So, if you'll just follow me," Douglas said as he turned to walk away.

"We're not going anywhere," Ethan recoiled expecting anything.

"Who is this Mister Randolph?" Carl said.

"Director in charge of the United States District for World Technologies," Jake finally spoke. "And your new boss's boss. So if you want to stay employed, I suggest you and your friend here follow us."

"Don't mean dittle to either one of us." Douglas kept walking.

Jake fell into step next to him.

Carl looked at Ethan. Both of them were confounded.

"Wait up," Ethan called out.

16

Sixty year old Leonard Randolph handed his empty Bourbon glass to the woman sitting next to him. "Gentlemen," the gray haired, World Technologies Director lowered the rear window of the black, mini-stretch Limousine and cheerfully beckoned Ethan and Carl closer.

With reserve, Ethan cautiously approached the Limo, leaned forward, peering through the half lowered window into the expanded back seat area of the Cadillac. Within the vehicle, nothing appeared threatening; Two, black leather, bench seats facing each other; an old man, dressed in an expensive looking, dark blue, pin striped, three piece suit and sitting on the rear most seat. Next to him, separated by an opened, black, briefcase, a pretty, red headed woman, in a mint green pants suit, Ethan guessed in her late twenties.

He leaned back trying to look through the heavily tinted side windows into the front seat, but couldn't. He leaned back in again, hoping to see through the thick, sliding glass partition that separated the driver's area from the passenger's. It too was visually impregnable.

Nevertheless, despite not knowing who, or what was in the front seat, Ethan felt the greater threat came from without, in the persons of the two men that they had followed out to the car.

"Come in," Leonard motioned again. Jake reached behind Ethan opening the vehicle's center door.

Ethan straightened up and backed away, letting Carl climb into the limousine ahead of him. To Ethan's relief, he noticed Douglas and Jake backing away and standing at a distance when he followed Carl in and closed the door.

Despite the heat of the summer's early afternoon in the airport parking lot the air conditioning inside the limo was cold. Cold enough to cause goose bumps to rise up on Ethan's arms. He rubbed them down. *Any colder*, he thought, and *the windows would frost up.*

The Cadillac started to move as Hilda set the empty Bourbon glass in a holder recessed in the side panel of the modified Cadillac.

"Let me introduce myself, Leonard Randolph." He extended his hand out to Ethan first and then Carl. "This is my personal secretary Hilda Aldous."

Hilda raised a delicate hand to Ethan but just nodded toward Carl.

From the look on Ethan's face, Leonard could see that there was a concern over the moving car. "Don't be alarmed, Mister Blake," Mister Randolph said. "You gentlemen are in need of rides home are you not?"

Carl nodded, letting his eyes slowly climb up Hilda's legs to her red, silky hair, pulled up in a bun atop her head and wondered what she would look like if she let it fall down around her shoulders.

"This will give us a chance to meet each other and talk. And provide you with a service too."

Upset by the audacity of World Technologies, Ethan said, "It's just all this 'cloak n' dagger' stuff that has gotten me a little concerned." Learning that he was being watched by the company, invading his privacy, didn't make him feel all too comfortable either.

Leonard chuckled. "You must mean Kolar and Miller?" He threw his thumb up and used it to point behind him. "Quite a pair aren't they? Take their work a bit seriously, I tell them."

"That's the understatement of the year," said Carl, while looking at Hilda's face to see if she had noticed him visually disrobing her. She hadn't. At least not that he could tell.

"But at times, I have to admit, it can come in right handy," Leonard said.

Ethan's narrowed eyes told Leonard that he didn't understand. "I can't see why they would be watching us anyway. I saw them in Detroit, New York and now here."

"We at World Technologies work all around the world," Leonard's face took on a stern demeanor as he tried to justify Douglas and Jake. "Because of that, we can find ourselves in some pretty hostile places, dealing with some quite unfriendly people at times." He leaned back deeper into the plush seat. "We like to know a little bit about who the people are we're dealing with before we connect with them. Mister Kolar and Mister Miller are just doing their jobs."

"I assume that we passed the test," Ethan relaxed a little himself.

"You're here are you not," Hilda said, with a tone of condescension.

"Be nice," Mister Randolph said to her.

Hilda smirked. "One of them arrogant, the other already has me naked and stretched out on the bed in some sleazy motel."

Carl quickly turned his head looking out the side window at the passing traffic.

"What is this I hear that World Technologies has purchased ESI?" Ethan said, looking with disdain at the back of Carl's head.

"You have heard correctly," Leonard said. "Though we haven't actually purchased the company, we just bought enough stock to own a controlling interest...And that will not be officially announced until Monday morning."

A bit sneaky of you wasn't it, Ethan thought but didn't say it. Instead, he asked why nobody at ESI knew of the intentions of World Technologies.

"Such is life," Mister Randolph said. "We have been keeping an eye on ESI for some time now. The stock became available and we just made a snap decision."

What he didn't tell Ethan was that World Technologies had to pay nearly double the going price for the stock they needed to obtain the fifty-one percent of ESI.

Ethan's thoughts wandered as he wondered just how long Douglas and Jake had been watching him. He searched his memory for where he may have seen them before, but couldn't recall seeing them before the Detroit presentation.

"So, there has got to be more to this than just giving us a ride home?" Carl rejoined the conversation, purposely avoiding eye contact with Hilda.

Matter-of-factly Leonard said, "Now that you asked," and leaned forward in the seat. "Because you two are the most familiar with the Signa-Chip. We would like for you and Ethan to fly to the World Technologies headquarters in Munich and hold some 'Train the Trainer' sessions on the presentation process. We are going to take the Signa-Chip world wide and we need you two gentlemen to help us build up a staff of people capable of holding convincing seminars, wherever we send them…Success means a promotion."

"And how long do you think this is going to take?" Ethan asked.

"We have allotted two weeks to the program," Hilda said. "Give or take a day or so. The more efficient you are, the less time it should take."

Wiggling uncomfortably in his seat, Carl said, "That's a long time away from home."

"We can have your two lady friends flown over if you'd like?" Hilda was still sarcastic toward him.

Carl's mind went into a fury as the realization that his escapades with Beverly and Delia were witnessed and Hilda was privy to that. No doubt, he surmised, by way of Douglas and Jake.

Ethan had the same revelation, glad again that he had distanced himself from the trio back in New York.

"What I do in my private life is just that...private," Carl snapped back.

"People," Mister Randolph said firmly. He leaned back into the seat again. "Let's just try to get along. We're going to be seeing a lot of each other in the near future."

"So, why couldn't this all wait until Monday," Ethan asked, hoping to ease the mounting tension. "This could have been done at ESI."

"Well, for one thing, Hilda and I are flying back to Munich as soon as we are done here and we won't be around Monday. For another, Ryan Page is out. Herbert Hannson will be taking over the position of CEO at ESI. And I thought it better if I talked to you in person first."

Carl, still angry with the thoughts of his privacy being invaded by his employer, made no attempt to hide his feelings in the tone of his voice when he asked, "Are you meeting with all the ESI managers?".

"No! For now just you two...I saw no real need for that at this time. You two were the more important. Especially, since I needed you to go to Germany for me."

"When is all this supposed to take place?" Ethan fidgeted in his seat.

"We would like to get started with the Train the Trainer classes A.S.A.P.," Hilda said. "Preferably Monday or Tuesday morning. But we would like you and Carl in Munich tomorrow night."

"That's not much notice for such a long trip," Ethan protested.

"If you can't do it," Mister Randolph leaned forward again, paused, then settled back. "I'm sure we can find somebody who can."

Hilda said, "I have your tickets right here." She reached into the open briefcase, extracted two envelopes, each containing two non-dated, round trip airline tickets. "Two for use at your discretion," she added, extending her hand out.

Carl took his tickets immediately.

Ethan paused, he didn't like the intonation of Leonard's comment and what it implied. But, having no desire to become among the unemployed, Ethan reached out, reluctantly grasping the envelope and slowly pulled it back toward him.

"Good," Mister Randolph said. "We will be expecting you than…no later than Sunday night?"

"And don't forget," Hilda added. Munich is six hours ahead of you.

Ethan glanced over to Carl who was inspecting the contents of his envelope. "We'll be there."

"Oh by the way," Leonard said, as the Limousine turned onto Ethan's block. "Doctor Reece will be there too."

Ethan forced an insincere smile. Something he was getting good at lately.

"Call me later," Carl said as Ethan climbed out after the limo had stopped in front of his house. "We need to talk."

Ethan nodded he would but knew he wouldn't. Every minute of his time, he intended on spending with his family, not on the telephone with Carl, listening to him complain about the unethical practices of World Technologies and the injustices he felt.

∴

Nicole shouted, "I want to know why it is you have to go?" She turned away from Ethan and went into the kitchen. "You just got home last night and you've got to leave already. And of all places Germany. Half the way around the world."

Ethan followed her. And torn between wanting to go and feeling the need to remain at home said, "It's my job." Though the excitement of being part of Signa-Chip becoming international, carried much more weight with it than the threat of losing his job. "I have no real choice in the mater," he added for impact.

Nicole turned and looked out of the window above the kitchen sink at the rays of the early Sunday morning sun casting its shadows across the uncut lawn.

"A new company has taken control of ESI and they want Carl and I to go to Munich," Ethan explained and turned the argument around. "What did you expect me to say to them, no?"

Nicole turned back to him and Ethan could plainly see from the look on her face, his words did little to comfort her.

The stress Renee's kidnapping had on her left her feeling alone and paranoid. Those feelings, augmented by Ethan being out of town and the lack of time he spent with her, or his children the past weeks, increased with the news her husband was leaving the country. And it showed on her face.

Ethan knew why Nicole felt neglected. But, he was looking at the chance of a lifetime and he wasn't going to let it pass him by.

"Are you guys fighting again?" Renee' suddenly appeared in the kitchen. Awakened by the 'heated' tone in her parent's conversation, she stood in the kitchen doorway, dressed in an ankle length night shirt rubbing her eyes.

"No sweetie," Nicole forced a smile at her. "Daddy and I are just talking about a trip he has to make.

"Are you going away again?" Renee' innocently asked, obviously troubled by the thought.

"Why don't you go back to bed for a little while," Nicole told her without answering the question. "We'll talk about it later."

Renee' retreated.

"I don't know what to expect from you anymore," Nicole started to cry. "It just seems like all that's important to you lately is your job."

Ethan hated it when Nicole cried. He always felt so guilty when she did.

"Just look at it this way," he went over to hug her. More to stop her from crying, so he didn't have to feel guilty, than to comfort her. "If I hadn't worked so much," he wrapped his arms around her, "and everything had been delayed by just one day, Renee' might not be here with us now."

"I know," whimpered Nicole. "I just feel so helpless lately and Renee', the poor child, is scared out of her mind and I think her daddy should be around for her."

"And I would. Except this new company has taken over and if I don't go to Germany, I could very well lose my job. Then what? I would be no good to you or the kids. You wouldn't want that now would you?"

Feeling ambivalent, Nicole pulled away from his embrace. "I guess not." She turned to the sink for a glass of water. "Do you have any idea how long you're going to be gone?"

"Shouldn't be more than a couple of days," Ethan lied. Knowing that he would have to call Nicole later in the week and provide her with an excuse as to why it was taking longer than he had originally promised it would, he set it up. "I'll call if it's going to be any longer than that."

"I think I'm going to take the kids and go stay by my parents while you're gone." Nicole took a long drink, knowing that Ethan's, 'a couple of days', would probably turn into a couple of weeks.

"Sounds like a good idea to me," Ethan smiled, feeling victorious. "But, in the mean time, I still have a few hours before I have to leave, what do you say we get the kids and go out for some breakfast?"

⋮

Adam was up late again, watching the national news. Along with the typical news, there were two stories on kidnapped victims. One six year old child, implanted with the Signa-Chip, was recovered twenty minutes after her abduction in Portland, Oregon. The police also had arrested her captor, a twenty-nine year old man wanted in connection with two other kidnappings.

The other, a four year old boy in Atlanta, Georgia, with no chip, was still missing. The child's parents came on the television screen, giving a heart wrenching plea to whoever had taken their son, begging for them to return him. More mixed emotions about the virtues of the chip flooded into Adam's mind, as his heart went out to the tearful mother.

After the clip, Adam got up and went into the kitchen for a glass of Vernors. He stood leaning against the sink drinking most of it before he returned to the living room couch. He was just in time to hear the tail end of a story about a seventy-eight year old man who had wander away from a senior citizens hospice in Denver and who had not yet been located.

Gary L. Dewey

He took another sip of his drink, pointing the remote at the television, he changed channels to the local news. The local broadcast was nearly over. The sports announcer giving a wrap-up of the Detroit Tigers, six, one, loss to the Toronto Blue Jays.

He pushed the off button on the remote and the television went dead. For a moment he sat there in the stillness, staring at the blank screen. No thoughts at all going through his mind.

Carol who had gone to bed an hour ago, unable to fall into much of a sleep, was awakened by the deep 'boomp' sound of the stereo TV going off and the ensuing quietness. As she walked into the room, her voice broke the silence of the moment, startling him. "You still up?" She asked, sitting heavily on the couch next to him.

"Couldn't sleep?" Adam answered her obvious question with one of his own.

"Naw," she shook her head sleepily. "Too much on my mind I guess."

"Where's that brochure I got when I went to that presentation of the chip?"

Groggy, Carol thought for a moment. "On top of the refrigerator," she said, yawning.

"You coming to bed soon?" She asked, when he got up to get it.

"Soon," he answered, disappearing around the corner of the dinning room wall.

"I'm going back to bed," Carol said, to no one there.

Adam got back to the living room, in time to see Carol, half walking, half sliding her way back toward the bedroom. "I'll be just a few minutes," he said.

Weakly she raised her hand, waved at him over her shoulder.

Forty-five minutes later, Adam set the Signa-Chip brochure down on the couch next to him. With a heightened interest he had read every descriptive word in the brochure. Not as he had lightly scanned it the first time.

The more he read, the more he found the potential of the chip fascinating. The words: 'Just about any application your mind can imagine an implantable, micro-chip could be used for', intrigued him most. His mind struggled though, with how much liberty those benefits would cost.

At twelve-thirty in the morning, Adam climbed into bed with Carol. His mental energy for the day spent, he curled up next to her, falling asleep within minutes. It was the best night of sleep he had for the week.

He was the last to arise, in the morning. The smell of fresh coffee tickling his nostrils was what eventually woke him.

"Can I go to Sunday School today?" Lindsey bounced on the bed next to him and completed the job of awakening him totally.

"We girls were talking about it this morning," Carol, standing in the bedroom doorway in her flowered housecoat smiled. "If we could get you up and talk you into it."

"What time is it?" Adam got up on an elbow and squinted toward the alarm clock on the mirrored dresser across the room.

"Almost nine," Carol answered.

Adam, collapsed back down on his pillow.

"Come on sleepy head," Lindsey continued to bounce.

"What time does Sunday School start?" Adam reached out, gently grabbing Lindsey by the shoulders to stop her from jouncing him around anymore.

"Jack said eleven, remember?" Carol said. "That gives us a couple of hours to get ready. Lindsey and I have already eaten…had our showers too."

He really didn't want to go, but could see from the look on their faces, tell from the excitement in their voices, that if he said 'no', both of the women in his life would be very disappointed.

"Well, I can't very well get up with you two women standing there staring at me, now can I?"

When they departed, leaving him alone in the room, Adam rolled out from between the sheets. He buried his face back into his pillow, reluctant to get up. Not because he was tired, he felt well rested. But it meant that he was going to go to church, something he never thought he would ever do again.

It would be the first time, in a long enough time, that Adam couldn't remember when the last time it was he had been in a church. A spans of time he wasn't anxious to come to an end. Especially since he didn't even know what kind of church Jack and Melissa Elsworth attended. *It would be an unfamiliar one at best,* he thought, */ hope it's not some kind of cult we'll have to fight our way out of. Or worse yet, one with a screaming preacher, we'll have to endure for hours.*

Climbing from the bed, Adam smiled at himself. Amused by the ridiculous excuses he came up with for not wanting to go.

After a lite breakfast of scrambled eggs and toast, Adam took his coffee and went into the living room. While the 'girls' dressed, he turned on the Sunday Morning news. The news, for the most part: a re-scripted version of last night's stories, except for the one on the big fire that had broken out in the central California national forest.

"Aided by a strong Southwesterly wind, the fast moving fire has engulfed several thousand acres already," the news-reporter read the transcript. "Trapping at least thirty-five people, many of which are families who had been hiking and camping in the area."

The thirty-ish, blonde haired television reporter looked up at the camera as she turned the pages on the desk in front of her. "Rescue crews are desperately searching for them." She dropped her eyes to read. "Before the growing flames totally consume everyone and thing in its path." She looked up again for effect. "Impeded by the scorching heat and bellowing, clouds of black smoke filling the region, rescuers are not very optimistic."

Tired of hearing so much bad news, Adam switched channels, searching for something more lighthearted, finally settling for the cartoon station. But even that was filled with violence. He shut the TV set off as Lindsey danced into the room. Spinning for him, adorned in a white, sun dress with a puppy in a playful pose printed on the skirt, her blonde hair, in tight little curls, bouncing as she came in, Lindsey grinned at him.

"Wow! Don't we look pretty," Adam teased her.

"Your turn," Carol said, stepping through the doorway two steps behind Lindsey's 'Grand Entrance'.

"Look at you," Adam exclaimed. "I'm not worthy."

The eggshell white, knee length dress Carol wore, matched her lightly tanned skin and shimmering golden hair perfectly. She looked like a goddess to Adam as she swayed into the room.

"Oh stop," Carol said, walking over to him. She bent down and kissed him on the cheek, leaving a smudge of pale pink, lipstick on the stubble.

"I don't need church," Adam leaned back in his seat, a slight scent of Carol's perfume wafting through the air. "I have died and am already in heaven. Surrounded by two beautiful angles."

"Stop," Carol blushed.

Lindsey grabbed his hand trying to pull him to his feet. "Come on!" She tugged.

Carol turned her wrist, looked at her watch. "Yeah, come on," she said. "It's almost ten o'clock already."

:

The parking lot of the little non-denominational church on seventeen mile road was nearly full. Adam pulled Carol's Pontiac Grand Am into the back section of the lot behind the white church building. It appeared more like a house, to Adam, than a church,

"It looks like we're too late already," Adam said, parking in one of the few remaining spaces. "Everybody is inside already."

"We still have ten minutes," Carol glanced at her watch again. "According to Jack and Melissa services don't start until eleven."

Another vehicle came into the lot, parking two rows over from them. A mid-aged couple climbed from the red, Ford Escort, casually dressed in blue jeans and matching tops. Each carried a bible in hand. They waved hello to Adam, Carol, and Lindsey as they walked past in front of them.

"Think we might be a little over dressed," Adam looked in the rearview mirror and adjusted his tie.

"Are we getting out?" Lindsey questioned from the back seat.

17

World Technologies Headquarters in Munich; a massive, octagon shaped building, with a dark, tinted glass exterior, towered twelve stories above the next tallest structure in the vicinity. Miniaturizing everything else around it, the edifice gleamed in the Monday morning sun like a huge diamond. Inside the ten foot high, solid glass entrance doors on the ground floor, a highly polished, black and white, marbled interior, greeted Ethan and Carl. Straight ahead of them, centralized in the open space of the reception area, a large, marbled, circular counter stood. On either side of the counter, two, three cushioned, white leather couches sat, separated by oak end tables from matching over stuffed chairs.

On one of the couches sat a man in a brown suit talking with a woman dressed in a pale yellow pants suit. They mulled over the contents of several open folders, setting on the rectangular table in front of them.

Behind the counter an armed guard and a receptionist sat. Both turning to look at Ethan and Carl as they neared.

Carl brushed the palm of his hand against one of the half dozen, eight foot thick, interior support pillars that dotted the twenty-five hundred square foot area. His eyes following the pillar upwards until it disappeared, into the ceiling two stories above them.

"Ethan Blake and Carl Torre from Electronic Solutions, of the United States," Ethan said, placing his hands on the waist high, counter top.

The couple on the couch glanced up momentarily.

The pretty, twenty-four year old, naturally blonde telephone operator/receptionist shuffled through a few sheets of paper on the lower desk top, next to the vertical telephone board. She found the one that listed the persons expected to come in for the day. Finding Ethan's name on the list and the contact person's extension number next to it, she plugged in the phone jack.

"Misters Blake and Torre are here," she said into the mouthpiece of the headset she wore.

Her lack of accent surprised Ethan. The receptionist's perfect English made him feel like he could be in 'anyplace' USA.

"Have a seat," she said to Ethan, glancing up at them. "Someone will be down to get you in a few moments."

Within five minutes, a smartly dressed man in his early forties came up to them. "Mister Blake?" The dark haired man, with deep set eyes, extended his hand toward Carl.

Carl stood, taking the hand. "I'm Mister Torre."

"Welcome," the man said, then turned to Ethan. "Mister Blake?"

"Good morning," Ethan said shaking his hand.

"William Schehr," the slightly heavy set man introduced himself. "Would you come with me."

They followed him across the reception area toward a wall of dark, smoked glass. Next to a pair of matching brass door handles, William stopped at a small numbered keypad, fastened to the glass. He punched in several numbers and waited for the telltale click of the lock opening.

Ethan smiled inwardly, recalling ESI's, antiquated, pre-Signa-Chip, security system.

Beyond the tinted glass door wall, a bustle of activity replaced the relative complacency of the reception area. At least a hundred people moved back and forth across the marbled floor. Along the western exterior wall, a large indoor garden, complete with indigenous plants and trees, a twelve-hundred gallon fountain pool, and white, marble and stone benches, graced the enclosure.

On one side of the garden, an open, spiraling, iron stairway lead up to the second level that held several retail shops. Ethan was surprised to see the familiar McDonalds fast food restaurant emblem outside one of the shops.

William led them over to a bank of elevators. Again punching his identification code into a numeric pad mounted next to the up/down button for the conveyance.

The ninth floor of the building, where the conference room Ethan and Carl were to give the first of many Train the Trainer' seminars, was totally different from what Ethan had expected. Instead of the unburdened, open areas of the first and second floors, the ninth was a series of long, connected hallways. Each dotted with numerous, closed, wood grain, office doors and each office door equipped with its own four by six inch keypad mounted on the wall next to it.

Ethan noted that the beautiful, polished marble walls and floors of the reception area had given way to inexpensive, smooth painted wallboard and black flecked, commercial tile.

Their escort led them down the first hallway to the left of the elevators. "Here we are," William stopped walking, again he punched his security code into the keypad before reaching for the brass handle on the door marked with a plaque: 'Conference Room' 904.

Ethan wondered, as William swung the door of the large, centralized room open, if it was Mister Schehr's exclusive job to pick people up from 'Reception' and take them where they needed to go or if he had other responsibilities.

Stepping into the room, Ethan noticed right away, that despite all the glass he saw surrounding the building, there were no windows in Room 904. Rows of recessed neon ceiling lights were providing all the illumination.

"Good Morning Gentlemen," came from beside them.

Ethan and Carl turned.

"I take it your flight was pleasant and uneventful?" Hilda Aldous, the only other occupant in the room, smiled.

They both nodded their response.

From the six foot long, folding table in front of her, Hilda picked up two matching, leather folders, handing one each to Ethan and Carl. "Inside," Hilda explained, "and of major importance, You will find a security form. I need you both to sign it. Basically, it says that whatever you hear, see, or discuss pertaining to the business within World Technologies while you are here...stays here. Under the threat of immediate termination of employment and, or possible prosecution, your signature verifies that you are aware of and agree to those terms."

Hilda saw from the hesitancy that Ethan and Carl were reluctant.

William stepped into the room letting the door close behind him.

Suddenly, Ethan got the feeling that escorting people around was not William's only job. Unconsciously, he looked around to see if Douglas and Jake were nearby too.

"Everyone who works up here has signed one," Hilda added, hoping to ease the reluctance. "We need it to get you clearance to work above the fifth floor."

"And if we don't sign?" Carl, took the folder from her, ignoring William. His animosity toward Hilda still lingering from they're first meeting. But, his training as a Public Relations Manager over-rode his personal feelings and Carl was genuinely curious to know if there were alternatives in World Technologies's employment policies to signing the form.

"Your employment with ESI will be terminated. Effective immediately," Hilda answered instantly, misinterpreting the intent of the question. And regarding it as a snide comment. "Company policy," she turned toward Ethan. "Besides, our automatic security system will not allow you into certain areas of our company, unless you have the proper clearance, and we can not give you that clearance until you sign the agreement."

"Where do we sign?" Ethan took his folder and opened it.

"Print your name here," Hilda pointed to the line on the bottom left corner. "Date it and sign here." She moved her finger to the right side of the form. "Press hard," she added. "There are three copies."

"I'd like to read some of this over before I sign," Carl interrupted Hilda. "My policy," he returned her forced smile.

"Sure. Why don't you two just have a seat.?" She swung her hand in a motion toward any of the six other empty, long, rectangular tables in the room. "Take as long as you need."

Ethan followed Hilda's hand over the two rows of tables that matched the one she occupied. Opting for the nearest, Ethan sat.

"Am I done here Miss Aldous?" William asked.

"I think so," Hilda nodded. "But, don't wander too far. After these gentlemen sign the security forms. You can start bringing some of the people in."

Presumptuous, Carl thought with disdain, while seating himself next to Ethan. Another trait he disliked in Hilda. Adding it to the growing list of negatives he planned on keeping in her regard.

"Also, in that same folder," Hilda said. "You will find a printout of a list of items concerning the Signa-Chip that I think we need to address during the seminars. If you would look those items over, eliminating those that you think unnecessary and adding any that you think pertinent, I would appreciate it."

Ethan glanced over the security form, signed it and turned to the list of items Hilda wanted addressed. The list was complete in his eyes and he told her so.

"Good," she said, moving between the tables. She took Ethan's original folder back, and exchanged it with another. This one constructed of a thick, almost cardboard cover, in a brilliant blue. "We took the liberty to have these printed," she added, dropping the other one on the table in front of Carl. "Everyone participating in the training sessions will get one."

Ethan quickly thumbed through the folder's pages.

"Basically it explains the Signa-Chip and some of its intended uses," Hilda said. "Feel free to use it as a guide to assist you…if you find anything helpful."

After he had signed the security form, Carl said, "Here," and handed the leather folder he had back to her.

Hilda reopened it. She verified that he had actually signed it, before setting it down on the table behind her, atop Ethan's. "Well, if you don't have any questions," she said. "Why don't we get started?"

"Is Doctor Reece here yet?" Carl asked.

"Yes," Hilda answered. "But, he will not be joining us."

Ethan looked up at her.

"He is up on the fifteenth floor. They are working on a way to make the chip non-removable once implanted and activated. We want to be absolutely as sure as possible that once the ID number is assigned to someone and is in the system, it stays there."

"How about malfunctioning chips or in the event the person dies?" Ethan wondered.

"Oh you misunderstand Mister Blake. Malfunctioning chips will be replaceable, but under closely monitored conditions. As far as in the event the persons dies, we will have to discontinue that number and completely destroy the chip itself. What I'm referring to is unauthorized removal."

"Sounds like this could get complicated," Ethan said.

"Well, we'll let the geniuses upstairs figure out the details. But you can rest assured that every possible scenario imaginable will be looked at, studied, and resolved before we move ahead with production."

"Still seems like with all the possibilities, times the amount of people you hope to get implanted," Ethan shook his head slowly and left his sentence unfinished.

"Just don't forget, Signa-Chip now has the European Union and one of the biggest organizations in Western Europe behind it. Within a short period of time the Signa-Chip will be ready for whatever application we want, or need to apply it to."

⋮

Adam, still groggy, climbed from bed. He would have slept right through the alarm clock buzzing on the dresser across the room had it not been for, Carol repeatedly elbowing him in the side.

"Don't forget to reset it for seven-thirty," Carol mumbled as he stood on unsteady legs. "We forgot to set the other clock up last night."

A flash of envy hit him. Adam wished, like her, that he too didn't have to get out of bed for another two hours.

No matter how many vacations he had taken over the years, with Kendell Industries, getting up for the first day back to work, after one of those vacations, was difficult for him.

Adam reached for the incessant clock, shut it off, resetting the alarm for seven-thirty. He headed for the shower, hoping the water would invigorate him.

That notorious 'first day back' was not being made any easier by the lack of sleep he had the night before. Tossing and turning all through the night with the preacher's Sunday sermon echoing through his head.

He realized, standing in the shower, the cool water splashing over him, that his whole outlook was changing. Something was happening to him. Something was making him feel elated and heavy-hearted simultaneously. Something he was fighting and the more he fought it, the stronger the feelings became of a needed change.

The preacher's closing words to the Sunday sermon came back to him again. Haunting. "The wheat shall be separated from the chaff," the middle aged Reverend had said, emphasizing the word 'shall'.

Adam relived the moment, word for word.

"People, we are on the thrashing floor of the Lord." Reverend James Tyke paused for everyone in the congregation to think about what he had just said. "The time is come," he paused again briefly, "when all will make their final decision."

In Adam's mind he saw Reverend Tyke move away from the podium, stop abruptly, turn back to the microphone mounted atop the oak lectern and say; "What will your choice be? '...as for me and my house...we will serve the Lord.'"

Adam knew what was happening; he was being backed into a corner, spiritually. A month ago, he wouldn't have given the preacher's words, or the feelings a second's thought. He would have simply laughed, turning away, content with his agnostic beliefs. But, the Signa-Chip was changing everything...the chip and the prophecy. The chip compelled him one-way, the prophecies another. He was being forced into a decision he was neither ready, nor willing to make.

The chip wasn't an evil thing, he tried to compromise. *Just an electronic computer chip. Why, such a controversial issue?*

The more he thought about it though, the more he realized, the reality of the prophecy and the truth it brought to light; The final choice. With those thoughts, the more undeniable the existence of a God became to him. And the more undeniable, the more intense Adam's introverted thoughts were becoming. The guilt, he felt because of his life long rejection of this God was consuming him.

He reached for the shampoo on the shower rack in front of him for a distraction. But, the only relief from the mental burden of the conviction he felt, was when he renewed his dogma of disbelief.

Though, those tenets of disbelief crumbled quickly in the face of the prophecies he was knowledgeable of. And the reality of the events of the world around him, like the water dissolving the suds of shampoo from his hair, dissolved his skepticism.

Turning his face upwards, Adam leaned in toward the invigorating spray.

From nowhere the words, "Lord help me," came out of his mouth. Surprising him. The first words, of the first prayer he had ever prayed as an adult…involuntary.

Adam leaned even farther forward putting his hand against the front wall of the shower.

What more would you have me to do? The response to his plea for help flashed through his mind. So vivid the thought, it appeared spoken.

Adam recoiled, almost falling. His hands grasping for something to hold on to. Slipping on the suds in the tub, he opened his eyes to get his spatial bearings. Instantly, the residue of un-rinsed, medicated shampoo poured into his eyes. They burned, but still he fought to keep them open. Preferring the pain of the soap in the eyes to falling, Adam grabbed the shower head for stability. He let the water pelt his face until the burning was gone.

Is it not hard for you to kick against the stones? The thought/voice came again. So indistinguishable between a thought and spoken words, Adam opened the sliding glass shower door and glanced around the bathroom. He expected, hoped to see someone, anyone, but as he had feared, he was alone.

"Great!" he said out loud as he slid the shower door closed. "On top of it all, now I'm hearing voices. Do dut, do dut, do dut." Adam imitated the musical score of a popular horror movie, just before the shark struck another victim.

His deep throated, whimsical rendition did little to alleviate the magnitude of what had just happened and he finished his shower feeling even more guilt, that he may have made light of the possible voice of God speaking to him.

:

Everyone was seated, facing forward, anxiously awaiting the Americans to begin the explanation of the Signa-Chip their company invented. Some of them rifled through the blue folders on the tables, hoping for a preview of the Train the Trainer session. Others, enjoying the time away from the drudgery of their usual daily routine, content to talk amongst themselves.

"Can we get started?" Ethan addressed Hilda. He too anxious to begin.

Sitting between him and Carl at the head table, Hilda shook her head; no.

"We're waiting for our interpreters," she said, without looking at him. "Not everyone here understands your language."

Ethan scanned the mixed gender and ethnic group of twenty people, all of which appeared aged in their late twenties to mid thirties. The scene reminded him of his college days and a windowless, Trigonometry classroom he attended twice a week. Except this time, he was the professor, not 'Ole Man Larson'.

Turning toward Ethan, Hilda said, "If all goes well, we'll move up to the eleventh floor conference room by mid-week. Security is much tighter up there, but the room has headsets that will automatically translate. However, until we get clearance from above for you two, we'll just have to make do the old fashioned way."

Ethan smiled at Hilda. He understood the simplistic, yet effective philosophy of completely separating the more sensitive projects World Technologies was working on from its everyday operations. Utilizing different floors of the building to do so.

Conversely, Carl, sitting just beyond her, pursed his lips at the back of her head, offended by the implied mistrust. His theory was for complete openness of all inner-company departments, and employee involvement in all areas of operation. His training; the more involvement, the more input from everyone, the better the chances for success. The idea of segregation in all areas appalled him to no end.

All eyes turned to the opening conference room door as the two interpreters entered, followed closely by three other men.

Ethan recognized Leonard Randolph immediately among the trailing trio and leading the way for the two others. It was apparent the 'others' were military men: in full dress uniforms.

Hilda jumped up, meeting Leonard just inside the door. They exchanged conversation in German. A language Ethan knew none of.

Mister Randolph had the last words and Hilda returned to her seat, obviously distraught over the unexpected arrival of the military officers.

Ethan turned to her questioningly.

"They weren't supposed to be here until midweek," was all she said.

There was a short disturbance as Leonard rearranged the occupants of the back table, allowing seating for himself and the two men with him.

"This is Van Volkenberg and Steward Mann," Hilda introduced the language interpreters, standing behind them.

Ethan and Carl nodded toward the two, blonde men that looked barely twenty.

Both of the interpreters of the same tall, thin stature, and muscularly build could have easily passed for brothers. In unison they nodded back.

"Kinda young for interpreters," Carl looked at Ethan, doubtful of the men's capabilities.

"Don't let their looks fool you," said Hilda. "They just look young. Both of them have been with us for several years and both are quite fluent in many languages."

The bustle at the rear of the room ceased.

Everyone settled into their seats, Hilda stood. "Ladies and Gentlemen," she said. "Welcome to our first "Train the Trainer" seminar on the attributes of the new Signa-Chip." She repeated her introduction in German and waited for Steward to voice it in Arabic.

The translation in German and Arabic occurring concurrently, Hilda spoke slightly louder than Van and Steward did as she began again. "As you all may have heard, World Technologies has officially purchased controlling interest in the American company that invented the Signa-Chip, Electronic Solutions Incorporated. Intending to expand ESI's manufacturing capabilities, by including one of our own state-of-the-art facilities in that process, we hope to meet the rapidly increasing demand for that product. Making Signa-Chip available on a world-wide basis." Hilda paused waiting for the translation to catch up. When it did, she resumed. "It is also the intention of World Technologies, in the near future, to put into orbit two satellites. Each dedicated to servicing the projected data demands of the chip. Therewith insuring that all present and future world-wide applications are provided for with adequate computing power." Hilda spread out her arms low. "And here, from the United States to introduce us to and explain some of the aspects of the Signa-Chip are Ethan Blake, Marketing Manager." She placed one of her outstretched hands on Ethan's shoulder. "And Carl Torre, Public Relations Manager." She placed the other on Carl's.

A short applause erupted as Hilda retook her seat.

"Implantable, tractable, miniaturized, personal Identification," Ethan started as he stood. "Words that describe the Signa-Chip. Its uses as varied and versatile as those words imply."

Ethan reached into his inside suit jacket pocket. He pulled out a small clear plastic bag. He fumbled with the bag tearing it open. "Ladies and Gentlemen...the Signa-Chip." He held the twenty millimeter by four millimeter microchip lengthwise between his thumb and index finger.

The sounds of chairs scraping against the tiled floor could be heard as everyone, including the two military men seated in the back, leaned forward, trying to get their first look of the rice sized chip. Ethan stepped out from around the table and walked down the aisles between the rows of other tables. Slowly he waved his hand with the chip in it back and forth so all could get a glimpse.

He returned to the front again and placed the chip back in the bag and set it on the table. It was the only visual aide he and Carl had for the first session, but it was all they needed. The slides and other paraphernalia used in the stateside presentations would come the next day, making the Train the Trainer seminars even easier.

Two hours later, Ethan and Carl, switching back and forth between who was speaking, completed their first task in Germany. Telling the conference room full of people, everything they could about the Signa-Chip as it stood. Including the radio frequency that it worked on. Though Ethan thought, less the time it took for the interpreters to restate verbatim their words in two different languages, the seminar could have been completed in half that time.

In closing, Ethan had announced that both him and Carl had been already implanted with the chip. Both of them showed their right palms to the captive audience. Most found it difficult to believe, because of the total absence of any sign the chip was there, until Carl explained that the actual incision was done along the 'lifeline' of the palm print making any scarring invisible.

Ethan added, "We should have a handheld, portable scanner by the next session and a display screen. Enabling you to see the readout from the chips."

A question and answer period followed the session and lasted another hour before Hilda stood up and released the group back to their usual jobs.

Leonard and the two military men remained behind. Patiently sitting at their table as the group of employees left.

"Excellent job," Leonard said, when the last of the staff had left. "Hilda," he added, "Why don't you take Mister Torre down to the Executive's lunchroom and treat him to some of our fine German cooking."

Hilda frowned as she looked up from gathering the left over folders off the front table.

"You can leave them there," Leonard smiled at her. "I'll have someone bring them up to your office."

"Yes sir," she said, reluctant about the lunch she was ordered to have with the one of the two Americans she personally disliked.

Carl, wasn't too pleased with the idea either. Though Hilda was by no means unpleasant to look at and under a different set of circumstances he would have jumped at the chance to be alone with her. He didn't, however, like being forced into a stressful, social position with Hilda. And for how long, he didn't know either. But mostly, he didn't like not knowing what Leonard Randolph and the military men wanted with Ethan. Especially, since they obviously didn't want him a party to it.

18

Ethan felt the thrill of excitement as he shook the General's hand.

"This is General Matoso," Leonard introduced him. "He is the General in charge of the Tunisia military forces in north central Africa."

"General," Ethan said in response. He could feel the physical strength and political power in the six foot tall, dark skinned man's prolonged handshake.

"Both he and Mohammed Asuri Ben Jari here are interested in utilizing the Signa-Chip as the means of identification for their military forces," Leonard continued. "An electronic equivalent to the American 'Dog Tag'."

"Excellent," Ethan said, exchanging the African's hand for the shorter, stockier Arabs.

"Mister Jari here, for security reasons, would like to maintain the anonymity of his country's origin," Leonard said.

All eyes in the room went to Ethan.

"No problem," Ethan said, without really thinking about it. His mind more focused on the millions of units the possible sales would encompass than any implications.

"I'd guess the real reason they are here is the assurance that Signa-Chip is capable of handling the demands of equipping their armies."

Ethan smiled. "If that is all you need, let me say with all certainty…with the backing of the resources of World Technologies and ESI the Signa-Chip is capable of exceeding any needs you may have."

Gary L. Dewey

"Especially, with the launching of the two proposed satellites," Leonard added. "And both of them dedicated to servicing the data needs of Signa-Chip."

"You see gentlemen," Ethan explained convincingly. "It's not really the chip that does anything much. The chip is just the means of electronically communicating with the computers and accessing the data linked with it. The abilities of Signa-Chip are not within the chip itself but within the computers and software behind it."

Both military men nodded their comprehension, both of their minds already made up that the Signa-Chip would be the new method of identifying their military personnel.

"Thank you," Leonard said, dismissing Ethan. "Mister Schehr should be outside to show you the way down to the Executive's lunchroom."

Ethan turned to the exit.

"Mister Blake," Leonard stepped away from the Generals and caught up to him. "This stays in here," he said, softly enough that only Ethan could hear.

:

The restricted dinning area for the upper management at World Technologies reminded Ethan of a fancy restaurant. The dozen, or so evenly spaced, cloth covered tables, surrounded by four, padded wooden chairs were not what he had expected to see in a company provided lunchroom. Neither was the virtual smorgasbord, in the form of a covered, heated, stainless steel food bar standing along the back wall and filled with various ethnic cuisines from around the world, nor was the piped in classical music, playing softly in the background. Also, surprising to Ethan, because it was long past the typical lunch hour, the tables were mostly filled.

262

The patrons though were engaged more in business conversations and not really eating, Ethan learned as he walked by their tables. And he surmised the relaxed, eloquent atmosphere of the room served a double purpose for company executives: Entertaining perspective clients as well as dinning.

Hilda and Carl were sitting along the back wall. One of the few table where actual eating was going on. A condition Hilda appreciated; engaged in eating, she had to do little socializing.

"Ethan," Carl called out, waving his hand. He was finishing up his bowl of a Belgian Beef and Beer Stew as Ethan joined them.

William diverted to a table on the other side of the room.

"What was all that about back there?" Carl started as soon as Ethan pulled out a chair.

"Nothing," Ethan sat. "Just a few technical questions about the chip."

"Why did they want just you?"

"I don't know."

"Who were those military men?"

"I need some coffee." Ethan ignored Carl's inquest, standing, looking toward the food bar.

"Around the back," Hilda pointed toward the partially hidden large stainless steel urn filled with coffee. "The Espresso Machine is back there too, if you so desire," she added, when she realized that Ethan's move was to avoid Carl's questions and not any real interest in the coffee.

She also knew the answers to Carl's questions as to who the Generals were and what they wanted. She also knew why Ethan was singled out and that Ethan was told to keep what they had talked about quiet.

It was no big deal if he didn't. The after the session meeting was a planned move, designed in part as a test to Ethan's ability to keep company business to himself. She smiled inwardly at Ethan's successful diversion.

"I don't know what the big deal is," Carl looked up at Hilda. He too realized Ethan's rejection but didn't understand why.

"Company business I suppose," Hilda forced a smile. "If he was told to keep quiet about the meeting, that is what he needs to do. And no matter how much you drill him…you're not going to get anything from him."

"That's a bunch of crap," Carl snarled. "I know you and I didn't get off on the right foot," his tone softened. "And I'm sorry for that. But, I'm an employee of this company too and I have the right to know what's going on just as much as anybody else."

Several heads turned toward their table.

"You have a right to know what the company wants you to know," Hilda responded. "And that's it. No more. No less."

"Who's running this outfit? Hitler?" Carl's timbre regained its animosity.

Ethan returned with his coffee in time to divert the conversation before it became heated. "Aren't you two ever going to get along?"

"I don't like all this secrecy," Carl said.

"It's not secrecy," Ethan said and sipped his coffee. "It's 'need to know' and certain things you just don't need to know."

Ethan's words did nothing to soothe Carl's feelings. Carl felt 'left out in the cold' and he didn't like it.

:

Lunch hour for Adam was typically spent alone in his crowded second floor office. Normally, he rushed out at lunch time to the 'fast food' restaurant, about a mile from Kendell Industries, down eighteen mile road. He'd bring back a hot sandwich of some kind and eat by himself, among the piles of Electrician's manuals stacked on his gray metal desk. The manuals for the Computer Numerically Controlled machines, typically were his only lunch time companions.

He didn't mind the loneliness, nor was he anti-social, Adam just liked the little reprieve his office afforded him from the din the computer controlled, metal cutting machines produced while running. Which most did, unmanned, during lunch. A reprieve, the ground floor, company break room, where the majority of plant employees ate, didn't provide.

Adam broke from the usual though, as he occasionally did, deciding to buy his lunch off the 'roach coach' that came by twice a day and eat with the machinists in the company's lunchroom.

Most times he did it because he wanted to hear the latest company gossip, or pickup, through the casual conversations, insight into a particular electronical problem the machinists where having with the machines during the production process. This time though, he just didn't want to be alone.

The day was not going too well. Adam was finding it increasingly difficult for him to stay focused on the intricate repair tasks he was engaged in. His mind kept wanting to relive the shower incident where he thought he had heard God speaking to him. And that was something he could not afford to do. Repairing, or re-wiring a mal-functioning CNC machine demanded his full concentration. Attempting a repair with a preoccupied mind could mean trouble for him, or the operator. And that was something Adam wasn't willing to chance.

He thought, perhaps breaking the routine by having lunch among the machinist and participating in the usual lunchroom camaraderie he might distract his mind enough to allow him to stay centered.

To his surprise, the 'hot' topic of the lunchroom was the Signa-Chip. He was also surprised to learn that six of the twenty-five machinist who worked at Kendell's, along with two ladies; one in the Shipping and Receiving Department, the other a Secretary in Employee Benefits, had already had the chip implanted in themselves and their families.

Sheila, the clerk from Shipping and Receiving and one of the women, was adamant when asked 'why' she and her family had the implants. "Why should I take the chance of havin' one of my kids gettin' lost, runnin' off, or gettin' kidnapped, or God knows what else happenin' to them and me not knowin' where they are," she said, "when the cops can use the chip to find them?"

Adam sitting at the end seat on one of the five, long folding tables that were dotted around the twenty by forty foot tiled room, set his unopened tuna salad sandwich down in front of him. He intently listened to the conversation going on at the half filled table, hanging on Sheila's every word.

Jim Fowler, one of the lead machinists, sitting mid-table, directly across from Sheila, asked the red headed, middle aged clerk, "I can see it for the kids. But why you?"

"I plan on goin' all computerized," Sheila proudly announced in her Southern accent. "Startin' next pay period, I'm gonna have my checks automatically deposited. Pay all my bills through automatic deductions."

"You coulda done that anyway without paying for the surgery to have that chip put in you," Kenneth Whitman, sitting on the opposite end of the table from Adam, joined the conversation. "I do that already and I don't have 'the chip'."

"Surgery?" Sheila laughed. "More like a poke. Two minutes in and out. 'Sides I didn't have to pay a cent. Bank paid for mine and my old man's. Insurance paid for the two kids."

Jim set his sandwich down on the brown paper bag he brought it in, chewed for a moment, swallowed. "Your bank paid for it?"

"Yep! Said if I'd open one of them new accounts with them they'd pay for it."

Adam's eyes widened as he reached to open the cellophane wrapper around his sandwich. He wanted to ask her what 'new' account, but didn't have to; Whitman beat him to it.

"All electronic," Sheila scooped up a spoonful of the macaroni salad she was eating. "No cards to loose, no checks to write, no bank books to balance. Swoosh," she waved her free hand over the top of the paper plate her lunch was on. "No fuss, no muss. Just slam, blam thank ya mam."

Adam watched the crass, over-weight woman stuff the rounded tablespoon full of macaroni into her mouth.

Not getting to the Shipping and Receiving Department at the rear of the building much, he barely recognized her. Blaming his lack of familiarity with her on that department having a fair turn-over of workers and assuming that Sheila was somewhat of a new employee.

"What you starin' at? Ain't never saw nobody eat before?" Sheila stopped chewing and returned Adam's look.

Embarrassed by the woman's forwardness, Adam's eyes dropped as he fumbled with his own sandwich.

"What do you think Adam," Kenneth relived his embarrassment. "You're the electronics expert around here."

"Think about what?"

"About the chip?"

"Can't say I think anything about it," Adam lied. "Can't talk about what I don't know. But, I'm sure it's everything they say it is and more."

Nathaniel Jenkins walked by the table and Adam looked up at the shy, quiet man.

"Nat," Adam said, standing up as he passed. "I need to talk to you."

The elderly black man who was the janitor at Kendell Industries stopped and turned.

"Not here," Adam scooped up his sandwich. "I'd like to see you in my office."

Nathaniel glanced at his watch. He, like the rest of the first floor workers who got half an hour for lunch, still had ten minutes of his time left.

"This isn't work related," Adam leaned toward him and whispered.

"Oh," Nat said and headed for the exit.

Once they were a few steps outside of the lunchroom, Adam caught up to Nathaniel. "We don't have to go up to my office," he said, "but, I need to ask you something."

"What can I do for you?" the always friendly, near retirement, Nathaniel said.

Adam looked around the shop suspiciously, checking to see that no one was near enough to hear. "I've seen you a few times reading your bible here at work."

"I know it's against company policy," Nathaniel immediately felt defensive. "But only on my time."

"That's okay," Adam said, pulling him a couple of steps closer to one of the CNC pallet machines. "That's not what this is about."

Nathaniel let himself be led.

"I assume that you're one of those 'Christian' people." Adam glanced at his eyes and saw that he had Nat's full attention. "And I wanted to ask you," Adam looked around the shop again.

"Is this 'bout dat chip they was takin' about in the lunchroom?"

"No...yes...no," Adam stammered. "Does God ever talk to you? I mean do you ever hear him speaking? Does he do that kind of stuff?"

Nathaniel's mouth broadened into a full smile. "Only when he wants your attention or something special."

The high pitched squeal of a rotating tool bit cutting its way along a block of steel in the machine made both men cringe. Adam walked away from the machine.

Nathaniel right behind him. "What did God say to you?"

"I don't know that he said anything." Adam headed for the coin operated coffee machine near the main entrance door to the factory. "I just wondered if he ever actually talked to you."

"Actually," Nathaniel admitted. "I kant really say. Sometime I kant tell if it be him, or just me thinkin'."

Despite the heat inside the un-air conditioned building, Adam felt a shiver course through him; goose bumps raising on his arms. He walked faster toward the coffee machine.

"What'd he say?" Nathaniel kept up with him.

Reaching the machine, Adam said, "Want coffee? I'll buy."

"I wanta hear what God said to you."

"Nathan," Adam turned to face him. "Until my mother died, I didn't even believe in a God. Now two days after we buried her, He wants to have a conversation with me?"

269

Nathaniel's broad smile returned. "Don't much matter to him what you used to believe," Nathaniel refused the coffee. "What he say?"

"I don't know." Adam nervously dropped the coins into the slot and pressed the coffee with cream button. "If it was him...something about kicking some stones."

"Ain't it hard for thee to kick against the stones?"

"Something like that." There was a pause as Adam reached down for his coffee. "What does it mean?" He straightened up and took a sip.

"He be axing you if it be hard for you to be a non-believer," Nathaniel said, as the buzzer signaling the time for the machinists to return to work sounded. "Said da same thin to Paul once."

"Who is Paul?"

"Only da guy who ust to kill Christians. Ended up writin' most of the New Testament of da Bible."

As usual, Jack Edwards, the plant manager, appeared at the edge of the second floor balcony over-looking the shop floor. He miraculously appeared at the same spot every work day, just after the buzzer ended the lunch break. His purpose: to make sure everyone who was supposed to, was returning to work.

Nathaniel turned away from Adam, headed for his floor sweeper.

"Nat," Adam called out to him. "Our little secret."

"Your secret is mine," Nathaniel waved over his shoulder.

Adam took another sip of coffee and went up to his office to finish eating his Tuna salad sandwich.

The remainder of the afternoon went by quickly and without much distraction by his thoughts. Nonetheless, when

Adam flopped down in the seat of his truck to go home, the thoughts came rushing back.

He drove toward home feeling spiritually worse. Convinced even more, after talking with Nathaniel, that not only was there a God that he had denied all of his adult life, but that God, despite those years of denial, had found him still 'special' enough to actually try to speak to him.

By the time Adam pulled into the driveway of his home the emotional weight of his burden of guilt was so heavy, his despair so overwhelming, he was near tears. He squared his shoulders against the emotional load and took several deep breaths before he gathered enough strength to climb out of his truck.

He walked heavy footed across his browning lawn. Stopping, he peered down at the dying grass then glanced upward. He saw little hope for precipitation in the bright blue, cloudless sky.

His was not the only yard in the neighborhood that resembled a hay field all the yards up and down his street were showing the effects of the hot, dry, summer. A summer that had not produced much rain except for an occasional, quick thunder storm that the parched ground absorbed the moisture from as quickly as it fell. And the outdoor watering restrictions, in place since early summer, prevented him from doing anything to save his once flourishing lawn.

Adam headed into the house, went straight for the refrigerator. The prospects of a cold beer his only hope of consolation.

The sticky note Carol put on the front of the refrigerator on her way out to work, greeted him: Have to work late, it read. Can you PLEASE pick Lindsey up from the Daycare? LOVE Carol.

Twenty-five minutes later and ten minutes after the business had closed for the day, Adam pulled up in front of the Early Learning Daycare Center. Lindsey was standing with Melissa next to the gate, awaiting him.

"Sorry," Adam apologized to both of them.

"That's okay," Lindsey smiled. "Sometimes Mom's late too."

"Thank you for waiting," Adam said to Melissa.

"No problem Mister Garrett. Lindsey and I were just chatting."

"Well, thanks anyway." Adam took Lindsey's hand and lead her out of the chain link gate.

"You're welcome," Melissa said, following Lindsey out and re-locking the gate behind her.

"Can I drop you anywhere?"

"No thank you," Melissa said. "I have my own car parked just around the corner."

"Listen," Adam said as he helped Lindsey up into the passenger seat of his pickup. "I'm very sorry for the way I behaved when you and your husband came by. I'd like to offer you and Jack an invitation for dinner tonight at our place. I'd like to make it up to you."

"That's awful nice," Melissa smiled. "You don't have to make anything up to us. But, I have to turn you down…for tonight anyway."

"Other plans?"

"Well, actually we have another function going on at church tonight."

"Oh." Adam felt disappointed. He really wanted to talk with them some more, one on one, hoping to find an answer for the spiritual turmoil he felt inside.

"A Revival, Prayer Meeting." Melissa beamed.

"What's that?"

"Some preaching, singing, praising the Lord and a lot of praying." Melissa beamed even more. "You and your family are welcome to come and join us."

Adam hesitated. "What time?" He eventually asked.

"Seven-thirty."

"'Till?"

"Until whenever."

Adam hesitated again for a moment.

"Can we go?" Lindsey said. "Please!"

"Let me ask you mother. See if she wants to go."

:

To Adam's surprise, Carol was not only willing to attend the Church Service, after working late, but anxious too. Tirelessly, she made a supper of salad, spaghetti, and garlic bread, took a quick shower and was ready to go half an hour before they had to.

Adam was on the couch watching the evening news when Carol and Lindsey, dressed alike in blue jeans and white blouses, sat next to him.

"We're ready when you are?" Carol announced.

"Is that what you're going to wear?" Adam said.

"Why not? It's comfortable. And we should fit right in. Besides, I called the Elsworth's and Melissa said it didn't matter. 'Just to come as we were'."

"Let me finish watching this." Adam said, and pointed at the television.

"The wild fires in Colorado, New Mexico, and Central Montana, driven by high winds," the newscaster on the television reported, "have destroyed over a hundred and eighty-five thousand acres of forest in the three states and are blamed for the deaths of a hundred and forty-three people."

"Wow! That's bad," Carol said.

"Can I go outside and…?" Lindsey started to ask.

"Shhhh," Adam mouthed.

Answering Lindsey silently, Carol shook her head no.

"Firefighters are praying for rain in the drought stricken areas as the fires close in on several, small, rural towns," the newscaster continued. "But, forecasters have not given them much hope for that and National Guard troops have been sent in to help evacuate the townspeople and protect against loot-ing."

The news station broke for commercials and Adam got up to take his shower. He had heard enough 'bad' news for one day. His brain refusing to deal with anymore of it, he shut the devastation of the wildfires out. During his shower, Adam found himself becoming angry with this all powerful, loving, merciful God for not causing it to rain and at least helping to contain the consuming fires. Angry almost to the point, that by the end of his shower, he was having second thoughts about attending the church service. Somehow, it seemed hypocritical to him, to go sing praises to a God who sat idly by as the destructive infernos raged.

Shampoo bubbles in his hair, he leaned into the spray of water to rinse when Carol pounded on the bathroom door and burst in.

"What is that?" Carol frantically asked.

"What?" Adam pulled back from the shower. Unable to open his eyes, for the streams of soap still cascading down his face, he reached for the wall to steady himself.

"Can't you feel that?" Carol almost screamed at him.

Adam stuck his face back into the water. "Feel what?" He garbled.

"The whole house is shaking! I think we're having an earthquake!"

"In Detroit?" Adam backed away from the water. He could hear Lindsey whining for fear. But from inside the shower, he could perceive no shaking. "Let me get out," he said, shutting the water off. "Hand me my robe."

By the time Adam was out the aftershock was over, but Carol and Lindsey were still trembling, visibly shaken. He lifted Lindsey out of Carol's arms and held them both close until some of their fear abated.

"It's over, whatever it was," Adam tried reassuring them, though he knew nothing of what caused their anxiety.

Lindsey said, un-burying her head from his shoulder. "The light on the ceiling was swinging back and forth. Then the lights went out. I was scared."

"I can't believe you didn't feel it," Carol said. "The whole house was shaking and I thought it was going to collapse."

"Well, thank God it didn't," Adam said, catching himself. He set Lindsey back down on the floor, concurrently feeling the totally contrasting emotions of anger and thankfulness. The thoughts confusing him for a moment, before the anger completely disappeared from his mind.

Gary L. Dewey

19

Waiting until after midnight, fighting sleep and jet-lag, Ethan called his in-laws house from his hotel room. He refrained from making the call earlier because Ethan knew his in-laws rarely ate out and it was more certain that they would be home around their typical dinner time. First, he talked with his children, the conversations light and lasting only a few minutes each. To his pleasant surprise, when he was finished talking with Erin and Renee', Nicole wanted to talk with him too.

"Here mom is," he heard Renee' handing the telephone over to Nicole.

There was a muffled sound and despite Nicole putting her hand over the mouth piece, Ethan heard her sending the children into the other room. It was his first hint that the conversation wasn't going to be a congenial one.

Nicole placed the phone to her mouth. Without even saying hello first, she said, "I suppose about now you're going to tell me you have to stay longer than a few days?"

Nicole braced herself, expecting a heated response. Instead her words were followed by a prolonged silence.

Ethan found words difficult. "Well, ah, um, Hello to you too," he stammered.

"Okay. Hello. Now tell me."

"Well, I really still don't know," Ethan lied to take the pressure off. "We had our first session this morning and it went very well. How many more sessions they have planned, they haven't even told me yet."

"How naive do you think I am Ethan? After ten years of marriage, I'd think you would at least give me enough credit to know when you are toying with me."

"Toying with you?" Ethan echoed and felt himself getting angry. The telephone call wasn't the gratifying conversation he expected and though Nicole was right, he didn't like the accusations. "You're taking this a little too far aren't you?" Ethan said.

"Too far?" It was Nicole's turn to echo him. "Our daughter gets kidnapped and you can't even spend a little time with her to help her? Too far? Your wife needs you around now more than she ever has in her whole life and the best you can do is run off to Germany, all in the name of the chip? Too far?"

Ethan found himself speechless again.

"What? Got nothing to say?"

"I thought I already explained that to you?" Ethan responded. "This new company…"

"New!" Nicole cut him off. "You couldn't have explained to them about Renee' and delayed this for a day or two?"

Ethan knew his wife was right. He probably could have delayed his trip, but didn't even try. Too much was at stake to argue with Leonard, he thought then and still did. An opportunity to advance, career-wise, and financially, he wouldn't jeopardize by debating the issue. Figuring that Renee' and Nicole would get over their fears without him, Ethan went along with the plan. There was nothing he felt he could do anyway and the likelihood of anything else bad happening was so remote, there was no real need for him to hang around, especially at so high a price.

In the silence, Nicole felt a lump coming up in her throat. Ethan's first priority, she had realized had become the chip, the children running second and her a distant third. She swallowed the lump down. "There's no sense in carrying this out any farther," she said. "It's obvious, your job is more important to you and that's that."

"Come on Nicole," Ethan tried reasoning with her. "You know how important this is."

Nicole brushed away the tear she felt trickling down her cheek. "Yeah, I know," she said. "More important than me and your family."

Silence filled the telephone line again. "I hope it's worth it," Nicole said and hung up.

:

He never lost consciousness, but he was drifting in and out of the awareness of his surroundings.

During the times of cognizance he heard voices. Several voices. Chanting. Though he couldn't discern the words.

While he strained to comprehend the prayers, he felt several pairs of hands upon his shoulders. Some softly rubbing. Some holding on firmly. Others barely touching.

At times he felt an invisible weight pressing him downward. Oppressing. Other times, a weightlessness, that if it were not for the hands holding him down, he would have floated away.

Then all was gone again and he was racing across a muddy field toward a slowly closing, distant door, a door too far away to reach in time before it slammed shut. What lay beyond the door, he didn't know, but only knew he had to get there before it shut completely and he was left this side of it. If it were not for the muck he could have ran faster. He struggled to move ahead. His movement restricted by the quagmire of his own making.

Then cognizance again, the chanting, the hands. He was crying, sobbing uncontrollably between words of compunction. Then all was gone again and the door returned. Nearer. Reachable. But barely ajar. The muddy field replaced with solid ground. A pierced, bodiless hand, appeared from behind the door. He reached out for it. Felt a power like none other surge through him when he touched it. The hand enclosed his, pulling him inward.

On the other side of the door he became aware again of his surroundings. Though he couldn't remember exactly how he had got where he was: on his knees at the alter, his arms outstretched, his face lifted upwards, the Reverend James Tyke, Jack Elsworth and several other men kneeling around him, fervently praying.

Adam's last recollection: standing at the close of the sermon and the Reverend Tyke, beckoning the heavyhearted; the burdened; those seeking the Christ, to step forward; to come down to the alter at the front of the sanctuary. He did remember standing in the aisle next to the last row of church pews, where Carol, Lindsey and himself had sat, and fitting all three of the reverend's conditions. His spirit heavy with self-condemnation; his soul encumbered with guilt, felt dirty. Standing there, his eyes wet with tears, he sought to settle in his heart, once and for all, the question of the existence of a God.

How he gotten from the rear, to the front of the chapel, he didn't know. Didn't care. The heaviness was gone, the feelings of reproach, no more. He felt free, clean, alive.

Adam let his head fall slowly forward until it lightly touched the padded rail at the top of the wooden alter. He knew in his heart, it was the hand of the Son of God that had pulled him down the aisle and through 'salvation's door' just before the opportunity for him forever vanished. Adam whispered a heartfelt "Thank You", before he was weeping again.

This time his tears were not of shame, but of gratitude. Never again would he struggle with the question of the existence of God; he had touched the nail pierced hand of God's son. Neither would he ever again doubt the depth of love God had for him. He felt it deep within his soul. Overflowing his spirit.

Adam lifted his head and looked through tear stained eyes at Jack Elsworth, kneeing in front of him. Adam's smile spoke volumes.

"Praise the Lord," Jack said to him, helping Adam to his feet. "Praise the Lord!"

The congregation fell silent as Adam turned to face the small group of parishioners.

His visual search through the back rows of pews for Carol was futile. Of all those in attendance, he couldn't see the one he most wanted to share his experience with. He felt a wave of fear rush through him, thinking that she may have been embarrassed by the display, taken Lindsey and left.

A soft hand reached up and touched his.

With the magnitude of his encounter with the Son of God, Adam had not noticed that Carol was on the alter with him, praying, her too finding spiritual salvation. She rose slowly to stand next to him. They embraced, as Reverend Tyke lead the congregation, all of them standing, in a verse of the classical hymn, 'Amazing Grace'.

One of the elders of the church, a sweet looking, gray haired woman in her early sixties, lead Lindsey by the hand up to Carol, then disappeared back into the group.

When the singing was over, the Reverend handed Adam a printed brochure explaining what had just happened to them and what they were to expect next. But, Adam knew what to expect; all the things his mother had ever told him over the years about Salvation's Plan; God; his Son, and the Holy Spirit; things he had ignored, conveniently blocking them out of his mind, returned with the same clarity as if she had just explained them to him yesterday.

:

At three-thirty Tuesday morning, the half mile wide Ganges River could hold no more of the relentless rain that had been falling for the last five days in southern Asia. It overran its banks four miles upstream from the Danpur Dam. The flood of river water gained width, depth, and momentum as it raced down the mountain slopes toward the populated, valley city of Danpur, washing out farm crops and live stock as it went. When, at four AM, the rushing waters hit the dam, the massive, concrete structure could not withstand the force nor the weight of it. It burst. Hurling a forty-three foot high wall of water, traveling upwards of sixty miles an hour at the sleeping people of Danpur a mile downstream.

By four-thirty AM it was all over, a major part of Danpur; gone. Along with the quaint homes and small businesses carried away, so were thirty-two thousand of its residents. The remainder of the people in the town of ninety thousand, whose homes had not been demolished or completely washed away by the unstoppable wall of water, stood in three feet of residual flood, contemplating their future. Most would disperse into the higher ground in the surrounding hills. Few of the elderly and toddlers would survive the week.

The Ganges River in India was only one of several rivers that would overflow its banks. Danpur, only one of many cities to suffer the effects of the torrential, unrelenting rains in South Asia and Central Europe.

The Indus and Brahmaputra Rivers would also swell beyond their banks. In the Czech Republic the Elbe and Vitava would also flood. All tolled the waters would destroy over fifteen million acres of precious food crops, three-hundred thousand homes and displace twenty-five million people.

:

Three stationary video cameras on tripods dotted the back wall of the conference room the second day of the Train the Trainer sessions. World Technologies deciding to put together a training video of the Signa-Chip using taped segments of the live presentations. Their philosophy; better utilization of Ethan's skills in the 'field', not tied up internally.

It was not the best of days for Ethan to be filmed. He was mentally, physically, and emotionally tired before the sessions ever started. Nor did he look his best. By lunch time, he was exhausted, ready to call it a day.

"Why don't we take a couple of hours break?" Hilda announced to everyone at quarter after twelve. She looked at her watch. "Let's say we meet back here at two." She too, along with Carl, had noticed Ethan's lack of enthusiasm and they both thought it best if they broke for a while.

"Sorry," Ethan responded to their inquiry, when everyone except them and the man who ran the video cameras had left the room. "Had a bad night and probably some jet-lag catching up to me."

"Anything we can do?" Hilda said.

"Naw, not really. Just need some time to let me catch up to myself."

"Not much chance of that happening," Carl snickered.

They turned toward the opening entrance door and saw Leonard Randolph heading their way.

"Good afternoon," he smiled, when he got close enough.

"Good afternoon," Hilda said.

Ethan and Carl just nodded.

"I have some really good news," Leonard said, "that you may want to incorporate into you session." Leonard paused for a moment. "Doctor Reece, along with 'Design and Engineering' has already come up with a new coating for the Signa-Chip that deteriorates upon contact with air, rendering the chip nonfunctional. So, once it's implanted it can't be removed without destroying it. Also, we're also going to start encoding the chips at manufacture." Leonard added. "Enabling only those chips made by World Technologies to access our computer systems." He smiled confidently. "The W.T. systems will then be secure."

"Sounds like monopolizing in the name of security," Carl said.

Ethan and Hilda both sent a disparaging look his way.

"How do they intend on getting Signa-Chip from manufacture to implantation, if the new coating is destroyed by air?" Ethan questioned. Both to resolve his wondering as to how they had devised exposing the chip during implantation, without exposing it, and to break the tension Carl's derogatory comment had initiated.

"Quite simply," Leonard smiled. "It will be double sealed inside a hard protein coating. The outer coating protecting the inner one until implantcd. Thcn, once inside the body, the protein coating will dissolve and be consumed."

"I'm going to lunch," the cameraman, walked passed them. "I'll be back before two."

"Great," Hilda nodded. "We're right behind you Edward."

Leonard waited until the door closed behind Ed. "While we're all here together," he said. "I can save us a trip up to my office...After the taped sessions this afternoon," Leonard unflinching, looked Carl in the eyes. "We won't be needing you here in Germany and see no sense in keeping you away from home and your family."

Stunned, Ethan's head turned between Leonard and Carl, looking for reactions. Seeing nothing in either man, he glanced over to Hilda. She let her eyes fall toward the floor, avoiding his glance. She didn't want Ethan to know that she had foreknowledge of this and figured that if he saw her eyes, he would know for certain she had.

"We have made all the arrangements," Leonard continued. "Doctor Reece will join you and we'll have a cab pick you up in front of your hotel at around six-fifteen tonight. Your flight will leave out of Munich around seven-twenty."

"Am I included in this?" Ethan asked, concerned he was, but from the directness of Leonard's speech at Carl, doubted it.

No," Hilda answered, as suspected. "We're going to want you to stay for a few more days. We have more we need you to do."

"Fine with me," Carl finally responded, offended that he wasn't included in the 'things'.

Ethan wanted to tell Carl to watch his belligerent tones. Warn him that World Technologies might not be as tolerant to his openness of expression as ESI was.

It would have done no good though, Leonard's mind was already made up; Carl was history. His employment would be terminated two days after his return to Chicago. "'Loose lips, sink ships'" Leonard would later use the antiquated World War Two adage in justifying his decision to let Carl go. "Carl's convictions that company issues need to be openly discussed doesn't fit into World Technologies's methodology."

Leonard offered the explanation knowing he had no need to justify anything to anyone. He had the authority to hire or fire anybody within the World Technologies's conglomerate he wanted to. Being only second in the hierarchy to Warren Kilpatrick, the fifty-three year old president of World Technologies, who answered only to the heads of the European Union. But he did to ease Ethan's mind.

Carl really didn't care much. He wanted out of the 'Public Relations Game', as he called it. He was tired of the routine and looking for a career change anyway. And even more so, now that World Technologies had taken over the controlling interest in ESI. He figured that major changes in the structure of ESI were in-line for the very near future anyway and he didn't necessarily want to hang around for them.

∶

Zealous was the best word to fit Adam's disposition after his spiritual conversion. That was, except at work. There, since open religious conversation, considered a form of harassment, was banned from the workplace, the only person that knew Adam had 'found' the Lord was Nathaniel Jenkins. Others had sensed changes in Adam's demeanor but didn't know why. Attributing them to his, announced engagement to Carol and their planned, October wedding.

Adam and Nathan had many long, lunch time, spiritual talks during the next few weeks. Adam, gleaning every bit of scriptural knowledge from his coworker that he could. And even one afternoon, after their shift was over, they lingered in the privacy of Adam's office for over an hour, sitting across from each other at Adam's cluttered desk, discussing biblically, apostolic matters.

"Don't you think it a bit strange," Adam confessed at the end of their post-shift meeting. "All of my life, I've wanted nothing of God and now I can't seem to get enough of him. Carol too. All we want now is to learn, learn, learn. Our days and nights are filled with God. Either talking about him, reading about him, or in church listening about him."

Nathaniel smiled knowingly, in his warm, gentleman smile. "Time's short," he said. "We're gonna need all we can get to gets us through."

That's when it struck him, Adam, to that point, had not realized what it all meant. He had bits and pieces, little victories, but never saw the big picture. It was like the game show where a letter-less passage is given and one by one the letters to it are guessed and placed in their appropriate place. Each letter correctly guessed, a small victory in and of itself, but the phrase yet unknown. Unknown, until one more letter is placed and the phrase jumps into realization. Nathan's words, 'Time's short,' echoed in his head, making it abundantly clear to Adam that was exactly what was happening, time was 'short'.

"You all right?" Nathaniel noticed the paleness in Adam's face.

Adam didn't answer. He never heard the question.

Nathan asked again, a little louder.

"Insect borne diseases; the fires and drought's out West; the Floods in Europe and Asia; the One World Government; the tremors we felt in Detroit; the Signa-Chip," Adam frowned. "We'll never see Lindsey graduate, will we?"

"I don't know," Nathaniel answered. "Unless God slows things down, it doesn't look like it."

"Is that possible?" Adam's face lit up with the hope. Suddenly, he felt that he could make the difference...if he could slow the surging progress of the chip.

:

For the next few days, at seven o'clock, Adam was glued to the television. He would send Lindsey to her room to play, while he and Carol watched the Nightly CNN, World News Report, faithfully. Except for Wednesdays and the following Sunday night broadcasts, which aired while they were at church services. Those nights he taped the broadcasts in his VCR, watching them after they had gotten home and Lindsey had gone to bed. Both Adam and Carol determining that at her young age, Lindsey didn't need to hear and see so many frightening stories.

The CNN news reports of suicide bombers; wars; droughts; famines and new insect borne diseases read like chapters from the book of Revelations.

Two of the 'news stories' he taped one Wednesday night made Adam, particularly cringe: The first one was of a five mile in diameter and enlarging circle of bacteria scientist had discovered drifting in the ocean currents. The uncontrollable bacteria, at present fifty feet deep, was infecting and killing everything in its path. From the aerial view CNN provided, the bacteria had a deep reddish cast to it.

Revelation chapter eight, verse eight jumped into Adam's mind. "And the third part of the sea became as blood," he said, beneath his breath.

"What was that?" Carol asked.

"Nothing," Adam answered with tact. He had kept his 'end times' realization to himself, though he knew Carol must have come to the same conclusions herself. But if she hadn't, he didn't want to be the one to tell her. At least not yet: Fearing the reality of it might dampen her spiritual enthusiasm.

The other story, that caused Adam great distress, dealt with a breed of mosquitoes a group of American environmentalists had found in central Africa. The group, while on a grant from the University of Southern California, was studying the effects the prolonged monsoons were having on the African continent, when they inadvertently discovered the mosquitoes that had built up an immunity to and were carrying the AIDS virus. The flying insects from the AIDS stricken region were now capable of infecting everyone they bit with the incurable disease.

Carol sat quietly listening to the AIDS story. CNN providing the scenes of the sick and dying in the remote villages, while inside her heart she was silently weeping. The thoughts of the dread the people of Central Africa lived under caused her heart to ache. Her mind began to wonder: with international transportation, how long it would take for the mosquitoes to spread to other, more densely populated, parts of the world. She turned to look at Adam, a tear trickling down her cheek, she brushed away before Adam saw it. To her relief the telephone rang and she got up to answer it.

The rest of the tape, Adam watched alone. It contained an interview with the United States Secretary of Defense, trying to convince any who would listen, that the President's campaign to gain international approval to attack a middle eastern country, harboring a known terrorist group, was justifiable.

Adam listened to the interview, contemplating the 'campaign', he himself wanted to start.

"This country is in the process of obtaining nuclear weapons," the Secretary defended the President's urgent quest. "Weapons of mass destruction! And they don't have the least bit of resolve in using them."

"Mom wants to know if we will come over for dinner, Friday night?" Carol came back in the room with the portable phone in her hand.

"Sure," Adam answered, without taking his eyes off the television.

"There are several countries that are known to harbor terrorist in that region," the balding, middle aged, interviewer said to the Secretary of Defense. "Is the President proposing that the international community attack all of them?"

"What time is good for you?" Carol asked Adam.

He turned toward her and never heard the first part of the Secretary's response. "Whenever you want to," he said.

Adam turned back to the ending interview. "Would you have us wait until we experience another nine-eleven? Only this time, ten times as bad! Contrary to the popular, head buried in the sand belief," the Secretary closed. "We are not immune in this country to chemical, nuclear or biological attack." He paused, turned directly at the television camera recording the interview. "How soon we forget."

:

After a delicious dinner of baked pork chops, mashed potatoes, and fresh corn on the cob, the ladies disappeared into the kitchen to clean up the mess the feast had caused. Adam, and Carol's dad, Robert, moved to the solitude of the living room. Adam headed for the light brown colored, overstuffed couch, Robert; his favorite, tan, leather recliner.

Adam melted into the comfortable sofa, its high back and side arms enveloping him in a den of cushions. "I just love this couch," he said, as he sunk deeper into its softness.

"Too soft for me," Robert smiled, his sixty year old lower back preferring the more solid support of the recliner. "But Ma, likes it. Spends more time on it than anywhere else in the house."

They both chuckled.

Exchanging small talk about their respective jobs, the subject of conversation focused on Robert's job at the automotive plant.

"Starting next week, they want to go with direct deposit at GM," Robert said. "No more paychecks. Just some little stub thing, tells ya how much they took."

Adam sat up straight, a difficult task in the overly pliant couch. The hairs on the nape of his neck went straight too. Robert had his full attention.

"No big thing," Robert said and thought Adam's reaction was a bit much. "It's the wave of the future. The only trouble is my damn bank has those new type of accounts and you need that computer thing to get your money out."

"You haven't got it have you?" Adam surprised himself and blurted out.

"Not yet. Why?"

"Don't"

"Don't what?" Carol asked, coming through the curved archway that separated the dinning area from the living room of the old house. Lindsey and her mother following behind her.

"Your dad is thinking about getting the chip." Adam looked at her with a frown.

Carol froze. Stunned by the announcement.

"No thinking about it." Susan said. "We're both scheduled for Wednesday at Doctor Ramas office, when your father gets off work."

Carol turned abruptly. "Ma you can't!"

"And why not?" Robert said.

Lindsey climbed up in her favorite spot on her Grandpapa's lap.

Adam looked up at Carol and she at him. Both wondering who should speak. Neither did.

Adam knew Carol had not yet told her agnostic parents about their conversion to Christianity and felt that it was her call when and how she did eventually inform them. Carol, on the other hand, felt that Adam, as future head of the household, had the responsibility.

Adam allowed himself to sink back into the comfort of the couch again as Carol sat next to him. Neither of them were unwilling to speak. Actually, both were anxious to share their conversions, but from inexperience didn't know how, or where to start.

Carol's parents eyed them suspiciously and with confusion.

"Well?" asked Susan as she sat in the arm chair that matched the sofa.

"Well," Carol nodded toward Lindsey. "I really don't want to get into it too much right now."

Lindsey looked up at her Grandfather, tugged on his shirt pocket. "She doesn't want me to know about the Mark of the Beast."

20

Each day that passed Ethan felt a little better. He dealt with Nicole's growing reproach by immersing himself even farther into his work. Which included several retakes of the taped Train the Trainer sessions.

By week's end, Carl's contributions to the tape had been completely edited out of the finished product. Every verbal glitch, awkward moment, and hesitation by Ethan had also been redone, until the film flowed smoothly from start to end. Multiple DVD copies of the tape, entitled simply, Signa-Chip, were then made and distributed throughout the World Technologies organization.

Knowing that Nicole and the children had returned from the in-laws and were back home, while he was still in Munich, also helped ease Ethan's feelings of guilt. He called every other night, that first week, talking with Erin and Renee' at length. And though he tried, twice during those calls to talk with Nicole, she steadfastly refused to speak with him.

Late Friday afternoon, Hilda showed up in the small, temporary office World Technologies, had given Ethan to use while he was there. The office was not much: an oversized closet, crowded with the gray metal desk and the swivel chair he was appropriated.

Ethan looked up from the laptop computer and the rough outline of the sales proposal he was working on at General Matoso's request. The outline, more Purchase Agreement than Sales Proposal, approximated the six month delivery schedule for the initial one million Signa-Chips the General had ordered; Giving quantities and approximate shipping dates.

He did a double take at Hilda standing in the narrow doorway. The overhead light in the hallway behind her danced in her hair, casting an auburn halo around her face. In the neon light, even the shoulders of the off-white, one piece dress she wore took on a reddish glow from her hair.

For the first time since they met, Ethan noticed how pretty she was.

"Mister Randolph would like to see you in his office," Hilda announced, in a voice softer, more sensual than Ethan had ever heard from her before.

Must be the weekend woman in her, Ethan thought. *One Hilda for the workplace. Yet quite another privately.*

"I'm almost finished here," Ethan smiled. He glanced down at the laptop. "Give me a minute."

"That can wait," Hilda's harsher, more demanding work voice almost returned, but vanished just as quickly as it surfaced. "Besides, it's late Friday afternoon," she smiled. "Time to stop working."

As a manager, Ethan resented being ordered around by a secretary. It was a new experience for him and he thought of putting Hilda in her place. Letting her know that; just because she was the boss's 'gofer' it was still disrespectful and unacceptable. But he held his tongue. *She might have a lot more 'pull' with Mister Randolph than I think,* he thought. And she did. Ethan would later learn that Hilda's job title of Personal Secretary was deceptive. She was actually: Assistant to the vice-president of World Technologies. And as such carried with her the 'King's Ring'.

Ethan followed her up to Leonard's, office in silence.

When he, for the first time, stepped through the double, oak wood doors that led into Leonard's opulent office, Ethan stopped in amazement. The size of the room astonished him: It was twice as large as the suite he was living in at the hotel in town.

"Come in," Leonard said from behind his large, Black Walnut desk. He motioned toward one of the two, white, leather couches in front of the desk. "Have a seat."

Ethan hesitated. Not knowing whether or not he should take his shoes off before stepping in on the office's beige colored carpeting.

Hilda headed into her office, just to the left of the double entrance doors. A much smaller room, contained within the main office,.

Ethan heard his own voice coming from his right and turned to see himself, life sized, on one of the several big screen televisions, flush mounted in the wall. A portion of the Train the Trainer video played.

"Excellent job," Leonard commented on the filmed sessions, shutting the DVD player off by remote control. "Come sit, relax," he motioned again.

Still astonished by the grandeur of the office decor, Ethan moved to a couch and sat.

"I'll get right to the point," Mister Blake, Leonard leaned forward, placing his elbows on his desktop. "If it is possible...I would like for you to stay in Germany for a while longer..."

Ethan didn't know if he should respond during the pause, or wait to hear more. When the pause continued long enough that he realized the statement was actually a question, Ethan said, "It's possible." Though he didn't know how he was going to explain it to his already disgruntled wife and children.

"Good," Leonard smiled.

"So you will spend another week or so with us?"

"Sure," said Ethan. "Whatever it takes."

Gary L. Dewey

In her office, Hilda stopped tiding up her desk, a usual Friday afternoon task for her, and smiled.

Leonard, unaware of Ethan's growing personal problems back in Chicago, interpreted the choice as a show of his devotion to the company. "Excellent," he said. "The reason I asked is I'd like to put together an international sales team whose purpose is solely the promotion of the Signa-Chip. And of course I'd like you to head up that team...If you're interested?"

A long time ago, Ethan learned not to over-react in situations like these; Not to appear to enthusiastic. He sat straight faced and waited, utilizing that learned ability.

"Of course there will be more travel and responsibilities with the position."

Come on say it, Ethan thought, his excitement growing.

"And of course along with those responsibilities...a significant salary increase."

Yes, Ethan cheered inwardly. *How much?*

Leonard answered the unspoken urging as if he had heard Ethan's thoughts. "Say...twenty-five percent?"

Ethan did the quick math. The raise, he figured would put his annual salary at just over a hundred thousand dollars.

"How's that sound?" Leonard said.

"Sounds like we have us a deal," Ethan said with enough excitement to let Leonard know that he was pleased, but without appearing too elated. *That ought to appease Nicole,* Ethan thought, but never said.

"Very well then," Leonard stood, extending his right hand. "We'll get started on assembling the sales team Monday morning."

Ethan grabbed the offered hand with his. Leonard winced. "Sorry sir," Ethan apologized though he didn't know what he did.

"Oh, that's okay," Leonard withdrew and turned his palm upward. "I just had the chip implanted this morning and the site is still a little tender. I forgot all about it until we shook hands."

"Sorry," Ethan said again.

"No problem," Leonard offered his left hand. "Doctor Reece said it might be sore for a day or so."

"Mine was," Ethan showed off his palm. "Now I can't even tell it's there."

"Hilda?" Leonard called, as the handshake broke. "Are you ready to go?"

"Yes, Mister Randolph," she appeared from her office, umbrella in hand.

"Could you show Mister Blake down?"

:

"So you're going to spend some more time with us?" Hilda said, as they stood waiting for the down elevator.

"Looks like it," Ethan smiled.

The elevator arrived and they stepped in together.

The elevator door slid closed. "What are you doing later?" Hilda asked, her softer tone had returned.

Ethan didn't answer.

Hilda gently placed her left hand on his shoulder, reached around him and pressed the button marked; Ground Floor, with her right. "Would you like to have dinner with me to-night? I could show you around Munich a little bit after-wards."

:

Gary L. Dewey

When they had left the Dewalt's, Adam and Carol knew there were ill feelings and unfinished business between the four of them. The spiritual conversation Lindsey's words had sparked, became heated. Robert and Susan, both practicing evolutionist, were quite disconcerted when they had found out that their daughter and future son-in-law had become Christians. Robert concerned that they were being taken in by some dangerous religious cult; Susan; more afraid that Lindsey would be coerced into the same 'views' without having a chance to even consider an alternative. And, in Susan's eyes, the more scientific based beliefs.

Before the conversation had turned into an all out argument, which was exactly where it was headed, Adam wisely announced that he was quite tired and wanted to get home. And although there were the same good-bye hugs and kisses, the same words of thanks for the wonderful meal, Adam and Carol knew their relationship with Robert and Susan would never be the same.

The first half of the drive back home, was in silence except for the occasional comment about how 'crazy' everyone was driving on the interstate.

Adam couldn't shake off the effects of the derogatory comments his future father-in-law had made when Carol had tired to use prophecy and current events to convince him of the existence of God.

"This kind of nonsense has been happening since forever," Robert had said in reply to his daughter. "And fanatics have been standing on the street corners yelling it's the end of the world for centuries. And we're all still here aren't we?"

"But…," Adam had jumped in and started to tell about the rebuilt Roman Empire, the Mark, and the other biblical

298

warnings that had never happened in the past. And the precise detail with which they were foretold.

"But nothing," Robert cut him off quickly. "It's like a weatherman that comes on and says it's going to be warm and sunny today, everyday! Sooner or later, he's bound to get the forecast right."

Adam felt a wave of frustration and settled back into his seat on the couch, content to say no more.

"Would anyone like some coffee?" Susan asked to ease the mounting sense of ire.

Adam refused and made the announcement that he was tired again. He realized that there was no convincing anyone who wouldn't listen and surely anyone who wouldn't even give him a chance to speak. He sat quietly as Carol gathered up Lindsey. Adam seeing the role reversal and a not to distant vision of his mother trying to talk to him and his total rejection of her words.

On the last half of the trip home, Lindsey, sitting between them, confused by what she had heard, again sparked the conversation. She tugged on the side of her mother's blouse and innocently asked. "Is it the end of the world?"

Carol put an arm around her young daughter, pulling the child in tighter to her side. "I don't think so," she said, kissing the top of her head. Long faced, Carol looked over to Adam.

Adam glanced back at Carol, catching the sparkle of a tear rolling down her cheek in the headlights of a tractor-trailer speeding past them. He knew that she realized all the ramifications of what 'end times' meant.

"I think God is going to give us a new world," Adam tried to console all three of them. Himself included. He reached out his hand and placed it where Carol's arm crossed Lindsey's shoulder, touching both of them. "A new world where everybody is happy all the time. Nobody will ever get sick or die again. And we can live forever and ever."

"Yeah," Carol joined in, the lump still in her throat. "It will be a very nice place."

"When?" Lindsey looked up at Adam.

Adam withdrew his hand, putting it back on the steering wheel. "Nobody knows for sure sweetie. But, we might have to go through some hard days until it gets here."

The concept of a 'new world' was impossible for Lindsey's young mind to grasp. Especially, one 'coming'. She envisioned a giant globe, like the one in her second grade classroom at school, floating through space with angles arduously pushing and pulling it closer and closer. "What's God going to do with the old one?" she asked. "When the new one gets here."

The innocent sincerity of the question along with the tensions of the night were enough to elicit a stress relieving laugh from Adam that eventually had them all giggling. A contagious laugh that grew and continued until Adam turned off the interstate at the nineteen mile road exit. "Anyone want an ice cream cone?" He was already pulling into the Double Dip Ice Cream Parlor near the I-94 exit.

While standing in line, in the crowded ice cream parlor and waiting to place his order for the Strawberry milk shakes, he and Carol wanted and the Chocolate ice cream cone Lindsey had asked for, Adam overheard the couple in front of him talking about the 'new Signa-Chip', boasting of its virtues. He felt sickened by their misguided praise.

He held his peace as long as he could. When he had heard more than he could bare, he leaned in toward the middle-aged couple. "You know, that chip you're talking so highly about is going to be your demise."

The couple and everyone else within earshot turned to look at him.

Adam felt a strange empowering confidence, an inner-strength, a courage to continue. "You sing praises of it without knowing its ramifications." Not knowing where the strength or the words were coming from he boldly spoke. His volume growing unconsciously louder with each sentence. "For eons God has patiently warned you and still you willfully continue to ignore his counsel. You will reap the consequences of your choices people."

The interior of the Double Dip, where Adam's 'campaign' started, fell silent. Every eye was on him.

"Preach it preacher," someone shouted mockingly.

Adam scanned the group of patrons unsuccessfully, for the source of the mockery.

"Laugh," he said in response. "Signa-Chip will rob you of your freedom, rob you of life. Look around you. Is it not hard for you to kick against the stones?" The familiar words stunned him more than they did the un-hearing audience. Slowly he backed away, surprised to hear the very words God spoke to him coming from his own mouth. He exited when he neared the door.

"Where's our ice creams," Carol asked him when he climbed back into the truck without the treats.

"Too busy in there," Adam said. "I know another place down the street we can try."

Adam backed out of the parking spot, feeling that he had just done something important, something that God had wanted him to do, though he didn't know what that something was.

"Hey!" A young woman dressed in cut-off shorts and a sleeveless tank top, flagged him down as he started to pull away.

Adam stopped and rolled his window down.

"I think what you did in there was great and took a lot of courage on your part," the young woman said. "Something I think people need to hear more about, including me."

Adam glanced over to Carol, then back to the young woman. *So, you are what my public testimony was all about,* he thought. *God wants you to 'hear' and had used me to do it.*

"I have so many questions about the chip," her head dropped low when she said 'the chip' and Adam could see she was distraught. "I wish we could talk more."

"What's your name?" Adam asked the blonde haired woman.

"Rebecca...Rebecca Reid," her head still low.

"Well, Rebecca, I really don't like to give out our telephone number." Adam turned to see Carol's reaction to the conversation.

Carol was rummaging through her purse for a pen and a scrap piece of paper to write on.

"Do you have an e-mail address?" Rebecca looked up at him. "We could e-mail each other, or maybe get on-line and chat."

"I'm sorry," Adam answered. "We're not connected either."

"To bad," Rebecca said, backing away. "You could reach a lot of people."

Adam looked back to Carol again. Her search for some scrap paper had shifted from her purse to the vehicle's glove compartment.

"What are you looking for?" Adam said.

"Something to write on. Maybe we could get her number and call her."

"You won't find anything in there. You wouldn't happen to have…". Adam turned to ask Rebecca if she had anything to write on, but she was gone.

He caught a glimpse of her disappearing back into the Double Dip though the front doors. "Never mind," he said to Carol. "She's gone."

Carol looked up from her rummaging. "Well, you just can't let her go. That's a soul that needs our help. Go back and get her telephone number."

Adam re-parked and went inside again.

The line was gone and only a scant number of people sat in the dinning area, enjoying their treats. Rebecca wasn't among them.

Baffled by her disappearance, Adam scanned the seating area again, to no avail. She was gone. He walked up to the counter and asked one of the people working there, if they had seen the young lady who had just came in, describing her in detail. The young counter-person looked at her coworker, furrowing her eyes in question.

"Nobody has come here in the last ten minutes," the co-worker responded.

"Wait a minute," Adam said, an eerie feeling coming over him. "I was just in here myself five minutes ago."

"I've never seen you before in my life mister."

Stunned, the uneasiness deepening, Adam almost shouted, "There was a long line of people in here, I was argu-ing with some people about the Signa-Chip."

A look of fear came over the two counter worker's faces.

"Nothing like that happened in here," one of them said. "We haven't had a line in here all night. In fact, its been real slow."

Adam stumbled back. He stood there for a moment in silence, trying to collect his thoughts. An older couple came through the doors and stopped behind him; waiting.

"I'll um," Adam stammered as he stepped back up to the counter. "I'll have two Strawberry Shakes and a small Chocolate cone."

"You get her number?" Carol asked as soon as Adam returned.

"She wasn't in there," Adam said, handing Lindsey her ice cream cone and Carol her milkshake.

Carol squinted in question. "Not there? Are you sure? We seen her go in and I didn't see anybody leave."

"What do you want me too say? She wasn't in there," Adam took a sip of his milkshake. "According to the people working in there, she never was."

"Did you check the rest room?" Carol asked, hearing but not believing.

She had saw the woman with own eyes and knew Rebecca wasn't an apparition.

"In fact I did," Adam grinned. "I saw a lady coming out and I asked her. I was a bit embarrassed, but she told me that other than her, there wasn't anybody else in the room."

"That's ridiculous," Carol said as Adam backed the truck out again.

"Maybe she was ah angel," Lindsey said innocently, as she looked up from her ice cream.

Adam stopped the truck at the parking lot exit. Though he could have, due to the absence of crossing traffic, pulled right out and headed toward home. But he lingered hoping Rebecca would mysteriously reappear as she had vanished. When she didn't, he slowly pulled out onto nineteen mile road and resumed his homeward trek. He glanced up into his rearview mirror several times as the Double Dip faded away, to make sure Rebecca wasn't there.

He turned back onto 1-94, headed east, wondering if he had, as Hebrews 13:2 said; '...entertained angels unawares'? He relived the meeting, Rebecca's words concerning the Internet echoing in his head.; 'Too bad!' he recalled her saying. 'You could reach a lot of people.'

"I think I'm going to setup the computer in the living room and get on the Internet," Adam announced as he slowed for the 23 mile road exit. "I'm going to use it to start telling people about Signa-Chip and the Mark."

"That's fine by me," Carol responded. "But where are you going to put it? In the living room?"

"I think if we move the couch around, that desk will fit along the back wall by the window."

By midnight, Adam had rearranged the living room, moved the computer and its desk from Lindsey's bedroom and had it connected and ready to go. He clicked on the Internet Connection Wizard icon that came with his Widows Operating System and following the on-screen menus, chose the local Internet Service Provider.

"I'm going to bed," Carol declared as Adam was in the process of signing on for the first time. "I need to get up in the morning."

She got up from the couch and walked over to him, kissing him on the cheek.

"I do too," Adam said. "I won't be much longer."

Two hours later, Adam logged off. With an uneasy boldness, he had spent the one hundred and twenty minutes stumbling from chat room to chat room, 'chatting' very little. His primary interests; more in learning to navigate his way around and how to utilized the Internet than actually partici-

305

pating in it. *There is plenty of time for that,* he thought. *Once I know a little bit more of what I'm doing.*

He did try once though to start a conversation about the Signa-Chip in one of the chat rooms, but was quickly ejected from the room as soon as he started expressing God's view of it. The mere mention of God in the room, elicited an onslaught of derogatory comments from the other room members, ending in his being barred.

Tomorrow's another day, his final thought as he logged off.

:

The One Peoples Bank, OPB, a European based financial institution, opened its first United States branch in Los Angles, California. OPB offering customers, who had the Signa-Chip, the first completely exclusive electronic banking experience.

To those who did not have the required chip, and who opened an account of twenty-five hundred dollars or more, the bank agreed, as a bonus, to pay for the cost of the implant. Additionally, to draw as many customers as they could, OPB was offering interest, on all new accounts, three percent above the average rate. Touting that the money it would not loose through claims on lost debit cards, theft, and fraud with the ultra secure accounts, it was passing on to its customers.

It was a tactic that met with overwhelming success. By Labor day, four thousand new accounts had been opened at the bank, forcing the local, competitive institutions in the area to adopt an all electronic, cash-less system of funds transfer or face serious financial problems. All due to a shrinking customer base.

"It's the wave of the future:", "Get on the train or get left behind:", "It's about time:", "We've needed something like this for a long time," some of the comments elicited from people by street reporters and 'aired' in televised commercials designed to help promote the transference from the standard type accounts to the OPB accounts.

⋮

Signa-Chip was gaining world-wide acceptance at a rate faster than anyone had anticipated. So fast, that even the massive resources of World Technologies were unable to keep up with the production demands. A growing backlog of three weeks on orders for Signa-Chip resulted. And that despite turning the ESI, Chicago Administrative and Engineering facility into a one thousand units a day, Manufacturing and Warehousing site. The move, which brought production capabilities up to nearly ten thousand units per day, was still not enough. And as a result of the Supply and Demand factor, the cost of the chip soared, nearly tripling to six hundred dollars each, since its release.

Fueling the unprecedented demand for Signa-Chip, other than the added interest rates banks were offering on the electronic accounts and the ninety-five percent drop in unsolved kidnapping cases in the United States, the chip also carried the CE emblem from the European Economic Community. It achieved 'emblem status', when testing showed the product had met the Community's, established, Universal Products Standards Directives. This emblem of approval allowed the Signa-Chip to flow freely throughout the world market place unaffected by international trade controls, creating unprecedented demand.

Gary L. Dewey

Along with the worldwide demand and causing an even deeper backlog of purchase orders, several states, within the United States had also adopted new laws requiring all convicted prisoners in their legal systems to be implanted with two chips. One in the right palm, for the typical identification purposes, the second, slightly modified, non-removable, and in an inaccessible location along the spinal cord, for tracking purposes. The modification, allowed the chip to automatically administer a painful, low voltage shock, whenever the prisoners were not where they should be.

The modified chip worked miracles for keeping those prisoners on work release, or under house arrest from wandering too far from the programmed locations at the times they were allowed to be there. Also, the tracking abilities, accredited to the communication between Signa-Chip and the Global Positioning System, cut repeat offensives by eighty-six percent and aided law enforcement in quickly locating and re-arresting the implanted offenders.

The new controls had a snowballing effect, reducing street crimes, namely; illegal drug sales, prostitution, and robbery. Enough so to prompt England; France; Germany; Japan, several other smaller countries, and the remaining states, to advocate similar regulations. All delighting in a comparable reduction in major crime statistics. The savings, in greatly reduced law enforcement costs, reached into the hundreds of millions of dollars.

Close to the time, World Technologies's production capabilities began to catch up to the demand rate for the Signa-Chip, and as a natural occurrence, in the expanding use of the chip; forty, state run pubic education systems obligated, along with social security numbers and up-to-date immunization records, all of its students to have the implant. This action maintained the three week delay for shipment of available Signa-Chip units.

The Federal government, promising to subsidize the cost, helped the states decision makers enact the legislation requiring the chip and kept the demand growing.

Additionally, data demands increased, so quickly that World Technologies found itself lagging behind in that respect too and turned to the European Union to assist them in launching the two satellites responsible for meeting those data demands. Simultaneously, the world community, through a charter resulting from a United Nations World Summit meeting in Johannesburg, originally held on the issue of Global Warming and Ecological reform concerning deforestation of the worlds shrinking Rainforests, unilaterally agreed to sponsor the launching, placement, and maintenance, of three new G.P.S. system satellites. Making it possible to cover, at any given point it time, every square inch of the earth's surface with the needed computer processing power.

Gary L. Dewey

21

Ethan as head of the newly formed, Munich based, International Sales Department was invited by Leonard Randolph to accompany Leonard and Hilda to Brussels and the emergency meeting of the Board of European Union Directors. The proposed launching of its own two data processing satellites, the topic of the meeting.

Ethan beamed with enthusiasm. "I'd love to go," he responded, when Leonard posed the opportunity.

And even though the trip to Brussels would delay his return to Chicago by at least another week, he really didn't care. Ethan, already in Munich for several weeks, was growing accustomed to the German lifestyle and liked it. World Technologies had also upgraded him to a very spacious, windowed, well furnished office on the eighteenth floor, and a private secretary. And his personal relationship with Hilda had also developed to the point where he wasn't too anxious to return to Nicole, nor the marital trouble he knew awaited him when he eventually would have to.

"You wouldn't be neutral," Leonard wanted him to understand. "We would expect you to provide supportive input."

"I have no problem with that," Ethan said with confidence. "I can think of millions of reasons why we need those satellites up there now. And that list is growing larger, even as we speak."

:

Once in Brussels, Ethan would meet Leonard's superior, Warren Kilpatrict, along with the charismatic, and politically influential, Agustus A. Neitoso. Meeting Mister Kilpatrict was definitely impressive for Ethan. Meeting the thirty-three year old, black haired, Agustus Neitoso, European Economic Community representative from Spain, and Consul General of the Peoples Commerce Commission, — a consulate of extremely wealthy businessmen from all parts of the world — would forever change Ethan's life.

"Just make sure you address him as Lord Agustus," or "Potentate Neitoso," Leonard instructed Ethan. "In the unlikely event that you should happen to meet him personally."

"A little extravagant isn't it?" Ethan smiled at the thought of calling someone 'Lord'.

The stern look he got from Leonard told him to take the advice seriously.

:

When the scan of their implanted Signa-chips had provided enough positive identification data to satisfy the security guards, Ethan, Leonard and Hilda were x-rayed and scanned again, by machine, for contraband, weapons and drugs. Without, positive identification and clearance from the multi-function security machine they would not have been allowed to pass any deeper into the Brussels Conference Building, where they were to meet up with Warren Kilpatrict.

As soon as they had received that clearance, they stepped through the locked doors just beyond the security station into the inner first floor area of the building. The wide open, windowless space, Ethan noticed was devoid of any furnishings. And except for the bank of elevators, he saw along the back wall, the area was completely empty. *Probably another buffer zone against unauthorized entry*, Ethan surmised. *A place to trap any and all unwanted visitors who made it passed the front station.*

Ethan was correct in his assumptions: the elevators, controlled by security, and back through the manned security station itself were the only ways in or out of the massive building.

The door to one of the elevators silently slid open. Warren Kilpatrict, and the security guard accompanying him, stepped out. Immediately Warren withdrew to a distant corner with Leonard, while Ethan, Hilda and the armed guard waited near the elevators for their personal conference to end. When they had finished talking they returned and Leonard introduced Ethan.

"So this is the gentleman I've been hearing so much about?" Warren said.

Ethan extended his hand in greeting "Mister Kilpatrict."

"How was your flight?"

"Fine. Everything was perfect"

"Excellent," Warren smiled. "And how is Miss Aldous treating you?"

"No complaints sir," Ethan smiled back and felt a bit self-conscious. He was glad the elevator doors reopened an instant later and broke the awkwardness he felt.

At no time, until they were inside the Conference Room, where the meeting was to occur, were they without the armed escort. The uniformed security guard even accompanying them on the elevator.

"As soon as we enter the conference room," Warren told Ethan on the ride up to the fifth floor conference room, "an attendant will take us to the far end of the conference table.

Several men, will be already seated around the table. Don't make visual contact with them and keep your eyes down."

Fighting the urge to look, Ethan did no more than take an occasional, quick, sideways glance at the men. All of them dressed in either very expensive suits or the colorful robes typical of their native countries. He kept his eyes on the heals of Leonard, half a step in front of him. The humility Ethan displayed was unfeigned, he knew he was in the presence of some of the worlds richest and most prestigious men. And his meekness earned him a level of respect.

Once the noise of their entrance subsided, the room again grew silent. But Ethan felt like he could still feel the eyes of everyone in the room on him.

Hilda, though she had the appropriate security clearance, was not allowed to enter with the men. Instead, through no choice of her own, she was escorted to another room on the same floor. Where along with several other female "assistants", she was allowed to view the proceedings of the meeting via video cameras. Having prior knowledge; accepting the fact that due to the diversities of cultures involved, the presence of women in the Conference was offensive to some, Hilda offered no resistance.

The triad representing World Technologies was seated behind triangular name plates placed atop the table in front of padded, high backed, chairs. The sumptuous seating reminded Ethan more of thrones than quintessential conference room chairs.

Once seated, Ethan glanced around reading the displayed name plates in front of the delegates for the nations present. He stopped at Greece the tenth such plate. Mentally he perused the names again, the more difficult ones several times, until he was satisfied he could correctly pronounce them if he addressed the person directly.

The seat, closest to the door and behind the plate marked Spain was empty and it was obvious they were awaiting whoever it was that was supposed to sit there before starting the conference. Ethan squinted to read the name: Agustus A. Neitoso. He wondered what the A. stood for.

In less than a minute, the Conference room door opened. A stocky, suspicious looking man stuck his head in, quickly glanced around the room, then retracted it. Seconds later a six foot tall, bronze skinned, finely dressed man stepped in. Instantly, Ethan detected, what he interpreted as an aura of divinity surrounding the man and just as quickly fell captive to its invisible force.

Accompanied by two personal bodyguards the representative from Spain stopped behind his chair, his shoulders square, his head held high, almost arrogant. "Gentlemen," he nodded, as one of the bodyguards pulled out his seat.

The guard stepped back with his cohort against the door. Collectively, the two guards effectively, prevented further entrance or exit.

For the first time since their arrival, Ethan felt anxious. More so when he allowed himself to envision the group of powerful men questioning him for his input as to why he thought the EEC should help finance the two satellites, World Technologies hoped to launch.

When the questions did come, three-quarters of the way through the two hour meeting, they came faster and more furious than even Ethan had envisioned. Notwithstanding, Warren and Leonard thought Ethan handled each one of them, including the ones from Spain, flawlessly.

"Why is it that you can not delay the completion and launch of the satellites until World Technologies can finance the operation?" The representative from Greece asked the first question of Ethan.

"We could," Ethan said and looked for the representative's name. "Mister Hyatt. However, at a much greater cost than the price of the actual satellites themselves."

"Why is that?" Italy asked.

"The reputation of the Signa-Chip…"

The room grew quiet. Waiting.

"The demand for Signa-Chip is greatly exceeding what was anticipated," Ethan explained. "As we speak, more people now have it than we can provide guaranteed satellite support for. When the demands for data are not met, people will start to become disenchanted with the benefits and doubt the effectiveness of our claims and the abilities of Signa-Chip."

"Sales will most certainly suffer," Leonard supported Ethan.

"Why has more capital not been allocated to the satellites. You surely knew you would need them?" The representative from Turkey asked.

"Again," Ethan said. "With the unexpected demand, all liquid assets have been used to try to meet the required production increases. We faced a difficult choice: focus on the satellites at the cost of production or retool for manufacturing."

"Not to mention the huge outlay of money required to purchase the controlling interest in Electronic Solutions Incorporated. The American based company that invented the original chip," Warren said, defending Ethan's response.

"Had it not been for the unforeseen drastic increase in demand, we could have easily accomplished both tasks simultaneously. However…"

"How many units daily are we taking about?" Agustus Neitoso asked.

"We're producing between forty and fifty thousand units a day Lord Agustus, "Ethan beamed. "At six hundred Euro dollars per. And we're looking at a growing backlog on purchase order delivery dates of over three weeks. With a half a million Signa-Chips already implanted, sales of twelve million more already on the books and the potential for hundreds of millions more. It is mathematically plain to see that we need your help in meeting this demand while the demand is there."

The questions continued for a few more minutes until they tapered off to the technicalities of any help the EEC would extend, World Technologies, if it had so inclined. Questions beyond Ethan's scope. But, he had accomplished his end of the bargain.

In fact, so expertly did Ethan respond, that by the end of the meeting, everyone present was impressed with his performance. Including Agustus.

The meeting over and World Technologies successfully obtaining the financial support they sought from the EEC, Ethan did meet Agustus personally. He was led to the standing representative from Spain by Warren and extended his right hand in greeting. "Lord Agustus," Ethan said.

"Call me Abaddon, Agustus said, "Everyone close to me calls me that. And I could use someone with your verbal expertise close."

:

Adam reached down the sides of the chair he sat in and pulled out the remote control. He pointed it at the television like he was aiming a pistol. A deep, subtle bump was heard as the twenty-seven inch stereo console shut off. He relaxed back into the reclining chair in the sudden quietness, pulling the lever on the chair's right side so the foot rest lifted his feet off the floor.

He had heard enough of the CNN Nightly Newscast. The stories of floods in Europe, Central Asia, and Africa; the scenes of terrorist, suicide bombers in Israel; Arab conflicts in the Middle East and their senseless killing of innocent people, all played on his mind. But, those stories were happening to a distant people. A people with which he felt no personal bond, no kindred. The news stories of the two month long droughts out west and the raging forest fires though, hit closer to heart, and he felt a deeper compassion for the thousands of American people chased from their residences by the fires. His earnest sadness for them, came from knowing that most of the fire's victims would return to either looted homes, or ashes.

The millions of acres of crops the droughts had destroyed, he knew would effect everybody nationwide eventually, with less produce at the market place, and soaring prices for what little there would be.

The 'news' was not over when he shut the television off, but his heart felt heavy in his chest and he just couldn't bare to hear anymore 'bad' news. He closed his eyes, listening to the voices of Carol and Lindsey, in the other room, as Carol sat, supervising Lindsey's evening bath. The sounds of the light-hearted 'bath time' camaraderie between a loving mother and her daughter helped him relax.

How could a loving God allow such things to happen to his people? Adam thought. A twinge of anger at his new found God welled up in his head. He started to open his mouth to put substance to his thought, but stopped himself before any sound occurred.

"All clean," Lindsey dashed out of the bathroom, her still damp hair hanging limp to her shoulders.

Adam lifted her up on his lap and hugged her.

It was a nightly ritual that Lindsey had initiated a couple of weeks ago: after her bath, and before her mother tucked her in for the night, a dash to the Living room for a hug and a good night kiss.

Typically, right after, Adam would log on to the Internet and continue to spread the word of the spiritual ramifications of accepting the Signa-Chip.

"Ummm," Adam sniffed her hair while he was holding her close. "You smell good too."

"It's my new shampoo," Lindsey drew back and beamed. "Mom got it for me today at the store."

"You smell like flowers."

Lindsey said in her young voice, "Tropical Bouquet," then pulled a strand around to her nose.

Carol finished restoring the bathroom to its pre-bath condition. "Say Good night," she said, as she stepped through the archway.

"Good night," Lindsey quickly leaned over and kissed Adam on the cheek.

Adam leaned back and closed his eyes again. He thanked God for the blessing of Carol and Lindsey in his life and felt the irony of being angry with God and thankful at the same time.

He relaxed, letting his mind wander. Signa-Chip jumped into his thoughts, the Mark, 'end times'. Instantly, the pain of realizing that he would probably never see Lindsey graduate from high school, or grow into a woman tore at his heart again. He jerked his eyes open and sat forward, snapping the leg support on the recliner closed. Suddenly he felt angry again. More than angry he felt hurt; cheated.

He stood up as Carol returned from tucking Lindsey in.

"What's the matter, honey?" Carol said.

Adam knew his feelings showed. "Nothing," he said. "I just need to go out in the yard for a walk."

"Do you want me to go with you?" Carol asked.

"Naw. I'm just going out in the backyard. I need some air and want to be alone for a few minutes."

"Did I do something? You're not mad at me are you?"

"Come here," Adam answered her and wrapped his arms around her. Holding her tight, he gently kissed her on the lips. "I love you," he whispered. "And no I'm not angry with you. I just want to be alone for a few minutes."

It never really got dark in the city. Wherever an unlit spot was, someone was trying to illuminate it with some form of lighting, mostly for safety's sake. And either from the brightness from the many streetlights, those in the neighbor's yards, or from the constant parade of automobile headlights passing by, it stayed twilight-like all through the night. Adam's yard was no exception.

Fact was, crime was rampant everywhere, even in the quiet suburban area where Adam lived and that fact inspired the excessive lighting. The thought was: The better things were lit, the less chance one had of becoming a victim of crime. Though that thought rarely rang true: The boldness of most criminals was not swayed by the presence of light.

Adam walked across the narrow strip of lawn he called his backyard, his shadow from the motion detector spotlight mounted high on the back wall of his house proceeding him. He stopped at the back fence, separating his yard from the neighbors on the other street, and stood perfectly still, hoping the automatic light would go out. After a few minutes the timer turned it off and he stood in the pale, vague seclusion. The sound of the traffic on twenty-three mile, the main east/west thoroughfare, two blocks away, hummed.

It was a clear, warm, late August night and Adam looked skyward at the few visible stars bright enough to show through the thick haze of city pollution. "Why Jesus," he spoke into the air. "Why does it have to be now?" He kept his eyes upward, like he was expecting the Son of God to suddenly appear in the haziness and personally answer his questions.

When he didn't, Adam let his face turn toward the ground, feeling ashamed for thinking that God owed him an explanation. And knowing that if God had provided him with one, in all probability, he wouldn't have openly accepted it anyway.

Adam laid his forearms along the top bar of the chain-link fence and let his head hang low. For the next few minutes of denial, he stood there in the relative quiet, trying to convince himself that the events on CNN were indeed 'just' natural occurrences and not related to the 'End Times' prophecy he was learning about. The pain of thinking that it might all be coming to an end soon was more than he wanted to accept.

Still, he argued with himself, and couldn't comprehend why a loving God would allow such atrocities to happen.

And where were you when I laid the foundations of the world that you might contend with ME, that I might have taken consul from you, jumped into his head.

"What?" Adam jerked his head upright and spun around, the thought so real, he again mistook it for a voice.

With his movement, the motion activated light on the back of the house came on.

The neighbor's dog, a full grown, four year old German Shepherd, three houses down barked out viciously. Warning anyone in the area that if they ventured his way, the sixty pound beast would be considerably less than congenial.

Within half a minute several flood lights in nearby yards came on illuminating everything and two other neighborhood dogs began barking. A ruckus that would last until the dogs were brought inside by their owners. Adam, slightly embarrassed, felt the eyes of his neighbors watching him from behind the safety of their closed doors. He hoped that everyone who had saw him recognized him and hadn't already called the police. Slowly, methodically, he walked back to his house and went in.

"What's all the fuss about out there?" Carol asked as soon as Adam was in.

"Me," Adam said, as he closed the front door behind him. "Can't even go out and stand in my own yard."

Carol, in her pink, flowered house coat, sitting on the couch, refocused on the bible she held in her lap.

"Do you think God talks to people?" Adam walked past her, sat in his recliner. His tone serious.

She looked up at him puzzled. Somehow he looked different: Pale, almost frighteningly so.

"I think God spoke to me…out there in the yard."

"What'd He say?"

"He asked me where I was when He was making the world." Adam reworded the vivid thought. "So He could've ask me to help Him."

A smile started to cross Carol's face but the look on Adam's face erased it before it happened. "What'd you say back?"

"Nothing."

A long moment passed with neither changing their position, nor speaking.

"I was feeling sad about all the bad things I'd been hearing on the news lately," Adam began. "Thinking, why would a loving God let so much suffering happen."

Using her finger to keep her place, Carol folded the Bible closed. Her eyes were glued to Adam.

"Then out of nowhere I get this thought. So strong I imagined it sounded like a voice."

"Maybe it was God letting you know that you shouldn't question Him. That He knows what He's doing."

"I'm sure that's what it was," Adam stood up. He headed for the kitchen and the refrigerator. "You want anything to drink?"

"I'll have a soda."

While he was pouring the two glasses of Ginger Ale, the telephone rang. He looked up at the clock on the wall next to the stove. Wondering who would be calling them at bed time.

Carol said, "I'll get it."

He heard Carol say, "No. We're still up...That's all right." Then a little chuckle before she added, "Adam and I were just talking."

"Who is it?" Adam set Carol's glass on the end table next to the couch where she had returned with the portable phone.

Melissa, Carol mouthed without actually saying it.

Adam retreated to his recliner with his Ginger Ale and re-lived his episode in the back yard.

"Jack wants to talk to you," Carol said, slid to the side of the couch nearest him and handed Adam the telephone.

"Hello Jack," Adam spoke into the phone.

"Evening, Adam."

"What's up?"

"I don't know," Jack Elsworth said. "Melissa and I were in prayer, as we usually do just before bed. God spoke to my heart and told me to call you and find out how you were do-ing."

A chill coursed its way through Adam, raising goose bumps on his arms and causing the tiny hairs on the nape of his neck to stand up. "So, I'm not going crazy?" He said, glad to hear Jack confirm his suspicions. "God does talk to people?"

"Well, not like you and I are talking," Jack clarified. "He speaks to our hearts. Sometimes so strongly that you think He's actually verbally speaking."

Carol picked up her Bible and started reading it again. But out of concern, paid more attention to the conversation going on next to her, than the words she was reading.

"But, if you're hearing voices…" Jack took the opportunity to jokingly rib Adam. He realized he shouldn't have, when Adam didn't respond. He waited for a moment then asked Adam directly, "How are things?"

Adam hesitated before he told Jack everything relevant about his evening. Starting with the CNN newscast. Even his thoughts.

Jack listened patiently on the other end of the phone. When Adam was done, Jack told him to read the last five or so chapters of the book of Job. "Where God dealt with Job and his friends who had complained a bit too much. As for the rest of it," Jack continued to explain. "I don't know what to tell you except be thankful you and your loved ones got saved when you did and you've had chance to be prepared. This is just the beginning. Things are going to get much, much worse."

That was not what Adam wanted to hear. He fidgetcd uncomfortably in his seat.

"I feel sorry for them too," Jack said in a softer voice, Adam knew was sincere. "But, they have wanted a world without God in it for a long, long time…And He is going to give it to them."

"But," Adam choked out. "Why now?"

"That I don't know Adam. But God has given man thousands of years to get it together and the longer He waits, the worse it gets."

Adam nodded his agreement.

"He even sent his only begotten Son to help man find his way. And what did we do? We denied and mocked Him, tortured and ended up killing Him."

A lump grew in Adam's throat as the impact of Jack's words struck home. A life time of memories came crashing in. *Guilty as Charged.* He reached for his soda.

"And have no doubt about it, Adam, man's sins impaled Jesus then and just as if their hands had personally drove in the original spikes, the sins of the people today, are just as much to blame."

Adam swallowed hard. "I can't help but think though that this Signa-Chip isn't to blame for all of this. It all started when the chip came out."

"This has been coming for a long time Adam," Jack said. "Perhaps the chip was the last straw, or it was the last piece of the puzzle. God sees the future, not us."

"I can see it," Adam set his glass down. "The more this chip spreads, the worse things are starting to occur.

:

Adam tossed and turned late into the night, reliving the chapters he had read in Job, the telephone conversation with Jack Elsworth, and God speaking to his heart in his backyard. In the quiet darkness, listening to Carol's gentle breathing as she slept, and still troubled by his 'End Times' realizations, he wept inwardly. It was painful for Adam. Life as he knew it, was crumbling to pieces all around him. Especially painful, was not having a real comprehension as to what lay ahead for him, Carol and Lindsey.

He got up and logged on to the Internet, reading his e-mail and checking into how many 'hits' he had on the simple, Anti-Signa-Chip web page he created. Most of the e-mails were short notes that either complimented, or belittled his efforts. The majority fit the later category and some of those even going so far as being threatening. *At least I'm getting some attention,* Adam thought of the forty visitors to his on-line site. But the number was way less than he thought he would have.

He was about to log off and try going to bed again when he opened one more of the e-mails he had still left unread. The short note from Carl Torre, neither really praising, nor condemning his web page, caught his attention.

Antibeast3:, the note started with Adam's screen name, was followed by: Idea good, approach weak, ended with: I may be of help. E-mail me. C. Torre.

The name sounded familiar, though Adam couldn't recall how or from where. He clicked on the Reply option his mail browser provided.

Dear CT9883: Interested in you comments. How can you help? Please email me at AG4CW@aol. com. (a more private address), he typed and sent it.

He went and laid back down, peaceful sleep came a few short moments later.

:

Surprisingly, despite only a few hours sleep, Adam awoke alert and rested, ready for another day at Kendell Industries.

He showered and dressed, convincing himself that he had a real chance to expose the Chip for what it was. If not turning the people against it, surely prolonging its acceptance.

Adam headed off to work, wondering who Carl Torre was and where he had met him. Confident that Carl's input just might make a difference, Adam set his mind: *Signa-Chip might gain world-wide acceptance. But not without a fight.*

He pulled into the parking lot at Kendell Industries and rushed in, anxious to converse with Nathaniel prior to the start of the shift.

Nathaniel and several of the machinists were huddled around the time clock, mid-plant, waiting for the shift to begin, and reading two bulletins pinned to the two foot square cork board just above the official company clock.

Adam worked his way into the group and read the first bulletin. Stunned, he read it twice. He couldn't believe his own eyes; Kendell Industries was going to a compulsory electronic deposit of all employee paychecks beginning the first of the month.

Kenneth Whitman, who followed Adam into the plant wiggled his way through the group blocking access to the clock. "Excuse me," he said, waving his, company issued, Personal Identification Card and needing to punch in via the computerized clock.

Adam took the card from him and slid it through the slot atop the small rectangular timepiece. The metallic strip on the card, containing Ken's social security and employee numbers, activated the scanner beam that read the embedded information. Instantly the Time Clock transferred the data of Ken's arrival to the Payroll Department server.

Nathaniel and Adam exchanged solemn glances as Kenneth stepped away. The janitor threw his head back while turning to reface the bulletin board. A gesture for Adam to read the other company note.

Adam leaned over, whispering to Nathaniel that he wanted to see him in his office for a moment before they started work. "I have something I want to discuss with you that you might be interested in."

The near retirement Janitor nodded, without taking his eyes off the bulletin.

Adam read the second bulletin, stumbled back in disbelief, a look of horror on his face. How could it be? No! He turned to look at Nathaniel. Nat's eyes were still glued to the cork board. Adam reread the bulletin hoping beyond hope that he had read it wrong the first time, that somehow the words would change.

They didn't:

> The Plant will close after the shift on Friday August 29th for the Labor day holiday and re-tooling. It will reopen at its regular time on September 8th. Employees may use sick days or vacation time during this shut down. Please see Diane Lynwood in Payroll, before Friday, for the proper forms.
> ************************************
> Required to report on the day after the holiday: Tuesday September 2nd.
> Joseph O'Harris … Shop Floor Supervisor
> Adam Garrett … Maintenance/Electrician
> Kenneth Whitman … Lead Machinist
> Nathaniel Jenkins … Maintenance/Janitorial
> Sheila Cummings … Shipping and Receiving.

They will assist the visiting representatives
from Electronic Solutions Inc. in retooling
three of our machines to manufacture components for the new high volume Signa-Chip
production machines.

****

Have a Safe and Happy Holiday.

Adam reeled. Staggered to his office and sat heavily behind his desk. Instead of hindering the propagation of the
chip, he was being told he had to assist it. And become a step
closer to being part of it, through Direct Deposit. His
thoughts bounced between anger, fear, determination, and
defeat.

"You wanted to see me?" Nathaniel stepped into his office.

He glanced up to him. "Why? Why is God doing this?"

"God ain't," Nathaniel said, as he closed the door behind
him. "Man is."

"But, He's letting it happen," Adam's head drooped low.

"If you beat your head against the desk," Nathaniel
moved in close to him. "Would God give you a headache?"

"No." Adam lifted his head.

"Dat's right," Nathaniel said. "You'd suffer the consequences of your own actions. And mankind is going to suffer
the consequences of their actions too. Actions God has been
warning them against for generations."

Adam looked up again. Astonished. The wisdom of the
Janitor answering a myriad of his questions.

"Man has chosen to ignore those warnin's. Even tryin' to
disprove the existence of God with their Evolutionary, Dar-
winism theories."

Gary L. Dewey

Adam nodded. "I was thinking about starting a group of believers that would help me slow down the spread of this chip and now they want me to help them make more of them."

A smirk crossed Nathaniel's face. Nathaniel placed his callused hands on the edge of the desk and leaned toward Adam. "Why you think Christians would be interested in anythin' like dat?...We've been praying for generations dat Jesus' Kingdom would come. Why would we want to stop it when it got here?"

The viability of Adam's idea crumbled.

"As for the other thin', I guess you and I are goin' to have to make a choice, aren't we?" Nathaniel turned and walked out of his office. It was the last time Adam would ever see him. The last words he would hear him speak.

22

Vibrations from the Surround Sound speakers, on the sixty-two inch projection screen television in Leonard's office, sent a ripple across the top of Ethan's glass of Bourbon. The unadulterated volume of the roar during lift off was near deafening. Orange and red flames trailed five hundred feet behind the winged, German built space shuttle as it arced upward into the clear blue, afternoon sky.

Satellite number one," Leonard said, hoisting his glass of bourbon as the roar waned and the shuttle became a shrinking black dot on the screen.

"Cheers," Ethan smiled triumphantly.

Hilda turned as their glasses converged and added hers to the symbolic victory salute.

After they gulped down the shot of whiskey, they stood together in front of the big screen television and watched until the dot was little more than a speck.

"Less than thirty-six hours from now the ship will rendezvous with the coordinates and deposit our satellite," Leonard, the first to turn away from the television, said.

"When is the next one scheduled for launch," Hilda asked.

"Two months," Ethan answered.

"And you're both invited back here again to watch it with me," Leonard added. He reached for the bottle of Kentucky's best on his desk. He poured them another shot.

Hilda glanced at her watch.

"Don't worry about it," Leonard smiled. "Our work for the day is over and it's time for a little celebration."

Ethan placed his hand over the top of his glass. "I need to check on that acquisition and make sure everything is going all right with that before I can call it a day,"

Leonard stopped his pour. "You mean the Connelly deal?"

Ethan nodded and stepped over to put his empty glass down on the desk. The last thing he wanted to do was to get inebriated before closing the biggest deal of his life. He cleared his still burning throat.

The asking price of one-hundred and eighty million dollars for the three manufacturing plants in the Connelly Group, Hilda knew was still beyond what World Technologies was capable of paying. She thought the deal 'dead' from lack of liquid capital. "I didn't know we were still interested in that," she said.

Leonard moved to his chair. "The bean counters did some studies and we figured if World Technologies purchased the Connelly factories with the moneys we didn't have to invest in the satellites, we could give the production of Signa-Chip a real boost."

"I thought we had a deal with the EEC to supply several of its companies with orders for the Chip as part of the deal. In exchange for their help with the satellites?"

"We did," Ethan responded to Hilda. He took a seat on the couch and looked at Leonard. "And we're not going to back out on that deal. But even at the rate of the half-a-million chips a day the EEC companies can give us, it would still take over two years to make enough chips for the people in the United States alone. If Signa-Chip takes off world wide, as it looks like it has, it would take over thirty years at that rate to manufacture enough chips to go around."

"That's an awful ambitious vision," Hilda said, as she sat next to Ethan on the couch. "There's six billion people in this world."

"And from the looks of things everyone of them are going to eventually need a chip of some sort." With visions of trillions of dollars in potential profit dancing in his head, Leonard beamed.

"Surely you can't think that we are going to sell that many Signa-Chips?" Hilda frowned.

"No," Ethan said and stood up. He nervously paced the office. "Other companies are going to jump on the money wagon and come out with their own versions of the chip. Before you know it the market place will be flooded with them." He stopped and turned toward Hilda. "We just need to get as much of this initial blast as we can before they do. And to do that we must produce a lot of chips and produce them fast."

"Sold," Hilda said. "You don't have to convince me. I was just curious as to why we were still interested in the Connelly Group. More so, since it hasn't yet been long enough to realize a profitable return on our initial investments, in Signa-Chip, where the money was coming from."

"Well, now you know," Leonard sipped at his Bourbon and offered to pour Hilda another.

She accepted, stood and moved over to the edge of Leonard's desk.

"Yeah, I suppose," she said, extending her glass. "One never knows when the bottom might fall out of a boon like this and we need to 'strike while the iron is hot'…to coin the American phrase."

Leonard poured; looked over to Ethan and said confidently, "I don't think the bottom is going to fall out of this one any time soon."

Too confident, Hilda thought. *The chip, though a 'hot' item now, is no different than any other product.* She knew from past experience that the buying public was a fickle bunch that could change over night. She also knew that Leonard and Ethan both knew that too. She returned to her seat, confused by the over-confidence. "How can you be so sure about that?"

"Cashless Society," Leonard answered. "No chip, no access to funds."

"You either have Signa-Chip or a version of it," Ethan said and started pacing again, "or you cannot function financially in the coming one world economic community. Plain and simple."

Hilda said, "Well, there's already somebody in the United States that has started an anti-Signa-Chip website that is drawing some local attention."

∶

Halfheartedly, Adam dawdled around his office for two hours before he became so upset with Kendell Industries that he wanted to leave. He faked illness to get the rest of the day off and walked up to the Payroll Department and put in for the last week of vacation time he had coming. He needed time to think. Time to put it all together. Time to distinguish just what it was he could do.

What AM I going to do? He asked himself many times, his thoughts emphasizing the word am.

He knew he couldn't just quit working. He had truck payments; a mortgage; a planned marriage seven weeks away; a family that depended upon him. Neither could he keep working there and help them make the very machines that would make Signa-Chips. *Another job* was an option he thought of. *Another place of employment. Somewhere that didn't know about Direct Deposit or the Signa-Chip.* But, 'another job' like that, he also realized, was quickly becoming increasingly difficult to get in the city. Another job also meant throwing away all his seniority, pension, medical benefits and starting all over.

He meandered out to his pickup a confused man. Sat behind the wheel, staring across the filled parking lot for several minutes before he started the engine. He leaned back in the seat and closed his eyes. The air conditioning fan blowing warm air over him, Adam opened the side window and looked for Nathaniel's vehicle. An older model, red, Mercury Cougar. It wasn't to be seen and he figured that Nathaniel had went home too, feeling much the same as he did. Eventually the AC unit began blowing cooler air. Adam rolled up the window and pulled away from the lot, headed no where in particular.

Traffic was heavy for the late morning as he drove east, down 21 mile road. The five lanes of road teaming with vehicles. Just a few short hours ago he was steadfast, his mind set; contemplating raising an army of believers to help him hinder the propagation of the chip. Now he was faced with assisting it, or face financial ruin. His mind numbed by the turn of events.

Traffic buzzed past him as he poked along just under the speed limit, in no hurry to get anywhere. The driver of the blue Pontiac behind him, a dark skinned man in his late twenties, had another agenda. It suddenly whipped out from behind his pickup, horn blowing, the driver yelling some profanity that Adam choose to ignore.

More horns and screeching tires as the driver of the car, the Pontiac had cut-off with the unexpected lane change, slammed its brakes to avoid certain impact. That driver yelling unheard profanities at the Pontiac, while extending his middle finger.

Adam glanced away nonchalantly, pretending not to notice the near collision. But he saw enough to know that the second driver, a younger, lighter skinned man was full of rage. Three blocks away, when the vehicles came to a complete stop at a traffic light, Adam mocked their impatience. "I hope it was worth it," he said to no one. He let the Dodge roll to a stop a few vehicles behind them.

In a flash the driver of the second vehicle was out, standing along side the driver's door of the blue, Pontiac, screaming. He violently kicked the front of the Pontiac, denting the fender.

Adam lowered his window as the dark skinned driver flung open his door, knocking the other man to the pavement. Just as quickly the man was out of his car and on top of the man that had damaged his car, pounding him with his fist. No one else moved as they watched the beating taking place. Adam noticed some were even laughing, enjoying the display of violence.

Adam reached to open his door to get out, when he spotted the glint of shiny steel in the younger man's hand. The five inch long knife blade was in the chest of the man on top of him so fast, Adam wasn't sure of what he had witnessed. The man recoiled, the knife dangling from his bloodied shirt. The younger man regained his feet, sprinted back into his car and made a U-turn, disappearing into the traffic behind them.

Adam jumped from his truck and rushed over toward the bleeding man as traffic began pulling away like nothing had happened. For them the show was over. It was back to business as usual. Some of the cars in the back actually blowing their horns, trying to hasten other vehicles to get out of their way.

The man staggered back into the Pontiac and sped away toward the nearest hospital Emergency Room, before Adam reached him. Leaving Adam standing alone in the middle of the busy road.

With disdain, for a moment, Adam stood there watching the traffic drive around him. Their apathy disturbed him. Some vehicles so close, they nearly brushed against him as they hurried past. He had to wait for the traffic light to turn red again, stopping the rush of vehicles once more, before he could weave his way through them, back to his pickup.

He looked at his watch to make note of the exact time. Just in case he was ever needed to give testimony of the incident, he would at least know what time it occurred. He would never need the information though, the event would go unrecorded.

Adam spotted a public telephone sign in the first Service Station after the traffic light and he pulled his truck into the station next to it. He called Carol at work to see if he could meet her somewhere for lunch.

"Why aren't you at work?" Carol asked in response to the invitation.

"We'll talk at lunch…if you want to meet somewhere."

"Sure!" Carol said, surprised, worried, and delighted all at once by the unexpected call. "There's a place called The Pelican on the corner of sixteen mile and Mound road. I'll meet you there at noon or a little after."

Adam looked at his watch again. It was 11:32. "I know the place," he said. "I should be able to make it there by then."

When he arrived, just after twelve o'clock, Carol already had a booth in the back section of The Pelican restaurant. A small privately owned dinner near where she worked. She

Gary L. Dewey

sat staring out through the large plate glass window, next to the table, at the constant stream of traffic on Mound road.

Adam picked his way through an unrelenting mob of impatient workers in the over crowded establishment. Most of who, unlike Carol who had an hour for lunch, only had thirty minutes to get a table, their food, eat it, and get back to wherever it was they worked by 12:30.

The drone of noise within the restaurant drowned out the mocking comments some made, as Adam pushed his way past those begrudging and unwilling to give way.

"Could you have picked a busier place?" Adam commented to Carol, as he slid into the seat across the table from her. Relieved to have a seat before a melee erupted, Adam sighed.

She smiled. "Around here, they're all busy now. It's lunch-time."

Instantly a haggard looking waitress was standing next to their table. "What'll it be?" She said indifferently.

Adam glanced around for a non-existent menu.

"We'll have burgers, fries and coffees," Carol answered for him before the waitress had time to react to the slight delay.

Just as quickly as she appeared, the waitress disappeared back into the throng of patrons.

Straight-faced, Carol listened as Adam retold her the accounts of his morning, starting with the stabbing. She was not one for holding back her emotions usually, and Adam knew the event had more impact on her than she was willing to show.

Carol waited until he was finished telling the story. "You're lucky you didn't get hurt too," she said, her expression still blank "You can't let yourself get involved in those

338

things. As crazy as people have gotten, it's a wonder you didn't get stabbed too."

"Well, I just couldn't sit there like everybody else and watch them kill each other either."

Carol's face, for the first time showed emotion. She reached out and took his hand in hers.

"Excuse me," the waitress returned with their food. Carol withdrew her hand as the woman set the matching plates of food on the table in front of them.

"That was quick," Adam smiled up at the young waitress as she poured their coffees.

"They make them up beforehand," she said. "That's why they call it 'Fast Food'."

He was going to respond but before Adam could, she was gone again.

The three men at the table across the aisle, their lunch gobbled rose to leave. Immediately two more took their place before the bus boy even had a chance to clear away the soiled dishes.

"So, how come you're not at work?" Carol asked, reaching for the catsup and mustard.

Adam dropped his head and silently gave thanks for their lunch. "They want me to help them make the machines that make the chip."

Carol stopped chewing her bite of hamburger. She swallowed hard. "When?"

"The first of the month."

They sat there silent amid the jumbled voices of the other patrons.

Adam spoke first, explaining all the details of Kendell's intentions concerning Direct Deposit and Signa-Chip, while Carol listened, her heart sinking further with each narration.

"What do you plan on doing?" Carol finally gathered the strength to ask.

"Don't know yet," Adam shrugged. "I took vacation for the rest of this week..." He looked across at her evident despondency. This time he took her hand, reassuringly he gently squeezed it. "I'll think of something,"

:

Half a world away, Israel's Prime Minister didn't have to 'think' anymore. Nor did the weary, angry people of his country. The last terrorist, suicide bombing: a vicious explosion in a crowded hotel lobby that killed twelve and wounded, or maimed twenty-three other innocent Israeli men, women, and children, was enough to answer the Israeli question as to 'what they were going to do'.

The Prime Minister's command went out and within hours, several divisions of Israeli tanks, along with air support from three squadrons of fighter jets, were leveling Palestinian border settlements. Their intent: annihilate the Palestinians and forever silence the terrorist threat.

Cries of Jihad reverberated through the Arab states as the Heads of States, Kings, and Princes held emergency meetings to formulate a united counter-offensive against Israel. "Stop, Instantly," their demand, "or face the wrath of a Holy war."

In response to the United Arab's warnings, Israel's Prime Minister announced Israel's concerted reply, "If it's Jihad you want...Jihad we will give you!"

World leaders scrambled feverishly, to avoid the inevitable slaughter of millions of people, if the Israeli advance was not checked. The United Nations Security Council, in their own emergency meeting in Geneva, denounced Israel's actions. The world community demanding, Israel cease all aggressive military actions against the Palestinian people immediately.

The Israeli envoy, attending the UN. meeting, listened to the condemnations and demands without any intent of compliance. Neither argument posed did anything to sway their sentiment, nor Israel's resolve to rid themselves of the plague of terrorism. "At any cost", one representative coldly stated Israel's intention. "They will kill no more of our women and children."

Tempers flared at Israel's indifference. Accusations and threats flew from everywhere. Even talk of ejecting Israel from the U.N. and considering them a threat to world peace erupted.

Calmly, the designate from Spain, Agustus (Abaddon) Neitoso, who had requested the floor, was announced. "Gentlemen," he started, stepping up to the podium at the front of the large, open, auditorium. The curved, enjoined, multiple rows of occupied stations stretching out below and in front of him, each seat filled with a murmuring occupant. Agustus focused his stare at the Israeli ambassador. "I have a viable plan to solve your country's terrorist problems without the loss of one innocent life."

The U.N. assemblage instantly went silent.

The microphone Agustus was speaking into squealed for a second, until the person in charge of monitoring its volume, who had turned it up to accommodate the din, adjusted the power to a lower level. Every eye and ear present focused on Agustus.

"And if I told you I had a way for you to monitor every movement of every terrorist on the face of the earth. Would you be interested?" Agustus confidently beamed. Still directing his words toward the Israeli emissary. But, knowing that every country there would be drawn into his 'sales pitch'.

"To know, who they are, where they are, where they have been and where they are headed, twenty-four hours a day, three-hundred and sixty-five days a year, anywhere in the world. And...at a minimal monetary cost. Would that be enough to ease your fears? To cause you to step back for a moment and listen? These retaliatory acts of aggression need not be!"

A low verbal hum ensued as everyone mumbled ambiguously among their contemporaries, including the skeptical Israelites. Agustus stepped back from the podium for a moment while they haggled the concept.

Agustus stepped back to the microphone. "Gentlemen." He waited until everyone focused on him again. "Signa-Chip, an inexpensive, implantable device, when used in conjunction with the Global Positioning System, will allow you to track virtually every individual on the face of the earth. Who they associate with, where they are and what they are doing. Stopping them before they ever even enter your country."

More mumbling.

"Satellites equipped with computers will even log their past locations, allowing you to know where they have been...Every terrorist cell, every hiding place, every meeting place exposed. Down to even what they buy, where they buy it, and from whom." Agustus stepped back again.

You could hear a pin drop in the crowded hall. Every leader stunned by the concept of having that much control of the world's citizenry.

On cue, as planned, the designate from Turkey shouted out, "It will never work!"

Agustus smiled. His programmed response to the pre-arranged statements from the countries in the European Economic Community already rehearsed.

"The terrorists won't allow themselves to be implanted."

"Then you will know that too," Agustus answered. "It is an admission of guilt, an act of treason. Expel them and not allow them back into your borders."

"And how do you propose that we force compliance on those countries who refuse?" The representative of Greece asked.

"That is the wonderful part...We have to 'force' no one into anything."

Agustus leaned back and waited for complete silence. Until every UN. member present was on the edge of their seats, eager to hear his response. Agustus didn't make them wait too long. "The world economic community is on the verge of emerging as a cashless entity, a totally electronic funds transfer system. No chip. No trade. No access to world markets. Complete isolation from the economic world. No import, export trade without Signa-Chip, or an approved version of it. And no country can survive that. At least not any that I know of. All will comply!" Agustus spoke confidently, unequivocally, letting the word 'will' drag out. "But, what you need to do," Agustus stared at the three Israeli delegates. "Is stop this aggression and loss of life and give this system the opportunity to work. Which I personally guarantee will. Signa-Chip will resolve this terrorist problem once and for all."

A din of excited arguing came forth from the delegates as they perused the concept. Agustus waited for a lull.

"This system will also work to control, among many other things," Agustus said, knowing he had the United Nations meeting in his control and his for the manipulation. "The international transportation of illegal drugs and other contraband. Not only for the Jewish people, but for the rest of the world."

"This is quite an ambitious undertaking," Italy said, again on cue. "I see it as taking more than mere words to accomplish."

Agustus smiled. "Thank you for your insightful comment," he said. "And I am in total agreement with you." He paused, squaring his shoulder. "That is why I would like to propose, that we as a governing unit, establish a branch of world government for undertaking and overseeing those responsibilities."

Agustus was going to add: *That I would be more than honored to head.* But didn't, knowing full well that if his idea was accepted by the assemblage, the position as head of the new governing branch, was all but automatically his. Instead he said, "Gentlemen. I have offered a viable solution to the problems, both to those at hand and to those that are yet unforeseen. The decision now lay in your hands," he pointed to Israel's UN representatives. "Solve them peaceably through Signa-Chip, or escalate them through the bloodshed of more innocent people?"

An energetic, resounding applause, ignited by the countries of the EEC, coursed through the auditorium. Agustus stepped down from the podium and returned to his designated station behind the embossed emblem for Spain.

All three of Israel's representatives were already on the telephones to their respective, homeland counter-parts by the time he sat. An hour later the divisions of Israeli tanks were withdrawing from Pakistani settlements and villages, the first of the fighter jets were returning to their air bases.

Before the emergency UN. session ended, a private conference was arranged between Agustus and Israel's Prime Mister for the next day.

Agustus immediately called Warren Kilpatrict, CEO of World Technologies, demanding the presence of Ethan Blake, to accompany him in Israel.

"I need an expert, knowledgeable in all aspects of the Signa-Chip with me," Agustus told Warren. "And Ethan is my man. I don't care what it takes. Get him there ASAP. This is our greatest chance to take the chip to the world and I want nothing to hinder that,"

Two hours later Ethan was airborne in the company's privately owned airliner; destination Jerusalem. In his absence, Leonard and Hilda would handle the Connelly deal. The importance of his meeting with Agustus and going over the details of the Signa-Chip deal Agustus would promote to Israel's Prime Minister, far outweighing the Connelly acquisitions.

Ethan's task was to support Agustus and he was brilliant, helping to convince the Israeli cabinet that the technology of the chip, would help end their terrorism problems. "Especially," Ethan ended his supportive argument, "when backed by the resources of the proposed branch of The One World Government, headed by Agustus."

Within the week, Israel's government would officially approve the plan. Passing, unanimously the law requiring all citizens within their boundaries to be implanted with Signa-Chip. And adding that every border site, every point of entry, every police vehicle, be equipped with Signa-Chip detection scanners.

A four month time constraint was placed on compliance. After which, to be on Israel soil and not implanted, meant immediate arrest for treason and/or deportation.

After the highly successful Israeli meeting, averting a disastrous Jihad, Agustus leaped ahead in world renown. The branch of World government, he had hoped for was approved by the United Nation Assembly and so was his election as its head.

23

After the Labor Day holiday, Adam never returned to Kendell Industries, except to collect his last paycheck and his tools. Through the friend of a friend of Jack Elsworth, Adam found a good job opportunity at a small, five man, electrical repair shop, on the outskirts of New Baltimore. The new place of employment was just eleven miles from where he lived and he took it.

The new job didn't pay as much as his position at Kendell Industries did. But his salary, coupled with Carol's, would give them enough money to make ends meet and he wouldn't have to think about the Direct Deposit issue for a while.

The pension and retirement benefits he would lose by quitting Kendell, were never factors in his decision to leave. He knew, in his heart of hearts, that the way Signa-Chip was progressing, they would not be collectable anyway. Life as he knew it would end long before he ever retired.

Although Adam did give as much of himself as he could to his new job, his commitment to his secular work fell to a distant fifth place behind his relationship with God, his family, the church, and his blossoming, Internet, Anti-Signa-Chip website. Work would never again hold the importance it once did: Adam would center his extra energy into the website.

Carl Torre's return e-mail was responsible for the website taking up so much of Adam's time. Carl's answer to Adam's request for help, suggested that instead of approaching the Signa-Chip from a 'Christian's point of view', Adam bring to light the 'Big Brother is watching you' concept. Carl even promised in the process to add several pages of his own to the website, focusing on governmental control and the total loss of personal freedom, implantation with the Signa-Chip would mean.

Adam had prayed about the theory for several nights before he incorporated Carl's thoughts. Adam eventually deciding as an alternative to Carl posting his own pages, that they should co-write a newsletter every other day and post that on the website instead. Carl providing insight into the adverse capabilities of Signa-Chip, in the short newsletters, Adam a touch of the spiritual.

Carl's notions proved successful. The information on the web page was contagious. From all around the world, thousands visited the site daily to read the letters.

Even Carol got in on Adam's 'campaign', designing and printing out fliers that she posted in store windows, telephone and street light poles, and anywhere else she could stick them. The one page flier expressing Anti-Signa-Chip sentiments and giving the website address, inviting any who wanted to know the 'truth', to visit the site.

Adam was two weeks into running the site before he ever remembered who Carl was. One night, while adding his commentary to the first rough draft of the newsletter and wondering how Carl had so much insight into the Signa-Chip, it came to him. His Internet partner was the one he had seen with Ethan Blake at the presentation on the chip and the one he had seen on the television news broadcast from New York, when World Technologies took over the controlling interest in ESI. His first intuition, after the realization, was to e-mail Carl and tell Mister Torre, who he was and reintroduce himself. But, Adam thought the better of it. *Why mess with something that's working?* He reasoned away his insight. He kept the knowledge to himself, not even telling Carol. Adam content kept his secret his.

:

It had been almost a month since Ethan had seen his wife and children. The extra long stay over in Munich and the sudden command for him to accompany Abaddon to Israel had preoccupied his mind to the point that he had nearly forgotten about them. Hilda's companionship had also played a major role in keeping his mind off his troubles at home. Her long tours around Germany when they weren't working and her nightly visits to his hotel room had kept his mind absorbed most of the time.

Sitting in the hotel lobby in Jerusalem, awaiting his ride to the airport and the flight back to Munich, it was Hilda that Ethan missed, not Nicole. Nonetheless, he promised himself that he would call Erin and Renee' as soon as he got back to Germany.

Ethan glanced around the ornate lobby, watching the bellhops tend to the incoming and outgoing patrons. The bellhops carrying luggage bags to and from the line of taxi cabs outside the main entrance of the hotel. *Americans tourist, for the most part,* Ethan guessed.

He leaned back in the light gray, two cushion sofa he was sitting in, thinking about how important of a man he was becoming, thanks to the Signa-Chip. His pride swelled as he watched the 'lowly' tourists, forced into depending on the common taxis for transportation, knowing a private limousine was on its way for him.

As he reached for a magazine on the table next to the sofa, the large, floor-to-ceiling plate glass windows that made up the front wall of the lobby fractured, sending huge shards of glass sailing in all directions. The flying glass was followed instantly by a deafening explosion. An explosion so loud, Ethan felt it more than he heard it.

Ethan instinctively dived for the floor as the second suicide bomber, at the back of the lobby, detonated the band of explosives strapped around his waist.

Something or someone hit Ethan hard in his back as he fell forward trying to get as low as he could. It knocked the breath out of him. The pain of the contact was excruciating and Ethan could feel the extreme weight of whatever, whoever it was on him.

In an instant the rumble of the explosions subsided. The cries and screams of the injured took its place. Ethan tried to stand but couldn't. The weight was too much. He opened his eyes to an impenetrable cloud of thick, black smoke and found it hard to take a breath. He tried to roll out from under the heaviness, but the weight was unrelenting. With his hands he scrapped and clawed his way from beneath whatever it was on top of him, until he was free enough from it to stand.

The smoke too thick to see through, Ethan stumbled over the mounds of rubble that littered the lobby floor as he headed in the direction of the gapping hole where the glass wall once stood. As he neared it, he felt someone grab his arm and pull him out into the street. Free of the building, he continued to stumble forward until he found himself in the road itself. He stood there oblivious to his surroundings.

Feeling something warm running down his leg, Ethan looked down. Half of the way between his knee and his hip on his left leg, a six inch long glass shard was protruding from his pants. Dazed, he stared at it and the pool of dripping blood, that had formed around his foot for several seconds, before he even realized that it was his leg and his blood.

Ethan winced in pain when he grabbed the shard and pulled it out. Instantly, unrestricted, the blood gushed from the wound. Instinctively, he pressed his hand hard against the gash in his leg. Slowly, unwillingly, he sat in the middle of the street and heard the distant sound of sirens drawing nearer.

⋮

Hilda stepped across Leonard's office and sat on the couch. "We have got to do something about this guy in Detroit before Abaddon hears," she said to Leonard. "His Anti-Signa-Chip website is getting more and more popular everyday and causing lots of problems."

Leonard looked up from his desk, his face drawn taunt, expressionless.

"We're getting reports of open protests and some fighting between pro, and anti-chip groups in the US," Hilda expounded. "Just small little incidences right now, but they're escalating." Hilda paused. "The whole scene is starting to have an adverse effect on sales over there."

"We expected a little resistance," Leonard said. "What makes you think this guy's web page is causing it?"

"This is a lot more than 'a little resistance', it's starting to spread to where there have been reports of acts of vandalism against some religious groups. And this web page is touting the Signa-Chip as the focal point for that violence. And I have no idea where he's getting his information but he's even putting out a newsletter with some inside stuff in it, fueling that growing animosity even more."

With the news of Ethan's serious injury only hours old and now this added problem, the usually complacent Leonard

351

could stand no more. He barked angrily from across his desk. "What kinds of 'stuff?"

"How the chip has two way communication capabilities for one thing, and how it can be used to record and store tracking information. It's frightening a lot of people away."

"How is he getting that information?" Leonard lowered his voice a few decibels, softened the tone, but kept the dominance.

"We're not sure yet, but I've had a couple of our computer people doing some backtracking and I think Carl Torre is helping him."

"Carl Torre? You mean the PR guy that came over here with Ethan and I fired?"

"One and the same."

"Do we know who this other guy is?"

"Just some religious fanatic from Detroit, Michigan...Adam Garrett."

Leonard stood up and walked around to the front of his desk. "Can't we just shut the site down? Send him some wicked virus, or something?"

"Can't. He's using one of the biggest Internet Service Providers in the world and they got more firewalls protecting them than you could imagine. Besides if we did shut him down like that, he'd just start up another site."

"Well," Leonard turned around and picked up his telephone. "Let's see if Douglas Kolar and Jake Miller can't have a little talk with Carl Torre and this Mister Garrett and convince them to find themselves another hobby."

Hilda rose from the couch and headed for her office. "Any more news on Ethan?"

"Last I've heard was he's lost some blood and he's in shock. But, Ethan's tough He'll just be down for a few days."

Hilda forced a smile.

"I'm going to send him back home when he gets out of the hospital and give him some time to rest," Leonard said.

Hilda's smile turned downward.

"Transfer me to security," Leonard spoke into the telephone.

:

Adam reached over the five foot long, wooden workbench, closed the lid on his tool box, and locked it. He picked up the digital, electronic component he had been working on, rolling the faulty, machine controller over in his hands. And trying to decide if the expensive part was non-repairable and needed replacement or if he should try to fix it.

Everyone else had already left for home and it was ten minutes after closing.

"You going home? Or you going to hang around here all night?" Art Schafer, Adam's new boss, called out to him from the shop doorway.

Adam glanced up from the component at the owner of Schafer Electronics. "Just trying to figure out what to do with this part," he said and set it back down on the workbench.

Standing at the doorway, keys in hand and anxious to leave, Art called back. "Tomorrow's another day."

"Tomorrow's Saturday, Adam walked up and reminded him. "I don't work weekends, remember?".

Art stepped out into the small, gravel parking lot of the rural shop. "Then you can decide on Monday what we need to do."

Adam followed. A slight breeze, blowing across the open, ten acre field next to the shop building, carried with it the scent of the Timothy Hay growing there and tickled Adam's nostrils. He took a deep breath of the fresh air.

"I'll be in tomorrow for a few hours," Art said, as he climbed into his car parked right next to the door. "I'll take a look at it. If it isn't any good, it isn't any good."

Adam nodded his agreement. "Have a good weekend," he waved as Art drove away, leaving him alone.

He walked the few yards to where his pickup sat, nose against the building, and climbed in. Adam never noticed the black Sedan, with the two men in it, idling a hundred yards or so down the road.

By the time he started the pickup's engine, the Sedan had pulled in behind him, blocking his exit. Fortunately, Adam checked his outside rearview mirrors for adjustment, before he backed up, and spotted the vehicle, or he would have accidentally crushed the front end of it.

"Adam Garrett?" The passenger of the smaller, much lower car, jumped out and walked up to Adam's door.

Surprised by the sudden appearance, of the dark suited man, Adam hesitated, then slowly lowered his window an inch or two. "Yes?" He answered.

Distracted, as planned, by the first man, Adam didn't see Jake Miller, also wearing a black suit jacket, coming around on the passenger side. Jake, opening the door and climbing into the seat, before Adam had chance to react.

"Hey!" Adam said, turning quickly to see the intruder. "What's going on," had just started to come out of his mouth when the driver's door was jerked open. Adam spun back quickly, to push Douglas Kolar back.

In an instant, Jake reached over and turned off the truck engine, extracting the ignition key.

Douglas, more powerful and unmoved by Adam's awkward attempt at shoving him away, sternly said, "We need to talk."

Adam went to swing his fist at him, but his arm was grabbed from behind and stopped.

"This can be easy, or it can be difficult," Douglas said. "Which ever way you like, don't much matter to us."

Adam relaxed his fist and jerked his arm free.

Jake, twice as strong, could have easily prevented it, released his grip, but remained ready to spring into action if Adam tried to resist again.

Adam didn't. He let his hand fall to the seat, an outward act of submission. It was obvious, he was out powered, and he also knew, from a sitting position, he couldn't mount much of a counter offensive against his two attackers. So, he chose, at least temporarily, to hear them out.

"That's better," Douglas said.

"Who are you guys?" Adam asked, as he looked straight ahead, trying to keep one eye on each of them.

"Doesn't matter," Jake said. "It's you we're interested in."

"You started a web page," Douglas joined in. "You wanted some attention and now you've got it. Ours. And we're not very happy about it either."

"So that is what this is about?"

"No," Douglas said, very coldly. "This is about you and us right now."

From the tone in the man's voice, Adam knew to keep silent and just listen.

"You are going to shut down that website and put an end to this nonsense, stirring people up," Jake said while tauntingly shaking Adam's ring of keys.

Adam glanced over at his keys, thinking the 'or' was coming next. It didn't. The intruder dropped the keys on the driver's side floor and climbed out.

"You, your girlfriend, and her daughter," Douglas said to Adam then redirected toward Jake, "What's her name?"

"Lindsey," Jake answered, purposely leaning back into the truck.

"Have a nice evening," Douglas finished his sentence and stepped back.

Adam spun to face Jake, his face contorted with anger. It was one thing, he felt, to threaten him, quite another to include Carol and Lindsey in that threat. And he had heard enough. "You...," he started to verbally lash back when he saw, hanging inside Jack's suit jacket the handle of the pistol.

Jake, knowing Adam had seen, what he had intended him to see by leaning over, said, "Yes?"

Adam turned back, facing forward.

Jake straightened up and said, "I didn't think so."

In silence, all three of them maintained their positions for a moment. The distant noise of the occasional traffic passing on 26 mile road the only sounds heard.

"I hope we don't have to have another one of our little talks," Douglas finally said and slowly backed away from the truck.

Adam never acknowledged the parting comment. He maintained his forward stare for several minutes after the black sedan had drove away.

He found the keys at his feet, started the truck again, and pulled the doors closed without thought, his mind still stunned. Adam leaned his head forward, letting it rest on the top of the steering wheel. When his thoughts returned, seconds later, he didn't know whether to blame God for the incident, or thank Him for getting him through it without serious injury.

On the short drive home, Adam 'thanked' Him repeatedly.

The house was empty, as it usually was, when Adam got there. Carol was still at work and Lindsey, still at Day Care. He logged onto the Internet right away and typed off a letter to CT9883, warning Carl of the encounter with the two men and wondering if Carl had the pleasure of meeting them yet. When Adam clicked to send the email, a pop-up message window appeared on the monitor.

The message box read: Unable to send mail. Address invalid.

Adam quickly rechecked the address, resending the email when he was sure it was correct. Again the same 'window' appeared and Adam knew his warning was too late. He switched over from the ISP Home Page to his own. It already had over three thousand visitors for the day and the day was still young.

For a moment he thought of heeding the attacker's admonition. He though felt a bit of shame for even entertaining the thought. For a few more moments Adam sat, blankly staring at the web page. Slowly he began recalling the biblical stories he had read about the hardships and troubles Christians had endured, through the centuries, getting God's word out. The remembrance strengthened his resolve. Attackers, or no attackers, Carl or no Carl, he was going to keep the website going.

Adam had decided to keep his incident with the two men to himself and spent a typical evening enjoying the company of Carol and Lindsey. Later that same evening, after Carol and Lindsey had retired, Adam composed a letter that he posted on his web page. The letter, appealing to those who could: 'to start other Anti-Signa-Chip websites, in the event, something should happen to this one. There are forces out there that don't want this information public', Adam concluded his letter. 'And they will do, and use whatever means it takes, to make sure it doesn't.'

:

"Whatever they did, it didn't work," Hilda spoke into her cell phone. Her Saturday morning call to Leonard's residence in response to the latest posting she read on Adam's web page. "He's even telling other people to start their own web pages now," she added.

"That's too bad," Leonard said.

"We need to put an end to this, before it gets out of hand."

Leonard, let his fingertips slide back and forth across his forehead as he listened, agreeing. "Well, let me get in contact with Douglas and Jake again and see if they can't come up with something a little more convincing."

:

Several thousand miles southwest of Germany, in the warm waters of the North Atlantic, Hannah, as the meteorologists named the eighth tropical depression of the season, sat, slowly spinning counter-clockwise. The eye of the massive, category three, storm, presently one-hundred-ninety miles, north and east of Cuba was stationary, but deepening and gaining strength. At 11:30AM, Munich time, as Leonard hung up from his second call to Douglas Kolar, the central barometric pressure of Hannah quickly dropped, bottoming out at nine-hundred even. Hannah, quickly blossoming into a category five Hurricane, packing one-hundred and ninety-five mile an hour winds and a storm surge of twenty-three feet, started moving southward at twenty-two miles an hour. The storm, threatening to wash parts of Haiti, The Dominican Republic, and Cuba off the map.

With winds, still at one-hundred and sixty miles an hour, a hundred miles from the eye and pushing a wave nearing fifteen feet in front of them, the storm licked the coastlines of all three countries, destroying homes, businesses, and killing one hundred-seventy-three, unprepared people, before it veered northwest into the still warmer waters of the gulf of Mexico.

:

He had put the dreaded task off as long as he could, so after lunch, Adam, announced he wanted to go by his mother's house and sort through her things. And decide which of her belongings he would keep, what he could sell, and what he would throw away.

He really didn't want to make those choices and considered putting it all into storage. But Carol convinced him that the fifty dollars a month it would take to store it seemed wasteful. Especially considering, that since he had left Kendell Industries, they didn't have a whole lot of extra fifty dollars.

"Why don't we just go through it today?" Carol suggested. "Separate the things you want to save and we can have an Estate sale next weekend for the rest. And what we don't sell, we can donate to the church she went to. I'm sure there are a lot of people that could really use some of it."

"I need to get that stuff out of there," Adam said. His head drooped as he spoke. "I want to put that house up for sale too," he forced himself to say. "Before the taxes come due on it again." He lifted his eyes to hers. "We could surely use the money right now."

A lump grew in Carol's throat as she caught a sense of his lingering pain. "We can put this off for a while," she said. "Give you more of a chance to deal with it."

He hesitated, contemplating the option to procrastinate. To revisit the places, through memorabilia, where his mother once lived and to relive the things they did together was more pain than he wanted to endure. But Adam knew, for closure, it was something he needed to do. "Naw," Adam said. "The sooner I get this part over with the better."

:

Just after six o'clock that evening, the bed of the truck loaded with the things Adam wanted to keep, Carol and Lindsey next to him, he backed the vehicle out of the drive-way of his mother's old house. It was a difficult day for Adam: deciding what to keep, what to get rid of. He felt his mother's spiritual presence in each article, a little part of her life in every piece, no matter how small or inconsequential the item. He wanted to keep it all but knew he couldn't.

Still fighting the emotional exhaustion he felt spending the day picking through his mother's personal things, like it was so much 'junk', Adam said to his passengers, "What say we stop and get some dinner? Maybe some take out chicken?"

Lindsey sensing his sorrow looked up at him. "Sure,"

"I can still cook," Carol said. "I'd really like to just get home and put this stuff in the basement."

Adam glanced down at Lindsey, pursed his lips, faking disappointment. She frowned back at him.

The thoughts of not having to go through the added work of preparing a meal, appealed Carol too. She relented. "Maybe after we get this stuff put away, we can go get something,".

"Yay!" Adam and Lindsey responded as the truck turned onto the I -75 interstate. Adam choose the I-75 alternate route home from downriver, to avoid the multiple weekend construction sites he knew they'd have to endure, if he took the more direct I -94.

An hour later, Adam turned up into his driveway, feeling famished. "Why don't you and Lindsey run up to the take-out place and get some chicken," he said stopping next to Carol's car. "I'm starving and by the time you guys get back, I'll have most of this stuff downstairs and we can eat."

"Okay," Carol said, transferring herself and Lindsey from the truck to her vehicle. The long ride home, diminishing even further her willingness to engage in the task of unloading the truck.

Twenty-five minutes later, when she and Lindsey returned with their dinner, she could see that not an item had been removed from the truck. It sat just as full as when they left. She let out a gasp as she entered the front door of the house, ready to scold, and saw Adam, face in hands, sitting, dazed and distraught, in the middle of the living room floor. Every item in the room around him either over-turned, maliciously strewn everywhere, or smashed.

Adam stood, his eyes glaring with anger, the pieces of his completely destroyed computer strewn at his feet.

Lindsey started to whimper.

For her daughter's sake, Carol steadied herself and held back her own tears. "Is it all like this?

"Every room," Adam said.

"Who? Why?"

Adam shook his head, but knew both the 'who' and the 'why'. "I want you and Lindsey to go stay at your parent's tonight," he said. "I'll feel much better knowing you guys are safe."

"I'm not leaving you here alone!" Carol said.

"I'll be over in a little bit," Adam said. "There's just a few things I need to take care of first. But, I want you to take Lindsey and go...now."

Reluctant, Carol agreed. But only after Adam had promised her again that he would join them shortly.

As soon as they were gone, Adam went to the basement and dug Carol's computer out from the boxes of her stuff. Within half an hour, amid the debris in his living room, he logged on to his web page and typed out another newsletter. This letter explaining his attack and the ransacking of his house, attributing both to the evil surrounding the chip. He also added another appeal for others to start web pages like his. He posted the letter then logged off.

Adam contemplated calling the police, but knew there wouldn't be a thing they could, or would do about the vandalism, except make out a report. He decided against it. Instead, he started straightening things back up.

Carol called as soon as she got to her parents, interrupting his work. Her insistence, making him close up the house and join her and Lindsey as he had promised.

24

Adam glanced up from his seat around the black flecked, white Formica table, at the clock above the refrigerator and yawned. The clock in his future in-law's kitchen, where the four of them had spent most of the night talking, read 1:30AM.

"I'm getting tired too, Susan announced, when she saw the prolonged yawn and turned toward Carol's father, sitting next to her. "We should let these kids get to sleep. I'm sure they have lots of things to do tomorrow and it's getting late."

To Adam's delight, Robert Dewalt nodded and stood. Adam usually enjoyed talking with them, the older couple's topic's typically inspiring. But hours ago, he had grown weary of tonight's subject: the plundering of his and Carol's belongings.

He had said nothing to anyone about the two men who assaulted him; who he was positive were also responsible for the damage to his house. His intention was to tell Carol, but waiting until they were alone before he did.

Quietly, Adam went upstairs to the guest room of the two story dwelling and checked in on the sleeping Lindsey, while Carol and her parents said their 'good nights'. Passing Carol, on the stairwell, on his way back down, he said, "There's some thing I need to talk to you about."

"Give me a few minutes," she sleepily said and continued up, as Adam headed for the living room and the more comfortable couch.

"I hadn't told you," Adam started when she rejoined him minutes later and continued to relate the incident were he was confronted by the two men in the parking lot at work. "I'm sure," he told Carol, "it was those same two guys that broke into our house and smashed my computer."

Despite her tiredness, Carol stood up and paced around the living room. "Why didn't you call the police?" she eventually asked.

"And tell them what; Two guys asked me to stop my web page?"

"Yes! And now this," she referred to the break in. "They could put two and two together."

"So, what if they did? What do you think the police are supposed to do? Bring out a swat team? Or armed body guards to follow me around?"

Carol sat back down next to him.

Adam said, "It's all just circumstantial anyway. There's no proof these guys were the ones."

"Come on," Carol leaned back in the couch. "It's so obvious."

"Maybe, but we have got to prove it…and we can't."

Carol posed the next logical question. "So, what are you going to do about the website?"

It was Adam's turn to stand and nervously pace.

:

The news of the bombing in the tourist filled hotel lobby in Jerusalem, killing eight Americans, injuring twelve others, among whom was Ethan, traveled around the world. The event, sensationalized by the media, sparked retaliatory attacks by groups of angry Americans, against Muslims living in the United States. The most violent, occurring in the largest Muslim community in America: Dearborn, Michigan: The attacks and subsequent responses, blossoming into full blown neighborhood riots in the Detroit area, as Adam, just a few miles away, paced, considering his dilemma.

"What can I do?" Adam said, answering Carol's question with questions of his own. "Is it better to obey God, or our fears? What do you think God would have me to do?"

Carol didn't respond. Her head slung lower. In her mind, she answered Adam's questions.

"Thousands of people around the world are getting God's warning about the chip from the website. I just can't stop. How many thousands more won't, if I do?"

"Well, you can rest assured," Carol lifted her head," these guys aren't just going to go away. They'll be back around. And, in all probability, get rougher every time they do."

Adam stopped pacing. He stood next to the front room window and stared out through the lace curtains into the darkness beyond.

Silence permeated the room. Both knew there was little choice Adam had. He had to keep the website going. The eternal lives and souls of possibly thousands depended on it.

"The only thing we can do," Adam said, turning back toward her. "I can get a laptop with a modem in it that allows me to plug into a telephone line anywhere and stay on the move."

"Do you know what you're saying?" Carol looked up at him, her face showing the impact of the realization. "I'd have no problem with that, but we have a six year old daughter we have to think about. What kind of life is that for her?"

Adam turned back to the window. "What kind of life is it for her…?" He froze mid-sentence. A black sedan with two men in it slowly cruised by the window. Both of the vehicle's occupants looking at his pickup truck sitting in the driveway. "Go get Lindsey," he said quietly, staring at the familiar vehicle.

"But, she's…"

"Just do as I say," Adam's voice trembled with sternest. "We've got company."

Carol jumped up.

"No," Adam said, "on second thought, I'm going to go." He swung open the front door. "I'll lead them away." He quickly stepped back and kissed her on the mouth. "Call the Elsworth's, tell them what's going on and see if Jack will come and pick you and Lindsey up."

Carol responded with a nervous "Adam I'm scared."

"Don't be. Everything will be all right. Just do as I say. I love you," he said and trotted out to his truck. He locked the front hubs into four wheel drive before he jumped in and started it up.

Adam didn't have to go far to find the black sedan. It was sitting, engine idling a block away. Adam slowed as he passed it. He looked out of his window at the driver and snarled his lip, then sped away.

The vehicle immediately did a U-turn in pursuit.

:

To Carol's surprise, the telephone only rang twice, before Melissa Elsworth answered it.

"We were up," Melissa said when Carol apologized for the 2:30AM call. "In fact, we have been trying to call you and Adam at your house for the last two hours."

"What's going on?" Carol asked.

"The church was severely damaged by a fire earlier this evening."

Carol reeled and sat back down on the couch. "There's no services tomorrow?"

"Not tomorrow, or any other day."

"Is that why you were trying to call?"

"No," Melissa said. "Matthew, twenty-four, verses six-teen through twenty-one is why I've needed to call."

Carol thought for a minute trying to remember the verses. She couldn't.

"Pastor thinks it's time and at sunrise we're leaving," Melissa continued.

"Leaving? Leaving where?" Carol almost shouted.

Melissa knew then that Carol didn't know the verses. "Our Lord tells us when we see these things happening to flee and that is what we are doing," she said. "Like I said, Pastor thinks it's time and we as a congregation agree…it's time for those 'in Judaea, to flee into the mountains'. And we were calling to invite Adam, Lindsey, and you to join us."

"Adam isn't here," Carol answered. "Which is why I've called." Carol then filled Melissa in on the events of the night. "And Adam wanted me to call you guys…wondering if you, or Jack could come and get Lindsey and I until he got back." Carol was trembling and Melissa could hear it in her voice as she listened to her friend's plea. "But, you guys are leaving in a few hours."

:

The sedan was no match in speed, maneuverability, or power to the Dodge Ram. Adam could have left them far be-hind at any moment. He though, only kept far enough ahead of them to keep them chasing. He lead the Sedan down one street and up another taking them westward, farther away from the city. Toward the nearest open back-roads he knew. The plan: get them to a place where he knew the Dodge would go with ease and the bulky, low swung, sedan would bog down and get stuck. Detaining them long enough to allow him to get back to the Carol and Lindsey and take them to safety.

The well laid plan went bad. He made his mistake when he turned down an unlit, residential, dirt road in Farmington Hills, the Sedan, half-a-block behind him. The road continued for only five hundred more feet, before it dead ended against a deep, tree lined, drainage ditch, he would have had trouble crossing even if he had been driving a bulldozer. The Sedan spun sideways across the one-lane, residential road and stopped. Adam was trapped.

:

In the darkness beneath the waters of the North Pacific, the Eurasian, Philippine, and Pacific tectonic plates, shifted by a subduction earthquake, measuring 10.2 on the Richter scale, slammed violently together. The Pacific plate forcing itself over the other two so aggressively, a one hundred foot tsunamis instantly spread in all directions from the epicenter, ninety miles southeast of Tokyo, Japan.

The southern arc of the wave, headed, unrelenting, toward the islands of Manila and the Philippines, while the western edge raced at two hundred miles an hour toward mainland Japan. The merciless wall of water struck twenty minutes later. Simultaneously, thousands of miles away, Carol heard the sounds of a vehicle pulling up into the driveway to her parents house. She jumped to the window, expecting to see Adam's truck.

:

There weren't many available options for Adam to take: he could put the Ram in reverse and floor it, knowing the pickup had the ground clearance and power to push the Sedan out of the way, or climb right over it. That option, Adam knew would probably bring gunfire and he would be at point blank range for the shooters. He let the idea pass from his thoughts. *I could try driving around it, through the front lawns*, he thought. *But again, that would take me right past the men and make me an easy target again.* He let that thought pass too. He chose to simply wait.

The sound of two quick shots, startled him. The Dodge jumped to the force of its two rear tires being suddenly, simultaneously blown out by gunshots. The truck was still rocking when one of the men jerked open the driver's door of the disabled pickup. The other grabbed Adam's arm, dragged him out and in one move flung him face down onto the dirt road.

"You'll just never learn will you?" One of them said.

Adam struggled to get to his feet. A sharp, painful kick to the ribs prevented that. He rolled over onto his back to see the faces of his attackers. He was surprised to see that they were not the same two men that had confronted him in the parking lot of Schafer Electronics. Fears for Carol and Lindsey flooded his mind as he considered the possibility that he had been the one 'lead away'.

One of the men yelled. "Get up!"

Adam was kicked again, but not as hard. He struggled to his knees and was jerked to his feet. A vicious blow to his stomach, just below the sternum doubled him over and again he was thrown face first onto the road.

"Maybe we just oughta take that kid of his," the second man said to the first. "He put outs the web page again…we send her back to him in a bag."

Adam started back up to his knees. He screamed out in pain, amid the crunching sound of bones breaking.

"Can't type much either without fingers," the first man said, as he withdrew his foot after stomping it down on Adam's hand.

The distant sound of an approaching police car siren caught the ears of his attackers, cutting their assault short.

"We better get outta here," the second man advised.

The men turned away, hurried back to the Sedan, and drove away.

Adam laid there, face down in the street, his hand and ribs throbbing. He thanked God again for sparing his life.

The Farmington hills police car turned the corner moments later and Adam was lifted to his feet a second time.

"What's going on?" The officer who helped him up asked.

"You need an ambulance?" The other asked.

Adam glanced to the officer's badge. "No," he said, more anxious to get back to Carol and Lindsey and make sure they were all right over tending to his own needs.

"What happened here?" The first officer asked again.

"Just a difference of opinion," Adam winced.

"Have you been drinking?"

Adam held tightly to his right wrist hoping to reduce the pain. "Look officers I really need to get home," he said. "And no I haven't been drinking."

"Don't look like you're going anywhere," Officer Freeport said, nodding toward the two flat tires. "Why don't you let us take you over to the hospital and have a doctor take a look at that hand of yours. It looks broken to me."

"We got a report of gunshots," the first officer said.

Adam thought for a moment and tried to give another, less suspicious explanation. "Probably my two back tires when they blew. I must've ran over something in the road."

The officers furrowed their eyes and looked at him, dubious of his answer.

"Isn't there a service station around here, where I can buy a couple of tires?"

"You're not going to press any charges?" Officer Freeport said.

"No!"

"We have to at least make out a report."

Adam forced himself to smile, despite the pain. "Just a little scuffle between two guys that's all. No big deal."

"What's your name?" the first officer pulled out a pad of paper and an ink pen.

"Adam Garrett."

"Do you know who did this?"

"No I don't."

Officer Freeport bent down to look at the license plate on the Dodge. Michigan, G...V...C, nine, one, seven," he read the plate.

"Let me see your driver's license," the officer stopped writing.

The pain in his hand was excruciating. Nonetheless, Adam dug his wallet out of his back pocket. Using the forearm on his 'bad hand' to hold it against his stomach, Adam got the license out.

"Can't we hurry this up?" Adam asked, watching the officer walk back to the scout car with his license.

"There's an all night truck stop up on the six-ninety-six service drive, about a mile or so from here," Freeport said, pointing beyond the ravine. "We'll follow you up there."

"He's clean," the officer returned within a few minutes and handed Adam's driver's license back.

Sunlight was breaking over the eastern horizon when, Adam pulled out of the truck stop, his right hand, black and blue, swollen to twice its size, two new tires on the back of the Dodge. His repeated telephone calls to the Elsworth's and Carol's parent's, while he waited for the tires to be replaced went unanswered. He sped back to the Dewalt's, the last place he saw Carol and Lindsey.

Half a block away he sighed heavily, encouraged by the site of Carol's car still in the driveway. He pulled to a stop beside it and went in the house.

He froze one step into the living room. Everything was turned upside down, the television screen and lamps smashed, glass from the items, strewn all over the floor.

"Carol," he yelled and ran in the house.

Silence was his answer.

In a frenzy, Adam dashed up the stairway, screaming Carol's name as he ran. The bedrooms were empty; the mattresses sliced in several places, the stuffing, protruding out from the slits; every dresser drawer pulled out and dumped on the floor.

The kitchen was in no better shape: the contents of the cupboards scattered viciously around the room. He ran to the door of the attached garage at the end of the kitchen and looked out the window; Robert's vehicle was still in its place, untouched.

He spun around, his mind near panic, unable to think clearly.

The only thing not broken, a beige wall phone started ringing. Adam lounged for it.

"Good morning Mister Garrett," a man's voice said.

Adam took a deep breath. "Who is…," he started.

"You just listen and listen good," the voice said, cutting him off.

Adam recognized it as belonging to one of those men who had first confronted him in his work parking lot.

"We have a couple of people here that you might be interested in," Douglas Kolar said. "Say hello."

Adam's heart stopped and jumped up into his throat.

"Adam!" Susan Dewalt's voice trembled.

"Susan," Adam yelled. "Is Carol and Lindsey with you?"

She never heard the question, Douglas pulled the telephone away from her ear before she had the chance.

"If we see the web page on the Internet tonight..." Douglas came back on and purposely didn't finish his sentence.

"If you hurt...," Adam tried to speak.

"You just behave yourself and take that Web page off the Internet and everything will work out just fine," Douglas cut him off again. "If you don't you're going to make a lot of people unhappy." Douglas paused for an instant. "Your decision," he added and hung up.

Adam turned to hang up the phone, banging his broken hand against the edge of the counter, in the process. He winced from the agonizing pain and grabbed for his wrist again, squeezing it tightly until the pain eased to bearable.

A flowered dish towel hung, drooped over the knob on one of the cupboard doors, Adam took it and filled it with ice cubes from the freezer and wrapped it gently around his hand. The sudden cold hurt too, but the throbbing abated.

Why didn't they put Carol or Lindsey on the telephone? Adam wondered, *instead of Susan, if whoever it was, wanted to get maximum impact. Maybe they don't have them?* His heart started to race again. *If they didn't where could they be?* He tried Jack and Melissa's again, with the same negative results. It's Sunday, he remembered. *They're probably at the church.*

Adam rushed out to the truck and drove over to the remains of the smoldering building that once held the songs and praises of the congregation. From the seat of his truck,

Adam could see through the busted, stained glass windows to the charred alter, where he gave his heart to the Lord. His eyes filled with tears at the sight. His hand was throbbing again.

"Dear God," he cried out into the emptiness as he drove away. *Maybe they went home?*

There too, Adam found only himself. Standing amid the upheaval, just as he had left it the night before, his body exhausted from the sleepless night, fighting shock from the pain of his injury, and emotional disasters, he righted his recliner. Collapsing into it, within minutes, he fell into a deep, trauma induced sleep.

:

The thunderstorms, offering a preview of the hurricane that produced them, raced inland from the gulf across southern Texas and Louisiana, reaching well up into the Mississippi delta before they began to dissipate.

The thunderstorms, a few hours ahead of Hannah, spawned twenty-three tornadoes over the two states. Nine of which touched down in populated areas. One completely leveled a trailer park in suburban San Antonio.

Before Hannah had ever touched American soil, twelve people were dead and three million dollars in damage was done by the preceding storms.

At 5:14PM the citizens of Corpus Christi felt the brunt of Hannah's fury: A fifteen foot high wall of water crashed ashore flattening everything in its path. What the surge had not completely destroyed along the Texas coastline, the winds did. Reaching well inland beyond the wave, the winds would all but annihilate the town of Corpus Christi killing seventeen-hundred of those who neither had the means or the time to evacuate.

The angle of trajectory the hurricane struck with, caused it to deflect away from the land back out into the gulf. Where once back over the warm gulf waters, Hannah regained some of the strength she had lost with her full frontal assault on Corpus Christi. For another seven hours it would geographically wobble like an animal stunned by the impact. The category five hurricane, fed by the warm gulf waters collected itself and headed back toward land again. This time due east, catching the unsuspecting residents of central Florida, completely unprepared.

The citizens of Tampa and St. Petersburg, who had thought, as typically Gulf hurricanes did, Hannah would continue on its northern trek and dissipate herself ashore, were coming home from their inland retreats and taken totally by surprise with the storm's sudden change in direction. And Hannah, without regard for life or property, raced across the narrow strip of land called Florida with a destructive vengeance, headed for the open waters of the Atlantic beyond.

:

Late afternoon, as hurricane Hannah bore down on the Florida peninsula Adam stirred. His mind muddled, his hand throbbing unbearably.

"Carol," he yelled the first word out of his mouth, hoping she answered, hoping it was all just a nightmare.

The grogginess gradually left him. Reality came crashing in. His house in shambles, just as he had left it the night before; his heart pounding in his broken, swollen hand, reminders of the validity of his fears.

He leaped up from the recliner, fumbled with the telephone, calling Jack and Melissa's again with the same negative results.

It was impossible for him to think clearly due to the tremendous pain in his hand and he knew, he had to get some relief before his mind could focus on anything else. The nearest hospital was the only chance for that. He drove to the Emergency Room there, hoping for a shot of morphine or something to ease his suffering. Finally, Adam said a quick prayer on his way into the ER, asking God to help him deal with the pain.

The young doctor in the ER, instead of the morphine injection Adam asked for, insisted first on x-rays. And after Adam had explained to him how he was injured, the doctor suspected multiple fractures needing surgery to repair. The x-rays confirmed, to the doctor's and Adam's surprise, there were no broken bones in his hand; the injury limited to the ligaments and soft tissue.

"Thank God," Adam exclaimed when he heard the heartening x-ray report.

"Thank the dirt road for being pliable enough to absorb the brunt of the force," the doctor looked up from the prescription he was writing.

The thought/voice occurred to Adam again. *Why did you wait so long to pray?*.

"You thank what you want, I'll thank the Lord," Adam responded to the doctor.

"Whatever, the doctor smirked and left the examination room.

The doctor was replaced a few minutes later by an older, heavyset nurse. The nurse, dressed in a white nylon pants suit, carried an elastic bandage under her arm and two, small, paper cups, one in each hand. "Here take these," she said, handing him one of the cups with two pain relievers in it, then the other filled with water.

Adam swallowed the contents of both cups.

The nurse loosely wrapped the bandage around his hand, careful not to get the bandage tight. "If this swells anymore you be sure to loosen this up," she said. She took a prescription for pain relievers with Codeine in them, from her oversized pocket and handed it to him. "And be sure to ice this hand down for fifteen to twenty minutes every couple of hours for the next few days."

Adam nodded.

"And go see your family doctor in about a week or so."

Adam nodded again, folded the 'script' and stuffed it into his pocket.

"You're all set," the nurse said and walked away.

By the time Adam had made it the short distance to the pharmacy near his house, the pain pills he had swallowed in the ER room were taking effect. The pain in his hand almost tolerable. He dropped the prescription off, intending on picking up the medicine later and drove home to telephone the police. The only option he had to locate Carol and Lindsey.

"There's nothing we can do yet," the officer he talked to told him. "They're not even considered missing 'til they've been gone for at least twenty-four hours."

"But, you don't understand," Adam tried arguing.

"No, you don't understand mister," the desk Sergeant interrupted sternly.

"Our hands are full with these riots in Detroit."

"Riots?" Adam blurted out. Unaware of the civil disorders because he had been preoccupied and had not listened to the Radio or watched any television for the past few days.

"If they don't show up by tomorrow, call us back. Then we can see about filling out a Missing Person's Report."

:

Amid chaos, Agustus Neitoso's private 727 landed at the Tokyo airport, just hours after the deadly tsunami had struck.

Three thousand were reported dead, ten thousand were listed as missing in the devastated, portal city. The citizenry either swept away by the unannounced, early morning tidal wave, or buried beneath the wreckage of the crushed structures it left in its wake. And that list was growing by the minute.

The world leader and his entourage, hoped to employ the disaster as a 'golden opportunity' to promote Signa-Chip to the Japanese government and its people.

Enthusiastically, welcomed, Agustus and his four man retinue found the concept of required implantation an 'easy sale'. The shattered, susceptible Japanese government, a mere four hours after the meeting in the Imperial Palace with the Emperor, the Japanese Prime Minister, and a select few from the House of Councilors, had started, was not only willing, but anxious to accept Signa-Chip as a viable tool to avoid such massive turmoil in the event of future disasters.

Agustus sealed the deal with his final comment when he said, "Signa-Chip would have been invaluable in locating missing loved ones. And the signals sent from Signa-Chip to the computers aboard the satellites, orbiting two hundred miles overhead, not only could tell you exactly where your missing 'loved ones' are, but if those 'loved ones' were still alive and in what condition."

The meeting with the Japanese government was considered by all, a successful one. The tentative contractual agreement for the future purchase of forty-five million Signa-Chips from the Japanese in their possession, Agustus and his entourage boarded the refueled jet and headed westbound for a scheduled meeting with the heads of the newly formed World Church, headquartered in Rome, Italy.

The proposed topic of the World Church meeting: To end the escalating discord between the various world religions by incorporating them into one peaceful congregation; Uniting them in the universal purpose of world peace. Little did any of the group of leaders realize the meeting was nothing more than a condensed, modern day version of the Ecumenical Councils of the Roman ruler, Constantine the Great.

Gary L. Dewey

25

Angered by his inability to get any help from the local authorities, and powerless to force them, Adam collapsed back into his recliner. Frustrated, by the knowledge that without the resources of the police department, there wasn't much he could do on his own to find his loved ones except wait and pray, he sobbed.

While the dim rays of fading daylight filtered through the opening between the drapes that hung over his living room windows, Adam closed his eyes in prayer. When he opened them again it was completely dark.

He sat in the total darkness thinking of the Anti-chip website and how much trouble it and his efforts to retard the progress of the chip had caused him. It hurt him even more to know, that despite those efforts, Signa-Chip's popularity had blossomed anyway.

Amid those qualms, he groped around for the table lamp he recalled seeing laying on the floor near his recliner. He found it and switched it on. The light illuminating the disheveled mess that once was his place of refuge.

He went over to Carol's computer and pressed the on button, aware for the first time that he hadn't eaten all day. His stomach protested the neglect with long warbling groans. Adam went to the kitchen and made himself a simple sandwich of cold-cuts and two slices of bread.

In the few steps it took him to return to the computer, the sandwich was three-quarters of the way gone. He stuffed the last two bites of it into his mouth and logged on to the Internet, intending to remove the trouble causing web page. He watched the monitor screen flashing, going through the motions of loading the home page of his ISP.

"Robert's got it," he blurted out, recalling the conversation with Carol's parents and their boasting that they were going to get the Signa-Chip implant. Quickly following his spoken thought, the realization that Susan probably had it too, came to him.

Adam immediately, shut the computer down, before it had completed loading the ISP Home Page. The phone line free, he dialed Chicago information.

"Carl Torre," Adam told the operator and held his breath, praying that the number wasn't unlisted.

His prayer was answered when the computer voice read off Carl's home telephone number to him. He dialed it, saying another quick prayer.

"Hello," a woman's voice answered the call and the prayer.

"Hello," Adam said, his heart racing. "Is Carl Torre there?"

"Who's calling?"

"Adam Garrett," he said. "I really need to talk to him!"

"Carl," Adam heard a muffled shout. "Pick up the phone."

After an anxious moment for Adam, Carl said, "Hello," into the phone.

"Hello Carl," Adam responded. "This is Adam Garrett."

"Who?"

Adam thought for a moment and realized that he and Carl had never met personally and Carl had no idea who he was. "Anti-beast-three," he said, hoping Carl would know, from his screen name, who he was.

He did.

"I have nothing…," Carl started to cut the conversation off, before it even began. He wanted no more to do with the anti-chip website, anti-beast-three, or Douglas and Jake. The latter two, had paid him an unwelcome visit and had 'advised' him, for health reasons, during that 'visit', to back away.

"Don't hang up PLEASE," Adam pleaded, interrupting him. "I really need to ask you something. Adam could hear Carl breathing through the phone line and knew he was considering disconnecting the call. "It may be a matter of life or death." With still no response, Adam continued. "What I need to do is locate someone who has the Signa-Chip in them and I need to know how to do that."

Adam paused, expecting to hear the phone detach at any second.

"You need the person's name and Social Security Number," Carl answered to Adam's relief. "And someone who has a computer that has the proper software that can access the data banks."

"Do you know anybody who has a computer like that?"

Again silence and Adam held his breath. "Carl please," Adam pleaded again after waiting for an answer as long as he could.

"Who are you trying to locate?"

Adam thought for a moment. He didn't want to lie but he wanted the most impact. Knowing the more sympathy he could invoke, the better his chances to get Carl's help, he choose Lindsey as his excuse. "My fiancee's her six year old daughter," he said.

"Can't the police in Detroit help you?"

"No," Adam explained. "The police are way over taxed with the riots going on around here and they said they won't even consider them missing until they have been gone for twenty-four hours. And I'm afraid Lindsey might be dead by then."

"Them? I thought you said the daughter was missing."

"They're both missing."

"And they have the chip? I thought you were totally against it…what's your girlfriend and her daughter doing with it?" Carl wondered.

"No," said Adam. Neither one of them have the chip. But one of the people she's with does."

A long silence ensued. Adam felt his heart skip a beat. "What's the name and Social Security number?"

Adam stammered.

"I can't promise you anything," Carl said. "But I can try to call my old buddy in the Computer Department at ESI and see if he will run it as a favor to me."

"Robert or Susan Dewalt," Adam nearly shouted, then lowered his voice. "But, I don't have either Social Security Number."

"Well, we have got to have that, or we can't run the program."

Adam felt his short-lived hope wane.

"Give me an hour or so, Adam said. "I'm headed over to their house now and let me see if I can find something with one of those numbers on it. I'll call you back as soon as I do."

"If you call back," Carl said. "Call me back at this number…755-9090. That's my cell phone."

Forty-five minutes later, Adam was rummaging through the dresser drawers in the Dewalt's bedroom, searching for anything that might contain the Social security Number of either future in-law.

Unsuccessful, his quest took him further out through the house: To the closet near the main entrance. There he found

Susan's purse. In it, her black leather wallet, containing her Social Security Card.

"Thank you Lord," Adam looked up, extracting the SSI card.

He rushed down to the wall phone in the kitchen and dialed Carl's cell phone number.

Carl answered and with Adam on his cell phone, he called Anthony Balford, his friend in the computer room at ESI, on his cordless home telephone. He relayed the information from Adam to Anthony and within five minutes Anthony came back with the location of the chip assigned to Susan Dewalt.

"I owe you big time," Adam told Carl after he jotted down the Detroit address.

"You know how you can pay me back?"

"How's that?"

"Don't ever contact me again," Carl answered, and hung up.

:

Despite treatment with the broad spectrum antibiotic cephalosporin, Ethan's body temperature had steadily climbed throughout the day, spiking at 104 degrees in the wee hours of the morning. His white-blood-count also raising sharply in response to the bacterial infection the contaminated shard of glass had caused when it punctured his left thigh. The gagged, sharp edged projectile, in addition to carrying the particularly resistant strain of staph into Ethan's body had also severed numerous blood vessels on its way in and even more when Ethan extracted it.

The life-threatening Staphylococcus pathogen had already invaded the blood starved tissue near the sutured wound and threatened to spread into Ethan's blood stream, if not stopped. And at the rate the bacteria was reproducing, stopped quickly, or Ethan would be in serious medical trouble.

A painful, lucid, red area had already surrounded the six inch long laceration that felt warm to the touch and was agonizing enough to make Ethan moan when it was touched.

If the infected leg was left on, and they couldn't find an effective antibiotic against the resistant Staphylococcus before it spread into Ethan's blood stream, the attending doctors knew it would probably infect a major organ system or the brain and be fatal. A probability of chance that increased with every passing hour. And a chance the doctors were not willing to take. A major medical decision had to be made and made quickly.

Ethan was scheduled for an emergency amputation as, thousands of miles away, Adam climbed into his truck. Ethan headed for the surgery room, Adam for the address Carl had given him.

:

From where he sat, driving through the older neighborhood in Southwest Detroit, the riot torn side streets looked more like mini war zones to Adam than residential areas: The remnants of burned out houses and vandalized automobiles lined the narrow roads. Some of the abandoned homes still smoldering from the gasoline bombs that had been tossed into them earlier in the day.

The small militant groups of people responsible for the malicious fires were still roaming the neighborhoods looking for vulnerable targets. And the fire departments responsible for extinguishing the fires they had started, either too busy fighting fires elsewhere, or too reluctant, without a police escort, to enter the neighborhoods where active rioting was still going on, to put them out.

Adam wondered as he sped past several of the small roving gangs, *how long it would take before the governor would call in the national guard to quell the violence.* And wondering, *why it was that the people who were most dissatisfied with their quality of life, destroyed even more of the little that they did have, making their own all ready rundown neighborhoods worse.*

Pennsylvania Avenue, where Carl told him Susan Dewalt was, came up suddenly. Adam turned quickly onto the street, the tires on his truck squealing from the abrupt change in directions. The narrow one lane road was completely dark, the few street lights that it once had, either smashed or shot out by the rioters long before he arrived.

The address he was looking for was another half a mile from where he turned and Adam hurried down the street feeling the tension mounting. He tried to postpone any thoughts of what he was going to do to get Carol, Lindsey, and his future in-laws out, once he got to the place where they were being held. But couldn't help imagining all sorts of possibilities—most, not with favorable outcomes.

Adam drove past the address with his headlights off, trying to avoid drawing any unwanted attention to himself. He counted the number of houses the old two family flat was from the next corner, then decided to go around the block, park on the next street, and sneak in from the alleyway.

He crouched low as he moved between the houses on Carolina street and through the dark alley. He eased his way around to the front of the house on Pennsylvania Avenue to verify the address. Satisfied he was at the right house, Adam slid back around to the side, ending up in the narrow, eight foot wide space between the closely constructed homes.

All window coverings on the house were drawn down tight, making it impossible to see in. Adam had no idea of who or what he was up against or where in the house the hostages were being kept, or for that matter, even if they were in the lower unit. Though he did see the shadow of someone repeatedly walking past one of the first floor windows near the back side of the house and Adam surmised it was probably the kitchen. He also got the impression from the rhythmic, back and forth movements, that whoever it was, they were nervously pacing.

It became obvious to Adam; if he had any hope of rescuing anybody, he had to get inside to do it. He took off his shirt, balled it up around the fist of his 'good' hand, and waited. Within a few minutes, he heard another vehicle coming down the street and placed his protected fist against one of the basement windows. When the loud vehicle passed the spot directly in front of the house, Adam punched the window, using the noise of the passing car to cover the sounds of the breaking glass.

To his surprise, and delight, the glass didn't shatter and come crashing out of the frame, but only cracked in several places that allowed him to carefully take out one piece at a time. Eventually he had the whole pane removed and he climbed in, undetected.

In the dark, damp basement, he could hear the pacing foot steps on the floor above him and wondered how long he should wait before he dared climb the basement stairway that led up to that very room.

Adam kneeled at the base of the steps and said a little prayer, asking God for strength and courage, then slowly climbed each of the steps. When he neared the top, he laid on his belly peering through the inch wide strip beneath the closed door and the floor.

His heart was pounding so loudly in his chest, he feared the man who's black oxfords he saw occasionally pass would hear it.

Just beyond the footsteps he could see the wooden baseboard of a wall and knew that the basement doorway opened into a short, narrow hallway.

Hearing no conversation to accompany the pacing and assuming because of that, that the oxfords belonged to the only person left behind to guard the captives, Adam's courage grew.

One on one, he felt his chances were better than if he were outnumbered, especially since for all intents and purposes, due to the injury of his hand, he was one armed.

The shadow of the man passed by the solid, maple wood door and Adam reached out and grabbed the door knob, slowly twisting it until it stopped. He waited. The figure turned and Adam knew from the increasing volume of the footsteps the man was headed back toward him.

Adam watched for the shadow under the door, coordinating the sound of the steps with the shadow to judge when the figure was directly adjacent him. And hoping whoever it was, wasn't beyond the arc of the heavy wood door.

When he figured the time was right, Adam took a deep breath, braced his feet, and with all the weight and force he could muster, he thrust himself against the door. It swung violently open. The edge of the door crashing squarely into the face of the man, breaking his nose and knocking him down. Adam leaped from behind the door and was atop him. Blood streamed from the stunned man's nostrils.

In an instant, against everything Adam believed in, against every vow he had made from his youth, Adam swung a tightly balled fist, intending to hurt.

The fist found its target against the man's jaw. With the man's head firmly against the hardwood floor, it had no place to go, nothing to absorb any of the force behind the blow. Adam heard and felt bone giving way beneath his fist and saw the man's eyes rolling back up into the head.

The man beneath him was still.

He straddled the unconscious man for a moment, watching the blood flow, regretting what he had done, regretting that whoever the man was, he had forced him to do this to him.

Gradually, Adam climbed off the man, pulling the pistol from the shoulder strap the man wore beneath his blood splattered jacket. He took the weapon, more so, that he knew the man wouldn't have it if he came to, than to have it himself. But, Adam did like the confident power he felt, holding the hefty weapon. Though he felt almost ashamed for that reckless confidence.

Two doors down the hallway from the kitchen, Adam found Robert and Susan, bound and gagged, huddled in the corner of an empty room that once served as a bedroom. Adam rushed to them, set the gun on the floor and removed Robert's gag. He almost shouted, "Where's Carol and Lindsey?"

"Untie me," Robert tugged against the rope.

"Where's Carol and Lindsey?" Adam asked again. His injured hands throbbing as he struggled against the tightly tied knots.

"We don't know," Robert excitedly answered, stripping the rope the rest of the way off of himself. "We thought they were with you."

As soon as Robert was free he turned to untie Susan.

"What's this all about?" Susan asked, as soon as her husband had the rag tied around her head and through her mouth removed.

Adam quickly stepped back to the door to make sure the man in the kitchen hallway wasn't moving.

"Is he the only one?" Adam nodded toward the still unconscious man.

"No!" Robert said. "The other three went out a while ago and are supposed to be back any minute."

"Then we'd better get out of here before they do," Adam said.

Susan pulled to her feet by her husband asked, "Are you going to tell us what this is all about?".

"Don't have the time now. Let's go."

They rushed away from the house, through the alley and started between the buildings that led to Carolina Avenue, Adam's truck and freedom. A group of four young men and a young girl stepped into the opening, blocking passage between the houses. Adam froze and started to retreat. He remembered the pistol. Frantically, he felt his waist, hoping he had stuck it there.

"We don't want any trouble," Adam said and backed up a step when he didn't feel the weapon. "We just want to leave."

The small gang of youths slowly advanced despite the plea.

"Hey, isn't that the guy from the hospital?" the girl said. "When Jamie was sick?"

Adam squinted his eyes and recognized the group as part of those who were at River Valley General the night his mother was brought in to the facility.

"Yeah, I remember you guys," Adam said, hoping to alleviate the situation. "How'd your friend come out?"

"She be okay," one of the guys said.

"I'm glad," Adam said. "My mother died." He let his head droop and glanced up.

The small gang stopped. After a moment one of them said "Get," and the group parted.

Slamming car doors and yelling voices from behind them on Pennsylvania caught everyone's attention and the group rushed past Adam and the Dewalts, drawn away by the commotion. "Don't be here when we come back," one of the guys in the gang stopped and snarled at them.

They didn't have to be told twice. They rushed to Adam's pickup, knowing the turmoil behind them was coming from the house they had just escaped.

As soon as the truck's engine started, Adam took off and sped away and didn't slow down until they had reached the northbound entrance to the 1-75 expressway.

When she saw the expanse of the open highway in front of them, Susan sighed. "That was close."

"Not as close as you think," Robert said and laid the .357 magnum he had picked up off the floor in the bedroom, on the dashboard.

"Where did you get that?" Susan squirmed nervously at the sight of the weapon.

"I took it off the guy back at the house," Adam said, pulling the gun down and stuffing it in his belt.

"Are you going to tell us what this is all about?" Susan said.

"They want me to stop the Internet web page and they'll do anything they need to do to make sure I do."

"Web page? What web page? And who are they?" Susan's questions flew in rapid succession.

Robert said, "More importantly where's Carol and Lindsey?"

Adam shook his head in silence and waited until he saw the Detroit city limits - the eight mile road exit - before he spoke again. Explaining the situation as best he could, without invoking an argument from his agnostic passengers, Adam told his story.

"So you don't have the slightest idea where my daughter and Grandchild are do you?" Susan started to cry.

Adam shook his head no.

"You're not going to keep running that web page are you," Robert's said. His voice a commanding statement and not a question.

Adam shook his head no again. "It has accomplished whatever it was intended to and at this point it's just an effort in futility."

"You have any tissue?" Susan snuffed.

"In the glove box," Adam pointed. "Still I think it best if you guys find someplace else to stay for a while," he added. "Until this settles down."

Just after eleven mile road, the 1-696 intersection came and Adam went east on the crossing freeway, headed toward where, he didn't know.

"We could go and stay by my brother's place out in Imlay City," Robert said. "I'm sure he and Kathy would let us stay out there for a few days."

Several miles and minutes of silence past.

"I'll need to go by the house and pick up a few things first," Susan said, confirming her agreement with her husband's suggestion.

"Then you want to go by there?" Adam said. The 1-94 interchange we need to take is coming up quick."

"What are you going to do about Carol?" Susan asked before she answered.

Adam shrugged. "I'll get the police on it first thing in the
morning and just wait to hear back from these people."

"Too bad, they don't have the chip implanted in them,"
Robert sarcastically said. "They could find them in minutes."

Adam turned quickly to retaliate but thought better of it.

"You're for sure taking that web page off the Internet?"
Susan asked.

"As soon as I get home," Adam said. "Which way do I
go?" He pointed at the upcoming exit sign.

"Take us by the house so we can get some things and our
own car," Robert answered.

26

The Dewalt house, unlike the majority of homes on the street, wasn't completely dark, when they drove past it at 2:15AM. All three of them scanning the dimly lit house and the area around it, looking for anything out of the ordinary, anything that might alert them to any awaiting danger.

"That car isn't right," Susan pointed to a dark blue compact parked on the street, two houses down. "I've never seen it around here before."

"Me either," Robert confirmed as they passed it.

Adam drove past the vehicle, down to the next corner and turned around. He came back from the other direction, and felt for the pistol in his belt.

They visually checked everything again with no clues.

"Let's change driver's," Adam said when he went passed again and down to the cross street. He turned the truck around again and pulled it over to the curb.

"What are you going to do?" Susan nervously asked as Robert and Adam changed places.

"Turn off the lights and wait for me down here," Adam instructed. "I'm going to walk down and check things out."

"I don't think that's a good idea," Susan tried to dissuade him.

"Don't worry," Adam responded. He climbed out of the truck again and patted the weapon. "If I see anything dangerous, I'll run out into the street and you come down and pick me up. If it's all clear, I'll signal and you can get your things and we can get out of here."

"I don't know about this," Susan shook her head.

"Give me a few minutes," Adam said to Robert, then quietly closed the truck door.

He went close to the front of the neighboring houses and sneaked, half standing, half crouched down to the Dewalt house. He peered in through the bottom edge of the front window. He stood instantly and frantically started waving at Robert.

Robert floored the gas pedal of the Ram and it leaped forward. To his surprise, Adam was pounding on the front door of the house when he pulled the truck up into the driveway seconds later.

"Carol," Susan screamed when her daughter opened the door and stepped out onto the small concrete stoop.

Carol quickly hugged Adam. "Oh my God what happened to you?" She said when she saw his injured hand and gently took it into hers.

Susan ran across the lawn. "Carol!" She called again,.

Adam nodded at Carol and she immediately turned to meet her mother's open arms.

Nervously Adam glanced up and down the street. Several porch lights in the area blinked on. "Let's get inside," he said and side stepped the doorway feeling again for the handle of the pistol.

Carol, first, Susan, Robert, then Adam stepped through the door into the house. The women, arms wrapped around each others shoulders, were in tears.

Most of the evidence of the earlier vandalism to the room had been cleaned up and Lindsey was sleeping on the couch, her head resting on Melissa Elsworth's lap, her feet on Jack's.

She awoke with a start. "Daddy," she cried and raced into Adam's arms.

He scooped her up in his arms. Adam hugged her tenderly and felt a tear running down his cheek. "Thank you God," he said, as his eyes rolled up toward the ceiling.

Carol hugged her dad at the same time and thought the same thing as Adam had said. Suddenly she pulled back. "What's going on?" she cried out in shock after spotting the wood grip handle of the weapon sticking out from Adam's belt.

Adam passed Lindsey over to her awaiting grandmother. "I'll explain later," he said and pushed the gun in deeper to better secure it in place.

"I think we all should just take a minute and praise the Lord," Jack stood and using his arms, gathered them all into a tight little circle.

When Jack said, "Amen", ending the prayer of thanks a few minutes later, everyone wanted to know what had happened to everyone else. Carol's eyes focusing on the butt of the pistol.

"All in due time," Adam responded to her insistence of an explanation for the gun. "And time is something I don't think we have a lot of. At least not here." Adam turned to Susan. "You need to get the things you're going to take together. Those guys are going to come looking again and this will probably be the first place they come."

"He's right," Robert agreed and led her away.

Despite her reluctance, Susan set Lindsey down, who went back to lay on the couch. The demands for rest from her tired little body were greater than her inquisitiveness.

"What guys?" Carol demanded, sternly glowering at Adam.

"All right," Adam said and glanced over at Lindsey to make sure she was falling back asleep and oblivious to what he had to say.

Melissa had returned to her place, the child's head on her lap, and was gently stroking Lindsey's forehead. The child was obviously just moments away from sleep.

Adam started to pace as he spoke. "But, only an abridged version because we really do need to get out of here and the sooner the better."

Stunned, Carol listened as Adam retold the events of the night with more detail than he had originally intended.

"Your turn," Adam said to Carol when he was finished.

Robert and Susan were coming down the stairs with the personal items they needed packed into three large suitcases and headed for their car parked in the garage.

"Wait," Carol's mother said. "I want to hear this too."

"All I know is I called the Elsworth's," Carol whimpered, fighting back tears. "Like you told me too. Jack came by to get us, despite having all ready made arrangements to leave town with the rest of the church. And after discussing things, we came back here and found this placed turned upside down. Mom and Dad were gone, and I got really scared. I thought everyone was dead."

"The rest of the church?" Adam questioned.

"Pastor feels it's time for the church to leave," Jack answered him. "That the Tribulation Period has started and since we weren't raptured away, as hoped, we need to go somewhere where we are safest, until the Lord returns for us. And we as a congregation agree with him. The feeling is it might be three and a half years from now or as long as seven. Nobody is sure."

Robert and Susan Dewalt furrowed their eyes at Jack and shook their heads.

"What a bunch of bull…," Robert started to argue.

Carol cut him off. "They wanted Lindsey and me to go with them. But we just couldn't leave without you. Even though Jack promised me he'd find you and tell you where we were."

Adam hugged her, holding her close for a moment.

When Carol stopped crying she backed up. "Jack said we would wait until daylight to see if anyone returned. Then we'd 'have' to go or be left behind."

"Speaking of going," Robert interrupted and set the suitcases he was holding down on the floor. The tiredness he felt overtook him. His will to argue with the 'religious fanatics' all gone from him.

"Where is it you think you're taking my grand baby?" Susan shouted. Her concern for Lindsey's safety outweighing her own exhaustion.

A vehicle passed the house; a neighborhood resident, innocently on his way home, and everyone froze. Adam fumbled for the pistol.

"We'd better get going," Adam relaxed when the vehicle continued past.

"Where are you going?" Carol nervously asked her parents.

"Your Uncle Ray and Aunt Kathy's," Robert said, picking the suitcases back up. He started heading for their car in the garage.

"We'll keep in touch and let you know where we are," Carol started to cry again when she hugged her mother. "You'll have to trust us mom," she sobbed. "We won't let anything bad happen to Lindsey."

Susan tried to back away from the embrace, but Carol held her tightly.

Carol knew in her heart of hearts that the Pastor was right, that it 'was' time for the church 'to flee'. But still she couldn't let go, couldn't bare the thoughts of knowing what, according to the scriptures, lay ahead for her parents. She sobbed bitterly.

"We'll see you again," Susan said, starting to cry too. "It's not like this is forever. Things will straighten out. You wait and see. Soon things will be back to normal."

But Carol, Adam, Melissa, and Jack knew it would never happen. That Earth's final countdown had begun. That "things", as they knew them, would never again be 'normal'. And that Carol's parents had made their choice, by taking the chip, and their fate was already sealed.

From somewhere Carol gathered the strength to regain her composure. "I love you," she whispered, and, unable to look her in the eyes, slowly turned away.

Melissa didn't have the strength to hold back her tears either and several cascaded down her cheeks as she watched and held hands with her husband. She thanked God, both her and Jack's parent's were believers and this was something she wouldn't have to endure.

Susan went over and tenderly kissed Lindsey on the cheek. "It was nice meeting you," she said to Melissa and Jack before turning to Adam. "You better take care of them," she said.

"God will," Melissa forced a smile through her tears.

Robert came back into the house from loading the suitcases in the car. "Are we ready?" he asked.

"I guess," Susan answered.

Carol walked up to her dad and wrapped her arms around him for the last time. "I love you," she said, fighting back more tears.

"I hate long teary good-byes," Robert blushed.

Adam reached out his hand and shook Robert's.

Moments later Carol stood in the doorway, watching her parents drive away, her heart torn to pieces.

"We need to get going too," Adam wrapped an arm around her shoulder, comforting her. "Well," Adam turned away from the doorway toward Jack and Melissa. "I suppose the only thing left for us is to say goodbye too."

Jack stood and said, "You're not going with us?"

"I don't think so," Adam replied.

Carol turned quickly and slowly closed the front door. "I thought we were going with the rest of the church?"

"I really don't think that it's time," Adam answered.

"If that is what you truly think, I suggest that you reread your scriptures," Jack stood and started to pace. "Three times the Lord has told us that when we saw these things happening to flee out of the cities. Once in Matthew, twenty-four, sixteen, then in Mark, thirteen, fourteen, and again in Luke, twenty-one, twenty-one."

Adam's head drooped. "If I remember those verses, the Lord said that when we saw the anti-Christ standing where he ought not, then we were to 'flee'. And I haven't seen that yet."

"The key word there is YET," Jack stopped pacing, but Adam started. "Look around you Adam," Jack said. "How long do you think it's going to be before that happens?"

Adam stopped, both men stood still and looked at each other.

"I still have some things I need to do before I can think of anything else," Adam said.

"'Let him which is on the housetop NOT come down to take any thing out of his house: Neither let him which is in the field return back to take his clothes," Melissa quoted the related scriptures from the book of Matthew.

Adam turned away and started to pace again. "I've got to go home and at least cancel that web page so those men stop looking for us."

Jack said, "Do what you feel you must," and motioned to Melissa that it was time for them to get going. "The church is gathering at the campground near Gaylord. We'll be there for a day or so as we try to figure out exactly the where's and what's of our options. If you decide to make it there before we leave…" Jack purposely cut his sentence short.

Melissa added, "We've already given Carol directions to the camp."

Another car drove past and sounded like it slowed down. Everyone froze again until the engine faded away into the distance.

"Let's gather for another word of prayer," Jack said and stretched out his arms to draw them together again.

They grouped together in a tight circle in the middle of the room, holding hands. Jack led the prayer, asking guidance from God and for wisdom, safety, and the courage to meet the times ahead. When they broke hands they hugged and parted.

"When God shows me it's time," Adam promised. "We too will go."

"He's already showing you Adam," Jack said. "I pray that you'll only see before it's too late."

Adam smiled a wry, self-conscious smile. "I'm sure I will," he added and scooped up Lindsey from the couch.

They followed Jack and Melissa eastbound, via 1-94, out just beyond Eleven mile road and the 1-696 interchange, where the Elsworth's exited heading west toward northbound 1-75 and Gaylord.

Adam tooted his horn and waved as the Elsworth's angled off on the interchange exit/entrance ramp. Watching with a heavy heart as his friends pulled away, Adam sighed.

When they were out of sight, he turned, glancing down at Lindsey. The child was asleep on the seat between them. He then looked up to Carol. Carol was nodding against the window.

"Sleepy?" Adam asked trying to make conversation.

Halfheartedly, without lifting her head, Carol responded, "Exhausted."

Feeling the tiredness, due to the ordeals of the last two days and his total lack of proper sleep during those days. Adam said, "Me too. But Thank God my hand isn't throbbing anymore."

"You have any idea where we're going to sleep tonight?"

"I'll drop you and Lindsey off at a motel once we get closer to the house then I'll go home and...,"

Carol sat up straight. "Oh no you won't! We're not going to get separated again. Where you go we go."

"Okay, okay," Adam said and glanced down at the clock on the radio, the soft green LED, on the radio's face showed 5:37. "We'll get us a place," he turned to reassure her. He refocused on the highway ahead as a flow of morning commuters merged in front of him from an entrance ramp. The occupants headed off to start another day of work, unaware of the turmoil brewing in their lives. Adam wondered how many of them had already been implanted with the chip.

And as it was in the days of Noah, so shall it be also in the days of the son of man, Adam recalled the biblical verse in the book of Luke, where Jesus spoke on the similarities between the people of the days of the flood and those of the end times. How they went about their daily business as usual, unaware, until suddenly they were swept away.

A chill went through him, raising goosebumps on the nape of his neck as he thought about it. He wanted to put down his window and shout out a warning, but knew it would either be ignored or everyone would think him a fool. Instead, he glanced over to Carol to tell her his thoughts, but she was dozing again, her head propped against the window.

The slowing of the truck startled her awake. "What's wrong?"

"Nothing," Adam said, turning on the exit. "I need to stop off at the twenty-four hour truck-stop on nineteen mile and get me some 'No Doze' caffeine pills or something, or I'll never stay awake long enough to take care of business."

The all night service station/restaurant was just a few blocks from the expressway and Adam pulled into the parking lot surprised to see the amount of people already in it. Most of them 'over the road' truck drivers who had stopped in for breakfast, or to get their thermos' refilled with fresh coffee for the road.

A 'World News' newspaper trucks was parked at the entrance. The driver and his helper, stacking bound bundles of the morning edition next to the doorway for the independent delivery people who would be by to pick them up for their routes.

Adam pulled up to the gas pumps and filled the Ram, the cool air of the morning invigorating him.

After he walked inside to pay for the fuel and get a package of caffeine pills, he glanced down at the headlines on one of the bundles of newspapers and froze. His eyes locked to the large, bold print. He read it twice unbelieving what it said. Again, a third time, just to be sure.

LORD AGUSTUS (ABADDON) NEITOSO
Chosen Head International Spokesman for the World Church Organization.

# # #

Epilogue

MATTHEW 24: 15-21, KJV, (King James Version),

When ye therefore shall see the abomination of desolation, spoken of by Daniel the prophet, stand in the holy place, (whoso readeth, let him understand:) Then let them which be in Judaea flee into the mountains:

Let him which is on the housetop not come down to take anything out of his house:

Neither let him which is in the field return back to take his clothes.

And woe unto them that are with child, and to them that give suck in those days!

But pray ye that your flight be not in the winter, neither on the Sabbath day:

For then shall be great tribulation, such as was not since the beginning of the world to this time, no, nor ever shall be.

REVELATION 13:16,17

And he causeth all, both small and great, rich and poor, free and bond, to receive a mark in their right hand or in their foreheads: And that no man might buy or sell, save he that had the mark, or the name of the beast, or the number of his name.

REVELATION, 16:1, (KJV)

And I heard a great voice out of the temple saying to the seven angels, Go thy ways, and pour out the vials of the wrath of God upon the earth.

About the Author

Born in Detroit, where he grew up with his five brothers and one sister, Gary Dewey worked as a precision machinist until his mid-thirties. In his early forties Gary enrolled in college, majoring in computer information systems where he gained intricate insight into computer functioning and programming. He began his writing career shortly afterwards and has completed five novels. Gary, now resides in the Upper Peninsula of Michigan with his wife Cynthia.